EDITH WHARTON

EDITH WHARTON

COLLECTED STORIES
1891–1910

THE LIBRARY OF AMERICA

Reprinted with permission of Scribner, an imprint
of Simon and Schuster, Inc.

The paper used in this publication meets the
minimum requirements of the American National Standard for
Information Sciences—Permanence of Paper for Printed
Library Materials, ANSI Z39.48—1984.

Distributed to the trade in the United States
by Penguin Putnam, Inc.
and in Canada by Penguin Books Canada Ltd.

Library of Congress Catalog Number: 00-057596
For cataloging information, see end of Notes.
ISBN 1–883011–93–0

First Printing
The Library of America—121

Manufactured in the United States of America

MAUREEN HOWARD
SELECTED THE CONTENTS AND WROTE THE NOTES
FOR THIS VOLUME

Contents

Mrs. Manstey's View 1

The Fulness of Life 12

The Lamp of Psyche 23

The Valley of Childish Things, and Other Emblems . . . 42

The Muse's Tragedy 50

A Journey 65

The Pelican 76

Souls Belated 95

The Twilight of the God 123

A Cup of Cold Water 136

The Touchstone 162

The Duchess at Prayer 234

The Angel at the Grave 254

The Recovery 271

The Rembrandt 290

The Moving Finger 307

Sanctuary 323

The Descent of Man 394

The Mission of Jane 414

The Other Two 433

The Reckoning 454

Expiation 476

The Lady's Maid's Bell 499

The House of the Dead Hand 520

The Introducers 548

The Hermit and the Wild Woman 578

The Last Asset 601

The Pretext 633

The Pot-Boiler 662

The Best Man 689

His Father's Son 714

The Daunt Diana 731

The Debt 744

Full Circle 758

The Legend 782

The Eyes 810

Afterward 830

The Letters 861

Chronology 901

Note on the Texts 920

Notes 924

COLLECTED STORIES 1891–1910

Mrs. Manstey's View

THE VIEW from Mrs. Manstey's window was not a striking one, but to her at least it was full of interest and beauty. Mrs. Manstey occupied the back room on the third floor of a New York boarding-house, in a street where the ash-barrels lingered late on the sidewalk and the gaps in the pavement would have staggered a Quintus Curtius. She was the widow of a clerk in a large wholesale house, and his death had left her alone, for her only daughter had married in California, and could not afford the long journey to New York to see her mother. Mrs. Manstey, perhaps, might have joined her daughter in the West, but they had now been so many years apart that they had ceased to feel any need of each other's society, and their intercourse had long been limited to the exchange of a few perfunctory letters, written with indifference by the daughter, and with difficulty by Mrs. Manstey, whose right hand was growing stiff with gout. Even had she felt a stronger desire for her daughter's companionship, Mrs. Manstey's increasing infirmity, which caused her to dread the three flights of stairs between her room and the street, would have given her pause on the eve of undertaking so long a journey; and without perhaps formulating these reasons she had long since accepted as a matter of course her solitary life in New York.

She was, indeed, not quite lonely, for a few friends still toiled up now and then to her room; but their visits grew rare as the years went by. Mrs. Manstey had never been a sociable woman, and during her husband's lifetime his companionship had been all-sufficient to her. For many years she had cherished a desire to live in the country, to have a hen-house and a garden; but this longing had faded with age, leaving only in the breast of the uncommunicative old woman a vague tenderness for plants and animals. It was, perhaps, this tenderness which made her cling so fervently to her view from her window, a view in which the most optimistic eye would at first have failed to discover anything admirable.

Mrs. Manstey, from her coign of vantage (a slightly projecting bow-window where she nursed an ivy and a succession of unwholesome-looking bulbs), looked out first upon the yard of her own dwelling, of which, however, she could get but a restricted glimpse. Still, her gaze took in the topmost boughs of the ailanthus below her window, and she knew how early each year the clump of dicentra strung its bending stalk with hearts of pink.

But of greater interest were the yards beyond. Being for the most part attached to boarding-houses they were in a state of chronic untidiness and fluttering, on certain days of the week, with miscellaneous garments and frayed table-cloths. In spite of this Mrs. Manstey found much to admire in the long vista which she commanded. Some of the yards were, indeed, but stony wastes, with grass in the cracks of the pavement and no shade in spring save that afforded by the intermittent leafage of the clothes-lines. These yards Mrs. Manstey disapproved of, but the others, the green ones, she loved. She had grown used to their disorder; the broken barrels, the empty bottles and paths unswept no longer annoyed her; hers was the happy faculty of dwelling on the pleasanter side of the prospect before her.

In the very next enclosure did not a magnolia open its hard white flowers against the watery blue of April? And was there not, a little way down the line, a fence foamed over every May by lilac waves of wistaria? Farther still, a horse-chestnut lifted its candelabra of buff and pink blossoms above broad fans of foliage; while in the opposite yard June was sweet with the breath of a neglected syringa, which persisted in growing in spite of the countless obstacles opposed to its welfare.

But if nature occupied the front rank in Mrs. Manstey's view, there was much of a more personal character to interest her in the aspect of the houses and their inmates. She deeply disapproved of the mustard-colored curtains which had lately been hung in the doctor's window opposite; but she glowed with pleasure when the house farther down had its old bricks washed with a coat of paint. The occupants of the houses did not often show themselves at the back windows, but the servants were always in sight. Noisy slatterns, Mrs. Manstey pronounced the greater number; she knew their ways and hated them. But to the quiet cook in the newly painted house, whose mistress bullied her, and who secretly fed the stray cats at nightfall, Mrs. Manstey's warmest sympathies were given. On one occasion her feelings were racked by the neglect of a house-maid, who for two days forgot to feed the parrot committed to her care. On the third day, Mrs. Manstey, in spite of her gouty hand, had just penned a letter, beginning: "Madam, it is now three days since your parrot has been fed," when the forgetful maid appeared at the window with a cup of seed in her hand.

But in Mrs. Manstey's more meditative moods it was the narrowing perspective of far-off yards which pleased her best. She loved, at twilight, when the distant brown-stone spire seemed melting in the fluid yellow of the west, to lose herself in vague memories of a trip to Europe, made years ago, and now reduced in her mind's eye to a pale phantasmagoria of indistinct steeples and dreamy skies. Perhaps at heart Mrs. Manstey was an artist; at all events she was sensible of many changes of color unnoticed by the average eye, and dear to her as the green of early spring was the black lattice of branches against a cold sulphur sky at the close of a snowy day. She enjoyed, also, the sunny thaws of March, when patches of earth showed through the snow, like ink-spots spreading on a sheet of white blotting-paper; and, better still, the haze of boughs, leafless but swollen, which replaced the clear-cut tracery of winter. She even watched with a certain interest the trail of smoke from a far-off factory chimney, and missed a detail in the landscape when the factory was closed and the smoke disappeared.

Mrs. Manstey, in the long hours which she spent at her window, was not idle. She read a little, and knitted numberless stockings; but the view surrounded and shaped her life as the sea does a lonely island. When her rare callers came it was difficult for her to detach herself from the contemplation of the opposite window-washing, or the scrutiny of certain green points in a neighboring flower-bed which might, or might not, turn into hyacinths, while she feigned an interest in her visitor's anecdotes about some unknown grandchild. Mrs. Manstey's real friends were the denizens of the yards, the hyacinths, the magnolia, the green parrot, the maid who fed the cats, the doctor who studied late behind his mustard-colored curtains; and the confidant of her tenderer musings was the church-spire floating in the sunset.

One April day, as she sat in her usual place, with knitting cast aside and eyes fixed on the blue sky mottled with round clouds, a knock at the door announced the entrance of her landlady. Mrs. Manstey did not care for her landlady, but she submitted to her visits with ladylike resignation. To-day, however, it seemed harder than usual to turn from the blue sky and the blossoming magnolia to Mrs. Sampson's unsuggestive face, and Mrs. Manstey was conscious of a distinct effort as she did so.

"The magnolia is out earlier than usual this year, Mrs. Sampson," she remarked, yielding to a rare impulse, for she seldom alluded to the absorbing interest of her life. In the first place it was a topic not likely to appeal to her visitors and, besides, she lacked the power of expression and could not have given utterance to her feelings had she wished to.

"The what, Mrs. Manstey?" inquired the landlady, glancing about the room as if to find there the explanation of Mrs. Manstey's statement.

"The magnolia in the next yard—in Mrs. Black's yard," Mrs. Manstey repeated.

"Is it, indeed? I didn't know there was a magnolia there," said Mrs. Sampson, carelessly. Mrs. Manstey looked at her; she did not know that there was a magnolia in the next yard!

"By the way," Mrs. Sampson continued, "speaking of Mrs. Black reminds me that the work on the extension is to begin next week."

"The what?" it was Mrs. Manstey's turn to ask.

"The extension," said Mrs. Sampson, nodding her head in the direction of the ignored magnolia. "You knew, of course, that Mrs. Black was going to build an extension to her house? Yes, ma'am. I hear it is to run right back to the end of the yard. How she can afford to build an extension in these hard times I don't see; but she always was crazy about building. She used to keep a boarding-house in Seventeenth Street, and she nearly ruined herself then by sticking out bow-windows and what not; I should have thought that would have cured her of building, but I guess it's a disease, like drink. Anyhow, the work is to begin on Monday."

Mrs. Manstey had grown pale. She always spoke slowly, so the landlady did not heed the long pause which followed. At last Mrs. Manstey said: "Do you know how high the extension will be?"

"That's the most absurd part of it. The extension is to be built right up to the roof of the main building; now, did you ever?"

Mrs. Manstey paused again. "Won't it be a great annoyance to you, Mrs. Sampson?" she asked.

"I should say it would. But there's no help for it; if people have got a mind to build extensions there's no law to prevent 'em, that I'm aware of." Mrs. Manstey, knowing this, was silent. "There is no help for it," Mrs. Sampson repeated, "but if I *am* a church member, I wouldn't be so sorry if it ruined Eliza Black. Well, good-day, Mrs. Manstey; I'm glad to find you so comfortable."

So comfortable—so comfortable! Left to herself the old woman turned once more to the window. How lovely the view was that day! The blue sky with its round clouds shed a brightness over everything; the ailanthus had put on a tinge of yellow-green, the hyacinths were budding, the magnolia flowers looked more than ever like rosettes carved in alabaster. Soon the wistaria would bloom, then the horse-chestnut; but not for her. Between her eyes and them a barrier of brick and mortar would swiftly rise; presently even the spire would disappear, and all her radiant world be blotted out. Mrs. Manstey sent away untouched the dinner-tray brought to her that evening. She lingered in the window until the windy sunset died in bat-colored dusk; then, going to bed, she lay sleepless all night.

Early the next day she was up and at the window. It was raining, but even through the slanting gray gauze the scene had its charm—and then the rain was so good for the trees. She had noticed the day before that the ailanthus was growing dusty.

"Of course I might move," said Mrs. Manstey aloud, and turning from the window she looked about her room. She might move, of course; so might she be flayed alive; but she was not likely to survive either operation. The room, though far less important to her happiness than the view, was as much a part of her existence. She had lived in it seventeen years. She knew every stain on the wall-paper, every rent in the carpet; the light fell in a certain way on her engravings, her books had grown shabby on their shelves, her bulbs and ivy were used to their window and knew which way to lean to the sun. "We are all too old to move," she said.

That afternoon it cleared. Wet and radiant the blue reappeared through torn rags of cloud; the ailanthus sparkled; the earth in the flower-borders looked rich and warm. It was Thursday, and on Monday the building of the extension was to begin.

On Sunday afternoon a card was brought to Mrs. Black, as she was engaged in gathering up the fragments of the boarders' dinner in the basement. The card, black-edged, bore Mrs. Manstey's name.

"One of Mrs. Sampson's boarders; wants to move, I suppose. Well, I can give her a room next year in the extension. Dinah," said Mrs. Black, "tell the lady I'll be upstairs in a minute."

Mrs. Black found Mrs. Manstey standing in the long parlor garnished with statuettes and antimacassars; in that house she could not sit down.

Stooping hurriedly to open the register, which let out a cloud of dust, Mrs. Black advanced to her visitor.

"I'm happy to meet you, Mrs. Manstey; take a seat, please," the landlady remarked in her prosperous voice, the voice of a woman who can afford to build extensions. There was no help for it; Mrs. Manstey sat down.

"Is there anything I can do for you, ma'am?" Mrs. Black continued. "My house is full at present, but I am going to build an extension, and——"

"It is about the extension that I wish to speak,"said Mrs. Manstey, suddenly. "I am a poor woman, Mrs. Black, and I have never been a happy one. I shall have to talk about myself first to—to make you understand."

Mrs. Black, astonished but imperturbable, bowed at this parenthesis.

"I never had what I wanted," Mrs. Manstey continued. "It was always one disappointment after another. For years I wanted to live in the country. I dreamed and dreamed about it; but we never could manage it. There was no sunny window in our house, and so all my plants died. My daughter married years ago and went away—besides, she never cared for the same things. Then my husband died and I was left alone. That was seventeen years ago. I went to live at Mrs. Sampson's, and I have been there ever since. I have grown a little infirm, as you see, and I don't get out often; only on fine days, if I am feeling very well. So you can understand my sitting a great deal in my window—the back window on the third floor——"

"Well, Mrs. Manstey," said Mrs. Black, liberally, "I could give you a back room, I dare say; one of the new rooms in the ex——"

"But I don't want to move; I can't move," said Mrs. Manstey, almost with a scream. "And I came to tell you that if you build that extension I shall have no view from my window—no view! Do you understand?"

Mrs. Black thought herself face to face with a lunatic, and she had always heard that lunatics must be humored.

"Dear me, dear me," she remarked, pushing her chair back a little way, "that is too bad, isn't it? Why, I never thought of that. To be sure, the extension *will* interfere with your view, Mrs. Manstey."

"You do understand?" Mrs. Manstey gasped.

"Of course I do. And I'm real sorry about it, too. But there, don't you worry, Mrs. Manstey. I guess we can fix that all right."

Mrs. Manstey rose from her seat, and Mrs. Black slipped toward the door.

"What do you mean by fixing it? Do you mean that I can induce you to change your mind about the extension? Oh, Mrs. Black, listen to me. I have two thousand dollars in the bank and I could manage, I know I could manage, to give you a thousand if——" Mrs. Manstey paused; the tears were rolling down her cheeks.

"There, there, Mrs. Manstey, don't you worry," repeated Mrs. Black, soothingly. "I am sure we can settle it. I am sorry that I can't stay and talk about it any longer, but this is such a busy time of day, with supper to get——"

Her hand was on the door-knob, but with sudden vigor Mrs. Manstey seized her wrist.

"You are not giving me a definite answer. Do you mean to say that you accept my proposition?"

"Why, I'll think it over, Mrs. Manstey, certainly I will. I wouldn't annoy you for the world——"

"But the work is to begin to-morrow, I am told," Mrs. Manstey persisted.

Mrs. Black hesitated. "It shan't begin, I promise you that; I'll send word to the builder this very night." Mrs. Manstey tightened her hold.

"You are not deceiving me, are you?" she said.

"No—no," stammered Mrs. Black. "How can you think such a thing of me, Mrs. Manstey?"

Slowly Mrs. Manstey's clutch relaxed, and she passed through the open door. "One thousand dollars," she repeated, pausing in the hall; then she let herself out of the house and hobbled down the steps, supporting herself on the cast-iron railing.

"My goodness," exclaimed Mrs. Black, shutting and bolting the hall-door, "I never knew the old woman was crazy! And she looks so quiet and ladylike, too."

Mrs. Manstey slept well that night, but early the next morning she was awakened by a sound of hammering. She got to her window with what haste she might and, looking out, saw that Mrs. Black's yard was full of workmen. Some were carrying loads of brick from the kitchen to the yard, others beginning to demolish the old-fashioned wooden balcony which adorned each story of Mrs. Black's house. Mrs. Manstey saw that she had been deceived. At first she thought of confiding her trouble to Mrs. Sampson, but a settled discouragement soon took possession of her and she went back to bed, not caring to see what was going on.

Toward afternoon, however, feeling that she must know the worst, she rose and dressed herself. It was a laborious task, for her hands were stiffer than usual, and the hooks and buttons seemed to evade her.

When she seated herself in the window, she saw that the workmen had removed the upper part of the balcony, and that the bricks had multiplied since morning. One of the men, a coarse fellow with a bloated face, picked a magnolia blossom and, after smelling it, threw it to the ground; the next man, carrying a load of bricks, trod on the flower in passing.

"Look out, Jim," called one of the men to another who was smoking a pipe, "if you throw matches around near those barrels of paper you'll have the old tinder-box burning down before you know it." And Mrs. Manstey, leaning forward, perceived that there were several barrels of paper and rubbish under the wooden balcony.

At length the work ceased and twilight fell. The sunset was perfect and a roseate light, transfiguring the distant spire, lingered late in the west. When it grew dark Mrs. Manstey drew down the shades and proceeded, in her usual methodical manner, to light her lamp. She always filled and lit it with her own hands, keeping a kettle of kerosene on a zinc-covered shelf in a closet. As the lamp-light filled the room it assumed its usual peaceful aspect. The books and pictures and plants seemed, like their mistress, to settle themselves down for another quiet evening, and Mrs. Manstey, as was her wont, drew up her armchair to the table and began to knit.

That night she could not sleep. The weather had changed and a wild wind was abroad, blotting the stars with close-driven clouds. Mrs. Manstey rose once or twice and looked out of the window; but of the view nothing was discernible save a tardy light or two in the opposite windows. These lights at last went out, and Mrs. Manstey, who had watched for their extinction, began to dress herself. She was in evident haste, for she merely flung a thin dressing-gown over her night-dress and wrapped her head in a scarf; then she opened her closet and cautiously took out the kettle of kerosene. Having slipped a bundle of wooden matches into her pocket she proceeded, with increasing precautions, to unlock her door, and a few moments later she was feeling her way down the dark staircase, led by a glimmer of gas from the lower hall. At length she reached the bottom of the stairs and began the more difficult descent into the utter darkness of the basement. Here, however, she could move more freely, as there was less danger of being overheard; and without much delay she contrived to unlock the iron door leading into the yard. A gust of cold wind smote her as she stepped out and groped shiveringly under the clothes-lines.

That morning at three o'clock an alarm of fire brought the engines to Mrs. Black's door, and also brought Mrs. Sampson's startled boarders to their windows. The wooden balcony at the back of Mrs. Black's house was ablaze, and among those who watched the progress of the flames was Mrs. Manstey, leaning in her thin dressing-gown from the open window.

The fire, however, was soon put out, and the frightened occupants of the house, who had fled in scant attire, reassembled at dawn to find that little mischief had been done beyond the cracking of window panes and smoking of ceilings. In fact, the chief sufferer by the fire was Mrs. Manstey, who was found in the morning gasping with pneumonia, a not unnatural result, as everyone remarked, of her having hung out of an open window at her age in a dressing-gown. It was easy to see that she was very ill, but no one had guessed how grave the doctor's verdict would be, and the faces gathered that evening about Mrs. Sampson's table were awe-struck and disturbed. Not that any of the boarders knew Mrs. Manstey well; she "kept to herself," as they said, and seemed to fancy herself too good for them; but then it is always disagreeable to have anyone dying in the house and, as one lady observed to another: "It might just as well have been you or me, my dear."

But it was only Mrs. Manstey; and she was dying, as she had lived, lonely if not alone. The doctor had sent a trained nurse, and Mrs. Sampson, with muffled step, came in from time to time; but both, to Mrs. Manstey, seemed remote and unsubstantial as the figures in a dream. All day she said nothing; but when she was asked for her daughter's address she shook her head. At times the nurse noticed that she seemed to be listening attentively for some sound which did not come; then again she dozed.

The next morning at daylight she was very low. The nurse called Mrs. Sampson and as the two bent over the old woman they saw her lips move.

"Lift me up—out of bed," she whispered.

They raised her in their arms, and with her stiff hand she pointed to the window.

"Oh, the window—she wants to sit in the window. She

used to sit there all day," Mrs. Sampson explained. "It can do her no harm, I suppose?"

"Nothing matters now," said the nurse.

They carried Mrs. Manstey to the window and placed her in her chair. The dawn was abroad, a jubilant spring dawn; the spire had already caught a golden ray, though the magnolia and horse-chestnut still slumbered in shadow. In Mrs. Black's yard all was quiet. The charred timbers of the balcony lay where they had fallen. It was evident that since the fire the builders had not returned to their work. The magnolia had unfolded a few more sculptural flowers; the view was undisturbed.

It was hard for Mrs. Manstey to breathe; each moment it grew more difficult. She tried to make them open the window, but they would not understand. If she could have tasted the air, sweet with the penetrating ailanthus savor, it would have eased her; but the view at least was there—the spire was golden now, the heavens had warmed from pearl to blue, day was alight from east to west, even the magnolia had caught the sun.

Mrs. Manstey's head fell back and smiling she died.

That day the building of the extension was resumed.

The Fulness of Life

FOR HOURS she had lain in a kind of gentle torpor, not unlike that sweet lassitude which masters one in the hush of
a midsummer noon, when the heat seems to have silenced the
very birds and insects, and, lying sunk in the tasselled
meadow-grasses, one looks up through a level roofing of
maple-leaves at the vast, shadowless, and unsuggestive blue.
Now and then, at ever-lengthening intervals, a flash of pain
darted through her, like the ripple of sheet-lightning across
such a midsummer sky; but it was too transitory to shake her
stupor, that calm, delicious, bottomless stupor into which she
felt herself sinking more and more deeply, without a disturbing impulse of resistance, an effort of reattachment to the
vanishing edges of consciousness.

The resistance, the effort, had known their hour of violence; but now they were at an end. Through her mind, long
harried by grotesque visions, fragmentary images of the life
that she was leaving, tormenting lines of verse, obstinate pre-
sentiments of pictures once beheld, indistinct impressions of
rivers, towers, and cupolas, gathered in the length of journeys
half forgotten—through her mind there now only moved a
few primal sensations of colorless well-being; a vague satisfaction in the thought that she had swallowed her noxious last
draught of medicine . . . and that she should never again
hear the creaking of her husband's boots—those horrible
boots—and that no one would come to bother her about the
next day's dinner . . . or the butcher's book. . . .

At last even these dim sensations spent themselves in the
thickening obscurity which enveloped her; a dusk now filled
with pale geometric roses, circling softly, interminably before
her, now darkened to a uniform blue-blackness, the hue of a
summer night without stars. And into this darkness she felt
herself sinking, sinking, with the gentle sense of security of one
upheld from beneath. Like a tepid tide it rose around her, glid-
ing ever higher and higher, folding in its velvety embrace her
relaxed and tired body, now submerging her breast and shoulders, now creeping gradually, with soft inexorableness, over

her throat to her chin, to her ears, to her mouth. . . . Ah, now it was rising too high; the impulse to struggle was renewed; . . . her mouth was full; . . . she was choking. . . . Help!

"It is all over," said the nurse, drawing down the eyelids with official composure.

The clock struck three. They remembered it afterward. Someone opened the window and let in a blast of that strange, neutral air which walks the earth between darkness and dawn; someone else led the husband into another room. He walked vaguely, like a blind man, on his creaking boots.

II

She stood, as it seemed, on a threshold, yet no tangible gateway was in front of her. Only a wide vista of light, mild yet penetrating as the gathered glimmer of innumerable stars, expanded gradually before her eyes, in blissful contrast to the cavernous darkness from which she had of late emerged.

She stepped forward, not frightened, but hesitating, and as her eyes began to grow more familiar with the melting depths of light about her, she distinguished the outlines of a landscape, at first swimming in the opaline uncertainty of Shelley's vaporous creations, then gradually resolved into distincter shape—the vast unrolling of a sunlit plain, aerial forms of mountains, and presently the silver crescent of a river in the valley, and a blue stencilling of trees along its curve—something suggestive in its ineffable hue of an azure background of Leonardo's, strange, enchanting, mysterious, leading on the eye and the imagination into regions of fabulous delight. As she gazed, her heart beat with a soft and rapturous surprise; so exquisite a promise she read in the summons of that hyaline distance.

"And so death is not the end after all," in sheer gladness she heard herself exclaiming aloud. "I always knew that it couldn't be. I believed in Darwin, of course. I do still; but then Darwin himself said that he wasn't sure about the soul—at least, I think he did—and Wallace was a spiritualist; and then there was St. George Mivart——"

Her gaze lost itself in the ethereal remoteness of the mountains.

"How beautiful! How satisfying!" she murmured. "Perhaps now I shall really know what it is to live."

As she spoke she felt a sudden thickening of her heart-beats, and looking up she was aware that before her stood the Spirit of Life.

"Have you never really known what it is to live?" the Spirit of Life asked her.

"I have never known," she replied, "that fulness of life which we all feel ourselves capable of knowing; though my life has not been without scattered hints of it, like the scent of earth which comes to one sometimes far out at sea."

"And what do you call the fulness of life?" the Spirit asked again.

"Oh, I can't tell you, if you don't know," she said, almost reproachfully. "Many words are supposed to define it—love and sympathy are those in commonest use, but I am not even sure that they are the right ones, and so few people really know what they mean."

"You were married," said the Spirit, "yet you did not find the fulness of life in your marriage?"

"Oh, dear, no," she replied, with an indulgent scorn, "my marriage was a very incomplete affair."

"And yet you were fond of your husband?"

"You have hit upon the exact word; I was fond of him, yes, just as I was fond of my grandmother, and the house that I was born in, and my old nurse. Oh, I was fond of him, and we were counted a very happy couple. But I have sometimes thought that a woman's nature is like a great house full of rooms: there is the hall, through which everyone passes in go-ing in and out; the drawing-room, where one receives formal visits; the sitting-room, where the members of the family come and go as they list; but beyond that, far beyond, are other rooms, the handles of whose doors perhaps are never turned; no one knows the way to them, no one knows whither they lead; and in the innermost room, the holy of holies, the soul sits alone and waits for a footstep that never comes."

"And your husband," asked the Spirit, after a pause, "never got beyond the family sitting-room?"

"Never," she returned, impatiently; "and the worst of it was that he was quite content to remain there. He thought it perfectly beautiful, and sometimes, when he was admiring its commonplace furniture, insignificant as the chairs and tables of a hotel parlor, I felt like crying out to him: 'Fool, will you never guess that close at hand are rooms full of treasures and wonders, such as the eye of man hath not seen, rooms that no step has crossed, but that might be yours to live in, could you but find the handle of the door?' "

"Then," the Spirit continued, "those moments of which you lately spoke, which seemed to come to you like scattered hints of the fulness of life, were not shared with your husband?"

"Oh, no—never. He was different. His boots creaked, and he always slammed the door when he went out, and he never read anything but railway novels and the sporting advertisements in the papers—and—and, in short, we never understood each other in the least."

"To what influence, then, did you owe those exquisite sensations?"

"I can hardly tell. Sometimes to the perfume of a flower; sometimes to a verse of Dante or of Shakespeare; sometimes to a picture or a sunset, or to one of those calm days at sea, when one seems to be lying in the hollow of a blue pearl; sometimes, but rarely, to a word spoken by someone who chanced to give utterance, at the right moment, to what I felt but could not express."

"Someone whom you loved?" asked the Spirit.

"I never loved anyone, in that way," she said, rather sadly, "nor was I thinking of any one person when I spoke, but of two or three who, by touching for an instant upon a certain chord of my being, had called forth a single note of that strange melody which seemed sleeping in my soul. It has seldom happened, however, that I have owed such feelings to people; and no one ever gave me a moment of such happiness as it was my lot to feel one evening in the Church of Or San Michele, in Florence."

"Tell me about it," said the Spirit.

"It was near sunset on a rainy spring afternoon in Easter week. The clouds had vanished, dispersed by a sudden wind, and as we entered the church the fiery panes of the high windows shone out like lamps through the dusk. A priest was at the high altar, his white cope a livid spot in the incense-laden obscurity, the light of the candles flickering up and down like fireflies about his head; a few people knelt near by. We stole behind them and sat down on a bench close to the tabernacle of Orcagna.

"Strange to say, though Florence was not new to me, I had never been in the church before; and in that magical light I saw for the first time the inlaid steps, the fluted columns, the sculptured bas-reliefs and canopy of the marvellous shrine. The marble, worn and mellowed by the subtle hand of time, took on an unspeakable rosy hue, suggestive in some remote way of the honey-colored columns of the Parthenon, but more mystic, more complex, a color not born of the sun's inveterate kiss, but made up of cryptal twilight, and the flame of candles upon martyrs' tombs, and gleams of sunset through symbolic panes of chrysoprase and ruby; such a light as illumines the missals in the library of Siena, or burns like a hidden fire through the Madonna of Gian Bellini in the Church of the Redeemer, at Venice; the light of the Middle Ages, richer, more solemn, more significant than the limpid sunshine of Greece.

"The church was silent, but for the wail of the priest and the occasional scraping of a chair against the floor, and as I sat there, bathed in that light, absorbed in rapt contemplation of the marble miracle which rose before me, cunningly wrought as a casket of ivory and enriched with jewel-like incrustations and tarnished gleams of gold, I felt myself borne onward along a mighty current, whose source seemed to be in the very beginning of things, and whose tremendous waters gathered as they went all the mingled streams of human passion and endeavor. Life in all its varied manifestations of beauty and strangeness seemed weaving a rhythmical dance around me as I moved, and wherever the spirit of man had passed I knew that my foot had once been familiar.

"As I gazed, the mediæval bosses of the tabernacle of Orcagna seemed to melt and flow into their primal forms, so that the folded lotus of the Nile and the Greek acanthus were braided with the runic knots and fish-tailed monsters of the North, and all the plastic terror and beauty born of man's hand from the Ganges to the Baltic quivered and mingled in

Orcagna's apotheosis of Mary. And so the river bore me on, past the alien face of antique civilizations and the familiar wonders of Greece, till I swam upon the fiercely rushing tide of the Middle Ages, with its swirling eddies of passion, its heaven-reflecting pools of poetry and art; I heard the rhythmic blow of the craftsmen's hammers in the goldsmiths' workshops and on the walls of churches, the party-cries of armed factions in the narrow streets, the organ-roll of Dante's verse, the crackle of the fagots around Arnold of Brescia, the twitter of the swallows to which St. Francis preached, the laughter of the ladies listening on the hillside to the quips of the Decameron, while plague-struck Florence howled beneath them—all this and much more I heard, joined in strange unison with voices earlier and more remote, fierce, passionate, or tender, yet subdued to such awful harmony that I thought of the song that the morning stars sang together and felt as though it were sounding in my ears. My heart beat to suffocation, the tears burned my lids, the joy, the mystery of it seemed too intolerable to be borne. I could not understand even then the words of the song; but I knew that if there had been someone at my side who could have heard it with me, we might have found the key to it together.

"I turned to my husband, who was sitting beside me in an attitude of patient dejection, gazing into the bottom of his hat; but at that moment he rose, and stretching his stiffened legs, said, mildly: 'Hadn't we better be going? There doesn't seem to be much to see here, and you know the table d'hôte dinner is at half-past six o'clock.' "

Her recital ended, there was an interval of silence; then the Spirit of Life said: "There is a compensation in store for such needs as you have expressed."

"Oh, then you *do* understand?" she exclaimed. "Tell me what compensation, I entreat you!"

"It is ordained," the Spirit answered, "that every soul which seeks in vain on earth for a kindred soul to whom it can lay bare its inmost being shall find that soul here and be united to it for eternity."

A glad cry broke from her lips. "Ah, shall I find him at last?" she cried, exultant.

"He is here," said the Spirit of Life.

She looked up and saw that a man stood near whose soul (for in that unwonted light she seemed to see his soul more clearly than his face) drew her toward him with an invincible force.

"Are you really he?" she murmured.

"I am he," he answered.

She laid her hand in his and drew him toward the parapet which overhung the valley.

"Shall we go down together," she asked him, "into that marvellous country; shall we see it together, as if with the self-same eyes, and tell each other in the same words all that we think and feel?"

"So," he replied, "have I hoped and dreamed."

"What?" she asked, with rising joy. "Then you, too, have looked for me?"

"All my life."

"How wonderful! And did you never, never find anyone in the other world who understood you?"

"Not wholly—not as you and I understand each other."

"Then you feel it, too? Oh, I am happy," she sighed.

They stood, hand in hand, looking down over the parapet upon the shimmering landscape which stretched forth beneath them into sapphirine space, and the Spirit of Life, who kept watch near the threshold, heard now and then a floating fragment of their talk blown backward like the stray swallows which the wind sometimes separates from their migratory tribe.

"Did you never feel at sunset——"

"Ah, yes; but I never heard anyone else say so. Did you?"

"Do you remember that line in the third canto of the 'Inferno?'"

"Ah, that line—my favorite always. Is it possible——"

"You know the stooping Victory in the frieze of the Nike Apteros?"

"You mean the one who is tying her sandal? Then you have noticed, too, that all Botticelli and Mantegna are dormant in those flying folds of her drapery?"

"After a storm in autumn have you never seen——"

"Yes, it is curious how certain flowers suggest certain

painters—the perfume of the carnation, Leonardo; that of the rose, Titian; the tuberose, Crivelli——"

"I never supposed that anyone else had noticed it."

"Have you never thought——"

"Oh, yes, often and often; but I never dreamed that anyone else had."

"But surely you must have felt——"

"Oh, yes, yes; and you, too——"

"How beautiful! How strange——"

Their voices rose and fell, like the murmur of two fountains answering each other across a garden full of flowers. At length, with a certain tender impatience, he turned to her and said: "Love, why should we linger here? All eternity lies before us. Let us go down into that beautiful country together and make a home for ourselves on some blue hill above the shining river."

As he spoke, the hand she had forgotten in his was suddenly withdrawn, and he felt that a cloud was passing over the radiance of her soul.

"A home," she repeated, slowly, "a home for you and me to live in for all eternity?"

"Why not, love? Am I not the soul that yours has sought?"

"Y-yes—yes, I know—but, don't you see, home would not be like home to me, unless——"

"Unless?" he wonderingly repeated.

She did not answer, but she thought to herself, with an impulse of whimsical inconsistency, "Unless you slammed the door and wore creaking boots."

But he had recovered his hold upon her hand, and by imperceptible degrees was leading her toward the shining steps which descended to the valley.

"Come, O my soul's soul," he passionately implored; "why delay a moment? Surely you feel, as I do, that eternity itself is too short to hold such bliss as ours. It seems to me that I can see our home already. Have I not always seen it in my dreams? It is white, love, is it not, with polished columns, and a sculptured cornice against the blue? Groves of laurel and oleander and thickets of roses surround it; but from the terrace where we walk at sunset, the eye looks out over woodlands and cool meadows where, deep-bowered under ancient boughs, a stream goes delicately toward the river. Indoors our favorite pictures hang upon the walls and the rooms are lined with books. Think, dear, at last we shall have time to read them all. With which shall we begin? Come, help me to choose. Shall it be 'Faust' or the 'Vita Nuova,' the 'Tempest' or 'Les Caprices de Marianne,' or the thirty-first canto of the 'Paradise,' or 'Epipsychidion' or 'Lycidas'? Tell me, dear, which one?"

As he spoke he saw the answer trembling joyously upon her lips; but it died in the ensuing silence, and she stood motionless, resisting the persuasion of his hand.

"What is it?" he entreated.

"Wait a moment," she said, with a strange hesitation in her voice. "Tell me first, are you quite sure of yourself? Is there no one on earth whom you sometimes remember?"

"Not since I have seen you," he replied; for, being a man, he had indeed forgotten.

Still she stood motionless, and he saw that the shadow deepened on her soul.

"Surely, love," he rebuked her, "it was not that which troubled you? For my part I have walked through Lethe. The past has melted like a cloud before the moon. I never lived until I saw you."

She made no answer to his pleadings, but at length, rousing herself with a visible effort, she turned away from him and moved toward the Spirit of Life, who still stood near the threshold.

"I want to ask you a question," she said, in a troubled voice.

"Ask," said the Spirit.

"A little while ago," she began, slowly, "you told me that every soul which has not found a kindred soul on earth is destined to find one here."

"And have you not found one?" asked the Spirit.

"Yes; but will it be so with my husband's soul also?"

"No," answered the Spirit of Life, "for your husband imagined that he had found his soul's mate on earth in you; and for such delusions eternity itself contains no cure."

She gave a little cry. Was it of disappointment or triumph?

"Then—then what will happen to him when he comes here?"

"That I cannot tell you. Some field of activity and happiness he will doubtless find, in due measure to his capacity for being active and happy."

She interrupted, almost angrily: "He will never be happy without me."

"Do not be too sure of that," said the Spirit.

She took no notice of this, and the Spirit continued: "He will not understand you here any better than he did on earth."

"No matter," she said; "I shall be the only sufferer, for he always thought that he understood me."

"His boots will creak just as much as ever——"

"No matter."

"And he will slam the door——"

"Very likely."

"And continue to read railway novels——"

She interposed, impatiently: "Many men do worse than that."

"But you said just now," said the Spirit, "that you did not love him."

"True," she answered, simply; "but don't you understand that I shouldn't feel at home without him? It is all very well for a week or two—but for eternity! After all, I never minded the creaking of his boots, except when my head ached, and I don't suppose it will ache *here*; and he was always so sorry when he had slammed the door, only he never *could* remember not to. Besides, no one else would know how to look after him, he is so helpless. His inkstand would never be filled, and he would always be out of stamps and visiting-cards. He would never remember to have his umbrella re-covered, or to ask the price of anything before he bought it. Why, he wouldn't even know what novels to read. I always had to choose the kind he liked, with a murder or a forgery and a successful detective."

She turned abruptly to her kindred soul, who stood listening with a mien of wonder and dismay.

"Don't you see," she said, "that I can't possibly go with you?"

"But what do you intend to do?" asked the Spirit of Life.

"What do I intend to do?" she returned, indignantly.

"Why, I mean to wait for my husband, of course. If he had come here first *he* would have waited for me for years and years; and it would break his heart not to find me here when he comes." She pointed with a contemptuous gesture to the magic vision of hill and vale sloping away to the translucent mountains. "He wouldn't give a fig for all that," she said, "if he didn't find me here."

"But consider," warned the Spirit, "that you are now choosing for eternity. It is a solemn moment."

"Choosing!" she said, with a half-sad smile. "Do you still keep up here that old fiction about choosing? I should have thought that *you* knew better than that. How can I help myself? He will expect to find me here when he comes, and he would never believe you if you told him that I had gone away with someone else—never, never."

"So be it," said the Spirit. "Here, as on earth, each one must decide for himself."

She turned to her kindred soul and looked at him gently, almost wistfully. "I am sorry," she said. "I should have liked to talk with you again; but you will understand, I know, and I dare say you will find someone else a great deal cleverer——"

And without pausing to hear his answer she waved him a swift farewell and turned back toward the threshold.

"Will my husband come soon?" she asked the Spirit of Life.

"That you are not destined to know," the Spirit replied.

"No matter," she said, cheerfully; "I have all eternity to wait in."

And still seated alone on the threshold, she listens for the creaking of his boots.

The Lamp of Psyche

DELIA CORBETT was too happy; her happiness frightened her. Not on theological grounds, however; she was sure that people had a right to be happy; but she was equally sure that it was a right seldom recognized by destiny. And her happiness almost touched the confines of pain—it bordered on that sharp ecstasy which she had known, through one sleepless night after another, when what had now become a reality had haunted her as an unattainable longing.

Delia Corbett was not in the habit of using what the French call *gros mots* in the rendering of her own emotions; she took herself, as a rule, rather flippantly, with a dash of contemptuous pity. But she felt that she had now entered upon a phase of existence wherein it became her to pay herself an almost reverential regard. Love had set his golden crown upon her forehead, and the awe of the office allotted her subdued her doubting heart. To her had been given the one portion denied to all other women on earth, the immense, the unapproachable privilege of becoming Laurence Corbett's wife.

Here she burst out laughing at the sound of her own thoughts, and rising from her seat walked across the drawing-room and looked at herself in the mirror above the mantelpiece. She was past thirty and had never been very pretty; but she knew herself to be capable of loving her husband better and pleasing him longer than any other woman in the world. She was not afraid of rivals; he and she had seen each other's souls.

She turned away, smiling carelessly at her insignificant reflection, and went back to her arm-chair near the balcony. The room in which she sat was very beautiful; it pleased Corbett to make all his surroundings beautiful. It was the drawing-room of his hotel in Paris, and the balcony near which his wife sat overlooked a small bosky garden framed in ivied walls, with a mouldering terra-cotta statue in the centre of its cup-shaped lawn. They had now been married some two months, and, after travelling for several weeks, had both desired to return to Paris; Corbett because he was really happier there than elsewhere, Delia because she passionately longed to enter as a wife the house where she had so often come and gone as a guest. How she used to find herself dreaming in the midst of one of Corbett's delightful dinners (to which she and her husband were continually being summoned) of a day when she might sit at the same table, but facing its master, a day when no carriage should wait to whirl her away from the brightly lit porte-cochère, and when, after the guests had gone, he and she should be left alone in his library, and she might sit down beside him and put her hand in his! The high-minded reader may infer from this that I am presenting him, in the person of Delia Corbett, with a heroine whom he would not like his wife to meet; but how many of us could face each other in the calm consciousness of moral rectitude if our inmost desire were not hidden under a convenient garb of lawful observance?

Delia Corbett, as Delia Benson, had been a very good wife to her first husband; some people (Corbett among them) had even thought her laxly tolerant of "poor Benson's" weaknesses. But then she knew her own; and it is admitted that nothing goes so far toward making us blink the foibles of others as the wish to have them extend a like mercy to ourselves. Not that Delia's foibles were of a tangible nature; they belonged to the order which escapes analysis by the coarse process of our social standards. Perhaps their very immateriality, the consciousness that she could never be brought to book for them before any human tribunal, made her the more restive under their weight; for she was of a nature to prefer buying her happiness to stealing it. But her rising scruples were perpetually being allayed by some fresh indiscretion of Benson's, to which she submitted with an undeviating amiability which flung her into the opposite extreme of wondering if she didn't really influence him to do wrong—if she mightn't help him to do better. All these psychological subtleties exerted, however, no influence over her conduct which, since the day of her marriage, had been a model of delicate circumspection. It was only necessary to look at Benson to see that the most eager reformer could have done little to improve him. In the first place he must have encountered the initial difficulty, most disheartening to reformers, of making his neophyte distinguish between right and wrong. Undoubtedly it was within the measure even of Benson's primitive perceptions to recognize that some actions were permissible and others were not; but his sole means of classifying them was to try both, and then deny having committed those of which his wife disapproved. Delia had once owned a poodle who greatly desired to sleep on a white fur rug which she destined to other uses. She and the poodle disagreed on the subject, and the latter, though submitting to her authority (when reinforced by a whip), could never be made to see the justice of her demand, and consequently (as the rug frequently revealed) never missed an opportunity of evading it when her back was turned. Her husband often reminded her of the poodle, and, not having a whip or its moral equivalent to control him with, she had long since resigned herself to seeing him smudge the whiteness of her early illusions. The worst of it was that her resignation was such a cheap virtue. She had to be perpetually rousing herself to a sense of Benson's enormities; through the ever-lengthening perspective of her indifference they looked as small as the details of a landscape seen through the wrong end of a telescope. Now and then she tried to remind herself that she had married him for love; but she was well aware that the sentiment she had once entertained for him had nothing in common with the state of mind which the words now represented to her; and this naturally diminished the force of the argument. She had married him at nineteen, because he had beautiful blue eyes and always wore a gardenia in his coat; really, as far as she could remember, these considerations had been the determining factors in her choice. Delia as a child (her parents were since dead) had been a much-indulged daughter, with a liberal allowance of pocket-money, and permission to spend it unquestioned and unadvised. Subsequently, she used sometimes to look, in a critical humor, at the various articles which she had purchased in her teens; futile chains and lockets, valueless china knick-knacks, and poor engravings of sentimental pictures. These, as a chastisement to her taste, she religiously preserved; and they often made her think of Benson. No one, she could not but reflect, would have blamed her if, with the

acquirement of a fuller discrimination, she had thrown them
all out of the window and replaced them by some object of
permanent merit; but she was expected not only to keep
Benson for life, but to conceal the fact that her taste had long
since discarded him.

It could hardly be expected that a woman who reasoned so
dispassionately about her mistakes should attempt to deceive
herself about her preferences. Corbett personified all those
finer amenities of mind and manners which may convert the
mere act of being into a beneficent career; to Delia he seemed
the most admirable man she had ever met, and she would
have thought it disloyal to her best aspirations not to admire
him. But she did not attempt to palliate her warmer feeling
under the mask of a plausible esteem; she knew that she loved
him, and scorned to disavow that also. So well, however, did
she keep her secret that Corbett himself never suspected it,
until her husband's death freed her from the obligation of
concealment. Then, indeed, she gloried in its confession; and
after two years of widowhood, and more than two months of
marriage, she was still under the spell of that moment of exquisite avowal.

She was reliving it now, as she often did in the rare hours
which separated her from her husband; when presently she
heard his step on the stairs, and started up with the blush of
eighteen. As she walked across the room to meet him she asked
herself perversely (she was given to such obliqueness of self-
scrutiny) if to a dispassionate eye he would appear as complete,
as supremely well-equipped as she beheld him, or if she walked
in a cloud of delusion, dense as the god-concealing mist of
Homer. But whenever she put this question to herself,
Corbett's appearance instantly relegated it to the limbo of
solved enigmas; he was so obviously admirable that she wondered that people didn't stop her in the street to attest her
good fortune.

As he came forward now, this renewal of satisfaction was so
strong in her that she felt an impulse to seize him and assure
herself of his reality; he was so perilously like the phantasms
of joy which had mocked her dissatisfied past. But his coat-
sleeve was convincingly tangible; and, pinching it, she felt the
muscles beneath.

"What—all alone?" he said, smiling back her welcome.

"No, I wasn't—I was with you!" she exclaimed; then fearing to appear fatuous, added, with a slight shrug, "Don't be alarmed—it won't last."

"That's what frightens me," he answered, gravely.

"Precisely," she laughed; "and I shall take good care not to reassure you!"

They stood face to face for a moment, reading in each other's eyes the completeness of their communion; then he broke the silence by saying, "By the way, I'd forgotten; here's a letter for you."

She took it unregardingly, her eyes still deep in his; but as her glance turned to the envelope she uttered a note of pleasure.

"Oh, now nice—it's from your only rival!"

"Your Aunt Mary?"

She nodded. "I haven't heard from her in a month—and I'm afraid I haven't written to her either. You don't know how many beneficent intentions of mine you divert from their proper channels."

"But your Aunt Mary has had you all your life—I've only had you two months," he objected.

Delia was still contemplating the letter with a smile. "Dear thing!" she murmured. "I wonder when I shall see her?"

"Write and ask her to come and spend the winter with us."

"What—and leave Boston, and her kindergartens, and associated charities, and symphony concerts, and debating clubs? You don't know Aunt Mary!"

"No, I don't. It seems so incongruous that you should adore such a bundle of pedantries."

"I forgive that, because you've never seen her. How I wish you could!"

He stood looking down at her with the all-promising smile of the happy lover. "Well, if she won't come to us we'll go to her."

"Laurence—and leave this!"

"It will keep—we'll come back to it. My dear girl, don't beam so; you make me feel as if you hadn't been happy until now."

"No—but it's your thinking of it!"

"I'll do more than think; I'll act; I'll take you to Boston to see your Aunt Mary."

"Oh, Laurence, you'd hate doing it."

"Not doing it together."

She laid her hand for a moment on his. "What a difference that does make in things!" she said, as she broke the seal of the letter.

"Well, I'll leave you to commune with Aunt Mary. When you've done, come and find me in the library."

Delia sat down joyfully to the perusal of her letter, but as her eye travelled over the closely written pages her gratified expression turned to one of growing concern; and presently, thrusting it back into the envelope, she followed her husband to the library. It was a charming room and singularly indicative, to her fancy, of its occupant's character; the expanse of harmonious bindings, the fruity bloom of Renaissance bronzes, and the imprisoned sunlight of two or three old pictures fitly epitomizing the delicate ramifications of her husband's taste. But now her glance lingered less appreciatively than usual on the warm tones and fine lines which formed so expressive a background for Corbett's fastidious figure.

"Aunt Mary has been ill—I'm afraid she's been seriously ill," she announced as he rose to receive her. "She fell in coming down-stairs from one of her tenement-house inspections, and it brought on water on the knee. She's been laid up ever since—some three or four weeks now. I'm afraid it's rather bad at her age; and I don't know how she will resign herself to keeping quiet."

"I'm very sorry," said Corbett, sympathetically; "but water on the knee isn't dangerous, you know."

"No—but the doctor says she mustn't go out for weeks and weeks; and that will drive her mad. She'll think the universe has come to a standstill."

"She'll find it hasn't," suggested Corbett, with a smile which took the edge from his comment.

"Ah, but such discoveries hurt—especially if one makes them late in life!"

Corbett stood looking affectionately at his wife.

"How long is it," he asked, "since you have seen your Aunt Mary?"

"I think it must be two years. Yes, just two years; you know I went home on business after——" She stopped; they never alluded to her first marriage.

Corbett took her hand. "Well," he declared, glancing rather wistfully at the Paris Bordone above the mantel-piece, "we'll sail next month and pay her a little visit."

II

Corbett was really making an immense concession in going to America at that season; he disliked the prospect at all times, but just as his hotel in Paris had reopened its luxurious arms to him for the winter, the thought of departure was peculiarly distasteful. Delia knew it, and winced under the enormity of the sacrifice which he had imposed upon himself; but he bore the burden so lightly, and so smilingly derided her impulse to magnify the heroism of his conduct, that she gradually yielded to the undisturbed enjoyment of her anticipations. She was really very glad to be returning to Boston as Corbett's wife; her occasional appearances there as Mrs. Benson had been so eminently unsatisfactory to herself and her relatives that she naturally desired to efface them by so triumphal a re-entry. She had passed so great a part of her own life in Europe that she viewed with a secret leniency Corbett's indifference to his native land; but though she did not mind his not caring for his country she was intensely anxious that his country should care for him. He was a New Yorker, and entirely unknown, save by name, to her little circle of friends and relatives in Boston; but she reflected, with tranquil satisfaction, that, if he were cosmopolitan enough for Fifth Avenue, he was also cultured enough for Beacon Street. She was not so confident of his being altruistic enough for Aunt Mary; but Aunt Mary's appreciations covered so wide a range that there seemed small doubt of his coming under the head of one of her manifold enthusiasms.

Altogether Delia's anticipations grew steadily rosier with the approach to Sandy Hook; and to her confident eye the Statue of Liberty, as they passed under it in the red brilliance of a winter sunrise, seemed to look down upon Corbett with her Aunt Mary's most approving smile.

Delia's Aunt Mary—known from the Back Bay to the South End as Mrs. Mason Hayne—had been the chief formative influence of her niece's youth. Delia, after the death of her parents, had even spent two years under Mrs. Hayne's roof, in direct contact with all her apostolic ardors, her inflammatory zeal for righteousness in everything from baking-powder to municipal government; and though the girl never felt any inclination to interpret her aunt's influence in action, it was potent in modifying her judgment of herself and others. Her parents had been incurably frivolous, Mrs. Hayne was incurably serious, and Delia, by some unconscious powers of selection, tended to frivolity of conduct, corrected by seriousness of thought. She would have shrunk from the life of unadorned activity, the unsmiling pursuit of Purposes with a capital letter, to which Mrs. Hayne's energies were dedicated; but it lent relief to her enjoyment of the purposeless to measure her own conduct by her aunt's utilitarian standards. This curious sympathy with aims so at variance with her own ideals would hardly have been possible to Delia had Mrs. Hayne been a narrow enthusiast without visual range beyond the blinders of her own vocation; it was the consciousness that her aunt's perceptions included even such obvious inutility as hers which made her so tolerant of her aunt's usefulness. All this she had tried, on the way across the Atlantic, to put vividly before Corbett; but she was conscious of a vague inability on his part to adjust his conception of Mrs. Hayne to his wife's view of her; and Delia could only count on her aunt's abounding personality to correct the one-sidedness of his impression.

Mrs. Hayne lived in a wide brick house on Mount Vernon Street, which had belonged to her parents and grandparents, and from which she had never thought of moving. Thither, on the evening of their arrival in Boston, the Corbetts were driven from the Providence Station. Mrs. Hayne had written to her niece that Cyrus would meet them with a "hack;" Cyrus was a sable factotum designated in Mrs. Hayne's vocabulary as a "chore-man." When the train entered the station he was, in fact, conspicuous on the platform, his smile shining like an open piano, while he proclaimed with abundant gesture the proximity of "de hack," and Delia, descending from the train into his dusky embrace, found herself guiltily wishing that he could have been omitted from the function of their arrival. She could not help wondering what her husband's valet would think of him. The valet was to be lodged at a hotel: Corbett himself had suggested that his presence might disturb the routine of Mrs. Hayne's household, a view in which Delia had eagerly acquiesced. There was, however, no possibility of dissembling Cyrus, and under the valet's depreciatory eye the Corbetts suffered him to precede them to the livery-stable landau, with blue shades and a confidentially disposed driver, which awaited them outside the station.

During the drive to Mount Vernon Street Delia was silent; but as they approached her aunt's swell-fronted domicile she said, hurriedly, "You won't like the house."

Corbett laughed. "It's the inmate I've come to see," he commented.

"Oh, I'm not afraid of her," Delia almost too confidently rejoined.

The parlor-maid who admitted them to the hall (a discouraging hall, with a large-patterned oil-cloth and buff walls stencilled with a Greek border) informed them that Mrs. Hayne was above; and ascending to the next floor they found her genial figure, supported on crutches, awaiting them at the drawing-room door. Mrs. Hayne was a tall, stoutish woman, whose bland expanse of feature was accentuated by a pair of gray eyes of such surpassing penetration that Delia often accused her of answering people's thoughts before they had finished thinking them. These eyes, through the close fold of Delia's embrace, pierced instantly to Corbett, and never had that accomplished gentleman been more conscious of being called upon to present his credentials. But there was no reservation in the uncritical warmth of Mrs. Hayne's welcome, and it was obvious that she was unaffectedly happy in their coming.

She led them into the drawing-room, still clinging to Delia, and Corbett, as he followed, understood why his wife had said that he would not like the house. One saw at a glance that Mrs. Hayne had never had time to think of her house or her dress. Both were scrupulously neat, but her gown might have been an unaltered one of her mother's, and her drawing-room wore the same appearance of contented archaism. There was a sufficient number of arm-chairs, and the tables (mostly marble-topped) were redeemed from monotony by their freight of books; but it had not occurred to Mrs. Hayne to substitute logs for hard coal in her fireplace, nor to replace by more personal works of art the smoky expanses of canvas "after" Raphael and Murillo which lurched heavily forward from the walls. She had even preserved the knotty antimacassars on her high-backed armchairs, and Corbett, who was growing bald, resignedly reflected that during his stay in Mount Vernon Street he should not be able to indulge in any lounging.

III

Delia held back for three days the question which burned her lip; then, following her husband upstairs after an evening during which Mrs. Hayne had proved herself especially comprehensive (even questioning Corbett upon the tendencies of modern French art), she let escape the imminent "Well?"

"She's charming," Corbett returned, with the fine smile which always seemed like a delicate criticism.

"Really?"

"Really, Delia. Do you think me so narrow that I can't value such a character as your aunt's simply because it's cast in different lines from mine? I once told you that she must be a bundle of pedantries, and you prophesied that my first sight of her would correct that impression. You were right; she's a bundle of extraordinary vitalities. I never saw a woman more thoroughly alive; and that's the great secret of living—to be thoroughly alive."

"I knew it; I knew it!" his wife exclaimed. "Two such people couldn't help liking each other."

"Oh, I should think she might very well help liking me."

"She doesn't; she admires you immensely; but why?"

"Well, I don't precisely fit into any of her ideals, and the worst part of having ideals is that the people who don't fit into them have to be discarded."

"Aunt Mary doesn't discard anybody," Delia interpolated.

"Her heart may not, but I fancy her judgment does."

"But she doesn't exactly fit into any of your ideals, and yet you like her," his wife persisted.

"I haven't any ideals," Corbett lightly responded. "*Je prends mon bien où je le trouve*; and I find a great deal in your Aunt Mary."

Delia did not ask Mrs. Hayne what she thought of her husband; she was sure that, in due time, her aunt would deliver her verdict; it was impossible for her to leave any one unclassified. Perhaps, too, there was a latent cowardice in Delia's reticence; an unacknowledged dread lest Mrs. Hayne should range Corbett among the intermediate types.

After a day or two of mutual inspection and adjustment the three lives under Mrs. Hayne's roof lapsed into their separate routines. Mrs. Hayne once more set in motion the complicated machinery of her own existence (rendered more intricate by the accident of her lameness), and Corbett and his wife began to dine out and return the visits of their friends. There were, however, some hours which Corbett devoted to the club or to the frequentation of the public libraries, and these Delia gave to her aunt, driving with Mrs. Hayne from one committee meeting to another, writing business letters at her dictation, or reading aloud to her the reports of the various philanthropic, educational, or political institutions in which she was interested. She had been conscious on her arrival of a certain aloofness from her aunt's militant activities; but within a week she was swept back into the strong current of Mrs. Hayne's existence. It was like stepping from a gondola to an ocean steamer; at first she was dazed by the throb of the screw and the rush of the parting waters, but gradually she felt herself infected by the exhilaration of getting to a fixed place in the shortest possible time. She could make sufficient allowance for the versatility of her moods to know that, a few weeks after her return to Paris, all that seemed most strenuous in Mrs. Hayne's occupations would fade to unreality; but that did not defend her from the strong spell of the moment. In its light her own life seemed vacuous, her husband's aims trivial as the subtleties of Chinese ivory carving; and she wondered if he walked in the same revealing flash.

Some three weeks after the arrival of the Corbetts in Mount Vernon Street it became manifest that Mrs. Hayne had overtaxed her strength and must return for an undetermined period to her lounge. The life of restricted activity to which this necessity condemned her left her an occasional hour of leisure when there seemed no more letters to be dictated, no more reports to be read; and Corbett, always sure to do the right thing, was at hand to speed such unoccupied moments with the ready charm of his talk.

One day when, after sitting with her for some time, he departed to the club, Mrs. Hayne, turning to Delia, who came in to replace him, said, emphatically, "My dear, he's delightful."

"Oh, Aunt Mary, so are you!" burst gratefully from Mrs. Corbett.

Mrs. Hayne smiled. "Have you suspended your judgment of me until now?" she asked.

"No; but your liking each other seems to complete you both."

"Really, Delia, your husband couldn't have put that more gracefully. But sit down and tell me about him."

"Tell you about him?" repeated Delia, thinking of the voluminous letters in which she had enumerated to Mrs. Hayne the sum of her husband's merits.

"Yes," Mrs. Hayne continued, cutting, as she talked, the pages of a report on state lunatic asylums; "for instance, you've never told me why so charming an American has condemned America to the hard fate of being obliged to get on without him."

"You and he will never agree on that point, Aunt Mary," said Mrs. Corbett, coloring.

"Never mind; I rather like listening to reasons that I know beforehand I'm bound to disagree with; it saves so much mental effort. And besides, how can you tell? I'm very uncertain."

"You are very broad-minded, but you'll never understand his just having drifted into it. Any definite reason would seem to you better than that."

"Ah—he drifted into it?"

"Well, yes. You know his sister, who married the Comte de Vitrey and went to live in Paris, was very unhappy after her marriage; and when Laurence's mother died there was no one left to look after her; and so Laurence went abroad in order to be near her. After a few years Monsieur de Vitrey died too; but by that time Laurence didn't care to come back."

"Well," said Mrs. Hayne, "I see nothing so shocking in that. Your husband can gratify his tastes much more easily in Europe than in America; and, after all, that is what we're all secretly striving to do. I'm sure if there were more lunatic asylums and poor-houses and hospitals in Europe than there are here I should be very much inclined to go and live there myself."

Delia laughed. "I knew you would like Laurence," she said, with a wisdom bred of the event.

"Of course I like him; he's a liberal education. It's very interesting to study the determining motives in such a man's career. How old is your husband, Delia?"

"Laurence is fifty-two."

"And when did he go abroad to look after his sister?"

"Let me see—when he was about twenty-eight; it was in 1867, I think."

"And before that he had lived in America?"

"Yes, the greater part of the time."

"Then of course he was in the war?" Mrs. Hayne continued, laying down her pamphlet. "You've never told me about that. Did he see any active service?"

As she spoke Delia grew pale; for a moment she sat looking blankly at her aunt.

"I don't think he was in the war at all," she said at length, in a low tone.

Mrs. Hayne stared at her. "Oh, you must be mistaken," she said, decidedly. "Why shouldn't he have been in the war? What else could he have been doing?"

Mrs. Corbett was silent. All the men of her family, all the men of her friends' families, had fought in the war; Mrs. Hayne's husband had been killed at Bull Run, and one of Delia's cousins at Gettysburg. Ever since she could remember it had been regarded as a matter of course by those about her that every man of her husband's generation who was neither lame, halt, nor blind should have fought in the war. Husbands had left their wives, fathers their children, young men their sweethearts, in answer to that summons; and those who had been deaf to it she had never heard designated by any name but one.

But all that had happened long ago; for years it had ceased to be a part of her consciousness. She had forgotten about the war; about her uncle who fell at Bull Run, and her cousin who was killed at Gettysburg. Now, of a sudden, it all came back to her, and she asked herself the question which her aunt had just put to her—why had her husband not been in the war? What else could he have been doing?

But the very word, as she repeated it, struck her as incongruous; Corbett was a man who never did anything. His elaborate intellectual processes bore no flower of result; he simply *was*—but had she not hitherto found that sufficient? She rose from her seat, turning away from Mrs. Hayne.

"I really don't know," she said, coldly. "I never asked him."

IV

Two weeks later the Corbetts returned to Europe. Corbett had really been charmed with his visit, and had in fact shown a marked inclination to outstay the date originally fixed for their departure. But Delia was firm; she did not wish to remain in Boston. She acknowledged that she was sorry to leave her Aunt Mary; but she wanted to get home.

"You turncoat!" Corbett said, laughing. "Two months ago you reserved that sacred designation for Boston."

"One can't tell where it is until one tries," she answered, vaguely.

"You mean that you don't want to come back and live in Boston?"

"Oh, no—no!"

"Very well. But pray take note of the fact that I'm very sorry to leave. Under your Aunt Mary's tutelage I'm becoming a passionate patriot."

Delia turned away in silence. She was counting the moments which led to their departure. She longed with an unreasoning intensity to get away from it all; from the dreary house in Mount Vernon Street, with its stencilled hall and hideous drawing-room, its monotonous food served in unappetizing profusion; from the rarefied atmosphere of philanthropy and reform which she had once found so invigorating; and most of all from the reproval of her aunt's altruistic activities. The recollection of her husband's delightful house in Paris, so framed for a noble leisure, seemed to mock the æsthetic barrenness of Mrs. Hayne's environment. Delia thought tenderly of the mellow bindings, the deep-piled rugs, the pictures, bronzes, and tapestries; of the "first nights" at the Français, the eagerly discussed *conférences* on art or literature, the dreaming hours in galleries and museums, and all the delicate enjoyments of the life to which she was returning. It would be like passing from a hospital-ward to a flower-filled drawing-room; how could her husband linger on the threshold?

Corbett, who observed her attentively, noticed that a change had come over her during the last two weeks of their stay in Mount Vernon Street. He wondered uneasily if she were capricious; a man who has formed his own habits upon principles of the finest selection does not care to think that he has married a capricious woman. Then he reflected that the love of Paris is an insidious disease, breaking out when its victim least looks for it, and concluded that Delia was suffering from some such unexpected attack.

Delia certainly was suffering. Ever since Mrs. Hayne had asked her that innocent question—"Why shouldn't your husband have been in the war?"—she had been repeating it to herself day and night with the monotonous iteration of a monomaniac. Whenever Corbett came into the room, with that air of giving the simplest act its due value which made episodes of his entrances she was tempted to cry out to him—"Why weren't you in the war?" When she heard him, at a dinner, point one of his polished epigrams, or smilingly demolish the syllogism of an antagonist, her pride in his achievement was chilled by the question—"Why wasn't he in the war?" When she saw him, in the street, give a coin to a crossing-sweeper, or lift his hat ceremoniously to one of Mrs. Hayne's maid-servants (he was always considerate of poor people and servants) her approval winced under the reminder—"Why wasn't he in the war?" And when they were alone together, all through the spell of his talk and the exquisite pervasion of his presence ran the embittering undercurrent, "Why wasn't he in the war?"

At times she hated herself for the thought; it seemed a disloyalty to life's best gift. After all, what did it matter now? The war was over and forgotten; it was what the newspapers call "a dead issue." And why should any act of her husband's youth affect their present happiness together? Whatever he might once have been, he was perfect now; admirable in every relation of life; kind, generous, upright; a loyal friend, an accomplished gentleman, and, above all, the man she loved. Yes—but why had he not been in the war? And so began again the reiterant torment of the question. It rose up and lay down with her; it watched with her through sleepless nights, and followed her into the street; it mocked her from the eyes of strangers, and she dreaded lest her husband should read it in her own. In her saner moments she told herself that she was under the influence of a passing mood, which would vanish at the contact of her wonted life in Paris. She had become over-strung in the high air of Mrs. Hayne's moral enthusiasms; all she needed was to descend again to regions of more temperate virtue. This thought increased her impatience to be gone; and the days seemed interminable which divided her from departure.

The return to Paris, however, did not yield the hoped-for alleviation. The question was still with her, clamoring for a reply, and reinforced, with separation, by the increasing fear of her aunt's unspoken verdict. That shrewd woman had never again alluded to the subject of her brief colloquy with Delia; up to the moment of his farewell she had been unreservedly cordial to Corbett; but she was not the woman to palter with her convictions.

Delia knew what she must think; she knew what name, in the old days, Corbett would have gone by in her aunt's uncompromising circle.

Then came a flash of resistance—the heart's instinct of self-preservation. After all, what did she herself know of her husband's reasons for not being in the war? What right had she to set down to cowardice a course which might have been enforced by necessity, or dictated by unimpeachable motives? Why should she not put to him the question which she was perpetually asking herself? And not having done so, how dared she condemn him unheard?

A month or more passed in this torturing indecision. Corbett had returned with fresh zest to his accustomed way of life, weaned, by his first glimpse of the Champs Élysées, from his factitious enthusiasm for Boston. He and his wife entertained their friends delightfully, and frequented all the "first nights" and "private views" of the season, and Corbett continued to bring back knowing "bits" from the Hôtel Drouot, and rare books from the quays; never had he appeared more cultivated, more decorative and enviable; people agreed that Delia Benson had been uncommonly clever to catch him.

One afternoon he returned later than usual from the club, and, finding his wife alone in the drawing-room, begged her for a cup of tea. Delia reflected, in complying, that she had never seen him look better; his fifty-two years sat upon him like a finish which made youth appear crude, and his voice, as he recounted his afternoon's doings, had the intimate inflections reserved for her ear.

"By the way," he said presently, as he set down his tea-cup, "I had almost forgotten that I've brought you a present— something I picked up in a little shop in the Rue Bonaparte. Oh, don't look too expectant; it's not a *chef-d'œuvre*; on the contrary, it's about as bad as it can be. But you'll see presently why I bought it."

As he spoke he drew a small, flat parcel from the breast-pocket of his impeccable frock-coat and handed it to his wife.

Delia, loosening the paper which wrapped it, discovered within an oval frame studded with pearls and containing the crudely executed miniature of an unknown young man in the uniform of a United States cavalry officer. She glanced inquiringly at Corbett.

"Turn it over," he said.

She did so, and on the back, beneath two unfamiliar initials, read the brief inscription:

"Fell at Chancellorsville, May 3, 1863."

The blood rushed to her face as she stood gazing at the words.

"You see now why I bought it?" Corbett continued. "All the pieties of one's youth seemed to protest against leaving it in the clutches of a Jew pawnbroker in the Rue Bonaparte.

It's awfully bad, isn't it?—but some poor soul might be glad
to think that it had passed again into the possession of fellow-
countrymen." He took it back from her, bending to examine
it critically. "What a daub!" he murmured. "I wonder who he
was? Do you suppose that by taking a little trouble one might
find out and restore it to his people?"

"I don't know—I dare say," she murmured, absently.

He looked up at the sound of her voice. "What's the matter, Delia? Don't you feel well?" he asked.

"Oh, yes. I was only thinking"——she took the miniature
from his hand. "It was kind of you, Laurence, to buy this—it
was like you."

"Thanks for the latter clause," he returned, smiling.

Delia stood staring at the vivid flesh-tints of the young man
who had fallen at Chancellorsville.

"You weren't very strong at his age, were you, Laurence?
Weren't you often ill?" she asked.

Corbett gave her a surprised glance. "Not that I'm aware
of," he said; "I had the measles at twelve, but since then I've
been unromantically robust."

"And you—you were in America until you came abroad to
be with your sister?"

"Yes—barring a trip of a few weeks in Europe."

Delia looked again at the miniature; then she fixed her eyes
upon her husband's.

"Then why weren't you in the war?" she said.

Corbett answered her gaze for a moment; then his lids
dropped, and he shifted his position slightly.

"Really," he said, with a smile, "I don't think I know."

They were the very words which she had used in answering
her aunt.

"You don't know?" she repeated, the question leaping out
like an electric shock. "What do you mean when you say that
you don't know?"

"Well—it all happened some time ago," he answered, still
smiling, "and the truth is that I've completely forgotten the
excellent reasons that I doubtless had at the time for remaining at home."

"Reasons for remaining at home? But there were none;
every man of your age went to the war; no one stayed at

home who wasn't lame, or blind, or deaf, or ill, or——" Her face blazed, her voice broke passionately.

Corbett looked at her with rising amazement.

"Or——?" he said.

"Or a coward," she flashed out. The miniature dropped from her hands, falling loudly on the polished floor.

The two confronted each other in silence; Corbett was very pale.

"I've told you," he said, at length, "that I was neither lame, deaf, blind, nor ill. Your classification is so simple that it will be easy for you to draw your own conclusion."

And very quietly, with that admirable air which always put him in the right, he walked out of the room. Delia, left alone, bent down and picked up the miniature; its protecting crystal had been broken by the fall. She pressed it close to her and burst into tears.

An hour later, of course, she went to ask her husband's forgiveness. As a woman of sense she could do no less; and her conduct had been so absurd that it was the more obviously pardonable. Corbett, as he kissed her hand, assured her that he had known it was only nervousness; and after dinner, during which he made himself exceptionally agreeable, he proposed their ending the evening at the Palais Royal, where a new play was being given.

Delia had undoubtedly behaved like a fool, and was prepared to do meet penance for her folly by submitting to the gentle sarcasm of her husband's pardon; but when the episode was over, and she realized that she had asked her question and received her answer, she knew that she had passed a milestone in her existence. Corbett was perfectly charming; it was inevitable that he should go on being charming to the end of the chapter. It was equally inevitable that she should go on being in love with him; but her love had undergone a modification which the years were not to efface.

Formerly he had been to her like an unexplored country, full of bewitching surprises and recurrent revelations of wonder and beauty; now she had measured and mapped him, and knew beforehand the direction of every path she trod. His answer to her question had given her the clue to the labyrinth; knowing what he had once done, it seemed quite simple to forecast his future conduct. For that long-past action was still a part of his actual being; he had not outlived or disowned it; he had not even seen that it needed defending.

Her ideal of him was shivered like the crystal above the miniature of the warrior of Chancellorsville. She had the crystal replaced by a piece of clear glass which (as the jeweller pointed out to her) cost much less and looked equally well; and for the passionate worship which she had paid her husband she substituted a tolerant affection which possessed precisely the same advantages.

The Valley of Childish Things, and Other Emblems

ONCE upon a time a number of children lived together in the Valley of Childish Things, playing all manner of delightful games, and studying the same lesson-books. But one day a little girl, one of their number, decided that it was time to see something of the world about which the lesson-books had taught her; and as none of the other children cared to leave their games, she set out alone to climb the pass which led out of the valley.

It was a hard climb, but at length she reached a cold, bleak table-land beyond the mountains. Here she saw cities and men, and learned many useful arts, and in so doing grew to be a woman. But the table-land was bleak and cold, and when she had served her apprenticeship she decided to return to her old companions in the Valley of Childish Things, and work with them instead of with strangers.

It was a weary way back, and her feet were bruised by the stones, and her face was beaten by the weather; but half way down the pass she met a man, who kindly helped her over the roughest places. Like herself, he was lame and weather-beaten; but as soon as he spoke she recognized him as one of her old playmates. He too had been out in the world, and was going back to the valley; and on the way they talked together of the work they meant to do there. He had been a dull boy, and she had never taken much notice of him; but as she listened to his plans for building bridges and draining swamps and cutting roads through the jungle, she thought to herself, "Since he has grown into such a fine fellow, what splendid men and women my other playmates must have become!"

But what was her surprise to find, on reaching the valley, that her former companions, instead of growing into men and women, had all remained little children. Most of them were playing the same old games, and the few who affected to be working were engaged in such strenuous occupations as building mudpies and sailing paper boats in basins. As for

the lad who had been the favorite companion of her studies, he was playing marbles with all the youngest boys in the
valley.

At first the children seemed glad to have her back, but soon
she saw that her presence interfered with their games; and
when she tried to tell them of the great things that were
being done on the table-land beyond the mountains, they
picked up their toys and went farther down the valley to play.

Then she turned to her fellow-traveler, who was the only
grown man in the valley; but he was on his knees before a
dear little girl with blue eyes and a coral necklace, for whom
he was making a garden out of cockle-shells and bits of glass,
and broken flowers stuck in sand.

The little girl was clapping her hands and crowing (she was
too young to speak articulately); and when she who had
grown to be a woman laid her hand on the man's shoulder,
and asked him if he did not want to set to work with her
building bridges, draining swamps, and cutting roads through
the jungle, he replied that at that particular moment he was
too busy.

And as she turned away, he added in the kindest possible
way, "Really, my dear, you ought to have taken better care of
your complexion."

II

There was once a maiden lady who lived alone in a commodious brick house facing north and south. The lady was
very fond of warmth and sunshine, but unfortunately her
room was on the north side of the house, so that in winter
she had no sun at all.

This distressed her so much that, after long deliberation,
she sent for an architect, and asked him if it would be possible to turn the house around so that her room should face the
south. The architect replied that anything could be done for
money; but the estimated cost of turning the house around
was so high that the lady, who enjoyed a handsome income,
was obliged to reduce her way of living and sell her securities
at a sacrifice to raise money enough for the purpose. At
length, however, the house was turned around, and she felt

almost consoled for her impoverishment by the first ray of sunlight which stole through her shutters the next morning.

That very day she received a visit from an old friend who had been absent a year; and this friend, finding her seated at her window in a flood of sunlight, immediately exclaimed:

"My dear, how sensible of you to have moved into a south room! I never could understand why you persisted so long in living on the north side of the house."

And the following day the architect sent in his bill.

III

There was once a little girl who was so very intelligent that her parents feared that she would die.

But an aged aunt, who had crossed the Atlantic in a sailing-vessel, said, "My dears, let her marry the first man she falls in love with, and she will make such a fool of herself that it will probably save her life."

IV

A thinly clad man, who was trudging afoot through a wintry and shelterless region, met another wrapped in a big black cloak. The cloak hung heavily on its wearer, and seemed to drag him back, but at least it kept off the cold.

"That's a fine warm cloak you've got," said the first man through his chattering teeth.

"Oh," said the other, "it's none of my choosing, I promise you. It's only my old happiness dyed black and made over into a sorrow; but in this weather a man must wear what he's got."

"To think of some people's luck!" muttered the first man, as the other passed on. "Now I never had enough happiness to make a sorrow out of."

V

There was once a man who married a sweet little wife; but when he set out with her from her father's house, he found that she had never been taught to walk. They had a long way to go, and there was nothing for him to do but to carry her; and as he carried her she grew heavier and heavier.

Then they came to a wide, deep river, and he found that she had never been taught to swim. So he told her to hold fast to his shoulder, and started to swim with her across the river. And as he swam she grew frightened, and dragged him down in her struggles. And the river was deep and wide, and the current ran fast; and once or twice she nearly had him under. But he fought his way through, and landed her safely on the other side; and behold, he found himself in a strange country, beyond all imagining delightful. And as he looked about him and gave thanks, he said to himself:

"Perhaps if I hadn't had to carry her over, I shouldn't have kept up long enough to get here myself."

VI

A soul once cowered in a gray waste, and a mighty shape came by. Then the soul cried out for help, saying, "Shall I be left to perish alone in this desert of Unsatisfied Desires?"

"But you are mistaken," the shape replied; "this is the land of Gratified Longings. And, moreover, you are not alone, for the country is full of people; but whoever tarries here grows blind."

VII

There was once a very successful architect who made a great name for himself. At length he built a magnificent temple, to which he devoted more time and thought than to any of the other buildings he had erected; and the world pronounced it his masterpiece. Shortly afterward he died, and when he came before the judgment angel he was not asked how many sins he had committed, but how many houses he had built.

He hung his head and said, more than he could count.

The judgment angel asked what they were like, and the architect said that he was afraid they were pretty bad.

"And are you sorry?" asked the angel.

"Very sorry," said the architect, with honest contrition.

"And how about that famous temple that you built just before you died?" the angel continued. "Are you satisfied with that?"

"Oh, no," the architect exclaimed. "I really think it has some good points about it,—I did try my best, you know,—but there's one dreadful mistake that I'd give my soul to go back and rectify."

"Well," said the angel, "you can't go back and rectify it, but you can take your choice of the following alternatives: either we can let the world go on thinking your temple a masterpiece and you the greatest architect that ever lived, or we can send to earth a young fellow we've got here who will discover your mistake at a glance, and point it out so clearly to posterity that you'll be the laughing-stock of all succeeding generations of architects. Which do you choose?"

"Oh, well," said the architect, "if it comes to that, you know—as long as it suits my clients as it is, I really don't see the use of making such a fuss."

VIII

A man once married a charming young person who agreed with him on every question. At first they were very happy, for the man thought his wife the most interesting companion he had ever met, and they spent their days telling each other what wonderful people they were. But by and by the man began to find his wife rather tiresome. Wherever he went she insisted upon going; whatever he did, she was sure to tell him that it would have been better to do the opposite; and moreover, it gradually dawned upon him that his friends had never thought so highly of her as he did. Having made this discovery, he naturally felt justified in regarding himself as the aggrieved party; she took the same view of her situation, and their life was one of incessant recrimination.

Finally, after years spent in violent quarrels and short-lived reconciliations, the man grew weary, and decided to divorce his wife.

He engaged an able lawyer, who assured him that he would have no difficulty in obtaining a divorce; but to his surprise, the judge refused to grant it.

"But—" said the man, and he began to recapitulate his injuries.

"That's all very true," said the judge, "and nothing would be easier than for you to obtain a divorce if you had only married another person."

"What do you mean by another person?" asked the man in astonishment.

"Well," replied the judge, "it appears that you inadvertently married yourself; that is a union no court has the power to dissolve."

"Oh," said the man; and he was secretly glad, for in his heart he was already longing to make it up again with his wife.

IX

There was once a gentleman who greatly disliked to assume any responsibility. Being possessed of ample means and numerous poor relatives, he might have indulged a variety of tastes and even a few virtues; but since there is no occupation that does not bring a few cares in its train, this gentleman resolutely refrained from doing anything.

He ceased to visit his old mother, who lived in the country, because it made him nervous to catch the train; he subscribed to no charities because it was a bother to write the checks; he received no visits because he did not wish to be under the obligation of returning them; he invited no guests to stay with him, for fear of being bored before they left; he gave no presents because it was so troublesome to choose them; finally, he even gave up asking his friends to dine because it was such a nuisance to tell the cook that they were coming.

This gentleman took an honest pride in his complete detachment from the trivial importunities of life, and was never tired of ridiculing those who complained of the weight of their responsibilities, justly remarking that if they really wished to be their own masters they had only to follow his example.

One day, however, one of his servants carelessly left the front door open, and Death walked in unannounced, and begged the gentleman to come along as quickly as possible, as there were a good many more people to be called for that afternoon.

"But I can't," cried the gentleman, in dismay. "I really can't, you know. I—why, I've asked some people to dine with me this evening."

"That's a little too much," said Death. And the devil carried the gentleman off in a big black bag.

X

There was once a man who had seen the Parthenon, and he wished to build his god a temple like it.

But he was not a skilful man, and, try as he would, he could produce only a mud hut thatched with straw; and he sat down and wept because he could not build a temple for his god.

But one who passed by said to him:

"There are two worse plights than yours. One is to have no god; the other is to build a mud hut and mistake it for the Parthenon."

The Muse's Tragedy

D ANYERS afterwards liked to fancy that he had recognized Mrs. Anerton at once; but that, of course, was absurd, since he had seen no portrait of her—she affected a strict anonymity, refusing even her photograph to the most privileged—and from Mrs. Memorall, whom he revered and cultivated as her friend, he had extracted but the one impressionist phrase: "Oh, well, she's like one of those old prints where the lines have the value of color."

He was almost certain, at all events, that he had been thinking of Mrs. Anerton as he sat over his breakfast in the empty hotel restaurant, and that, looking up on the approach of the lady who seated herself at the table near the window, he had said to himself, *"That might be she."*

Ever since his Harvard days—he was still young enough to think of them as immensely remote—Danyers had dreamed of Mrs. Anerton, the Silvia of Vincent Rendle's immortal sonnet-cycle, the Mrs. A. of the *Life and Letters*. Her name was enshrined in some of the noblest English verse of the nineteenth century—and of all past or future centuries, as Danyers, from the stand-point of a maturer judgment, still believed. The first reading of certain poems—of the *Antinous*, the *Pia Tolomei*, the *Sonnets to Silvia*,—had been epochs in Danyers's growth, and the verse seemed to gain in mellowness, in amplitude, in meaning as one brought to its interpretation more experience of life, a finer emotional sense. Where, in his boyhood, he had felt only the perfect, the almost austere beauty of form, the subtle interplay of vowel-sounds, the rush and fulness of lyric emotion, he now thrilled to the close-packed significance of each line, the allusiveness of each word—his imagination lured hither and thither on fresh trails of thought, and perpetually spurred by the sense that, beyond what he had already discovered, more marvellous regions lay waiting to be explored. Danyers had written, at college, the prize essay on Rendle's poetry (it chanced to be the moment of the great man's death); he had fashioned the fugitive verse of his own storm-and-stress period on the forms which

Rendle had first given to English metre; and when two years later the *Life and Letters* appeared, and the Silvia of the sonnets took substance as Mrs. A., he had included in his worship of Rendle the woman who had inspired not only such divine verse but such playful, tender, incomparable prose.

Danyers never forgot the day when Mrs. Memorall happened to mention that she knew Mrs. Anerton. He had known Mrs. Memorall for a year or more, and had somewhat contemptuously classified her as the kind of woman who runs cheap excursions to celebrities; when one afternoon she remarked, as she put a second lump of sugar in his tea:

"Is it right this time? You're almost as particular as Mary Anerton."

"Mary Anerton?"

"Yes, I never *can* remember how she likes her tea. Either it's lemon *with* sugar, or lemon without sugar, or cream without either, and whichever it is must be put into the cup before the tea is poured in; and if one hasn't remembered, one must begin all over again. I suppose it was Vincent Rendle's way of taking his tea and has become a sacred rite."

"Do you *know* Mrs. Anerton?" cried Danyers, disturbed by this careless familiarity with the habits of his divinity.

" 'And did I once see Shelley plain?' Mercy, yes! She and I were at school together—she's an American, you know. We were at a *pension* near Tours for nearly a year; then she went back to New York, and I didn't see her again till after her marriage. She and Anerton spent a winter in Rome while my husband was attached to our Legation there, and she used to be with us a great deal." Mrs. Memorall smiled reminiscently. "It was *the* winter."

"The winter they first met?"

"Precisely—but unluckily I left Rome just before the meeting took place. Wasn't it too bad? I might have been in the *Life and Letters*. You know he mentions that stupid Madame Vodki, at whose house he first saw her."

"And did you see much of her after that?"

"Not during Rendle's life. You know she has lived in Europe almost entirely, and though I used to see her off and on when I went abroad, she was always so engrossed, so preoccupied, that one felt one wasn't wanted. The fact is, she cared only about his friends—she separated herself gradually from all her own people. Now, of course, it's different; she's desperately lonely; she's taken to writing to me now and then; and last year, when she heard I was going abroad, she asked me to meet her in Venice, and I spent a week with her there."

"And Rendle?"

Mrs. Memorall smiled and shook her head. "Oh, I never was allowed a peep at *him*; none of her old friends met him, except by accident. Ill-natured people say that was the reason she kept him so long. If one happened in while he was there, he was hustled into Anerton's study, and the husband mounted guard till the inopportune visitor had departed. Anerton, you know, was really much more ridiculous about it than his wife. Mary was too clever to lose her head, or at least to show she'd lost it—but Anerton couldn't conceal his pride in the conquest. I've seen Mary shiver when he spoke of Rendle as *our poet*. Rendle always had to have a certain seat at the dinner-table, away from the draught and not too near the fire, and a box of cigars that no one else was allowed to touch, and a writing-table of his own in Mary's sitting-room—and Anerton was always telling one of the great man's idiosyncrasies: how he never would cut the ends of his cigars, though Anerton himself had given him a gold cutter set with a star-sapphire, and how untidy his writing-table was, and how the house-maid had orders always to bring the waste-paper basket to her mistress before emptying it, lest some immortal verse should be thrown into the dust-bin."

"The Anertons never separated, did they?"

"Separated? Bless you, no. He never would have left Rendle! And besides, he was very fond of his wife."

"And she?"

"Oh, she saw he was the kind of man who was fated to make himself ridiculous, and she never interfered with his natural tendencies."

From Mrs. Memorall, Danyers further learned that Mrs. Anerton, whose husband had died some years before her poet, now divided her life between Rome, where she had a small apartment, and England, where she occasionally went to stay with those of her friends who had been Rendle's. She had been engaged, for some time after his death, in editing some juvenilia which he had bequeathed to her care; but that task being accomplished, she had been left without definite occupation, and Mrs. Memorall, on the occasion of their last meeting, had found her listless and out of spirits.

"She misses him too much—her life is too empty. I told her so—I told her she ought to marry."

"Oh!"

"Why not, pray? She's a young woman still—what many people would call young," Mrs. Memorall interjected, with a parenthetic glance at the mirror. "Why not accept the inevitable and begin over again? All the King's horses and all the King's men won't bring Rendle to life—and besides, she didn't marry *him* when she had the chance."

Danyers winced slightly at this rude fingering of his idol. Was it possible that Mrs. Memorall did not see what an anticlimax such a marriage would have been? Fancy Rendle "making an honest woman" of Silvia; for so society would have viewed it! How such a reparation would have vulgarized their past—it would have been like "restoring" a masterpiece; and how exquisite must have been the perceptions of the woman who, in defiance of appearances, and perhaps of her own secret inclination, chose to go down to posterity as Silvia rather than as Mrs. Vincent Rendle!

Mrs. Memorall, from this day forth, acquired an interest in Danyers's eyes. She was like a volume of unindexed and discursive memoirs, through which he patiently plodded in the hope of finding embedded amid layers of dusty twaddle some precious allusion to the subject of his thought. When, some months later, he brought out his first slim volume, in which the remodelled college essay on Rendle figured among a dozen somewhat overstudied "appreciations," he offered a copy to Mrs. Memorall; who surprised him, the next time they met, with the announcement that she had sent the book to Mrs. Anerton.

Mrs. Anerton in due time wrote to thank her friend. Danyers was privileged to read the few lines in which, in terms that suggested the habit of "acknowledging" similar tributes, she spoke of the author's "feeling and insight," and was "so glad of the opportunity," etc. He went away disappointed, without clearly knowing what else he had expected.

The following spring, when he went abroad, Mrs. Memorall offered him letters to everybody, from the Archbishop of Canterbury to Louise Michel. She did not include Mrs. Anerton, however, and Danyers knew, from a previous conversation, that Silvia objected to people who "brought letters." He knew also that she travelled during the summer, and was unlikely to return to Rome before the term of his holiday should be reached, and the hope of meeting her was not included among his anticipations.

The lady whose entrance broke upon his solitary repast in the restaurant of the Hotel Villa d'Este had seated herself in such a way that her profile was detached against the window; and thus viewed, her domed forehead, small arched nose, and fastidious lip suggested a silhouette of Marie Antoinette. In the lady's dress and movements—in the very turn of her wrist as she poured out her coffee—Danyers thought he detected the same fastidiousness, the same air of tacitly excluding the obvious and unexceptional. Here was a woman who had been much bored and keenly interested. The waiter brought her a *Secolo*, and as she bent above it Danyers noticed that the hair rolled back from her forehead was turning gray; but her figure was straight and slender, and she had the invaluable gift of a girlish back.

The rush of Anglo-Saxon travel had not set toward the lakes, and with the exception of an Italian family or two, and a hump-backed youth with an *abbé*, Danyers and the lady had the marble halls of the Villa d'Este to themselves.

When he returned from his morning ramble among the hills he saw her sitting at one of the little tables at the edge of the lake. She was writing, and a heap of books and newspapers lay on the table at her side. That evening they met again in the garden. He had strolled out to smoke a last cigarette before dinner, and under the black vaulting of ilexes, near the steps leading down to the boat-landing, he found her leaning on the parapet above the lake. At the sound of his approach she turned and looked at him. She had thrown a black lace scarf over her head, and in this sombre setting her face seemed thin and unhappy. He remembered afterwards that her eyes, as they met his, expressed not so much sorrow as profound discontent.

To his surprise she stepped toward him with a detaining gesture.

"Mr. Lewis Danyers, I believe?"

He bowed.

"I am Mrs. Anerton. I saw your name on the visitors' list and wished to thank you for an essay on Mr. Rendle's poetry —or rather to tell you how much I appreciated it. The book was sent to me last winter by Mrs. Memorall."

She spoke in even melancholy tones, as though the habit of perfunctory utterance had robbed her voice of more spontaneous accents; but her smile was charming.

They sat down on a stone bench under the ilexes, and she told him how much pleasure his essay had given her. She thought it the best in the book—she was sure he had put more of himself into it than into any other; was she not right in conjecturing that he had been very deeply influenced by Mr. Rendle's poetry? *Pour comprendre il faut aimer*, and it seemed to her that, in some ways, he had penetrated the poet's inner meaning more completely than any other critic. There were certain problems, of course, that he had left untouched; certain aspects of that many-sided mind that he had perhaps failed to seize—

"But then you are young," she concluded gently, "and one could not wish you, as yet, the experience that a fuller understanding would imply."

II

She stayed a month at Villa d'Este, and Danyers was with her daily. She showed an unaffected pleasure in his society; a pleasure so obviously founded on their common veneration of Rendle, that the young man could enjoy it without fear of fatuity. At first he was merely one more grain of frankincense on the altar of her insatiable divinity; but gradually a more personal note crept into their intercourse. If she still liked him only because he appreciated Rendle, she at least perceptibly distinguished him from the herd of Rendle's appreciators.

Her attitude toward the great man's memory struck Danyers as perfect. She neither proclaimed nor disavowed

her identity. She was frankly Silvia to those who knew and
cared; but there was no trace of the Egeria in her pose. She
spoke often of Rendle's books, but seldom of himself; there
was no posthumous conjugality, no use of the possessive
tense, in her abounding reminiscences. Of the master's intellectual life, of his habits of thought and work, she never wea-
ried of talking. She knew the history of each poem; by what
scene or episode each image had been evoked; how many
times the words in a certain line had been transposed; how
long a certain adjective had been sought, and what had at
last suggested it; she could even explain that one impenetrable line, the torment of critics, the joy of detractors, the last
line of *The Old Odysseus*.

Danyers felt that in talking of these things she was no mere
echo of Rendle's thought. If her identity had appeared to be
merged in his it was because they thought alike, not because
he had thought for her. Posterity is apt to regard the women
whom poets have sung as chance pegs on which they hung
their garlands; but Mrs. Anerton's mind was like some fertile
garden wherein, inevitably, Rendle's imagination had rooted
itself and flowered. Danyers began to see how many threads
of his complex mental tissue the poet had owed to the blend-
ing of her temperament with his; in a certain sense Silvia had
herself created the *Sonnets to Silvia*.

To be the custodian of Rendle's inner self, the door, as it
were, to the sanctuary, had at first seemed to Danyers so comprehensive a privilege that he had the sense, as his friendship
with Mrs. Anerton advanced, of forcing his way into a life already crowded. What room was there, among such towering
memories, for so small an actuality as his? Quite suddenly, after this, he discovered that Mrs. Memorall knew better: his
fortunate friend was bored as well as lonely.

"You have had more than any other woman!" he had exclaimed to her one day; and her smile flashed a derisive light
on his blunder. Fool that he was, not to have seen that she
had not had enough! That she was young still—do years
count?—tender, human, a woman; that the living have need
of the living.

After that, when they climbed the alleys of the hanging
park, resting in one of the little ruined temples, or watching,

through a ripple of foliage, the remote blue flash of the lake, they did not always talk of Rendle or of literature. She encouraged Danyers to speak of himself; to confide his ambitions to her; she asked him the questions which are the wise woman's substitute for advice.

"You must write," she said, administering the most exquisite flattery that human lips could give.

Of course he meant to write—why not to do something great in his turn? His best, at least; with the resolve, at the outset, that his best should be *the* best. Nothing less seemed possible with that mandate in his ears. How she had divined him; lifted and disentangled his groping ambitions; laid the awakening touch on his spirit with her creative *Let there be light!*

It was his last day with her, and he was feeling very hopeless and happy.

"You ought to write a book about *him*," she went on gently.

Danyers started; he was beginning to dislike Rendle's way of walking in unannounced.

"You ought to do it," she insisted. "A complete interpretation—a summing-up of his style, his purpose, his theory of life and art. No one else could do it as well."

He sat looking at her perplexedly. Suddenly—dared he guess?

"I couldn't do it without you," he faltered.

"I could help you—I would help you, of course."

They sat silent, both looking at the lake.

It was agreed, when they parted, that he should rejoin her six weeks later in Venice. There they were to talk about the book.

III

Lago d'Iseo, August 14th.

When I said good-by to you yesterday I promised to come back to Venice in a week: I was to give you your answer then. I was not honest in saying that; I didn't mean to go back to Venice or to see you again. I was running away from you—and I mean to keep on running! If *you* won't, *I* must. Somebody must save you from marrying a disappointed woman of—well, you say years don't count, and why should they, after all, since you are not to marry me?

That is what I dare not go back to say. *You are not to marry me.* We have had our month together in Venice (such a good month, was it not?) and now you are to go home and write a book—any book but the one we—didn't talk of!—and I am to stay here, attitudinizing among my memories like a sort of female Tithonus. The dreariness of this enforced immortality!

But you shall know the truth. I care for you, or at least for your love, enough to owe you that.

You thought it was because Vincent Rendle had loved me that there was so little hope for you. I had had what I wanted to the full; wasn't that what you said? It is just when a man begins to think he understands a woman that he may be sure he doesn't! It is because Vincent Rendle *didn't love me* that there is no hope for you. I never had what I wanted, and never, never, never will I stoop to wanting anything else.

Do you begin to understand? It was all a sham then, you say? No, it was all real as far as it went. You are young—you haven't learned, as you will later, the thousand imperceptible signs by which one gropes one's way through the labyrinth of human nature; but didn't it strike you, sometimes, that I never told you any foolish little anecdotes about him? His trick, for instance, of twirling a paper-knife round and round between his thumb and forefinger while he talked; his mania for saving the backs of notes; his greediness for wild straw-berries, the little pungent Alpine ones; his childish delight in acrobats and jugglers; his way of always calling me *you—dear you*, every letter began— I never told you a word of all that, did I? Do you suppose I could have helped telling you, if he had loved me? These little things would have been mine, then, a part of my life—of our life—they would have slipped out in spite of me (it's only your unhappy woman who is al-ways reticent and dignified). But there never was any "our life;" it was always "our lives" to the end. . . .

If you knew what a relief it is to tell some one at last, you would bear with me, you would let me hurt you! I shall never be quite so lonely again, now that some one knows.

Let me begin at the beginning. When I first met Vincent Rendle I was not twenty-five. That was twenty years ago.

From that time until his death, five years ago, we were fast
friends. He gave me fifteen years, perhaps the best fifteen
years, of his life. The world, as you know, thinks that his
greatest poems were written during those years; I am supposed to have "inspired" them, and in a sense I did. From the
first, the intellectual sympathy between us was almost complete; my mind must have been to him (I fancy) like some
perfectly tuned instrument on which he was never tired of
playing. Some one told me of his once saying of me that I "always understood;" it is the only praise I ever heard of his giving me. I don't even know if he thought me pretty, though I
hardly think my appearance could have been disagreeable to
him, for he hated to be with ugly people. At all events he fell
into the way of spending more and more of his time with me.
He liked our house; our ways suited him. He was nervous, ir-
ritable; people bored him and yet he disliked solitude. He
took sanctuary with us. When we travelled he went with us;
in the winter he took rooms near us in Rome. In England or
on the continent he was always with us for a good part of the
year. In small ways I was able to help him in his work; he
grew dependent on me. When we were apart he wrote to me
continually—he liked to have me share in all he was doing or
thinking; he was impatient for my criticism of every new book
that interested him; I was a part of his intellectual life. The
pity of it was that I wanted to be something more. I was a
young woman and I was in love with him—not because he
was Vincent Rendle, but just because he was himself!

People began to talk, of course—I was Vincent Rendle's
Mrs. Anerton; when the *Sonnets to Silvia* appeared, it was
whispered that I was Silvia. Wherever he went, I was invited;
people made up to me in the hope of getting to know him;
when I was in London my door-bell never stopped ringing.
Elderly peeresses, aspiring hostesses, love-sick girls and struggling authors overwhelmed me with their assiduities. I
hugged my success, for I knew what it meant—they thought
that Rendle was in love with me! Do you know, at times, they
almost made me think so too? Oh, there was no phase of folly
I didn't go through. You can't imagine the excuses a woman
will invent for a man's not telling her that he loves her—
pitiable arguments that she would see through at a glance if

any other woman used them! But all the while, deep down, I knew he had never cared. I should have known it if he had made love to me every day of his life. I could never guess whether he knew what people said about us—he listened so little to what people said; and cared still less, when he heard. He was always quite honest and straightforward with me; he treated me as one man treats another; and yet at times I felt he *must* see that with me it was different. If he did see, he made no sign. Perhaps he never noticed—I am sure he never meant to be cruel. He had never made love to me; it was no fault of his if I wanted more than he could give me. The *Sonnets to Silvia*, you say? But what are they? A cosmic philosophy, not a love-poem; addressed to Woman, not to a woman!

But then, the letters? Ah, the letters! Well, I'll make a clean breast of it. You have noticed the breaks in the letters here and there, just as they seem to be on the point of growing a little—warmer? The critics, you may remember, praised the editor for his commendable delicacy and good taste (so rare in these days!) in omitting from the correspondence all personal allusions, all those *détails intimes* which should be kept sacred from the public gaze. They referred, of course, to the asterisks in the letters to Mrs. A. Those letters I myself prepared for publication; that is to say, I copied them out for the editor, and every now and then I put in a line of asterisks to make it appear that something had been left out. You understand? The asterisks were a sham—*there was nothing to leave out.*

No one but a woman could understand what I went through during those years—the moments of revolt, when I felt I must break away from it all, fling the truth in his face and never see him again; the inevitable reaction, when not to see him seemed the one unendurable thing, and I trembled lest a look or word of mine should disturb the poise of our friendship; the silly days when I hugged the delusion that he *must* love me, since everybody thought he did; the long periods of numbness, when I didn't seem to care whether he loved me or not. Between these wretched days came others when our intellectual accord was so perfect that I forgot everything else in the joy of feeling myself lifted up on the wings of his thought. Sometimes, then, the heavens seemed to be opened. . . .

All this time he was so dear a friend! He had the genius of friendship, and he spent it all on me. Yes, you were right when you said that I have had more than any other woman. *Il faut de l'adresse pour aimer*, Pascal says; and I was so quiet, so cheerful, so frankly affectionate with him, that in all those years I am almost sure I never bored him. Could I have hoped as much if he had loved me?

You mustn't think of him, though, as having been tied to my skirts. He came and went as he pleased, and so did his fancies. There was a girl once (I am telling you everything), a lovely being who called his poetry "deep" and gave him *Lucile* on his birthday. He followed her to Switzerland one summer, and all the time that he was dangling after her (a little too conspicuously, I always thought, for a Great Man), he was writing to *me* about his theory of vowel-combinations— or was it his experiments in English hexameter? The letters were dated from the very places where I knew they went and sat by waterfalls together and he thought out adjectives for her hair. He talked to me about it quite frankly afterwards. She was perfectly beautiful and it had been a pure delight to watch her; but she *would* talk, and her mind, he said, was "all elbows." And yet, the next year, when her marriage was announced, he went away alone, quite suddenly . . . and it was just afterwards that he published *Love's Viaticum*. Men are queer!

After my husband died—I am putting things crudely, you see—I had a return of hope. It was because he loved me, I argued, that he had never spoken; because he had always hoped some day to make me his wife; because he wanted to spare me the "reproach." Rubbish! I knew well enough, in my heart of hearts, that my one chance lay in the force of habit. He had grown used to me; he was no longer young; he dreaded new people and new ways; *il avait pris son pli*. Would it not be easier to marry me?

I don't believe he ever thought of it. He wrote me what people call "a beautiful letter;" he was kind, considerate, decently commiserating; then, after a few weeks, he slipped into his old way of coming in every afternoon, and our interminable talks began again just where they had left off. I heard later that people thought I had shown "such good taste" in not marrying him.

So we jogged on for five years longer. Perhaps they were the best years, for I had given up hoping. Then he died.

After his death—this is curious—there came to me a kind of mirage of love. All the books and articles written about him, all the reviews of the "Life," were full of discreet allusions to Silvia. I became again the Mrs. Anerton of the glorious days. Sentimental girls and dear lads like you turned pink when somebody whispered, "that was Silvia you were talking to." Idiots begged for my autograph—publishers urged me to write my reminiscences of him—critics consulted me about the reading of doubtful lines. And I knew that, to all these people, I was the woman Vincent Rendle had loved.

After a while that fire went out too and I was left alone with my past. Alone—quite alone; for he had never really been with me. The intellectual union counted for nothing now. It had been soul to soul, but never hand in hand, and there were no little things to remember him by.

Then there set in a kind of Arctic winter. I crawled into myself as into a snow-hut. I hated my solitude and yet dreaded any one who disturbed it. That phase, of course, passed like the others. I took up life again, and began to read the papers and consider the cut of my gowns. But there was one question that I could not be rid of, that haunted me night and day. Why had he never loved me? Why had I been so much to him, and no more? Was I so ugly, so essentially unlovable, that though a man might cherish me as his mind's comrade, he could not care for me as a woman? I can't tell you how that question tortured me. It became an obsession.

My poor friend, do you begin to see? I had to find out what some other man thought of me. Don't be too hard on me! Listen first—consider. When I first met Vincent Rendle I was a young woman, who had married early and led the quietest kind of life; I had had no "experiences." From the hour of our first meeting to the day of his death I never looked at any other man, and never noticed whether any other man looked at me. When he died, five years ago, I knew the extent of my powers no more than a baby. Was it too late to find out? Should I never know *why?*

Forgive me—forgive me. You are so young; it will be an episode, a mere "document," to you so soon! And, besides, it wasn't as deliberate, as cold-blooded as these disjointed lines have made it appear. I didn't plan it, like a woman in a book. Life is so much more complex than any rendering of it can be. I liked you from the first—I was drawn to you (you must have seen that)—I wanted you to like me; it was not a mere psychological experiment. And yet in a sense it was that, too—I must be honest. I had to have an answer to that question; it was a ghost that had to be laid.

At first I was afraid—oh, so much afraid—that you cared for me only because I was Silvia, that you loved me because you thought Rendle had loved me. I began to think there was no escaping my destiny.

How happy I was when I discovered that you were growing jealous of my past; that you actually hated Rendle! My heart beat like a girl's when you told me you meant to follow me to Venice.

After our parting at Villa d'Este my old doubts reasserted themselves. What did I know of your feeling for me, after all? Were you capable of analyzing it yourself? Was it not likely to be two-thirds vanity and curiosity, and one-third literary sentimentality? You might easily fancy that you cared for Mary Anerton when you were really in love with Silvia—the heart is such a hypocrite! Or you might be more calculating than I had supposed. Perhaps it was you who had been flattering *my* vanity in the hope (the pardonable hope!) of turning me, after a decent interval, into a pretty little essay with a margin.

When you arrived in Venice and we met again—do you remember the music on the lagoon, that evening, from my balcony?—I was so afraid you would begin to talk about the book—the book, you remember, was your ostensible reason for coming. You never spoke of it, and I soon saw your one fear was *I* might do so—might remind you of your object in being with me. Then I knew you cared for me! yes, at that moment really cared! We never mentioned the book once, did we, during that month in Venice?

I have read my letter over; and now I wish that I had said this to you instead of writing it. I could have felt my way then, watching your face and seeing if you understood. But, no, I could not go back to Venice; and I could not tell you (though I tried) while we were there together. I couldn't spoil that month—my one month. It was so good, for once in my life, to get away from literature. . . .

You will be angry with me at first—but, alas! not for long. What I have done would have been cruel if I had been a younger woman; as it is, the experiment will hurt no one but myself. And it will hurt me horribly (as much as, in your first anger, you may perhaps wish), because it has shown me, for the first time, all that I have missed. . . .

A Journey

As she lay in her berth, staring at the shadows overhead, the rush of the wheels was in her brain, driving her deeper and deeper into circles of wakeful lucidity. The sleeping-car had sunk into its night-silence. Through the wet window-pane she watched the sudden lights, the long stretches of hurrying blackness. Now and then she turned her head and looked through the opening in the hangings at her husband's curtains across the aisle . . .

She wondered restlessly if he wanted anything and if she could hear him if he called. His voice had grown very weak within the last months and it irritated him when she did not hear. This irritability, this increasing childish petulance seemed to give expression to their imperceptible estrangement. Like two faces looking at one another through a sheet of glass they were close together, almost touching, but they could not hear or feel each other: the conductivity between them was broken. She, at least, had this sense of separation, and she fancied sometimes that she saw it reflected in the look with which he supplemented his failing words. Doubtless the fault was hers. She was too impenetrably healthy to be touched by the irrelevancies of disease. Her self-reproachful tenderness was tinged with the sense of his irrationality: she had a vague feeling that there was a purpose in his helpless tyrannies. The suddenness of the change had found her so unprepared. A year ago their pulses had beat to one robust measure; both had the same prodigal confidence in an exhaustless future. Now their energies no longer kept step: hers still bounded ahead of life, preëmpting unclaimed regions of hope and activity, while his lagged behind, vainly struggling to overtake her.

When they married, she had such arrears of living to make up: her days had been as bare as the white-washed school-room where she forced innutritious facts upon reluctant children. His coming had broken in on the slumber of circumstance, widening the present till it became the encloser of remotest chances. But imperceptibly the horizon narrowed.

Life had a grudge against her: she was never to be allowed to spread her wings.

At first the doctors had said that six weeks of mild air would set him right; but when he came back this assurance was explained as having of course included a winter in a dry climate. They gave up their pretty house, storing the wedding presents and new furniture, and went to Colorado. She had hated it there from the first. Nobody knew her or cared about her; there was no one to wonder at the good match she had made, or to envy her the new dresses and the visiting-cards which were still a surprise to her. And he kept growing worse. She felt herself beset with difficulties too evasive to be fought by so direct a temperament. She still loved him, of course; but he was gradually, undefinably ceasing to be himself. The man she had married had been strong, active, gently masterful: the male whose pleasure it is to clear a way through the material obstructions of life; but now it was she who was the protector, he who must be shielded from importunities and given his drops or his beef-juice though the skies were falling. The routine of the sick-room bewildered her; this punctual administering of medicine seemed as idle as some uncomprehended religious mummery.

There were moments, indeed, when warm gushes of pity swept away her instinctive resentment of his condition, when she still found his old self in his eyes as they groped for each other through the dense medium of his weakness. But these moments had grown rare. Sometimes he frightened her: his sunken expressionless face seemed that of a stranger; his voice was weak and hoarse; his thin-lipped smile a mere muscular contraction. Her hand avoided his damp soft skin, which had lost the familiar roughness of health: she caught herself furtively watching him as she might have watched a strange animal. It frightened her to feel that this was the man she loved; there were hours when to tell him what she suffered seemed the one escape from her fears. But in general she judged herself more leniently, reflecting that she had perhaps been too long alone with him, and that she would feel differently when they were at home again, surrounded by her robust and buoyant family. How she had rejoiced when the doctors at last gave their consent to his going home! She knew, of course, what the decision meant; they both knew. It meant that he was to die; but they dressed the truth in hopeful euphuisms, and at times, in the joy of preparation, she really forgot the purpose of their journey, and slipped into an eager allusion to next year's plans.

At last the day of leaving came. She had a dreadful fear that they would never get away; that somehow at the last moment he would fail her; that the doctors held one of their accustomed treacheries in reserve; but nothing happened. They drove to the station, he was installed in a seat with a rug over his knees and a cushion at his back, and she hung out of the window waving unregretful farewells to the acquaintances she had really never liked till then.

The first twenty-four hours had passed off well. He revived a little and it amused him to look out of the window and to observe the humours of the car. The second day he began to grow weary and to chafe under the dispassionate stare of the freckled child with the lump of chewing-gum. She had to explain to the child's mother that her husband was too ill to be disturbed: a statement received by that lady with a resentment visibly supported by the maternal sentiment of the whole car . . . .

That night he slept badly and the next morning his temperature frightened her: she was sure he was growing worse. The day passed slowly, punctuated by the small irritations of travel. Watching his tired face, she traced in its contractions every rattle and jolt of the train, till her own body vibrated with sympathetic fatigue. She felt the others observing him too, and hovered restlessly between him and the line of interrogative eyes. The freckled child hung about him like a fly; offers of candy and picture-books failed to dislodge her: she twisted one leg around the other and watched him imperturbably. The porter, as he passed, lingered with vague proffers of help, probably inspired by philanthropic passengers swelling with the sense that "something ought to be done;" and one nervous man in a skull-cap was audibly concerned as to the possible effect on his wife's health.

The hours dragged on in a dreary inoccupation. Towards dusk she sat down beside him and he laid his hand on hers. The touch startled her. He seemed to be calling her from far off. She looked at him helplessly and his smile went through her like a physical pang.

"Are you very tired?" she asked.

"No, not very."

"We'll be there soon now."

"Yes, very soon."

"This time to-morrow—"

He nodded and they sat silent. When she had put him to bed and crawled into her own berth she tried to cheer herself with the thought that in less than twenty-four hours they would be in New York. Her people would all be at the station to meet her—she pictured their round unanxious faces pressing through the crowd. She only hoped they would not tell him too loudly that he was looking splendidly and would be all right in no time: the subtler sympathies developed by long contact with suffering were making her aware of a certain coarseness of texture in the family sensibilities.

Suddenly she thought she heard him call. She parted the curtains and listened. No, it was only a man snoring at the other end of the car. His snores had a greasy sound, as though they passed through tallow. She lay down and tried to sleep . . . Had she not heard him move? She started up trembling . . . The silence frightened her more than any sound. He might not be able to make her hear—he might be calling her now . . . What made her think of such things? It was merely the familiar tendency of an over-tired mind to fasten itself on the most intolerable chance within the range of its forebodings . . . Putting her head out, she listened; but she could not distinguish his breathing from that of the other pairs of lungs about her. She longed to get up and look at him, but she knew the impulse was a mere vent for her restlessness, and the fear of disturbing him restrained her. . . . The regular movement of his curtain reassured her, she knew not why; she remembered that he had wished her a cheerful good-night; and the sheer inability to endure her fears a moment longer made her put them from her with an effort of her whole sound tired body. She turned on her side and slept.

She sat up stiffly, staring out at the dawn. The train was rushing through a region of bare hillocks huddled against a lifeless sky. It looked like the first day of creation. The air of the car was close, and she pushed up her window to let in the keen wind. Then she looked at her watch: it was seven o'clock, and soon the people about her would be stirring. She slipped into her clothes, smoothed her dishevelled hair and crept to the dressing-room. When she had washed her face and adjusted her dress she felt more hopeful. It was always a struggle for her not to be cheerful in the morning. Her cheeks burned deliciously under the coarse towel and the wet hair about her temples broke into strong upward tendrils. Every inch of her was full of life and elasticity. And in ten hours they would be at home!

She stepped to her husband's berth: it was time for him to take his early glass of milk. The window-shade was down, and in the dusk of the curtained enclosure she could just see that he lay sideways, with his face away from her. She leaned over him and drew up the shade. As she did so she touched one of his hands. It felt cold . . .

She bent closer, laying her hand on his arm and calling him by name. He did not move. She spoke again more loudly; she grasped his shoulder and gently shook it. He lay motionless. She caught hold of his hand again: it slipped from her limply, like a dead thing. A dead thing? . . . Her breath caught. She must see his face. She leaned forward, and hurriedly, shrinkingly, with a sickening reluctance of the flesh, laid her hands on his shoulders and turned him over. His head fell back; his face looked small and smooth; he gazed at her with steady eyes.

She remained motionless for a long time, holding him thus; and they looked at each other. Suddenly she shrank back: the longing to scream, to call out, to fly from him, had almost overpowered her. But a strong hand arrested her. Good God! If it were known that he was dead they would be put off the train at the next station—

In a terrifying flash of remembrance there arose before her a scene she had once witnessed in travelling, when a husband and wife, whose child had died in the train, had been thrust out at some chance station. She saw them standing on the platform with the child's body between them; she had never forgotten the dazed look with which they followed the receding train. And this was what would happen to her. Within the next hour she might find herself on the platform of some strange station, alone with her husband's body. . . . Anything but that! It was too horrible— She quivered like a creature at bay.

As she cowered there, she felt the train moving more slowly. It was coming then—they were approaching a station! She saw again the husband and wife standing on the lonely platform; and with a violent gesture she drew down the shade to hide her husband's face.

Feeling dizzy, she sank down on the edge of the berth, keeping away from his outstretched body, and pulling the curtains close, so that he and she were shut into a kind of sepulchral twilight. She tried to think. At all costs she must conceal the fact that he was dead. But how? Her mind refused to act: she could not plan, combine. She could think of no way but to sit there, clutching the curtains, all day long . . .

She heard the porter making up her bed; people were beginning to move about the car; the dressing-room door was being opened and shut. She tried to rouse herself. At length with a supreme effort she rose to her feet, stepping into the aisle of the car and drawing the curtains tight behind her. She noticed that they still parted slightly with the motion of the car, and finding a pin in her dress she fastened them together. Now she was safe. She looked round and saw the porter. She fancied he was watching her.

"Ain't he awake yet?" he enquired.

"No," she faltered.

"I got his milk all ready when he wants it. You know you told me to have it for him by seven."

She nodded silently and crept into her seat.

At half-past eight the train reached Buffalo. By this time the other passengers were dressed and the berths had been folded back for the day. The porter, moving to and fro under his burden of sheets and pillows, glanced at her as he passed. At length he said: "Ain't he going to get up? You know we're ordered to make up the berths as early as we can."

She turned cold with fear. They were just entering the station.

"Oh, not yet," she stammered. "Not till he's had his milk. Won't you get it, please?"

"All right. Soon as we start again."

When the train moved on he reappeared with the milk. She took it from him and sat vaguely looking at it: her brain moved slowly from one idea to another, as though they were stepping-stones set far apart across a whirling flood. At length she became aware that the porter still hovered expectantly.

"Will I give it to him?" he suggested.

"Oh, no," she cried, rising. "He—he's asleep yet, I think—"

She waited till the porter had passed on; then she unpinned the curtains and slipped behind them. In the semi-obscurity her husband's face stared up at her like a marble mask with agate eyes. The eyes were dreadful. She put out her hand and drew down the lids. Then she remembered the glass of milk in her other hand: what was she to do with it? She thought of raising the window and throwing it out; but to do so she would have to lean across his body and bring her face close to his. She decided to drink the milk.

She returned to her seat with the empty glass and after a while the porter came back to get it.

"When'll I fold up his bed?" he asked.

"Oh, not now—not yet; he's ill—he's very ill. Can't you let him stay as he is? The doctor wants him to lie down as much as possible."

He scratched his head. "Well, if he's *really* sick—"

He took the empty glass and walked away, explaining to the passengers that the party behind the curtains was too sick to get up just yet.

She found herself the centre of sympathetic eyes. A motherly woman with an intimate smile sat down beside her.

"I'm real sorry to hear your husband's sick. I've had a remarkable amount of sickness in my family and maybe I could assist you. Can I take a look at him?"

"Oh, no—no, please! He mustn't be disturbed."

The lady accepted the rebuff indulgently.

"Well, it's just as you say, of course, but you don't look to me as if you'd had much experience in sickness and I'd have been glad to assist you. What do you generally do when your husband's taken this way?"

"I—I let him sleep."

"Too much sleep ain't any too healthful either. Don't you give him any medicine?"

"Y—yes."

"Don't you wake him to take it?"

"Yes."

"When does he take the next dose?"

"Not for—two hours—"

The lady looked disappointed. "Well, if I was you I'd try giving it oftener. That's what I do with my folks."

After that many faces seemed to press upon her. The passengers were on their way to the dining-car, and she was conscious that as they passed down the aisle they glanced curiously at the closed curtains. One lantern-jawed man with prominent eyes stood still and tried to shoot his projecting glance through the division between the folds. The freckled child, returning from breakfast, waylaid the passers with a buttery clutch, saying in a loud whisper, "He's sick;" and once the conductor came by, asking for tickets. She shrank into her corner and looked out of the window at the flying trees and houses, meaningless hieroglyphs of an endlessly unrolled papyrus.

Now and then the train stopped, and the newcomers on entering the car stared in turn at the closed curtains. More and more people seemed to pass—their faces began to blend fantastically with the images surging in her brain . . .

Later in the day a fat man detached himself from the mist of faces. He had a creased stomach and soft pale lips. As he pressed himself into the seat facing her she noticed that he was dressed in black broadcloth, with a soiled white tie.

"Husband's pretty bad this morning, is he?"

"Yes."

"Dear, dear! Now that's terribly distressing, ain't it?" An apostolic smile revealed his gold-filled teeth. "Of course you know there's no sech thing as sickness. Ain't that a lovely thought? Death itself is but a deloosion of our grosser senses. On'y lay yourself open to the influx of the sperrit, submit yourself passively to the action of the divine force, and disease and dissolution will cease to exist for you. If you could indooce your husband to read this little pamphlet—"

The faces about her again grew indistinct. She had a vague recollection of hearing the motherly lady and the parent of the freckled child ardently disputing the relative advantages of trying several medicines at once, or of taking each in turn; the motherly lady maintaining that the competitive system saved time; the other objecting that you couldn't tell which remedy had effected the cure; their voices went on and on, like bell-buoys droning through a fog . . . The porter came up now and then with questions that she did not understand, but that somehow she must have answered since he went away again without repeating them; every two hours the motherly lady reminded her that her husband ought to have his drops; people left the car and others replaced them . . .

Her head was spinning and she tried to steady herself by clutching at her thoughts as they swept by, but they slipped away from her like bushes on the side of a sheer precipice down which she seemed to be falling. Suddenly her mind grew clear again and she found herself vividly picturing what would happen when the train reached New York. She shuddered as it occurred to her that he would be quite cold and that some one might perceive he had been dead since morning.

She thought hurriedly:—"If they see I am not surprised they will suspect something. They will ask questions, and if I tell them the truth they won't believe me—no one would believe me! It will be terrible"—and she kept repeating to herself:—"I must pretend I don't know. I must pretend I don't know. When they open the curtains I must go up to him quite naturally—and then I must scream." . . . . She had an idea that the scream would be very hard to do.

Gradually new thoughts crowded upon her, vivid and urgent: she tried to separate and restrain them, but they beset her clamorously, like her school-children at the end of a hot day, when she was too tired to silence them. Her head grew confused, and she felt a sick fear of forgetting her part, of betraying herself by some unguarded word or look.

"I must pretend I don't know," she went on murmuring. The words had lost their significance, but she repeated them mechanically, as though they had been a magic formula, until suddenly she heard herself saying: "I can't remember, I can't remember!"

Her voice sounded very loud, and she looked about her in terror; but no one seemed to notice that she had spoken.

As she glanced down the car her eye caught the curtains of her husband's berth, and she began to examine the monotonous arabesques woven through their heavy folds. The pattern was intricate and difficult to trace; she gazed fixedly at the curtains and as she did so the thick stuff grew transparent and through it she saw her husband's face—his dead face. She struggled to avert her look, but her eyes refused to move and her head seemed to be held in a vice. At last, with an effort that left her weak and shaking, she turned away; but it was of no use; close in front of her, small and smooth, was her husband's face. It seemed to be suspended in the air between her and the false braids of the woman who sat in front of her. With an uncontrollable gesture she stretched out her hand to push the face away, and suddenly she felt the touch of his smooth skin. She repressed a cry and half started from her seat. The woman with the false braids looked around, and feeling that she must justify her movement in some way she rose and lifted her travelling-bag from the opposite seat. She unlocked the bag and looked into it; but the first object her hand met was a small flask of her husband's, thrust there at the last moment, in the haste of departure. She locked the bag and closed her eyes . . . his face was there again, hanging between her eyeballs and lids like a waxen mask against a red curtain . . .

She roused herself with a shiver. Had she fainted or slept? Hours seemed to have elapsed; but it was still broad day, and the people about her were sitting in the same attitudes as before.

A sudden sense of hunger made her aware that she had eaten nothing since morning. The thought of food filled her with disgust, but she dreaded a return of faintness, and remembering that she had some biscuits in her bag she took one out and ate it. The dry crumbs choked her, and she hastily swallowed a little brandy from her husband's flask. The burning sensation in her throat acted as a counter-irritant, momentarily relieving the dull ache of her nerves. Then she felt a gently-stealing warmth, as though a soft air fanned her, and the swarming fears relaxed their clutch, receding through the stillness that enclosed her, a stillness soothing as the spacious quietude of a summer day. She slept.

Through her sleep she felt the impetuous rush of the train. It seemed to be life itself that was sweeping her on with headlong inexorable force—sweeping her into darkness and terror, and the awe of unknown days.—Now all at once everything was still—not a sound, not a pulsation . . . She was dead in her turn, and lay beside him with smooth upstaring face. How quiet it was!—and yet she heard feet coming, the feet of the men who were to carry them away . . . She could feel too—she felt a sudden prolonged vibration, a series of hard shocks, and then another plunge into darkness: the darkness of death this time—a black whirlwind on which they were both spinning like leaves, in wild uncoiling spirals, with millions and millions of the dead . . .

She sprang up in terror. Her sleep must have lasted a long time, for the winter day had paled and the lights had been lit. The car was in confusion, and as she regained her self-possession she saw that the passengers were gathering up their wraps and bags. The woman with the false braids had brought from the dressing-room a sickly ivy-plant in a bottle, and the Christian Scientist was reversing his cuffs. The porter passed down the aisle with his impartial brush. An impersonal figure with a gold-banded cap asked for her husband's ticket. A voice shouted "Baig-gage *ex*press!" and she heard the clicking of metal as the passengers handed over their checks.

Presently her window was blocked by an expanse of sooty wall, and the train passed into the Harlem tunnel. The journey was over; in a few minutes she would see her family pushing their joyous way through the throng at the station. Her heart dilated. The worst terror was past . . .

"We'd better get him up now, hadn't we?" asked the porter, touching her arm.

He had her husband's hat in his hand and was meditatively revolving it under his brush.

She looked at the hat and tried to speak; but suddenly the car grew dark. She flung up her arms, struggling to catch at something, and fell face downward, striking her head against the dead man's berth.

The Pelican

S HE was very pretty when I first knew her, with the sweet
straight nose and short upper lip of the cameo-brooch divinity, humanized by a dimple that flowered in her cheek
whenever anything was said possessing the outward attributes
of humor without its intrinsic quality. For the dear lady was
providentially deficient in humor: the least hint of the real
thing clouded her lovely eye like the hovering shadow of an
algebraic problem.

I don't think nature had meant her to be "intellectual;" but
what can a poor thing do, whose husband has died of drink
when her baby is hardly six months old, and who finds her
coral necklace and her grandfather's edition of the British
Dramatists inadequate to the demands of the creditors?

Her mother, the celebrated Irene Astarte Pratt, had written
a poem in blank verse on "The Fall of Man;" one of her aunts
was dean of a girls' college; another had translated Euripides
—with such a family, the poor child's fate was sealed in advance. The only way of paying her husband's debts and keeping the baby clothed was to be intellectual; and, after some
hesitation as to the form her mental activity was to take, it was
unanimously decided that she was to give lectures.

They began by being drawing-room lectures. The first time
I saw her she was standing by the piano, against a flippant
background of Dresden china and photographs, telling a
roomful of women preoccupied with their spring bonnets all
she thought she knew about Greek art. The ladies assembled
to hear her had given me to understand that she was "doing
it for the baby," and this fact, together with the shortness of
her upper lip and the bewildering co-operation of her dimple,
disposed me to listen leniently to her dissertation. Happily, at
that time Greek art was still, if I may use the phrase, easily
handled: it was as simple as walking down a museum-gallery
lined with pleasant familiar Venuses and Apollos. All the later
complications—the archaic and archaistic conundrums; the
influences of Assyria and Asia Minor; the conflicting attribu-
tions and the wrangles of the erudite—still slumbered in the

bosom of the future "scientific critic." Greek art in those days began with Phidias and ended with the Apollo Belvedere; and a child could travel from one to the other without danger of losing his way.

Mrs. Amyot had two fatal gifts: a capacious but inaccurate memory, and an extraordinary fluency of speech. There was nothing she did not remember—wrongly; but her halting facts were swathed in so many layers of rhetoric that their infirmities were imperceptible to her friendly critics. Besides, she had been taught Greek by the aunt who had translated Euripides; and the mere sound of the αἶς and οἶς that she now and then not unskilfully let slip (correcting herself, of course, with a start, and indulgently mistranslating the phrase), struck awe to the hearts of ladies whose only "accomplishment" was French—if you didn't speak too quickly.

I had then but a momentary glimpse of Mrs. Amyot, but a few months later I came upon her again in the New England university town where the celebrated Irene Astarte Pratt lived on the summit of a local Parnassus, with lesser muses and college professors respectfully grouped on the lower ledges of the sacred declivity. Mrs. Amyot, who, after her husband's death, had returned to the maternal roof (even during her father's lifetime the roof had been distinctively maternal), Mrs. Amyot, thanks to her upper lip, her dimple and her Greek, was already esconced in a snug hollow of the Parnassian slope.

After the lecture was over it happened that I walked home with Mrs. Amyot. From the incensed glances of two or three learned gentlemen who were hovering on the door-step when we emerged, I inferred that Mrs. Amyot, at that period, did not often walk home alone; but I doubt whether any of my discomfited rivals, whatever his claims to favor, was ever treated to so ravishing a mixture of shyness and self-abandonment, of sham erudition and real teeth and hair, as it was my privilege to enjoy. Even at the opening of her public career Mrs. Amyot had a tender eye for strangers, as possible links with successive centres of culture to which in due course the torch of Greek art might be handed on.

She began by telling me that she had never been so frightened in her life. She knew, of course, how dreadfully learned I was, and when, just as she was going to begin, her hostess had whispered to her that I was in the room, she had felt ready to sink through the floor. Then (with a flying dimple) she had remembered Emerson's line—wasn't it Emerson's?—that beauty is its own excuse for *seeing*, and that had made her feel a little more confident, since she was sure that no one *saw* beauty more vividly than she—as a child she used to sit for hours gazing at an Etruscan vase on the book-case in the library, while her sisters played with their dolls—and if *seeing* beauty was the only excuse one needed for talking about it, why, she was sure I would make allowances and not be *too* critical and sarcastic, especially if, as she thought probable, I had heard of her having lost her poor husband, and how she had to do it for the baby.

Being abundantly assured of my sympathy on these points, she went on to say that she had always wanted so much to consult me about her lectures. Of course, one subject wasn't enough (this view of the limitations of Greek art as a "subject" gave me a startling idea of the rate at which a successful lecturer might exhaust the universe); she must find others; she had not ventured on any as yet, but she had thought of Tennyson—didn't I *love* Tennyson? She *worshipped* him so that she was sure she could help others to understand him; or what did I think of a "course" on Raphael or Michelangelo—or on the heroines of Shakespeare? There were some fine steel-engravings of Raphael's Madonnas and of the Sistine ceiling in her mother's library, and she had seen Miss Cushman in several Shakespearian *rôles*, so that on these subjects also she felt qualified to speak with authority.

When we reached her mother's door she begged me to come in and talk the matter over; she wanted me to see the baby—she felt as though I should understand her better if I saw the baby—and the dimple flashed through a tear.

The fear of encountering the author of "The Fall of Man," combined with the opportune recollection of a dinner engagement, made me evade this appeal with the promise of returning on the morrow. On the morrow, I left too early to redeem my promise; and for several years afterwards I saw no more of Mrs. Amyot.

My calling at that time took me at irregular intervals from one to another of our larger cities, and as Mrs. Amyot was also peripatetic it was inevitable that sooner or later we should cross each other's path. It was therefore without surprise that, one snowy afternoon in Boston, I learned from the lady with whom I chanced to be lunching that, as soon as the meal was over, I was to be taken to hear Mrs. Amyot lecture.

"On Greek art?" I suggested.

"Oh, you've heard her then? No, this is one of the series called 'Homes and Haunts of the Poets.' Last week we had Wordsworth and the Lake Poets, to-day we are to have Goethe and Weimar. She is a wonderful creature—all the women of her family are geniuses. You know, of course, that her mother was Irene Astarte Pratt, who wrote a poem on 'The Fall of Man'; N. P. Willis called her the female Milton of America. One of Mrs. Amyot's aunts has translated Eurip—"

"And is she as pretty as ever?" I irrelevantly interposed.

My hostess looked shocked. "She is excessively modest and retiring. She says it is actual suffering for her to speak in public. You know she only does it for the baby."

Punctually at the hour appointed, we took our seats in a lecture-hall full of strenuous females in ulsters. Mrs. Amyot was evidently a favorite with these austere sisters, for every corner was crowded, and as we entered a pale usher with an educated mispronunciation was setting forth to several dejected applicants the impossibility of supplying them with seats.

Our own were happily so near the front that when the curtains at the back of the platform parted, and Mrs. Amyot appeared, I was at once able to establish a comparison between the lady placidly dimpling to the applause of her public and the shrinking drawing-room orator of my earlier recollections.

Mrs. Amyot was as pretty as ever, and there was the same curious discrepancy between the freshness of her aspect and the staleness of her theme, but something was gone of the blushing unsteadiness with which she had fired her first random shots at Greek art. It was not that the shots were less uncertain, but that she now had an air of assuming that, for her purpose, the bull's-eye was everywhere, so that there was no need to be flustered in taking aim. This assurance had so facilitated the flow of her eloquence that she seemed to be performing a trick analogous to that of the conjuror who pulls hundreds of yards of white paper out of his mouth. From a large assortment of stock adjectives she chose, with unerring deftness and rapidity, the one that taste and discrimination would most surely have rejected, fitting out her subject with a whole wardrobe of slop-shop epithets irrelevant in cut and size. To the invaluable knack of not disturbing the association of ideas in her audience, she added the gift of what may be called a confidential manner—so that her fluent generalizations about Goethe and his place in literature (the lecture was, of course, manufactured out of Lewes's book) had the flavor of personal experience, of views sympathetically exchanged with her audience on the best way of knitting children's socks, or of putting up preserves for the winter. It was, I am sure, to this personal accent—the moral equivalent of her dimple—that Mrs. Amyot owed her prodigious, her irrational success. It was her art of transposing second-hand ideas into first-hand emotions that so endeared her to her feminine listeners.

To any one not in search of "documents" Mrs. Amyot's success was hardly of a kind to make her more interesting, and my curiosity flagged with the growing conviction that the "suffering" entailed on her by public speaking was at most a retrospective pang. I was sure that she had reached the point of measuring and enjoying her effects, of deliberately manipulating her public; and there must indeed have been a certain exhilaration in attaining results so considerable by means involving so little conscious effort. Mrs. Amyot's art was simply an extension of coquetry: she flirted with her audience.

In this mood of enlightened skepticism I responded but languidly to my hostess's suggestion that I should go with her that evening to see Mrs. Amyot. The aunt who had translated Euripides was at home on Saturday evenings, and one met "thoughtful" people there, my hostess explained: it was one of the intellectual centres of Boston. My mood remained distinctly resentful of any connection between Mrs. Amyot and intellectuality, and I declined to go; but the next day I met Mrs. Amyot in the street.

She stopped me reproachfully. She had heard I was in Boston; why had I not come last night? She had been told that I was at her lecture, and it had frightened her—yes, really, almost as much as years ago in Hillbridge. She never *could* get over that stupid shyness, and the whole business was as distasteful to her as ever; but what could she do? There was the baby—he was a big boy now, and boys were *so* expensive! But did I really think she had improved the least little bit? And why wouldn't I come home with her now, and see the boy, and tell her frankly what I had thought of the lecture? She had plenty of flattery—people were *so* kind, and every one knew that she did it for the baby—but what she felt the need of was criticism, severe, discriminating criticism like mine— oh, she knew that I was dreadfully discriminating!

I went home with her and saw the boy. In the early heat of her Tennyson-worship Mrs. Amyot had christened him Lancelot, and he looked it. Perhaps, however, it was his black velvet dress and the exasperating length of his yellow curls, together with the fact of his having been taught to recite Browning to visitors, that raised to fever-heat the itching of my palms in his Infant-Samuel-like presence. I have since had reason to think that he would have preferred to be called Billy, and to hunt cats with the other boys in the block: his curls and his poetry were simply another outlet for Mrs. Amyot's irrepressible coquetry.

But if Lancelot was not genuine, his mother's love for him was. It justified everything—the lectures *were* for the baby, after all. I had not been ten minutes in the room before I was pledged to help Mrs. Amyot carry out her triumphant fraud. If she wanted to lecture on Plato she should—Plato must take his chance like the rest of us! There was no use, of course, in being "discriminating." I preserved sufficient reason to avoid that pitfall, but I suggested "subjects" and made lists of books for her with a fatuity that became more obvious as time attenuated the remembrance of her smile; I even remember thinking that some men might have cut the knot by marrying her, but I handed over Plato as a hostage and escaped by the afternoon train.

The next time I saw her was in New York, when she had become so fashionable that it was a part of the whole duty of woman to be seen at her lectures. The lady who suggested that of course I ought to go and hear Mrs. Amyot, was not very clear about anything except that she was perfectly lovely, and had had a horrid husband, and was doing it to support her boy. The subject of the discourse (I think it was on Ruskin) was clearly of minor importance, not only to my friend, but to the throng of well-dressed and absent-minded ladies who rustled in late, dropped their muffs and pocket-books, and undisguisedly lost themselves in the study of each other's apparel. They received Mrs. Amyot with warmth, but she evidently represented a social obligation like going to church, rather than any more personal interest; in fact, I suspect that every one of the ladies would have remained away, had they been sure that none of the others were coming.

Whether Mrs. Amyot was disheartened by the lack of sympathy between herself and her hearers, or whether the sport of arousing it had become a task, she certainly imparted her platitudes with less convincing warmth than of old. Her voice had the same confidential inflections, but it was like a voice reproduced by a gramophone: the real woman seemed far away. She had grown stouter without losing her dewy freshness, and her smart gown might have been taken to show either the potentialities of a settled income, or a politic concession to the taste of her hearers. As I listened I reproached myself for ever having suspected her of self-deception in saying that she took no pleasure in her work. I was sure now that she did it only for Lancelot, and judging from the size of her audience and the price of the tickets I concluded that Lancelot must be receiving a liberal education.

I was living in New York that winter, and in the rotation of dinners I found myself one evening at Mrs. Amyot's side. The dimple came out at my greeting as punctually as a cuckoo in a Swiss clock, and I detected the same automatic quality in the tone in which she made her usual pretty demand for advice. She was like a musical-box charged with popular airs. They succeeded one another with breathless rapidity, but there was a moment after each when the cylinders scraped and whizzed.

Mrs. Amyot, as I found when I called on her, was living in a sunny flat, with a sitting-room full of flowers and a tea-table that had the air of expecting visitors. She owned that she had been ridiculously successful. It was delightful, of course, on Lancelot's account. Lancelot had been sent to the best school

in the country, and if things went well and people didn't tire
of his silly mother he was to go to Harvard afterwards.
During the next two or three years Mrs. Amyot kept her flat
in New York, and radiated art and literature upon the suburbs. I saw her now and then, always stouter, better dressed,
more successful and more automatic: she had become a
lecturing-machine.

I went abroad for a year or two and when I came back she
had disappeared. I asked several people about her, but life had
closed over her. She had been last heard of as lecturing—still
lecturing—but no one seemed to know when or where.

It was in Boston that I found her at last, forlornly swaying
to the oscillations of an overhead strap in a crowded trolley-
car. Her face had so changed that I lost myself in a startled
reckoning of the time that had elapsed since our parting. She
spoke to me shyly, as though aware of my hurried calculation,
and conscious that in five years she ought not to have altered
so much as to upset my notion of time. Then she seemed to
set it down to her dress, for she nervously gathered her cloak
over a gown that asked only to be concealed, and shrank into
a seat behind the line of prehensile bipeds blocking the aisle
of the car.

It was perhaps because she so obviously avoided me that I
felt for the first time that I might be of use to her; and when
she left the car I made no excuse for following her.

She said nothing of needing advice and did not ask me to
walk home with her, concealing, as we talked, her transparent
preoccupations under the guise of a sudden interest in all I
had been doing since she had last seen me. Of what concerned her, I learned only that Lancelot was well and that for
the present she was not lecturing—she was tired and her doctor had ordered her to rest. On the doorstep of a shabby
house she paused and held out her hand. She had been so
glad to see me and perhaps if I were in Boston again—the
tired dimple, as it were, bowed me out and closed the door
on the conclusion of the phrase.

Two or three weeks later, at my club in New York, I found
a letter from her. In it she owned that she was troubled, that
of late she had been unsuccessful, and that, if I chanced to be
coming back to Boston, and could spare her a little of that

invaluable advice which—. A few days later the advice was at her disposal.

She told me frankly what had happened. Her public had grown tired of her. She had seen it coming on for some time, and was shrewd enough in detecting the causes. She had more rivals than formerly—younger women, she admitted, with a smile that could still afford to be generous—and then her audiences had grown more critical and consequently more exacting. Lecturing—as she understood it—used to be simple enough. You chose your topic—Raphael, Shakespeare, Gothic Architecture, or some such big familiar "subject"—and read up about it for a week or so at the Athenæum or the Astor Library, and then told your audience what you had read. Now, it appeared, that simple process was no longer adequate. People had tired of familiar "subjects"; it was the fashion to be interested in things that one hadn't always known about—natural selection, animal magnetism, sociology and comparative folk-lore; while, in literature, the demand had become equally difficult to meet, since Matthew Arnold had introduced the habit of studying the "influence" of one author on another. She had tried lecturing on influences, and had done very well as long as the public was satisfied with the tracing of such obvious influences as that of Turner on Ruskin, of Schiller on Goethe, of Shakespeare on English literature; but such investigations had soon lost all charm for her too-sophisticated audiences, who now demanded either that the influence or the influenced should be quite unknown, or that there should be no perceptible connection between the two. The zest of the performance lay in the measure of ingenuity with which the lecturer established a relation between two people who had probably never heard of each other, much less read each other's works. A pretty Miss Williams with red hair had, for instance, been lecturing with great success on the influence of the Rosicrucians upon the poetry of Keats, while somebody else had given a "course" on the influence of St. Thomas Aquinas upon Professor Huxley.

Mrs. Amyot, warmed by my participation in her distress, went on to say that the growing demand for evolution was what most troubled her. Her grandfather had been a pillar of the Presbyterian ministry, and the idea of her lecturing on

Darwin or Herbert Spencer was deeply shocking to her mother and aunts. In one sense the family had staked its literary as well as its spiritual hopes on the literal inspiration of Genesis: what became of "The Fall of Man" in the light of modern exegesis?

The upshot of it was that she had ceased to lecture because she could no longer sell tickets enough to pay for the hire of a lecture-hall; and as for the managers, they wouldn't look at her. She had tried her luck all through the Eastern States and as far south as Washington; but it was of no use, and unless she could get hold of some new subjects—or, better still, of some new audiences—she must simply go out of the business. That would mean the failure of all she had worked for, since Lancelot would have to leave Harvard. She paused, and wept some of the unbecoming tears that spring from real grief. Lancelot, it appeared, was to be a genius. He had passed his opening examinations brilliantly; he had "literary gifts"; he had written beautiful poetry, much of which his mother had copied out, in reverentially slanting characters, in a velvet-bound volume which she drew from a locked drawer.

Lancelot's verse struck me as nothing more alarming than growing-pains; but it was not to learn this that she had summoned me. What she wanted was to be assured that he was worth working for, an assurance which I managed to convey by the simple stratagem of remarking that the poems reminded me of Swinburne—and so they did, as well as of Browning, Tennyson, Rossetti, and all the other poets who supply young authors with original inspirations.

This point being established, it remained to be decided by what means his mother was, in the French phrase, to pay herself the luxury of a poet. It was clear that this indulgence could be bought only with counterfeit coin, and that the one way of helping Mrs. Amyot was to become a party to the circulation of such currency. My fetish of intellectual integrity went down like a ninepin before the appeal of a woman no longer young and distinctly foolish, but full of those dear contradictions and irrelevancies that will always make flesh and blood prevail against a syllogism. When I took leave of Mrs. Amyot I had promised her a dozen letters to Western universities and had half pledged myself to sketch out a lecture on the reconciliation of science and religion.

In the West she achieved a success which for a year or more embittered my perusal of the morning papers. The fascination that lures the murderer back to the scene of his crime drew my eye to every paragraph celebrating Mrs. Amyot's last brilliant lecture on the influence of something upon somebody; and her own letters—she overwhelmed me with them—spared me no detail of the entertainment given in her honor by the Palimpsest Club of Omaha or of her reception at the University of Leadville. The college professors were especially kind: she assured me that she had never before met with such discriminating sympathy. I winced at the adjective, which cast a sudden light on the vast machinery of fraud that I had set in motion. All over my native land, men of hitherto unblemished integrity were conniving with me in urging their friends to go and hear Mrs. Amyot lecture on the reconciliation of science and religion! My only hope was that, somewhere among the number of my accomplices, Mrs. Amyot might find one who would marry her in the defense of his convictions.

None, apparently, resorted to such heroic measures; for about two years later I was startled by the announcement that Mrs. Amyot was lecturing in Trenton, New Jersey, on modern theosophy in the light of the Vedas. The following week she was at Newark, discussing Schopenhauer in the light of recent psychology. The week after that I was on the deck of an ocean steamer, reconsidering my share in Mrs. Amyot's triumphs with the impartiality with which one views an episode that is being left behind at the rate of twenty knots an hour. After all, I had been helping a mother to educate her son.

The next ten years of my life were spent in Europe, and when I came home the recollection of Mrs. Amyot had become as inoffensive as one of those pathetic ghosts who are said to strive in vain to make themselves visible to the living. I did not even notice the fact that I no longer heard her spoken of; she had dropped like a dead leaf from the bough of memory.

A year or two after my return I was condemned to one of the worst punishments a worker can undergo—an enforced holiday. The doctors who pronounced the inhuman sentence decreed that it should be worked out in the South, and for a whole winter I carried my cough, my thermometer and my idleness from one fashionable orange-grove to another. In the vast and melancholy sea of my disoccupation I clutched like a drowning man at any human driftwood within reach. I took a critical and depreciatory interest in the coughs, the thermometers and the idleness of my fellow-sufferers; but to the healthy, the occupied, the transient I clung with undiscriminating enthusiasm.

In no other way can I explain, as I look back on it, the importance I attached to the leisurely confidences of a new arrival with a brown beard who, tilted back at my side on a hotel veranda hung with roses, imparted to me one afternoon the simple annals of his past. There was nothing in the tale to kindle the most inflammable imagination, and though the man had a pleasant frank face and a voice differing agreeably from the shrill inflections of our fellow-lodgers, it is probable that under different conditions his discursive history of successful business ventures in a Western city would have affected me somewhat in the manner of a lullaby.

Even at the time I was not sure I liked his agreeable voice: it had a self-importance out of keeping with the humdrum nature of his story, as though a breeze engaged in shaking out a table-cloth should have fancied itself inflating a banner. But this criticism may have been a mere mark of my own fastidiousness, for the man seemed a simple fellow, satisfied with his middling fortunes, and already (he was not much past thirty) deep-sunk in conjugal content.

He had just started on an anecdote connected with the cutting of his eldest boy's teeth, when a lady I knew, returning from her late drive, paused before us for a moment in the twilight, with the smile which is the feminine equivalent of beads to savages.

"Won't you take a ticket?" she said sweetly.

Of course I would take a ticket—but for what? I ventured to inquire.

"Oh, that's *so* good of you—for the lecture this evening. You needn't go, you know; we're none of us going; most of us have been through it already at Aiken and at Saint Augustine and at Palm Beach. I've given away my tickets to some new people who've just come from the North, and some of us are going to send our maids, just to fill up the room."

"And may I ask to whom you are going to pay this delicate attention?"

"Oh, I thought you knew—to poor Mrs. Amyot. She's been lecturing all over the South this winter; she's simply *haunted* me ever since I left New York—and we had six weeks of her at Bar Harbor last summer! One has to take tickets, you know, because she's a widow and does it for her son—to pay for his education. She's so plucky and nice about it, and talks about him in such a touching unaffected way, that everybody is sorry for her, and we all simply ruin ourselves in tickets. I do hope that boy's nearly educated!"

"Mrs. Amyot? Mrs. Amyot?" I repeated. "Is she *still* educating her son?"

"Oh, do you know about her? Has she been at it long? There's some comfort in that, for I suppose when the boy's provided for the poor thing will be able to take a rest—and give us one!"

She laughed and held out her hand.

"Here's your ticket. Did you say *tickets*—two? Oh, thanks. Of course you needn't go."

"But I mean to go. Mrs. Amyot is an old friend of mine."

"Do you really? That's awfully good of you. Perhaps I'll go too if I can persuade Charlie and the others to come. And I wonder"—in a well-directed aside—"if your friend—?"

I telegraphed her under cover of the dusk that my friend was of too recent standing to be drawn into her charitable toils, and she masked her mistake under a rattle of friendly adjurations not to be late, and to be sure to keep a seat for her, as she had quite made up her mind to go even if Charlie and the others wouldn't.

The flutter of her skirts subsided in the distance, and my neighbor, who had half turned away to light a cigar, made no effort to reopen the conversation. At length, fearing he might have overheard the allusion to himself, I ventured to ask if he were going to the lecture that evening.

"Much obliged—I have a ticket," he said abruptly.

This struck me as in such bad taste that I made no answer; and it was he who spoke next.

"Did I understand you to say that you were an old friend of Mrs. Amyot's?"

"I think I may claim to be, if it is the same Mrs. Amyot I had the pleasure of knowing many years ago. My Mrs. Amyot used to lecture too—"

"To pay for her son's education?"

"I believe so."

"Well—see you later."

He got up and walked into the house.

In the hotel drawing-room that evening there was but a meagre sprinkling of guests, among whom I saw my brown-bearded friend sitting alone on a sofa, with his head against the wall. It could not have been curiosity to see Mrs. Amyot that had impelled him to attend the performance, for it would have been impossible for him, without changing his place, to command the improvised platform at the end of the room. When I looked at him he seemed lost in contemplation of the chandelier.

The lady from whom I had bought my tickets fluttered in late, unattended by Charlie and the others, and assuring me that she would *scream* if we had the lecture on Ibsen—she had heard it three times already that winter. A glance at the programme reassured her: it informed us (in the lecturer's own slanting hand) that Mrs. Amyot was to lecture on the Cosmogony.

After a long pause, during which the small audience coughed and moved its chairs and showed signs of regretting that it had come, the door opened, and Mrs. Amyot stepped upon the platform. Ah, poor lady!

Some one said "Hush!", the coughing and chair-shifting subsided, and she began.

It was like looking at one's self early in the morning in a cracked mirror. I had no idea I had grown so old. As for Lancelot, he must have a beard. A beard? The word struck me, and without knowing why I glanced across the room at my bearded friend on the sofa. Oddly enough he was looking at me, with a half-defiant, half-sullen expression; and as our glances crossed, and his fell, the conviction came to me that *he was Lancelot*.

I don't remember a word of the lecture; and yet there were enough of them to have filled a good-sized dictionary. The stream of Mrs. Amyot's eloquence had become a flood: one had the despairing sense that she had sprung a leak, and that until the plumber came there was nothing to be done about it.

The plumber came at length, in the shape of a clock striking ten; my companion, with a sigh of relief, drifted away in search of Charlie and the others; the audience scattered with the precipitation of people who had discharged a duty; and, without surprise, I found the brown-bearded stranger at my elbow.

We stood alone in the bare-floored room, under the flaring chandelier.

"I think you told me this afternoon that you were an old friend of Mrs. Amyot's?" he began awkwardly.

I assented.

"Will you come in and see her?"

"Now? I shall be very glad to, if—"

"She's ready; she's expecting you," he interposed.

He offered no further explanation, and I followed him in silence. He led me down the long corridor, and pushed open the door of a sitting-room.

"Mother," he said, closing the door after we had entered, "here's the gentleman who says he used to know you."

Mrs. Amyot, who sat in an easy-chair stirring a cup of bouillon, looked up with a start. She had evidently not seen me in the audience, and her son's description had failed to convey my identity. I saw a frightened look in her eyes; then, like a frost flower on a window-pane, the dimple expanded on her wrinkled cheek, and she held out her hand.

"I'm so glad," she said, "so glad!"

She turned to her son, who stood watching us. "You must have told Lancelot all about me—you've known me so long!"

"I haven't had time to talk to your son—since I knew he was your son," I explained.

Her brow cleared. "Then you haven't had time to say anything very dreadful?" she said with a laugh.

"It is he who has been saying dreadful things," I returned, trying to fall in with her tone.

I saw my mistake. "What things?" she faltered.

"Making me feel how old I am by telling me about his children."

"My grandchildren!" she exclaimed with a blush.

"Well, if you choose to put it so."

She laughed again, vaguely, and was silent. I hesitated a moment and then put out my hand.

"I see you are tired. I shouldn't have ventured to come in at this hour if your son—"

The son stepped between us. "Yes, I asked him to come," he said to his mother, in his clear self-assertive voice. "*I* haven't told him anything yet; but you've got to—now. That's what I brought him for."

His mother straightened herself, but I saw her eye waver.

"Lancelot—" she began.

"Mr. Amyot," I said, turning to the young man, "if your mother will let me come back to-morrow, I shall be very glad—"

He struck his hand hard against the table on which he was leaning.

"No, sir! It won't take long, but it's got to be said now."

He moved nearer to his mother, and I saw his lip twitch under his beard. After all, he was younger and less sure of himself than I had fancied.

"See here, mother," he went on, "there's something here that's got to be cleared up, and as you say this gentleman is an old friend of yours it had better be cleared up in his presence. Maybe he can help explain it—and if he can't, it's got to be explained to *him*."

Mrs. Amyot's lips moved, but she made no sound. She glanced at me helplessly and sat down. My early inclination to thrash Lancelot was beginning to reassert itself. I took up my hat and moved toward the door.

"Mrs. Amyot is under no obligation to explain anything whatever to me," I said curtly.

"Well! She's under an obligation to me, then—to explain something in your presence." He turned to her again. "Do you know what the people in this hotel are saying? Do you know what he thinks—what they all think? That you're doing this lecturing to support me—to pay for my education! They say you go round telling them so. That's what they buy the tickets for—they do it out of charity. Ask him if it isn't what they say—ask him if they weren't joking about it on the piazza before dinner. The others think I'm a little boy, but he's known you for years, and he must have known how old I was. *He* must have known it wasn't to pay for my education!"

He stood before her with his hands clenched, the veins beating in his temples. She had grown very pale, and her cheeks looked hollow. When she spoke her voice had an odd click in it.

"If—if these ladies and gentlemen have been coming to my lectures out of charity, I see nothing to be ashamed of in that—" she faltered.

"If they've been coming out of charity to *me*," he retorted, "don't you see you've been making me a party to a fraud? Isn't there any shame in that?" His forehead reddened. "Mother! Can't you see the shame of letting people think I was a d— beat, who sponged on you for my keep? Let alone making us both the laughing-stock of every place you go to!"

"I never did that, Lancelot!"

"Did what?"

"Made you a laughing-stock—"

He stepped close to her and caught her wrist.

"Will you look me in the face and swear you never told people you were doing this lecturing business to support me?"

There was a long silence. He dropped her wrist and she lifted a limp handkerchief to her frightened eyes. "I did do it—to support you—to educate you"—she sobbed.

"We're not talking about what you did when I was a boy. Everybody who knows me knows I've been a grateful son. Have I ever taken a penny from you since I left college ten years ago?"

"I never said you had! How can you accuse your mother of such wickedness, Lancelot?"

"Have you never told anybody in this hotel—or anywhere else in the last ten years—that you were lecturing to support me? Answer me that!"

"How can you," she wept, "before a stranger?"

"Haven't you said such things about *me* to strangers?" he retorted.

"Lancelot!"

"Well—answer me, then. Say you haven't, mother!" His voice broke unexpectedly and he took her hand with a gentler touch. "I'll believe anything you tell me," he said almost humbly.

She mistook his tone and raised her head with a rash clutch at dignity.

"I think you'd better ask this gentleman to excuse you first."

"No, by God, I won't!" he cried. "This gentleman says he knows all about you and I mean him to know all about me too. I don't mean that he or anybody else under this roof shall go on thinking for another twenty-four hours that a cent of their money has ever gone into my pockets since I was old enough to shift for myself. And he sha'n't leave this room till you've made that clear to him."

He stepped back as he spoke and put his shoulders against the door.

"My dear young gentleman," I said politely, "I shall leave this room exactly when I see fit to do so—and that is now. I have already told you that Mrs. Amyot owes me no explanation of her conduct."

"But I owe you an explanation of mine—you and every one who has bought a single one of her lecture tickets. Do you suppose a man who's been through what I went through while that woman was talking to you in the porch before dinner is going to hold his tongue, and not attempt to justify himself? No decent man is going to sit down under that sort of thing. It's enough to ruin his character. If you're my mother's friend, you owe it to me to hear what I've got to say."

He pulled out his handkerchief and wiped his forehead.

"Good God, mother!" he burst out suddenly, "what did you do it for? Haven't you had everything you wanted ever since I was able to pay for it? Haven't I paid you back every cent you spent on me when I was in college? Have I ever gone back on you since I was big enough to work?" He turned to me with a laugh. "I thought she did it to amuse herself—and because there was such a demand for her lectures. *Such a demand!* That's what she always told me. When we asked her to come out and spend this winter with us in Minneapolis, she wrote back that she couldn't because she had engagements all through the south, and her manager wouldn't let her off. That's the reason why I came all the way on here to see her. We thought she was the most popular lecturer in the United States, my wife and I did! We were awfully proud of it too, I can tell you." He dropped into a chair, still laughing.

"How can you, Lancelot, how can you!" His mother, forgetful of my presence, was clinging to him with tentative caresses. "When you didn't need the money any longer I spent it all on the children—you know I did."

"Yes, on lace christening dresses and life-size rocking-horses with real manes! The kind of thing children can't do without."

"Oh, Lancelot, Lancelot—I loved them so! How can you believe such falsehoods about me?"

"What falsehoods about you?"

"That I ever told anybody such dreadful things?"

He put her back gently, keeping his eyes on hers. "Did you never tell anybody in this house that you were lecturing to support your son?"

Her hands dropped from his shoulders and she flashed round on me in sudden anger.

"I know what I think of people who call themselves friends and who come between a mother and her son!"

"Oh, mother, mother!" he groaned.

I went up to him and laid my hand on his shoulder.

"My dear man," I said, "don't you see the uselessness of prolonging this?"

"Yes, I do," he answered abruptly; and before I could forestall his movement he rose and walked out of the room.

There was a long silence, measured by the lessening reverberations of his footsteps down the wooden floor of the corridor.

When they ceased I approached Mrs. Amyot, who had sunk into her chair. I held out my hand and she took it without a trace of resentment on her ravaged face.

"I sent his wife a seal-skin jacket at Christmas!" she said, with the tears running down her cheeks.

Souls Belated

Their railway-carriage had been full when the train left Bologna; but at the first station beyond Milan their only remaining companion—a courtly person who ate garlic out of a carpet-bag—had left his crumb-strewn seat with a bow.

Lydia's eye regretfully followed the shiny broadcloth of his retreating back till it lost itself in the cloud of touts and cab-drivers hanging about the station; then she glanced across at Gannett and caught the same regret in his look. They were both sorry to be alone.

"*Par-ten-za!*" shouted the guard. The train vibrated to a sudden slamming of doors; a waiter ran along the platform with a tray of fossilized sandwiches; a belated porter flung a bundle of shawls and band-boxes into a third-class carriage; the guard snapped out a brief *Partenza!* which indicated the purely ornamental nature of his first shout; and the train swung out of the station.

The direction of the road had changed, and a shaft of sunlight struck across the dusty red velvet seats into Lydia's corner. Gannett did not notice it. He had returned to his *Revue de Paris*, and she had to rise and lower the shade of the farther window. Against the vast horizon of their leisure such incidents stood out sharply.

Having lowered the shade, Lydia sat down, leaving the length of the carriage between herself and Gannett. At length he missed her and looked up.

"I moved out of the sun," she hastily explained.

He looked at her curiously: the sun was beating on her through the shade.

"Very well," he said pleasantly; adding, "You don't mind?" as he drew a cigarette-case from his pocket.

It was a refreshing touch, relieving the tension of her spirit with the suggestion that, after all, if he could *smoke*—! The relief was only momentary. Her experience of smokers was limited (her husband had disapproved of the use of tobacco) but she knew from hearsay that men sometimes smoked to get away from things; that a cigar might be the masculine

equivalent of darkened windows and a headache. Gannett, after a puff or two, returned to his review.

It was just as she had foreseen; he feared to speak as much
as she did. It was one of the misfortunes of their situation that
they were never busy enough to necessitate, or even to justify,
the postponement of unpleasant discussions. If they avoided a
question it was obviously, unconcealably because the question
was disagreeable. They had unlimited leisure and an accumu-
lation of mental energy to devote to any subject that presented itself; new topics were in fact at a premium. Lydia
sometimes had premonitions of a famine-stricken period
when there would be nothing left to talk about, and she had
already caught herself doling out piecemeal what, in the first
prodigality of their confidences, she would have flung to him
in a breath. Their silence therefore might simply mean that
they had nothing to say; but it was another disadvantage of
their position that it allowed infinite opportunity for the
classification of minute differences. Lydia had learned to distinguish between real and factitious silences; and under
Gannett's she now detected a hum of speech to which her
own thoughts made breathless answer.

How could it be otherwise, with that thing between them?
She glanced up at the rack overhead. The *thing* was there, in
her dressing-bag, symbolically suspended over her head and
his. He was thinking of it now, just as she was; they had been
thinking of it in unison ever since they had entered the train.
While the carriage had held other travellers they had screened
her from his thoughts; but now that he and she were alone
she knew exactly what was passing through his mind; she
could almost hear him asking himself what he should say to
her. . . .

The thing had come that morning, brought up to her in an
innocent-looking envelope with the rest of their letters, as
they were leaving the hotel at Bologna. As she tore it open,
she and Gannett were laughing over some ineptitude of the
local guide-book—they had been driven, of late, to make the
most of such incidental humors of travel. Even when she had
unfolded the document she took it for some unimportant
business paper sent abroad for her signature, and her eye

travelled inattentively over the curly *Whereases* of the preamble until a word arrested her:—Divorce. There it stood, an impassable barrier, between her husband's name and hers.

She had been prepared for it, of course, as healthy people are said to be prepared for death, in the sense of knowing it must come without in the least expecting that it will. She had known from the first that Tillotson meant to divorce her—but what did it matter? Nothing mattered, in those first days of supreme deliverance, but the fact that she was free; and not so much (she had begun to be aware) that freedom had released her from Tillotson as that it had given her to Gannett. This discovery had not been agreeable to her self-esteem. She had preferred to think that Tillotson had himself embodied all her reasons for leaving him; and those he represented had seemed cogent enough to stand in no need of reinforcement. Yet she had not left him till she met Gannett. It was her love for Gannett that had made life with Tillotson so poor and incomplete a business. If she had never, from the first, regarded her marriage as a full canceling of her claims upon life, she had at least, for a number of years, accepted it as a provisional compensation,—she made it "do." Existence in the commodious Tillotson mansion in Fifth Avenue—with Mrs. Tillotson senior commanding the approaches from the second-story front windows—had been reduced to a series of purely automatic acts. The moral atmosphere of the Tillotson interior was as carefully screened and curtained as the house itself: Mrs. Tillotson senior dreaded ideas as much as a draught in her back. Prudent people liked an even temperature; and to do anything unexpected was as foolish as going out in the rain. One of the chief advantages of being rich was that one need not be exposed to unforeseen contingencies: by the use of ordinary firmness and common sense one could make sure of doing exactly the same thing every day at the same hour. These doctrines, reverentially imbibed with his mother's milk, Tillotson (a model son who had never given his parents an hour's anxiety) complacently expounded to his wife, testifying to his sense of their importance by the regularity with which he wore galoshes on damp days, his punctuality at meals, and his elaborate precautions against burglars and contagious diseases. Lydia, coming from a smaller town, and entering New

York life through the portals of the Tillotson mansion, had mechanically accepted this point of view as inseparable from having a front pew in church and a parterre box at the opera. All the people who came to the house revolved in the same small circle of prejudices. It was the kind of society in which, after dinner, the ladies compared the exorbitant charges of their children's teachers, and agreed that, even with the new duties on French clothes, it was cheaper in the end to get everything from Worth; while the husbands, over their cigars, lamented municipal corruption, and decided that the men to start a reform were those who had no private interests at stake.

To Lydia this view of life had become a matter of course, just as lumbering about in her mother-in-law's landau had come to seem the only possible means of locomotion, and listening every Sunday to a fashionable Presbyterian divine the inevitable atonement for having thought oneself bored on the other six days of the week. Before she met Gannett her life had seemed merely dull: his coming made it appear like one of those dismal Cruikshank prints in which the people are all ugly and all engaged in occupations that are either vulgar or stupid.

It was natural that Tillotson should be the chief sufferer from this readjustment of focus. Gannett's nearness had made her husband ridiculous, and a part of the ridicule had been reflected on herself. Her tolerance laid her open to a suspicion of obtuseness from which she must, at all costs, clear herself in Gannett's eyes.

She did not understand this until afterwards. At the time she fancied that she had merely reached the limits of endurance. In so large a charter of liberties as the mere act of leaving Tillotson seemed to confer, the small question of divorce or no divorce did not count. It was when she saw that she had left her husband only to be with Gannett that she perceived the significance of anything affecting their relations. Her husband, in casting her off, had virtually flung her at Gannett: it was thus that the world viewed it. The measure of alacrity with which Gannett would receive her would be the subject of curious speculation over afternoon-tea tables and in club corners. She knew what would be said—she had heard it so often of others! The recollection bathed her in misery. The men would probably back Gannett to "do the decent thing"; but the ladies' eye-brows would emphasize the worthlessness of such enforced fidelity; and after all, they would be right. She had put herself in a position where Gannett "owed" her something; where, as a gentleman, he was bound to "stand the damage." The idea of accepting such compensation had never crossed her mind; the so-called rehabilitation of such a marriage had always seemed to her the only real disgrace. What she dreaded was the necessity of having to explain herself; of having to combat his arguments; of calculating, in spite of herself, the exact measure of insistence with which he pressed them. She knew not whether she most shrank from his insisting too much or too little. In such a case the nicest sense of proportion might be at fault; and how easy to fall into the error of taking her resistance for a test of his sincerity! Whichever way she turned, an ironical implication confronted her: she had the exasperated sense of having walked into the trap of some stupid practical joke.

Beneath all these preoccupations lurked the dread of what he was thinking. Sooner or later, of course, he would have to speak; but that, in the meantime, he should think, even for a moment, that there was any use in speaking, seemed to her simply unendurable. Her sensitiveness on this point was aggravated by another fear, as yet barely on the level of consciousness; the fear of unwillingly involving Gannett in the trammels of her dependence. To look upon him as the instrument of her liberation; to resist in herself the least tendency to a wifely taking possession of his future; had seemed to Lydia the one way of maintaining the dignity of their relation. Her view had not changed, but she was aware of a growing inability to keep her thoughts fixed on the essential point—the point of parting with Gannett. It was easy to face as long as she kept it sufficiently far off: but what was this act of mental postponement but a gradual encroachment on his future? What was needful was the courage to recognize the moment when, by some word or look, their voluntary fellowship should be transformed into a bondage the more wearing that it was based on none of those common obligations which make the most imperfect marriage in some sort a centre of gravity.

When the porter, at the next station, threw the door open, Lydia drew back, making way for the hoped-for intruder; but none came, and the train took up its leisurely progress through the spring wheat-fields and budding copses. She now began to hope that Gannett would speak before the next station. She watched him furtively, half-disposed to return to the seat opposite his, but there was an artificiality about his absorption that restrained her. She had never before seen him read with so conspicuous an air of warding off interruption. What could he be thinking of? Why should he be afraid to speak? Or was it her answer that he dreaded?

The train paused for the passing of an express, and he put down his book and leaned out of the window. Presently he turned to her with a smile.

"There's a jolly old villa out here," he said.

His easy tone relieved her, and she smiled back at him as she crossed over to his corner.

Beyond the embankment, through the opening in a mossy wall, she caught sight of the villa, with its broken balustrades, its stagnant fountains, and the stone satyr closing the perspective of a dusky grass-walk.

"How should you like to live there?" he asked as the train moved on.

"There?"

"In some such place, I mean. One might do worse, don't you think so? There must be at least two centuries of solitude under those yew-trees. Shouldn't you like it?"

"I—I don't know," she faltered. She knew now that he meant to speak.

He lit another cigarette. "We shall have to live somewhere, you know," he said as he bent above the match.

Lydia tried to speak carelessly. "*Je n'en vois pas la nécessité!* Why not live everywhere, as we have been doing?"

"But we can't travel forever, can we?"

"Oh, forever's a long word," she objected, picking up the review he had thrown aside.

"For the rest of our lives then," he said, moving nearer.

She made a slight gesture which caused his hand to slip from hers.

"Why should we make plans? I thought you agreed with me that it's pleasanter to drift."

He looked at her hesitatingly. "It's been pleasant, certainly; but I suppose I shall have to get at my work again some day. You know I haven't written a line since—all this time," he hastily emended.

She flamed with sympathy and self-reproach. "Oh, if you mean *that*—if you want to write—of course we must settle down. How stupid of me not to have thought of it sooner! Where shall we go? Where do you think you could work best? We oughtn't to lose any more time."

He hesitated again. "I had thought of a villa in these parts. It's quiet; we shouldn't be bothered. Should you like it?"

"Of course I should like it." She paused and looked away. "But I thought—I remember your telling me once that your best work had been done in a crowd—in big cities. Why should you shut yourself up in a desert?"

Gannett, for a moment, made no reply. At length he said, avoiding her eye as carefully as she avoided his: "It might be different now; I can't tell, of course, till I try. A writer ought not to be dependent on his *milieu*; it's a mistake to humor oneself in that way; and I thought that just at first you might prefer to be—"

She faced him. "To be what?"

"Well—quiet. I mean—"

"What do you mean by 'at first'?" she interrupted.

He paused again. "I mean after we are married."

She thrust up her chin and turned toward the window. "Thank you!" she tossed back at him.

"Lydia!" he exclaimed blankly; and she felt in every fibre of her averted person that he had made the inconceivable, the unpardonable mistake of anticipating her acquiescence.

The train rattled on and he groped for a third cigarette. Lydia remained silent.

"I haven't offended you?" he ventured at length, in the tone of a man who feels his way.

She shook her head with a sigh. "I thought you understood," she moaned. Their eyes met and she moved back to his side.

"Do you want to know how not to offend me? By taking it for granted, once for all, that you've said your say on this odious question and that I've said mine, and that we stand just where we did this morning before that—that hateful paper came to spoil everything between us!"

"To spoil everything between us? What on earth do you mean? Aren't you glad to be free?"

"I was free before."

"Not to marry me," he suggested.

"But I don't *want* to marry you!" she cried.

She saw that he turned pale. "I'm obtuse, I suppose," he said slowly. "I confess I don't see what you're driving at. Are you tired of the whole business? Or was I simply a—an excuse for getting away? Perhaps you didn't care to travel alone? Was that it? And now you want to chuck me?" His voice had grown harsh. "You owe me a straight answer, you know; don't be tender-hearted!"

Her eyes swam as she leaned to him. "Don't you see it's because I care—because I care so much? Oh, Ralph! Can't you see how it would humiliate me? Try to feel it as a woman would! Don't you see the misery of being made your wife in this way? If I'd known you as a girl—that would have been a real marriage! But now—this vulgar fraud upon society—and upon a society we despised and laughed at—this sneaking back into a position that we've voluntarily forfeited: don't you see what a cheap compromise it is? We neither of us believe in the abstract 'sacredness' of marriage; we both know that no ceremony is needed to consecrate our love for each other; what object can we have in marrying, except the secret fear of each that the other may escape, or the secret longing to work our way back gradually—oh, very gradually—into the esteem of the people whose conventional morality we have always ridiculed and hated? And the very fact that, after a decent interval, these same people would come and dine with us—the women who talk about the indissolubility of marriage, and who would let me die in a gutter to-day because I am 'leading a life of sin'—doesn't that disgust you more than their turning their backs on us now? I can stand being cut by them, but I couldn't stand their coming to call and asking what I meant to do about visiting that unfortunate Mrs. So-and-so!"

She paused, and Gannett maintained a perplexed silence.

"You judge things too theoretically," he said at length, slowly. "Life is made up of compromises."

"The life we ran away from—yes! If we had been willing to accept them"—she flushed—"we might have gone on meeting each other at Mrs. Tillotson's dinners."

He smiled slightly. "I didn't know that we ran away to found a new system of ethics. I supposed it was because we loved each other."

"Life is complex, of course; isn't it the very recognition of that fact that separates us from the people who see it *tout d'une pièce*? If *they* are right—if marriage is sacred in itself and the individual must always be sacrificed to the family—then there can be no real marriage between us, since our—our being together is a protest against the sacrifice of the individual to the family." She interrupted herself with a laugh. "You'll say now that I'm giving you a lecture on sociology! Of course one acts as one can—as one must, perhaps—pulled by all sorts of invisible threads; but at least one needn't pretend, for social advantages, to subscribe to a creed that ignores the complexity of human motives—that classifies people by arbitrary signs, and puts it in everybody's reach to be on Mrs. Tillotson's visiting-list. It may be necessary that the world should be ruled by conventions—but if we believed in them, why did we break through them? And if we don't believe in them, is it honest to take advantage of the protection they afford?"

Gannett hesitated. "One may believe in them or not; but as long as they do rule the world it is only by taking advantage of their protection that one can find a *modus vivendi*."

"Do outlaws need a *modus vivendi*?"

He looked at her hopelessly. Nothing is more perplexing to man than the mental process of a woman who reasons her emotions.

She thought she had scored a point and followed it up passionately. "You do understand, don't you? You see how the very thought of the thing humiliates me! We are together to-day because we choose to be—don't let us look any farther than that!" She caught his hands. "*Promise* me you'll never speak of it again; promise me you'll never *think* of it even," she implored, with a tearful prodigality of italics.

Through what followed—his protests, his arguments, his final unconvinced submission to her wishes—she had a sense of
his but half-discerning all that, for her, had made the moment
so tumultuous. They had reached that memorable point in
every heart-history when, for the first time, the man seems
obtuse and the woman irrational. It was the abundance of his
intentions that consoled her, on reflection, for what they
lacked in quality. After all, it would have been worse, incalcu-
lably worse, to have detected any over-readiness to understand her.

II

When the train at night-fall brought them to their journey's end at the edge of one of the lakes, Lydia was glad that
they were not, as usual, to pass from one solitude to another.
Their wanderings during the year had indeed been like the
flight of outlaws: through Sicily, Dalmatia, Transylvania and
Southern Italy they had persisted in their tacit avoidance of
their kind. Isolation, at first, had deepened the flavor of their
happiness, as night intensifies the scent of certain flowers; but
in the new phase on which they were entering, Lydia's chief
wish was that they should be less abnormally exposed to the
action of each other's thoughts.

She shrank, nevertheless, as the brightly-looming bulk of
the fashionable Anglo-American hotel on the water's brink
began to radiate toward their advancing boat its vivid suggestion of social order, visitors' lists, Church services, and
the bland inquisition of the *table-d'hôte*. The mere fact that
in a moment or two she must take her place on the hotel
register as Mrs. Gannett seemed to weaken the springs of her
resistance.

They had meant to stay for a night only, on their way to a
lofty village among the glaciers of Monte Rosa; but after the
first plunge into publicity, when they entered the dining-
room, Lydia felt the relief of being lost in a crowd, of ceasing
for a moment to be the centre of Gannett's scrutiny; and in
his face she caught the reflection of her feeling. After dinner,
when she went upstairs, he strolled into the smoking-room,
and an hour or two later, sitting in the darkness of her win-

dow, she heard his voice below and saw him walking up and down the terrace with a companion cigar at his side. When he came up he told her he had been talking to the hotel chaplain—a very good sort of fellow.

"Queer little microcosms, these hotels! Most of these people live here all summer and then migrate to Italy or the Riviera. The English are the only people who can lead that kind of life with dignity—those soft-voiced old ladies in Shetland shawls somehow carry the British Empire under their caps. *Civis Romanus sum.* It's a curious study—there might be some good things to work up here."

He stood before her with the vivid preoccupied stare of the novelist on the trail of a "subject." With a relief that was half painful she noticed that, for the first time since they had been together, he was hardly aware of her presence.

"Do you think you could write here?"

"Here? I don't know." His stare dropped. "After being out of things so long one's first impressions are bound to be tremendously vivid, you know. I see a dozen threads already that one might follow—"

He broke off with a touch of embarrassment.

"Then follow them. We'll stay," she said with sudden decision.

"Stay here?" He glanced at her in surprise, and then, walking to the window, looked out upon the dusky slumber of the garden.

"Why not?" she said at length, in a tone of veiled irritation.

"The place is full of old cats in caps who gossip with the chaplain. Shall you like—I mean, it would be different if—"

She flamed up.

"Do you suppose I care? It's none of their business."

"Of course not; but you won't get them to think so."

"They may think what they please."

He looked at her doubtfully.

"It's for you to decide."

"We'll stay," she repeated.

Gannett, before they met, had made himself known as a successful writer of short stories and of a novel which had achieved the distinction of being widely discussed. The reviewers called him "promising," and Lydia now accused herself of having too long interfered with the fulfilment of his promise. There was a special irony in the fact, since his passionate assurances that only the stimulus of her companionship could bring out his latent faculty had almost given the dignity of a "vocation" to her course: there had been moments when she had felt unable to assume, before posterity, the responsibility of thwarting his career. And, after all, he had not written a line since they had been together: his first desire to write had come from renewed contact with the world! Was it all a mistake then? Must the most intelligent choice work more disastrously than the blundering combinations of chance? Or was there a still more humiliating answer to her perplexities? His sudden impulse of activity so exactly coincided with her own wish to withdraw, for a time, from the range of his observation, that she wondered if he too were not seeking sanctuary from intolerable problems.

"You must begin to-morrow!" she cried, hiding a tremor under the laugh with which she added, "I wonder if there's any ink in the inkstand?"

Whatever else they had at the Hotel Bellosguardo, they had, as Miss Pinsent said, "a certain tone." It was to Lady Susan Condit that they owed this inestimable benefit; an advantage ranking in Miss Pinsent's opinion above even the lawn tennis courts and the resident chaplain. It was the fact of Lady Susan's annual visit that made the hotel what it was. Miss Pinsent was certainly the last to underrate such a privilege:—"It's so important, my dear, forming as we do a little family, that there should be some one to give *the tone*; and no one could do it better than Lady Susan—an earl's daughter and a person of such determination. Dear Mrs. Ainger now—who really *ought*, you know, when Lady Susan's away—absolutely refuses to assert herself." Miss Pinsent sniffed derisively. "A bishop's niece!—my dear, I saw her once actually give in to some South Americans—and before us all. She gave up her seat at table to oblige them—such a lack of dignity! Lady Susan spoke to her very plainly about it afterwards."

Miss Pinsent glanced across the lake and adjusted her auburn front.

"But of course I don't deny that the stand Lady Susan takes is not always easy to live up to—for the rest of us, I mean. Monsieur Grossart, our good proprietor, finds it trying at times, I know—he has said as much, privately, to Mrs. Ainger and me. After all, the poor man is not to blame for wanting to fill his hotel, is he? And Lady Susan is so difficult—so very difficult—about new people. One might almost say that she disapproves of them beforehand, on principle. And yet she's had warnings—she very nearly made a dreadful mistake once with the Duchess of Levens, who dyed her hair and—well, swore and smoked. One would have thought that might have been a lesson to Lady Susan." Miss Pinsent resumed her knitting with a sigh. "There are exceptions, of course. She took at once to you and Mr. Gannett—it was quite remarkable, really. Oh, I don't mean that either—of course not! It was perfectly natural—we *all* thought you so charming and interesting from the first day—we knew at once that Mr. Gannett was intellectual, by the magazines you took in; but you know what I mean. Lady Susan is so very—well, I won't say prejudiced, as Mrs. Ainger does—but so prepared *not* to like new people, that her taking to you in that way was a surprise to us all, I confess."

Miss Pinsent sent a significant glance down the long laurustinus alley from the other end of which two people—a lady and gentleman—were strolling toward them through the smiling neglect of the garden.

"In this case, of course, it's very different; that I'm willing to admit. Their looks are against them; but, as Mrs. Ainger says, one can't exactly tell them so."

"She's very handsome," Lydia ventured, with her eyes on the lady, who showed, under the dome of a vivid sunshade, the hour-glass figure and superlative coloring of a Christmas chromo.

"That's the worst of it. She's too handsome."

"Well, after all, she can't help that."

"Other people manage to," said Miss Pinsent skeptically.

"But isn't it rather unfair of Lady Susan—considering that nothing is known about them?"

"But, my dear, that's the very thing that's against them. It's infinitely worse than any actual knowledge."

Lydia mentally agreed that, in the case of Mrs. Linton, it possibly might be.

"I wonder why they came here?" she mused.

"That's against them too. It's always a bad sign when loud people come to a quiet place. And they've brought van-loads of boxes—her maid told Mrs. Ainger's that they meant to stop indefinitely."

"And Lady Susan actually turned her back on her in the *salon*?"

"My dear, she said it was for our sakes: that makes it so unanswerable! But poor Grossart *is* in a way! The Lintons have taken his most expensive *suite*, you know—the yellow damask drawing-room above the portico—and they have champagne with every meal!"

They were silent as Mr. and Mrs. Linton sauntered by; the lady with tempestuous brows and challenging chin; the gentleman, a blond stripling, trailing after her, head downward, like a reluctant child dragged by his nurse.

"What does your husband think of them, my dear?" Miss Pinsent whispered as they passed out of earshot.

Lydia stooped to pick a violet in the border.

"He hasn't told me."

"Of your speaking to them, I mean. Would he approve of that? I know how very particular nice Americans are. I think your action might make a difference; it would certainly carry weight with Lady Susan."

"Dear Miss Pinsent, you flatter me!"

Lydia rose and gathered up her book and sun-shade.

"Well, if you're asked for an opinion—if Lady Susan asks you for one—I think you ought to be prepared," Miss Pinsent admonished her as she moved away.

III

Lady Susan held her own. She ignored the Lintons, and her little family, as Miss Pinsent phrased it, followed suit. Even Mrs. Ainger agreed that it was obligatory. If Lady Susan owed it to the others not to speak to the Lintons, the others clearly owed it to Lady Susan to back her up. It was generally found expedient, at the Hotel Bellosguardo, to adopt this form of reasoning.

Whatever effect this combined action may have had upon the Lintons, it did not at least have that of driving them away. Monsieur Grossart, after a few days of suspense, had the satisfaction of seeing them settle down in his yellow damask *premier* with what looked like a permanent installation of palm-trees and silk sofa-cushions, and a gratifying continuance in the consumption of champagne. Mrs. Linton trailed her Doucet draperies up and down the garden with the same challenging air, while her husband, smoking innumerable cigarettes, dragged himself dejectedly in her wake; but neither of them, after the first encounter with Lady Susan, made any attempt to extend their acquaintance. They simply ignored their ignorers. As Miss Pinsent resentfully observed, they behaved exactly as though the hotel were empty.

It was therefore a matter of surprise, as well as of displeasure, to Lydia, to find, on glancing up one day from her seat in the garden, that the shadow which had fallen across her book was that of the enigmatic Mrs. Linton.

"I want to speak to you," that lady said, in a rich hard voice that seemed the audible expression of her gown and her complexion.

Lydia started. She certainly did not want to speak to Mrs. Linton.

"Shall I sit down here?" the latter continued, fixing her intensely-shaded eyes on Lydia's face, "or are you afraid of being seen with me?"

"Afraid?" Lydia colored. "Sit down, please. What is it that you wish to say?"

Mrs. Linton, with a smile, drew up a garden-chair and crossed one open-work ankle above the other.

"I want you to tell me what my husband said to your husband last night."

Lydia turned pale.

"My husband—to yours?" she faltered, staring at the other.

"Didn't you know they were closeted together for hours in the smoking-room after you went upstairs? My man didn't get to bed until nearly two o'clock and when he did I

couldn't get a word out of him. When he wants to be aggra-
vating I'll back him against anybody living!" Her teeth and
eyes flashed persuasively upon Lydia. "But you'll tell me what
they were talking about, won't you? I know I can trust you—
you look so awfully kind. And it's for his own good. He's
such a precious donkey and I'm so afraid he's got into some
beastly scrape or other. If he'd only trust his own old woman!
But they're always writing to him and setting him against me.
And I've got nobody to turn to." She laid her hand on
Lydia's with a rattle of bracelets. "You'll help me, won't you?"

Lydia drew back from the smiling fierceness of her brows.

"I'm sorry—but I don't think I understand. My husband
has said nothing to me of—of yours."

The great black crescents above Mrs. Linton's eyes met
angrily.

"I say—is that true?" she demanded.

Lydia rose from her seat.

"Oh, look here, I didn't mean that, you know—you mustn't
take one up so! Can't you see how rattled I am?"

Lydia saw that, in fact, her beautiful mouth was quivering
beneath softened eyes.

"I'm beside myself!" the splendid creature wailed, dropping into her seat.

"I'm so sorry," Lydia repeated, forcing herself to speak
kindly; "but how can I help you?"

Mrs. Linton raised her head sharply.

"By finding out—there's a darling!"

"Finding what out?"

"What Trevenna told him."

"Trevenna—?" Lydia echoed in bewilderment.

Mrs. Linton clapped her hand to her mouth.

"Oh, Lord—there, it's out! What a fool I am! But I supposed of course you knew; I supposed everybody knew." She
dried her eyes and bridled. "Didn't you know that he's Lord
Trevenna? I'm Mrs. Cope."

Lydia recognized the names. They had figured in a flam-
boyant elopement which had thrilled fashionable London
some six months earlier.

"Now you see how it is—you understand, don't you?" Mrs.
Cope continued on a note of appeal. "I knew you would—

that's the reason I came to you. I suppose *he* felt the same thing about your husband; he's not spoken to another soul in the place." Her face grew anxious again. "He's awfully sensitive, generally—he feels our position, he says—as if it wasn't *my* place to feel that! But when he does get talking there's no knowing what he'll say. I know he's been brooding over something lately, and I *must* find out what it is—it's to his interest that I should. I always tell him that I think only of his interest; if he'd only trust me! But he's been so odd lately—I can't think what he's plotting. You will help me, dear?"

Lydia, who had remained standing, looked away uncomfortably.

"If you mean by finding out what Lord Trevenna has told my husband, I'm afraid it's impossible."

"Why impossible?"

"Because I infer that it was told in confidence."

Mrs. Cope stared incredulously.

"Well, what of that? Your husband looks such a dear—any one can see he's awfully gone on you. What's to prevent your getting it out of him?"

Lydia flushed.

"I'm not a spy!" she exclaimed.

"A spy—a spy? How dare you?" Mrs. Cope flamed out. "Oh, I don't mean that either! Don't be angry with me—I'm so miserable." She essayed a softer note. "Do you call that spying—for one woman to help out another? I do need help so dreadfully! I'm at my wits' end with Trevenna, I am indeed. He's such a boy—a mere baby, you know; he's only two-and-twenty." She dropped her orbed lids. "He's younger than me—only fancy! A few months younger. I tell him he ought to listen to me as if I was his mother; oughtn't he now? But he won't, he won't! All his people are at him, you see— oh, I know *their* little game! Trying to get him away from me before I can get my divorce—that's what they're up to. At first he wouldn't listen to them; he used to toss their letters over to me to read; but now he reads them himself, and answers 'em too, I fancy; he's always shut up in his room, writing. If I only knew what his plan is I could stop him fast enough—he's such a simpleton. But he's dreadfully deep too—at times I can't make him out. But I know he's told

your husband everything—I knew that last night the minute
I laid eyes on him. And I *must* find out—you must help me—
I've got no one else to turn to!"

She caught Lydia's fingers in a stormy pressure.

"Say you'll help me—you and your husband."

Lydia tried to free herself.

"What you ask is impossible; you must see that it is. No
one could interfere in—in the way you ask."

Mrs. Cope's clutch tightened.

"You won't, then? You won't?"

"Certainly not. Let me go, please."

Mrs. Cope released her with a laugh.

"Oh, go by all means—pray don't let me detain you! Shall
you go and tell Lady Susan Condit that there's a pair of us—
or shall I save you the trouble of enlightening her?"

Lydia stood still in the middle of the path, seeing her antagonist through a mist of terror. Mrs. Cope was still laughing.

"Oh, I'm not spiteful by nature, my dear; but you're a little more than flesh and blood can stand! It's impossible, is it?
Let you go, indeed! You're too good to be mixed up in my
affairs, are you? Why, you little fool, the first day I laid eyes
on you I saw that you and I were both in the same box—
that's the reason I spoke to you."

She stepped nearer, her smile dilating on Lydia like a lamp
through a fog.

"You can take your choice, you know; I always play fair. If
you'll tell I'll promise not to. Now then, which is it to be?"

Lydia, involuntarily, had begun to move away from the
pelting storm of words; but at this she turned and sat down
again.

"You may go," she said simply. "I shall stay here."

IV

She stayed there for a long time, in the hypnotized contemplation, not of Mrs. Cope's present, but of her own past.
Gannett, early that morning, had gone off on a long walk—
he had fallen into the habit of taking these mountain-tramps
with various fellow-lodgers; but even had he been within
reach she could not have gone to him just then. She had to

deal with herself first. She was surprised to find how, in the last months, she had lost the habit of introspection. Since their coming to the Hotel Bellosguardo she and Gannett had tacitly avoided themselves and each other.

She was aroused by the whistle of the three o'clock steamboat as it neared the landing just beyond the hotel gates. Three o'clock! Then Gannett would soon be back—he had told her to expect him before four. She rose hurriedly, her face averted from the inquisitorial façade of the hotel. She could not see him just yet; she could not go indoors. She slipped through one of the overgrown garden-alleys and climbed a steep path to the hills.

It was dark when she opened their sitting-room door. Gannett was sitting on the window-ledge smoking a cigarette. Cigarettes were now his chief resource: he had not written a line during the two months they had spent at the Hotel Bellosguardo. In that respect, it had turned out not to be the right *milieu* after all.

He started up at Lydia's entrance.

"Where have you been? I was getting anxious."

She sat down in a chair near the door.

"Up the mountain," she said wearily.

"Alone?"

"Yes."

Gannett threw away his cigarette: the sound of her voice made him want to see her face.

"Shall we have a little light?" he suggested.

She made no answer and he lifted the globe from the lamp and put a match to the wick. Then he looked at her.

"Anything wrong? You look done up."

She sat glancing vaguely about the little sitting-room, dimly lit by the pallid-globed lamp, which left in twilight the outlines of the furniture, of his writing-table heaped with books and papers, of the tea-roses and jasmine drooping on the mantel-piece. How like home it had all grown—how like home!

"Lydia, what is wrong?" he repeated.

She moved away from him, feeling for her hatpins and turning to lay her hat and sunshade on the table.

Suddenly she said: "That woman has been talking to me."

Gannett stared.

"That woman? What woman?"

"Mrs. Linton—Mrs. Cope."

He gave a start of annoyance, still, as she perceived, not grasping the full import of her words.

"The deuce! She told you—?"

"She told me everything."

Gannett looked at her anxiously.

"What impudence! I'm so sorry that you should have been exposed to this, dear."

"Exposed!" Lydia laughed.

Gannett's brow clouded and they looked away from each other.

"Do you know *why* she told me? She had the best of reasons. The first time she laid eyes on me she saw that we were both in the same box."

"Lydia!"

"So it was natural, of course, that she should turn to me in a difficulty."

"What difficulty?"

"It seems she has reason to think that Lord Trevenna's people are trying to get him away from her before she gets her divorce—"

"Well?"

"And she fancied he had been consulting with you last night as to—as to the best way of escaping from her."

Gannett stood up with an angry forehead.

"Well—what concern of yours was all this dirty business? Why should she go to you?"

"Don't you see? It's so simple. I was to wheedle his secret out of you."

"To oblige that woman?"

"Yes; or, if I was unwilling to oblige her, then to protect myself."

"To protect yourself? Against whom?"

"Against her telling every one in the hotel that she and I are in the same box."

"She threatened that?"

"She left me the choice of telling it myself or of doing it for me."

"The beast!"

There was a long silence. Lydia had seated herself on the sofa, beyond the radius of the lamp, and he leaned against the window. His next question surprised her.

"When did this happen? At what time, I mean?"

She looked at him vaguely.

"I don't know—after luncheon, I think. Yes, I remember; it must have been at about three o'clock."

He stepped into the middle of the room and as he approached the light she saw that his brow had cleared.

"Why do you ask?" she said.

"Because when I came in, at about half-past three, the mail was just being distributed, and Mrs. Cope was waiting as usual to pounce on her letters; you know she was always watching for the postman. She was standing so close to me that I couldn't help seeing a big official-looking envelope that was handed to her. She tore it open, gave one look at the inside, and rushed off upstairs like a whirlwind, with the director shouting after her that she had left all her other letters behind. I don't believe she ever thought of you again after that paper was put into her hand."

"Why?"

"Because she was too busy. I was sitting in the window, watching for you, when the five o'clock boat left, and who should go on board, bag and baggage, valet and maid, dressing-bags and poodle, but Mrs. Cope and Trevenna. Just an hour and a half to pack up in! And you should have seen her when they started. She was radiant—shaking hands with everybody—waving her handkerchief from the deck—distributing bows and smiles like an empress. If ever a woman got what she wanted just in the nick of time that woman did. She'll be Lady Trevenna within a week, I'll wager."

"You think she has her divorce?"

"I'm sure of it. And she must have got it just after her talk with you."

Lydia was silent.

At length she said, with a kind of reluctance, "She was horribly angry when she left me. It wouldn't have taken long to tell Lady Susan Condit."

"Lady Susan Condit has not been told."

"How do you know?"

"Because when I went downstairs half an hour ago I met Lady Susan on the way—"

He stopped, half smiling.

"Well?"

"And she stopped to ask if I thought you would act as patroness to a charity concert she is getting up."

In spite of themselves they both broke into a laugh. Lydia's ended in sobs and she sank down with her face hidden. Gannett bent over her, seeking her hands.

"That vile woman—I ought to have warned you to keep away from her; I can't forgive myself! But he spoke to me in confidence; and I never dreamed—well, it's all over now."

Lydia lifted her head.

"Not for me. It's only just beginning."

"What do you mean?"

She put him gently aside and moved in her turn to the window. Then she went on, with her face turned toward the shimmering blackness of the lake, "You see of course that it might happen again at any moment."

"What?"

"This—this risk of being found out. And we could hardly count again on such a lucky combination of chances, could we?"

He sat down with a groan.

Still keeping her face toward the darkness, she said, "I want you to go and tell Lady Susan—and the others."

Gannett, who had moved towards her, paused a few feet off.

"Why do you wish me to do this?" he said at length, with less surprise in his voice than she had been prepared for.

"Because I've behaved basely, abominably, since we came here: letting these people believe we were married—lying with every breath I drew—"

"Yes, I've felt that too," Gannett exclaimed with sudden energy.

The words shook her like a tempest: all her thoughts seemed to fall about her in ruins.

"You—you've felt so?"

"Of course I have." He spoke with low-voiced vehemence. "Do you suppose I like playing the sneak any better than you do? It's damnable."

He had dropped on the arm of a chair, and they stared at each other like blind people who suddenly see.

"But you have liked it here," she faltered.

"Oh, I've liked it—I've liked it." He moved impatiently. "Haven't you?"

"Yes," she burst out; "that's the worst of it—that's what I can't bear. I fancied it was for your sake that I insisted on staying—because you thought you could write here; and perhaps just at first that really was the reason. But afterwards I wanted to stay myself—I loved it." She broke into a laugh. "Oh, do you see the full derision of it? These people—the very prototypes of the bores you took me away from, with the same fenced-in view of life, the same keep-off-the-grass morality, the same little cautious virtues and the same little frightened vices—well, I've clung to them, I've delighted in them, I've done my best to please them. I've toadied Lady Susan, I've gossipped with Miss Pinsent, I've pretended to be shocked with Mrs. Ainger. Respectability! It was the one thing in life that I was sure I didn't care about, and it's grown so precious to me that I've stolen it because I couldn't get it in any other way."

She moved across the room and returned to his side with another laugh.

"I who used to fancy myself unconventional! I must have been born with a card-case in my hand. You should have seen me with that poor woman in the garden. She came to me for help, poor creature, because she fancied that, having 'sinned,' as they call it, I might feel some pity for others who had been tempted in the same way. Not I! She didn't know me. Lady Susan would have been kinder, because Lady Susan wouldn't have been afraid. I hated the woman—my one thought was not to be seen with her—I could have killed her for guessing my secret. The one thing that mattered to me at that moment was my standing with Lady Susan!"

Gannett did not speak.

"And you—you've felt it too!" she broke out accusingly. "You've enjoyed being with these people as much as I have; you've let the chaplain talk to you by the hour about 'The Reign of Law' and Professor Drummond. When they asked you to hand the plate in church I was watching you—*you wanted to accept.*"

She stepped close, laying her hand on his arm.

"Do you know, I begin to see what marriage is for. It's to keep people away from each other. Sometimes I think that two people who love each other can be saved from madness only by the things that come between them—children, duties, visits, bores, relations—the things that protect married people from each other. We've been too close together—that has been our sin. We've seen the nakedness of each other's souls."

She sank again on the sofa, hiding her face in her hands.

Gannett stood above her perplexedly: he felt as though she were being swept away by some implacable current while he stood helpless on its bank.

At length he said, "Lydia, don't think me a brute—but don't you see yourself that it won't do?"

"Yes, I see it won't do," she said without raising her head.

His face cleared.

"Then we'll go to-morrow."

"Go—where?"

"To Paris; to be married."

For a long time she made no answer; then she asked slowly, "Would they have us here if we were married?"

"Have us here?"

"I mean Lady Susan—and the others."

"Have us here? Of course they would."

"Not if they knew—at least, not unless they could pretend not to know."

He made an impatient gesture.

"We shouldn't come back here, of course; and other people needn't know—no one need know."

She sighed. "Then it's only another form of deception and a meaner one. Don't you see that?"

"I see that we're not accountable to any Lady Susans on earth!"

"Then why are you ashamed of what we are doing here?"

"Because I'm sick of pretending that you're my wife when you're not—when you won't be."

She looked at him sadly.

"If I were your wife you'd have to go on pretending. You'd have to pretend that I'd never been—anything else. And our friends would have to pretend that they believed what you pretended."

Gannett pulled off the sofa-tassel and flung it away.

"You're impossible," he groaned.

"It's not I—it's our being together that's impossible. I only want you to see that marriage won't help it."

"What will help it then?"

She raised her head.

"My leaving you."

"Your leaving me?" He sat motionless, staring at the tassel which lay at the other end of the room. At length some impulse of retaliation for the pain she was inflicting made him say deliberately:

"And where would you go if you left me?"

"Oh!" she cried, wincing.

He was at her side in an instant.

"Lydia—Lydia—you know I didn't mean it; I couldn't mean it! But you've driven me out of my senses; I don't know what I'm saying. Can't you get out of this labyrinth of self-torture? It's destroying us both."

"That's why I must leave you."

"How easily you say it!" He drew her hands down and made her face him. "You're very scrupulous about yourself—and others. But have you thought of me? You have no right to leave me unless you've ceased to care—"

"It's because I care—"

"Then I have a right to be heard. If you love me you can't leave me."

Her eyes defied him.

"Why not?"

He dropped her hands and rose from her side.

"Can you?" he said sadly.

The hour was late and the lamp flickered and sank. She stood up with a shiver and turned toward the door of her room.

V

At daylight a sound in Lydia's room woke Gannett from a troubled sleep. He sat up and listened. She was moving about softly, as though fearful of disturbing him. He heard her push back one of the creaking shutters; then there was a moment's silence, which seemed to indicate that she was waiting to see if the noise had roused him.

Presently she began to move again. She had spent a sleepless night, probably, and was dressing to go down to the garden for a breath of air. Gannett rose also; but some undefinable instinct made his movements as cautious as hers. He stole to his window and looked out through the slats of the shutter.

It had rained in the night and the dawn was gray and lifeless. The cloud-muffled hills across the lake were reflected in its surface as in a tarnished mirror. In the garden, the birds were beginning to shake the drops from the motionless laurustinus-boughs.

An immense pity for Lydia filled Gannett's soul. Her seeming intellectual independence had blinded him for a time to the feminine cast of her mind. He had never thought of her as a woman who wept and clung: there was a lucidity in her intuitions that made them appear to be the result of reasoning. Now he saw the cruelty he had committed in detaching her from the normal conditions of life; he felt, too, the insight with which she had hit upon the real cause of their suffering. Their life was "impossible," as she had said— and its worst penalty was that it had made any other life impossible for them. Even had his love lessened, he was bound to her now by a hundred ties of pity and self-reproach; and she, poor child! must turn back to him as Latude returned to his cell . . .

A new sound startled him: it was the stealthy closing of Lydia's door. He crept to his own and heard her footsteps passing down the corridor. Then he went back to the window and looked out.

A minute or two later he saw her go down the steps of the porch and enter the garden. From his post of observation her face was invisible, but something about her appearance struck him. She wore a long travelling cloak and under its folds he detected the outline of a bag or bundle. He drew a deep breath and stood watching her.

She walked quickly down the laurustinus alley toward the gate; there she paused a moment, glancing about the little shady square. The stone benches under the trees were empty, and she seemed to gather resolution from the solitude about her, for she crossed the square to the steam-boat landing, and he saw her pause before the ticket-office at the head of the wharf. Now she was buying her ticket. Gannett turned his head a moment to look at the clock: the boat was due in five minutes. He had time to jump into his clothes and over-take her—

He made no attempt to move; an obscure reluctance restrained him. If any thought emerged from the tumult of his sensations, it was that he must let her go if she wished it. He had spoken last night of his rights: what were they? At the last issue, he and she were two separate beings, not made one by the miracle of common forbearances, duties, abnegations, but bound together in a *noyade* of passion that left them resisting yet clinging as they went down.

After buying her ticket, Lydia had stood for a moment looking out across the lake; then he saw her seat herself on one of the benches near the landing. He and she, at that moment, were both listening for the same sound: the whistle of the boat as it rounded the nearest promontory. Gannett turned again to glance at the clock: the boat was due now.

Where would she go? What would her life be when she had left him? She had no near relations and few friends. There was money enough . . . but she asked so much of life, in ways so complex and immaterial. He thought of her as walking bare-footed through a stony waste. No one would understand her —no one would pity her—and he, who did both, was power-less to come to her aid . . .

He saw that she had risen from the bench and walked to-ward the edge of the lake. She stood looking in the direction from which the steamboat was to come; then she turned to the ticket-office, doubtless to ask the cause of the delay. After that she went back to the bench and sat down with bent head. What was she thinking of?

The whistle sounded; she started up, and Gannett involun-tarily made a movement toward the door. But he turned back and continued to watch her. She stood motionless, her eyes on the trail of smoke that preceded the appearance of the boat. Then the little craft rounded the point, a dead-white object on the leaden water: a minute later it was puffing and backing at the wharf.

The few passengers who were waiting—two or three peasants and a snuffy priest—were clustered near the ticket-office. Lydia stood apart under the trees.

The boat lay alongside now; the gang-plank was run out and the peasants went on board with their baskets of vegetables, followed by the priest. Still Lydia did not move. A bell began to ring querulously; there was a shriek of steam, and some one must have called to her that she would be late, for she started forward, as though in answer to a summons. She moved waveringly, and at the edge of the wharf she paused. Gannett saw a sailor beckon to her; the bell rang again and she stepped upon the gang-plank.

Half-way down the short incline to the deck she stopped again; then she turned and ran back to the land. The gang-plank was drawn in, the bell ceased to ring, and the boat backed out into the lake. Lydia, with slow steps, was walking toward the garden . . .

As she approached the hotel she looked up furtively and Gannett drew back into the room. He sat down beside a table; a Bradshaw lay at his elbow, and mechanically, without knowing what he did, he began looking out the trains to Paris . . .

The Twilight of the God

A Newport drawing-room. Tapestries, flowers, bric-a-brac. Through the windows, a geranium-edged lawn, the cliffs and the sea. Isabel Warland *sits reading*. Lucius Warland *enters in flannels and a yachting-cap.*

Isabel. Back already?

Warland. The wind dropped—it turned into a drifting race. Langham took me off the yacht on his launch. What time is it? Two o'clock? Where's Mrs. Raynor?

Isabel. On her way to New York.

Warland. To New York?

Isabel. Precisely. The boat must be just leaving; she started an hour ago and took Laura with her. In fact I'm alone in the house—that is, until this evening. Some people are coming then.

Warland. But what in the world—

Isabel. Her aunt, Mrs. Griscom, has had a fit. She has them constantly. They're not serious—at least they wouldn't be, if Mrs. Griscom were not so rich—and childless. Naturally, under the circumstances, Marian feels a peculiar sympathy for her; her position is such a sad one; there's positively no one to care whether she lives or dies—except her heirs. Of course they all rush to Newburgh whenever she has a fit. It's hard on Marian, for she lives the farthest away; but she has come to an understanding with the housekeeper, who always telegraphs her first, so that she gets a start of several hours. She will be at Newburgh to-night at ten, and she has calculated that the others can't possibly arrive before midnight.

Warland. You have a delightful way of putting things. I suppose you'd talk of me like that.

Isabel. Oh, no. It's too humiliating to doubt one's husband's disinterestedness.

Warland. I wish I had a rich aunt who had fits.

Isabel. If I were wishing I should choose heart-disease.

Warland. There's no doing anything without money or influence.

Isabel (*picking up her book*). Have you heard from Washington?

Warland. Yes. That's what I was going to speak of when I asked for Mrs. Raynor. I wanted to bid her good-bye.

Isabel. You're going?

Warland. By the five train. Fagott has just wired me that the Ambassador will be in Washington on Monday. He hasn't named his secretaries yet, but there isn't much hope for me. He has a nephew—

Isabel. They always have. Like the Popes.

Warland. Well, I'm going all the same. You'll explain to Mrs. Raynor if she gets back before I do? Are there to be people at dinner? I don't suppose it matters. You can always pick up an extra man on a Saturday.

Isabel. By the way, that reminds me that Marian left me a list of the people who are arriving this afternoon. My novel is so absorbing that I forgot to look at it. Where can it be? Ah, here— Let me see: the Jack Merringtons, Adelaide Clinton, Ned Lender—all from New York, by seven P.M. train. Lewis Darley to-night, by Fall River boat. John Oberville, from Boston at five P.M. Why, I didn't know—

Warland (*excitedly*). John Oberville? John Oberville? Here? To-day at five o'clock? Let me see—let me look at the list. Are you sure you're not mistaken? Why, she never said a word! Why the deuce didn't you tell me?

Isabel. I didn't know.

Warland. Oberville—Oberville—!

Isabel. Why, what difference does it make?

Warland. What difference? What difference? Don't look at me as if you didn't understand English! Why, if Oberville's coming—(*a pause*) Look here, Isabel, didn't you know him very well at one time?

Isabel. Very well—yes.

Warland. I thought so—of course—I remember now; I heard all about it before I met you. Let me see—didn't you and your mother spend a winter in Washington when he was Under-secretary of State?

Isabel. That was before the deluge.

Warland. I remember—it all comes back to me. I used to hear it said that he admired you tremendously; there was a report that you were engaged. Don't you remember? Why, it was in all the papers. By Jove, Isabel, what a match that would have been!

Isabel. You *are* disinterested!

Warland. Well, I can't help thinking—

Isabel. That I paid you a handsome compliment?

Warland (*preoccupied*). Eh?—Ah, yes—exactly. What was I saying? Oh—about the report of your engagement. (*Playfully.*) He was awfully gone on you, wasn't he?

Isabel. It's not for me to diminish your triumph.

Warland. By Jove, I can't think why Mrs. Raynor didn't tell me he was coming. A man like that—one doesn't take him for granted, like the piano-tuner! I wonder I didn't see it in the papers.

Isabel. Is he grown such a great man?

Warland. Oberville? Great? John Oberville? I'll tell you what he is—the power behind the throne, the black Pope, the King-maker and all the rest of it. Don't you read the papers? Of course I'll never get on if you won't interest yourself in politics. And to think you might have married that man!

Isabel. And got you your secretaryship!

Warland. Oberville has them all in the hollow of his hand.

Isabel. Well, you'll see him at five o'clock.

Warland. I don't suppose he's ever heard of *me*, worse luck! (*A silence.*) Isabel, look here. I never ask questions, do I? But it was so long ago—and Oberville almost belongs to history—he will one of these days at any rate. Just tell me— did he want to marry you?

Isabel. Since you answer for his immortality—(*after a pause*) I was very much in love with him.

Warland. Then of course he did. (*Another pause.*) But what in the world—

Isabel (*musing*). As you say, it was so long ago; I don't see why I shouldn't tell you. There was a married woman who had—what is the correct expression?—made sacrifices for him. There was only one sacrifice she objected to making— and he didn't consider himself free. It sounds rather *rococo*, doesn't it? It was odd that she died the year after we were married.

Warland. Whew!

Isabel (*following her own thoughts*). I've never seen him since; it must be ten years ago. I'm certainly thirty-two, and I was just twenty-two then. It's curious to talk of it. I had put it away so carefully. How it smells of camphor! And what an old-fashioned cut it has! (*Rising.*) Where's the list, Lucius? You wanted to know if there were to be people at dinner to-night—

Warland. Here it is—but never mind. Isabel—(*silence*) Isabel—

Isabel. Well?

Warland. It's odd he never married.

Isabel. The comparison is to my disadvantage. But then I met you.

Warland. Don't be so confoundedly sarcastic. I wonder how he'll feel about seeing you. Oh, I don't mean any sentimental rot, of course . . . but you're an uncommonly agreeable woman. I daresay he'll be pleased to see you again; you're fifty times more attractive than when I married you.

Isabel. I wish your other investments had appreciated at the same rate. Unfortunately my charms won't pay the butcher.

Warland. Damn the butcher!

Isabel. I happened to mention him because he's just written again; but I might as well have said the baker or the candlestick-maker. The candlestick-maker—I wonder what he is, by the way? He must have more faith in human nature than the others, for I haven't heard from him yet. I wonder if there is a Creditor's Polite Letter-writer they all consult; their style is so exactly alike. I advise you to pass through New York incognito on your way to Washington; their attentions might be oppressive.

Warland. Confoundedly oppressive. What a dog's life it is! My poor Isabel—

Isabel. Don't pity me. I didn't marry you for a home.

Warland (*after a pause*). What *did* you marry me for, if you cared for Oberville? (*Another pause.*) Eh?

Isabel. Don't make me regret my confidence.

Warland. I beg your pardon.

Isabel. Oh, it was only a subterfuge to conceal the fact that I have no distinct recollection of my reasons. The fact is, a girl's motives in marrying are like a passport—apt to get mislaid. One is so seldom asked for either. But mine certainly couldn't have been mercenary: I never heard a mother praise you to her daughters.

Warland. No, I never was much of a match.

Isabel. You impugn my judgment.

Warland. If I only had a head for business, now, I might have done something by this time. But I'd sooner break stones in the road.

Isabel. It must be very hard to get an opening in that profession. So many of my friends have aspired to it, and yet I never knew any one who actually did it.

Warland. If I could only get the secretaryship. How that kind of life would suit you! It's as much for you that I want it—

Isabel. And almost as much for the butcher. Don't belittle the circle of your benevolence. (*She walks across the room.*) Three o'clock already—and Marian asked me to give orders about the carriages. Let me see—Mr. Oberville is the first arrival; if you'll ring I will send word to the stable. I suppose you'll stay now?

Warland. Stay?

Isabel. Not go to Washington. I thought you spoke as if he could help you.

Warland. He could settle the whole thing in five minutes. The President can't refuse him anything. But he doesn't know me; he may have a candidate of his own. It's a pity you haven't seen him for so long—and yet I don't know; perhaps it's just as well. The others don't arrive till seven? It seems as if— How long is he going to be here? Till to-morrow night, I suppose? I wonder what he's come for. The Merringtons will bore him to death, and Adelaide, of course, will be philandering with Lender. I wonder (*a pause*) if Darley likes boating. (*Rings the bell.*)

Isabel. Boating?

Warland. Oh, I was only thinking— Where are the matches? One may smoke here, I suppose? (*He looks at his wife.*) If I were you I'd put on that black gown of yours to-night—the one with the spangles.—It's only that Fred Langham asked me to go over to Narragansett in his launch to-morrow morning, and I was thinking that I might take Darley; I always liked Darley.

Isabel (*to the footman who enters*). Mrs. Raynor wishes the dog-cart sent to the station at five o'clock to meet Mr. Oberville.

Footman. Very good, m'm. Shall I serve tea at the usual time, m'm?

Isabel. Yes. That is, when Mr. Oberville arrives.

Footman (*going out*). Very good, m'm.

Warland (*to Isabel, who is moving toward the door*). Where are you going?

Isabel. To my room now—for a walk later.

Warland. Later? It's past three already.

Isabel. I've no engagement this afternoon.

Warland. Oh, I didn't know. (*As she reaches the door.*) You'll be back, I suppose?

Isabel. I have no intention of eloping.

Warland. For tea, I mean?

Isabel. I never take tea. (*Warland shrugs his shoulders.*)

II

The same drawing-room. Isabel *enters from the lawn in hat and gloves. The tea-table is set out, and the footman just lighting the lamp under the kettle.*

Isabel. You may take the tea-things away. I never take tea.

Footman. Very good, m'm. (*He hesitates.*) I understood, m'm, that Mr. Oberville was to have tea?

Isabel. Mr. Oberville? But he was to arrive long ago! What time is it?

Footman. Only a quarter past five, m'm.

Isabel. A quarter past five? (*She goes up to the clock.*) Surely you're mistaken? I thought it was long after six. (*To herself.*) I walked and walked—I must have walked too fast . . . (*To the Footman.*) I'm going out again. When Mr. Oberville arrives please give him his tea without waiting for me. I shall not be back till dinner-time.

Footman. Very good, m'm. Here are some letters, m'm.

Isabel (*glancing at them with a movement of disgust*). You may send them up to my room.

Footman. I beg pardon, m'm, but one is a note from Mme Fanfreluche, and the man who brought it is waiting for an answer.

Isabel. Didn't you tell him I was out?

Footman. Yes, m'm. But he said he had orders to wait till you came in.

Isabel. Ah—let me see. (*She opens the note.*) Ah, yes. (*A pause.*) Please say that I am on my way now to Mme Fanfreluche's to give her the answer in person. You may tell the man that I have already started. Do you understand? Already started.

Footman. Yes, m'm.

Isabel. And—wait. (*With an effort.*) You may tell *me* when the man has started. I shall wait here till then. Be sure you let me know.

Footman. Yes, m'm. (*He goes out.*)

Isabel (*sinking into a chair and hiding her face*). Ah! (*After a moment she rises, taking up her gloves and sun-shade, and walks toward the window which opens on the lawn.*) I'm so tired. (*She hesitates and turns back into the room.*) Where can I go to? (*She sits down again by the tea-table, and bends over the kettle. The clock strikes half-past five.*)

Isabel (*picking up her sunshade, walks back to the window*). If I *must* meet one of them . . .

Oberville (*speaking in the hall*). Thanks. I'll take tea first. (*He enters the room, and pauses doubtfully on seeing* Isabel.)

Isabel (*stepping towards him with a smile*). It's not that I've changed, of course, but only that I happened to have my back to the light. Isn't that what you are going to say?

Oberville. Mrs. Warland!

Isabel. So you really *have* become a great man! They always remember people's names.

Oberville. Were you afraid I was going to call you Isabel?

Isabel. Bravo! *Crescendo!*

Oberville. But you have changed, all the same.

Isabel. You must indeed have reached a dizzy eminence, since you can indulge yourself by speaking the truth!

Oberville. It's your voice. I knew it at once, and yet it's different.

Isabel. I hope it can still convey the pleasure I feel in seeing an old friend. (*She holds out her hand. He takes it.*) You know, I suppose, that Mrs. Raynor is not here to receive you? She was called away this morning very suddenly by her aunt's illness.

Oberville. Yes. She left a note for me. (*Absently.*) I'm sorry to hear of Mrs. Griscom's illness.

Isabel. Oh, Mrs. Griscom's illnesses are less alarming than her recoveries. But I am forgetting to offer you any tea. (*She hands him a cup.*) I remember you liked it very strong.

Oberville. What else do you remember?

Isabel. A number of equally useless things. My mind is a store-room of obsolete information.

Oberville. Why obsolete, since I am providing you with a use for it?

Isabel. At any rate, it's open to question whether it was worth storing for that length of time. Especially as there must have been others more fitted—by opportunity—to undertake the duty.

Oberville. The duty?

Isabel. Of remembering how you like your tea.

Oberville (*with a change of tone*). Since you call it a duty— I may remind you that it's one I have never asked any one else to perform.

Isabel. As a duty! But as a pleasure?

Oberville. Do you really want to know?

Isabel. Oh, I don't require and charge you.

Oberville. You dislike as much as ever having the *i*'s dotted?

Isabel. With a handwriting I know as well as yours!

Oberville (*recovering his lightness of manner*). Accomplished woman! (*He examines her approvingly.*) I'd no idea that you were here. I never was more surprised.

Isabel. I hope you like being surprised. To my mind it's an overrated pleasure.

Oberville. Is it? I'm sorry to hear that.

Isabel. Why? Have you a surprise to dispose of?

Oberville. I'm not sure that I haven't.

Isabel. Don't part with it too hastily. It may improve by being kept.

Oberville (*tentatively*). Does that mean that you don't want it?

Isabel. Heaven forbid! I want everything I can get.

Oberville. And you get everything you want. At least you used to.

Isabel. Let us talk of your surprise.

Oberville. It's to be yours, you know. (*A pause. He speaks gravely.*) I find that I've never got over having lost you.

Isabel (*also gravely*). And is that a surprise—to you too?

Oberville. Honestly—yes. I thought I'd crammed my life full. I didn't know there was a cranny left anywhere. At first, you know, I stuffed in everything I could lay my hands on— there was such a big void to fill. And after all I haven't filled it. I felt that the moment I saw you. (*A pause.*) I'm talking stupidly.

Isabel. It would be odious if you were eloquent.

Oberville. What do you mean?

Isabel. That's a question you never used to ask me.

Oberville. Be merciful. Remember how little practise I've had lately.

Isabel. In what?

Oberville. Never mind! (*He rises and walks away; then comes back and stands in front of her.*) What a fool I was to give you up!

Isabel. Oh, don't say that! I've lived on it!

Oberville. On my letting you go?

Isabel. On your letting everything go—but the right.

Oberville. Oh, hang the right! What is truth? We had the right to be happy!

Isabel (*with rising emotion*). I used to think so sometimes.

Oberville. Did you? Triple fool that I was!

Isabel. But you showed me—

Oberville. Why, good God, we belonged to each other— and I let you go! It's fabulous. I've fought for things since that weren't worth a crooked sixpence; fought as well as other men. And you—you—I lost you because I couldn't face a scene! Hang it, suppose there'd been a dozen scenes—I might have survived them. Men have been known to. They're not necessarily fatal.

Isabel. A scene?

Oberville. It's a form of fear that women don't understand. How you must have despised me!

Isabel. You were—afraid—of a scene?

Oberville. I was a damned coward, Isabel. That's about the size of it.

Isabel. Ah—I had thought it so much larger!

Oberville. What did you say?

Isabel. I said that you have forgotten to drink your tea. It must be quite cold.

Oberville. Ah—

Isabel. Let me give you another cup.

Oberville (*collecting himself*). No—no. This is perfect.

Isabel. You haven't tasted it.

Oberville (*falling into her mood*). You always made it to perfection. Only you never gave me enough sugar.

Isabel. I know better now. (*She puts another lump in his cup.*)

Oberville (*drinks his tea, and then says, with an air of reproach*). Isn't all this chaff rather a waste of time between two old friends who haven't met for so many years?

Isabel (*lightly*). Oh, it's only a *hors d'œuvre*—the tuning of the instruments. I'm out of practise too.

Oberville. Let us come to the grand air, then. (*Sits down near her.*) Tell me about yourself. What are you doing?

Isabel. At this moment? You'll never guess. I'm trying to remember you.

Oberville. To remember me?

Isabel. Until you came into the room just now my recollection of you was so vivid; you were a living whole in my thoughts. Now I am engaged in gathering up the fragments —in laboriously reconstructing you. . . .

Oberville. I have changed so much, then?

Isabel. No, I don't believe that you've changed. It's only that I see you differently. Don't you know how hard it is to convince elderly people that the type of the evening paper is no smaller than when they were young?

Oberville. I've shrunk then?

Isabel. You couldn't have grown bigger. Oh, I'm serious now; you needn't prepare a smile. For years you were the tallest object on my horizon. I used to climb to the thought of you, as people who live in a flat country mount the church steeple for a view. It's wonderful how much I used to see from there! And the air was so strong and pure!

Oberville. And now?

Isabel. Now I can fancy how delightful it must be to sit next to you at dinner.

Oberville. You're unmerciful. Have I said anything to offend you?

Isabel. Of course not. How absurd!

Oberville. I lost my head a little—I forgot how long it is since we have met. When I saw you I forgot everything except what you had once been to me. (*She is silent.*) I thought you too generous to resent that. Perhaps I have overtaxed your generosity. (*A pause.*) Shall I confess it? When I first saw you I thought for a moment that you had remembered—as I had. You see I can only excuse myself by saying something inexcusable.

Isabel (*deliberately*). Not inexcusable.

Oberville. Not—?

Isabel. I had remembered.

Oberville. Isabel!

Isabel. But now—

Oberville. Ah, give me a moment before you unsay it!

Isabel. I don't mean to unsay it. There's no use in repealing an obsolete law. That's the pity of it! You say you lost me ten years ago. (*A pause.*) I never lost you till now.

Oberville. Now?

Isabel. Only this morning you were my supreme court of justice; there was no appeal from your verdict. Not an hour ago you decided a case for me—against myself! And now—. And the worst of it is that it's not because you've changed. How do I know if you've changed? You haven't said a hundred words to me. You haven't been an hour in the room. And the years must have enriched you—I daresay you've doubled your capital. You've been in the thick of life, and the metal you're made of brightens with use. Success on some men looks like a borrowed coat; it sits on you as though it had been made to order. I see all this; I know it; but I don't *feel* it. I don't feel anything . . . anywhere . . . I'm numb. (*A pause.*) Don't laugh, but I really don't think I should know

now if you came into the room—unless I actually saw you. (*They are both silent.*)

Oberville (*at length*). Then, to put the most merciful interpretation upon your epigrams, your feeling for me was made out of poorer stuff than mine for you.

Isabel. Perhaps it has had harder wear.

Oberville. Or been less cared for?

Isabel. If one has only one cloak one must wear it in all weathers.

Oberville. Unless it is so beautiful and precious that one prefers to go cold and keep it under lock and key.

Isabel. In the cedar-chest of indifference—the key of which is usually lost.

Oberville. Ah, Isabel, you're too pat! How much I preferred your hesitations.

Isabel. My hesitations? That reminds me how much your coming has simplified things. I feel as if I'd had an auction sale of fallacies.

Oberville. You speak in enigmas, and I have a notion that your riddles are the reverse of the sphinx's—more dangerous to guess than to give up. And yet I used to find your thoughts such good reading.

Isabel. One cares so little for the style in which one's praises are written.

Oberville. You've been praising me for the last ten minutes and I find your style detestable. I would rather have you find fault with me like a friend than approve me like a *dilettante*.

Isabel. A *dilettante*! The very word I wanted!

Oberville. I am proud to have enriched so full a vocabulary. But I am still waiting for the word *I* want. (*He grows serious.*) Isabel, look in your heart—give me the first word you find there. You've no idea how much a beggar can buy with a penny!

Isabel. It's empty, my poor friend, it's empty.

Oberville. Beggars never say that to each other.

Isabel. No; never, unless it's true.

Oberville (*after another silence*). Why do you look at me so curiously?

Isabel. I'm—what was it you said? Approving you as a *dilettante*. Don't be alarmed; you can bear examination; I don't

see a crack anywhere. After all, it's a satisfaction to find that
one's idol makes a handsome *bibelot.*

Oberville (with an attempt at lightness). I was right then—
you're a collector?

Isabel (modestly). One must make a beginning. I think I
shall begin with you. (*She smiles at him.*) Positively, I must
have you on my mantel-shelf! (*She rises and looks at the clock.*)
But it's time to dress for dinner. (*She holds out her hand to him
and he kisses it. They look at each other, and it is clear that he
does not quite understand, but is watching eagerly for his cue.*)

Warland (coming in). Hullo, Isabel—you're here after all?

Isabel. And so is Mr. Oberville. (*She looks straight at
Warland.*) I stayed in on purpose to meet him. My husband —
(*The two men bow.*)

Warland (effusively). So glad to meet you. My wife talks of
you so often. She's been looking forward tremendously to
your visit.

Oberville. It's a long time since I've had the pleasure of seeing Mrs. Warland.

Isabel. But now we are going to make up for lost time. (*As
he goes to the door.*) I claim you to-morrow for the whole day.

Oberville bows and goes out.

Isabel. Lucius . . . I think you'd better go to Washington,
after all. (*Musing.*) Narragansett might do for the others,
though. . . . Couldn't you get Fred Langham to ask all the
rest of the party to go over there with him to-morrow morning? I shall have a headache and stay at home. (*He looks at her
doubtfully.*) Mr. Oberville is a bad sailor.

Warland advances demonstratively.

Isabel (drawing back). It's time to go and dress. I think you
said the black gown with spangles?

A Cup of Cold Water

IT WAS three o'clock in the morning, and the cotillion was at its height, when Woburn left the over-heated splendor of the Gildermere ball-room, and after a delay caused by the determination of the drowsy footman to give him a ready-made overcoat with an imitation astrachan collar in place of his own unimpeachable Poole garment, found himself breasting the icy solitude of the Fifth Avenue. He was still smiling, as he emerged from the awning, at his insistence in claiming his own overcoat: it illustrated, humorously enough, the invincible force of habit. As he faced the wind, however, he discerned a providence in his persistency, for his coat was fur-lined, and he had a cold voyage before him on the morrow.

It had rained hard during the earlier part of the night, and the carriages waiting in triple line before the Gildermeres' door were still domed by shining umbrellas, while the electric lamps extending down the avenue blinked Narcissus-like at their watery images in the hollows of the sidewalk. A dry blast had come out of the north, with pledge of frost before day-light, and to Woburn's shivering fancy the pools in the pavement seemed already stiffening into ice. He turned up his coat-collar and stepped out rapidly, his hands deep in his coat-pockets.

As he walked he glanced curiously up at the ladder-like door-steps which may well suggest to the future archæologist that all the streets of New York were once canals; at the spectral tracery of the trees about St. Luke's, the fretted mass of the Cathedral, and the mean vista of the long side-streets. The knowledge that he was perhaps looking at it all for the last time caused every detail to start out like a challenge to memory, and lit the brown-stone house-fronts with the glamor of sword-barred Edens.

It was an odd impulse that had led him that night to the Gildermere ball; but the same change in his condition which made him stare wonderingly at the houses in the Fifth Avenue gave the thrill of an exploit to the tame business of ball-going. Who would have imagined, Woburn mused, that such a situ-

ation as his would possess the priceless quality of sharpening
the blunt edge of habit?

It was certainly curious to reflect, as he leaned against the
doorway of Mrs. Gildermere's ball-room, enveloped in the
warm atmosphere of the accustomed, that twenty-four hours
later the people brushing by him with looks of friendly recognition would start at the thought of having seen him and slur
over the recollection of having taken his hand!

And the girl he had gone there to see: what would she
think of him? He knew well enough that her trenchant classi-
fications of life admitted no overlapping of good and evil,
made no allowance for that incalculable interplay of motives
that justifies the subtlest casuistry of compassion. Miss Talcott
was too young to distinguish the intermediate tints of the
moral spectrum; and her judgments were further simplified by
a peculiar concreteness of mind. Her bringing-up had fostered this tendency and she was surrounded by people who
focussed life in the same way. To the girls in Miss Talcott's
set, the attentions of a clever man who had to work for his living had the zest of a forbidden pleasure; but to marry such a
man would be as unpardonable as to have one's carriage seen
at the door of a cheap dress-maker. Poverty might make a
man fascinating; but a settled income was the best evidence of
stability of character. If there were anything in heredity, how
could a nice girl trust a man whose parents had been careless
enough to leave him unprovided for?

Neither Miss Talcott nor any of her friends could be
charged with formulating these views; but they were implicit
in the slope of every white shoulder and in the ripple of every
yard of imported tulle dappling the foreground of Mrs.
Gildermere's ball-room. The advantages of line and colour in
veiling the crudities of a creed are obvious to emotional
minds; and besides, Woburn was conscious that it was to the
cheerful materialism of their parents that the young girls he
admired owed that fine distinction of outline in which their
skilfully-rippled hair and skilfully-hung draperies coöperated
with the slimness and erectness that came of participating in
the most expensive sports, eating the most expensive food
and breathing the most expensive air. Since the process which
had produced them was so costly, how could they help being

costly themselves? Woburn was too logical to expect to give no more for a piece of old Sèvres than for a bit of kitchen crockery; he had no faith in wonderful bargains, and believed that one got in life just what one was willing to pay for. He had no mind to dispute the taste of those who preferred the rustic simplicity of the earthen crock; but his own fancy inclined to the piece of *pâte tendre* which must be kept in a glass case and handled as delicately as a flower.

It was not merely by the external grace of these drawing-room ornaments that Woburn's sensibilities were charmed. His imagination was touched by the curious exoticism of view resulting from such conditions. He had always enjoyed listening to Miss Talcott even more than looking at her. Her ideas had the brilliant bloom and audacious irrelevance of those tropical orchids which strike root in air. Miss Talcott's opinions had no connection with the actual; her very materialism had the grace of artificiality. Woburn had been enchanted once by seeing her helpless before a smoking lamp: she had been obliged to ring for a servant because she did not know how to put it out.

Her supreme charm was the simplicity that comes of taking it for granted that people are born with carriages and country-places: it never occurred to her that such congenital attributes could be matter for self-consciousness, and she had none of the *nouveau riche* prudery which classes poverty with the nude in art and is not sure how to behave in the presence of either.

The conditions of Woburn's own life had made him peculiarly susceptible to those forms of elegance which are the flower of ease. His father had lost a comfortable property through sheer inability to go over his agent's accounts; and this disaster, coming at the outset of Woburn's school-days, had given a new bent to the family temperament. The father characteristically died when the effort of living might have made it possible to retrieve his fortunes; and Woburn's mother and sister, embittered by this final evasion, settled down to a vindictive war with circumstances. They were the kind of women who think that it lightens the burden of life to throw over the amenities, as a reduced housekeeper puts away her knick-knacks to make the dusting easier. They

fought mean conditions meanly; but Woburn, in his resentment of their attitude, did not allow for the suffering which
had brought it about: his own tendency was to overcome difficulties by conciliation rather than by conflict. Such surroundings threw into vivid relief the charming figure of Miss
Talcott. Woburn instinctively associated poverty with bad
food, ugly furniture, complaints and recriminations: it was
natural that he should be drawn toward the luminous atmosphere where life was a series of peaceful and good-humored
acts, unimpeded by petty obstacles. To spend one's time in
such society gave one the illusion of unlimited credit; and
also, unhappily, created the need for it.

It was here in fact that Woburn's difficulties began. To
marry Miss Talcott it was necessary to be a rich man: even to
dine out in her set involved certain minor extravagances.
Woburn had determined to marry her sooner or later; and in
the meanwhile to be with her as much as possible.

As he stood leaning in the doorway of the Gildermere ball-
room, watching her pass him in the waltz, he tried to remember how it had begun. First there had been the tailor's
bill; the fur-lined overcoat with cuffs and collar of Alaska sable
had alone cost more than he had spent on his clothes for two
or three years previously. Then there were theatre-tickets;
cab-fares; florist's bills; tips to servants at the country-houses
where he went because he knew that she was invited; the
Omar Khayyám bound by Sullivan that he sent her at
Christmas; the contributions to her pet charities; the reckless
purchases at fairs where she had a stall. His whole way of life
had imperceptibly changed and his year's salary was gone before the second quarter was due.

He had invested the few thousand dollars which had been
his portion of his father's shrunken estate: when his debts began to pile up, he took a flyer in stocks and after a few months
of varying luck his little patrimony disappeared. Meanwhile
his courtship was proceeding at an inverse ratio to his financial ventures. Miss Talcott was growing tender and he began
to feel that the game was in his hands. The nearness of the
goal exasperated him. She was not the girl to wait and he
knew that it must be now or never. A friend lent him five
thousand dollars on his personal note and he bought railway

stocks on margin. They went up and he held them for a higher rise: they fluctuated, dragged, dropped below the level at which he had bought, and slowly continued their uninterrupted descent. His broker called for more margin; he could not respond and was sold out.

What followed came about quite naturally. For several years he had been cashier in a well-known banking-house. When the note he had given his friend became due it was obviously necessary to pay it and he used the firm's money for the purpose. To repay the money thus taken, he increased his debt to his employers and bought more stocks; and on these operations he made a profit of ten thousand dollars. Miss Talcott rode in the Park, and he bought a smart hack for seven hundred, paid off his tradesmen, and went on speculating with the remainder of his profits. He made a little more, but failed to take advantage of the market and lost all that he had staked, including the amount taken from the firm. He increased his over-draft by another ten thousand and lost that; he over-drew a farther sum and lost again. Suddenly he woke to the fact that he owed his employers fifty thousand dollars and that the partners were to make their semi-annual inspection in two days. He realized then that within forty-eight hours what he had called borrowing would become theft.

There was no time to be lost: he must clear out and start life over again somewhere else. The day that he reached this decision he was to have met Miss Talcott at dinner. He went to the dinner, but she did not appear: she had a headache, his hostess explained. Well, he was not to have a last look at her, after all; better so, perhaps. He took leave early and on his way home stopped at a florist's and sent her a bunch of violets. The next morning he got a little note from her: the violets had done her head so much good—she would tell him all about it that evening at the Gildermere ball. Woburn laughed and tossed the note into the fire. That evening he would be on board ship: the examination of the books was to take place the following morning at ten.

Woburn went down to the bank as usual; he did not want to do anything that might excite suspicion as to his plans, and from one or two questions which one of the partners had lately put to him he divined that he was being observed. At the bank the day passed uneventfully. He discharged his business with his accustomed care and went uptown at the usual hour.

In the first flush of his successful speculations he had set up bachelor lodgings, moved by the temptation to get away from the dismal atmosphere of home, from his mother's struggles with the cook and his sister's curiosity about his letters. He had been influenced also by the wish for surroundings more adapted to his tastes. He wanted to be able to give little teas, to which Miss Talcott might come with a married friend. She came once or twice and pronounced it all delightful: she thought it *so* nice to have only a few Whistler etchings on the walls and the simplest crushed levant for all one's books.

To these rooms Woburn returned on leaving the bank. His plans had taken definite shape. He had engaged passage on a steamer sailing for Halifax early the next morning; and there was nothing for him to do before going on board but to pack his clothes and tear up a few letters. He threw his clothes into a couple of portmanteaux, and when these had been called for by an expressman he emptied his pockets and counted up his ready money. He found that he possessed just fifty dollars and seventy-five cents; but his passage to Halifax was paid, and once there he could pawn his watch and rings. This calculation completed, he unlocked his writing-table drawer and took out a handful of letters. They were notes from Miss Talcott. He read them over and threw them into the fire. On his table stood her photograph. He slipped it out of its frame and tossed it on top of the blazing letters. Having performed this rite, he got into his dress-clothes and went to a small French restaurant to dine.

He had meant to go on board the steamer immediately after dinner; but a sudden vision of introspective hours in a silent cabin made him call for the evening paper and run his eye over the list of theatres. It would be as easy to go on board at midnight as now.

He selected a new vaudeville and listened to it with surprising freshness of interest; but toward eleven o'clock he again began to dread the approaching necessity of going down to the steamer. There was something peculiarly unnerving in the idea of spending the rest of the night in a stifling cabin jammed against the side of a wharf.

He left the theatre and strolled across to the Fifth Avenue. It was now nearly midnight and a stream of carriages poured up town from the opera and the theatres. As he stood on the corner watching the familiar spectacle it occurred to him that many of the people driving by him in smart broughams and C-spring landaus were on their way to the Gildermere ball. He remembered Miss Talcott's note of the morning and wondered if she were in one of the passing carriages; she had spoken so confidently of meeting him at the ball. What if he should go and take a last look at her? There was really nothing to prevent it. He was not likely to run across any member of the firm: in Miss Talcott's set his social standing was good for another ten hours at least. He smiled in anticipation of her surprise at seeing him, and then reflected with a start that she would not be surprised at all.

His meditations were cut short by a fall of sleety rain, and hailing a hansom he gave the driver Mrs. Gildermere's address.

As he drove up the avenue he looked about him like a traveller in a strange city. The buildings which had been so unobtrusively familiar stood out with sudden distinctness: he noticed a hundred details which had escaped his observation. The people on the sidewalks looked like strangers: he wondered where they were going and tried to picture the lives they led; but his own relation to life had been so suddenly reversed that he found it impossible to recover his mental perspective.

At one corner he saw a shabby man lurking in the shadow of the side street; as the hansom passed, a policeman ordered him to move on. Farther on, Woburn noticed a woman crouching on the door-step of a handsome house. She had drawn a shawl over her head and was sunk in the apathy of despair or drink. A well-dressed couple paused to look at her. The electric globe at the corner lit up their faces, and Woburn saw the lady, who was young and pretty, turn away with a little grimace, drawing her companion after her.

The desire to see Miss Talcott had driven Woburn to the Gildermere's; but once in the ball-room he made no effort to find her. The people about him seemed more like strangers than those he had passed in the street. He stood in the doorway, studying the petty manœuvres of the women and the resigned amenities of their partners. Was it possible that these were his friends? These mincing women, all paint and dye and whalebone, these apathetic men who looked as much alike as the figures that children cut out of a folded sheet of paper? Was it to live among such puppets that he had sold his soul? What had any of these people done that was noble, exceptional, distinguished? Who knew them by name even, except their tradesmen and the society reporters? Who were they, that they should sit in judgment on him?

The bald man with the globular stomach, who stood at Mrs. Gildermere's elbow surveying the dancers, was old Boylston, who had made his pile in wrecking railroads; the smooth chap with glazed eyes, at whom a pretty girl smiled up so confidingly, was Collerton, the political lawyer, who had been mixed up to his own advantage in an ugly lobbying transaction; near him stood Brice Lyndham, whose recent failure had ruined his friends and associates, but had not visibly affected the welfare of his large and expensive family. The slim fellow dancing with Miss Gildermere was Alec Vance, who lived on a salary of five thousand a year, but whose wife was such a good manager that they kept a brougham and victoria and always put in their season at Newport and their spring trip to Europe. The little ferret-faced youth in the corner was Regie Colby, who wrote the *Entre-Nous* paragraphs in the *Social Searchlight*: the women were charming to him and he got all the financial tips he wanted from their husbands and fathers.

And the women? Well, the women knew all about the men, and flattered them and married them and tried to catch them for their daughters. It was a domino-party at which the guests were forbidden to unmask, though they all saw through each other's disguises.

And these were the people who, within twenty-four hours, would be agreeing that they had always felt there was something wrong about Woburn! They would be extremely sorry for him, of course, poor devil; but there are certain standards, after all—what would society be without standards? His new friends, his future associates, were the suspicious-looking man whom the policeman had ordered to move on, and the drunken woman asleep on the door-step. To these he was linked by the freemasonry of failure.

Miss Talcott passed him on Collerton's arm: she was giving him one of the smiles of which Woburn had fancied himself sole owner. Collerton was a sharp fellow; he must have made a lot in that last deal; probably she would marry him. How much did she know about the transaction? She was a shrewd girl and her father was in Wall Street. If Woburn's luck had turned the other way she might have married him instead; and if he had confessed his sin to her one evening, as they drove home from the opera in their new brougham, she would have said that really it was of no use to tell her, for she never *could* understand about business, but that she did entreat him in future to be nicer to Regie Colby. Even now, if he made a big strike somewhere, and came back in ten years with a beard and a steam yacht, they would all deny that anything had been proved against him, and Mrs. Collerton might blush and remind him of their friendship. Well—why not? Was not all morality based on a convention? What was the stanchest code of ethics but a trunk with a series of false bottoms? Now and then one had the illusion of getting down to absolute right or wrong, but it was only a false bottom—a removable hypothesis—with another false bottom underneath. There was no getting beyond the relative.

The cotillion had begun. Miss Talcott sat nearly opposite him: she was dancing with young Boylston and giving him a Woburn-Collerton smile. So young Boylston was in the syndicate too!

Presently Woburn was aware that she had forgotten young Boylston and was glancing absently about the room. She was looking for some one, and meant the some one to know it: he knew that *Lost-Chord* look in her eyes.

A new figure was being formed. The partners circled about the room and Miss Talcott's flying tulle drifted close to him as she passed. Then the favors were distributed; white skirts wavered across the floor like thistle-down on summer air; men rose from their seats and fresh couples filled the shining *parquet*.

Miss Talcott, after taking from the basket a Legion of Honor in red enamel, surveyed the room for a moment; then she made her way through the dancers and held out the favor to Woburn. He fastened it in his coat, and emerging from the crowd of men about the doorway, slipped his arm about her. Their eyes met; hers were serious and a little sad. How fine and slender she was! He noticed the little tendrils of hair about the pink convolution of her ear. Her waist was firm and yet elastic; she breathed calmly and regularly, as though dancing were her natural motion. She did not look at him again and neither of them spoke.

When the music ceased they paused near her chair. Her partner was waiting for her and Woburn left her with a bow.

He made his way down-stairs and out of the house. He was glad that he had not spoken to Miss Talcott. There had been a healing power in their silence. All bitterness had gone from him and he thought of her now quite simply, as the girl he loved.

At Thirty-fifth Street he reflected that he had better jump into a car and go down to his steamer. Again there rose before him the repulsive vision of the dark cabin, with creaking noises overhead, and the cold wash of water against the pier: he thought he would stop in a café and take a drink. He turned into Broadway and entered a brightly-lit café; but when he had taken his whisky and soda there seemed no reason for lingering. He had never been the kind of man who could escape difficulties in that way. Yet he was conscious that his will was weakening; that he did not mean to go down to the steamer just yet. What did he mean to do? He began to feel horribly tired and it occurred to him that a few hours' sleep in a decent bed would make a new man of him. Why not go on board the next morning at daylight?

He could not go back to his rooms, for on leaving the house he had taken the precaution of dropping his latch-key into his letter-box; but he was in a neighborhood of discreet hotels and he wandered on till he came to one which was known to offer a dispassionate hospitality to luggageless travellers in dress-clothes.

II

He pushed upon the swinging door and found himself in a long corridor with a tessellated floor, at the end of which, in a brightly-lit enclosure of plate-glass and mahogany, the night-clerk dozed over a copy of the *Police Gazette*. The air in the corridor was rich in reminiscences of yesterday's dinners, and a bronzed radiator poured a wave of dry heat into Woburn's face.

The night-clerk, roused by the swinging of the door, sat watching Woburn's approach with the unexpectant eye of one who has full confidence in his capacity for digesting surprises. Not that there was anything surprising in Woburn's appearance; but the night-clerk's callers were given to such imaginative flights in explaining their luggageless arrival in the small hours of the morning, that he fared habitually on fictions which would have staggered a less experienced stomach. The night-clerk, whose unwrinkled bloom showed that he throve on this high-seasoned diet, had a fancy for classifying his applicants before they could frame their explanations.

"This one's been locked out," he said to himself as he mustered Woburn.

Having exercised his powers of divination with his accustomed accuracy he listened without stirring an eye-lid to Woburn's statement; merely replying, when the latter asked the price of a room, "Two-fifty."

"Very well," said Woburn, pushing the money under the brass lattice, "I'll go up at once; and I want to be called at seven."

To this the night-clerk profferred no reply, but stretching out his hand to press an electric button, returned apathetically to the perusal of the *Police Gazette*. His summons was answered by the appearance of a man in shirt-sleeves, whose rumpled head indicated that he had recently risen from some kind of makeshift repose; to him the night-clerk tossed a key, with the brief comment, "Ninety-seven;" and the man, after a sleepy glance at Woburn, turned on his heel and lounged toward the staircase at the back of the corridor.

Woburn followed and they climbed three flights in silence. At each landing Woburn glanced down the long passage-way lit by a lowered gas-jet, with a double line of boots before the doors, waiting, like yesterday's deeds, to carry their owners so many miles farther on the morrow's destined road. On the third landing the man paused, and after examining the number on the key, turned to the left, and slouching past three or four doors, finally unlocked one and preceded Woburn into a room lit only by the upward gleam of the electric globes in the street below.

The man felt in his pockets; then he turned to Woburn. "Got a match?" he asked.

Woburn politely offered him one, and he applied it to the gas-fixture which extended its jointed arm above an ash dressing-table with a blurred mirror fixed between two standards. Having performed this office with an air of detachment designed to make Woburn recognize it as an act of supererogation, he turned without a word and vanished down the passage-way.

Woburn, after an indifferent glance about the room, which seemed to afford the amount of luxury generally obtainable for two dollars and a half in a fashionable quarter of New York, locked the door and sat down at the ink-stained writing-table in the window. Far below him lay the pallidly-lit depths of the forsaken thoroughfare. Now and then he heard the jingle of a horse-car and the ring of hoofs on the freezing pavement, or saw the lonely figure of a policeman eclipsing the illumination of the plate-glass windows on the opposite side of the street. He sat thus for a long time, his elbows on the table, his chin between his hands, till at length the contemplation of the abandoned sidewalks, above which the electric globes kept Stylites-like vigil, became intolerable to him, and he drew down the window-shade, and lit the gas-fixture beside the dressing-table. Then he took a cigar from his case, and held it to the flame.

The passage from the stinging freshness of the night to the stale overheated atmosphere of the Haslemere Hotel had checked the preternaturally rapid working of his mind, and he was now scarcely conscious of thinking at all. His head was heavy, and he would have thrown himself on the bed had he not feared to oversleep the hour fixed for his departure. He thought it safest, instead, to seat himself once more by the table, in the most uncomfortable chair that he could find, and smoke one cigar after another till the first sign of dawn should give an excuse for action.

He had laid his watch on the table before him, and was gazing at the hour-hand, and trying to convince himself by so

doing that he was still wide awake, when a noise in the ad-
joining room suddenly straightened him in his chair and banished all fear of sleep.

There was no mistaking the nature of the noise; it was that
of a woman's sobs. The sobs were not loud, but the sound
reached him distinctly through the frail door between the two
rooms; it expressed an utter abandonment to grief; not the
cloud-burst of some passing emotion, but the slow down-
pour of a whole heaven of sorrow.

Woburn sat listening. There was nothing else to be done;
and at least his listening was a mute tribute to the trouble he
was powerless to relieve. It roused, too, the drugged pulses of
his own grief: he was touched by the chance propinquity of
two alien sorrows in a great city throbbing with multifarious
passions. It would have been more in keeping with the irony
of life had he found himself next to a mother singing her
child to sleep: there seemed a mute commiseration in the
hand that had led him to such neighborhood.

Gradually the sobs subsided, with pauses betokening an effort at self-control. At last they died off softly, like the intermittent drops that end a day of rain.

"Poor soul," Woburn mused, "she's got the better of it for
the time. I wonder what it's all about?"

At the same moment he heard another sound that made him
jump to his feet. It was a very low sound, but in that nocturnal
silence which gives distinctness to the faintest noises, Woburn
knew at once that he had heard the click of a pistol.

"What is she up to now?" he asked himself, with his eye on
the door between the two rooms; and the brightly-lit keyhole
seemed to reply with a glance of intelligence. He turned out
the gas and crept to the door, pressing his eye to the illuminated circle.

After a moment or two of adjustment, during which he
seemed to himself to be breathing like a steam-engine, he discerned a room like his own, with the same dressing-table
flanked by gas-fixtures, and the same table in the window.
This table was directly in his line of vision; and beside it stood
a woman with a small revolver in her hands. The lights being
behind her, Woburn could only infer her youth from her slender silhouette and the nimbus of fair hair defining her head.

Her dress seemed dark and simple, and on a chair under one of the gas-jets lay a jacket edged with cheap fur and a small travelling-bag. He could not see the other end of the room, but something in her manner told him that she was alone. At length she put the revolver down and took up a letter that lay on the table. She drew the letter from its envelope and read it over two or three times; then she put it back, sealing the envelope, and placing it conspicuously against the mirror of the dressing-table.

There was so grave a significance in this dumb-show that Woburn felt sure that her next act would be to return to the table and take up the revolver; but he had not reckoned on the vanity of woman. After putting the letter in place she still lingered at the mirror, standing a little sideways, so that he could now see her face, which was distinctly pretty, but of a small and unelastic mould, inadequate to the expression of the larger emotions. For some moments she continued to study herself with the expression of a child looking at a playmate who has been scolded; then she turned to the table and lifted the revolver to her forehead.

A sudden crash made her arm drop, and sent her darting backward to the opposite side of the room. Woburn had broken down the door, and stood torn and breathless in the breach.

"Oh!" she gasped, pressing closer to the wall.

"Don't be frightened," he said; "I saw what you were going to do and I had to stop you."

She looked at him for a moment in silence, and he saw the terrified flutter of her breast; then she said, "No one can stop me for long. And besides, what right have you—"

"Every one has the right to prevent a crime," he returned, the sound of the last word sending the blood to his forehead.

"I deny it," she said passionately. "Every one who has tried to live and failed has the right to die."

"Failed in what?"

"In everything!" she replied. They stood looking at each other in silence.

At length he advanced a few steps.

"You've no right to say you've failed," he said, "while you have breath to try again." He drew the revolver from her hand.

"Try again—try again? I tell you I've tried seventy times seven!"

"What have you tried?"

She looked at him with a certain dignity.

"I don't know," she said, "that you've any right to question me—or to be in this room at all—" and suddenly she burst into tears.

The discrepancy between her words and action struck the chord which, in a man's heart, always responds to the touch of feminine unreason. She dropped into the nearest chair, hiding her face in her hands, while Woburn watched the course of her weeping.

At last she lifted her head, looking up between drenched lashes.

"Please go away," she said in childish entreaty.

"How can I?" he returned. "It's impossible that I should leave you in this state. Trust me—let me help you. Tell me what has gone wrong, and let's see if there's no other way out of it."

Woburn had a voice full of sensitive inflections, and it was now trembling with profoundest pity. Its note seemed to re-assure the girl, for she said, with a beginning of confidence in her own tones, "But I don't even know who you are."

Woburn was silent: the words startled him. He moved nearer to her and went on in the same quieting tone.

"I am a man who has suffered enough to want to help others. I don't want to know any more about you than will enable me to do what I can for you. I've probably seen more of life than you have, and if you're willing to tell me your troubles perhaps together we may find a way out of them."

She dried her eyes and glanced at the revolver.

"That's the only way out," she said.

"How do you know? Are you sure you've tried every other?"

"Perfectly sure. I've written and written, and humbled myself like a slave before him, and she won't even let him answer my letters. Oh, but you don't understand"—she broke off with a renewal of weeping.

"I begin to understand—you're sorry for something you've done?"

"Oh, I've never denied that—I've never denied that I was wicked."

"And you want the forgiveness of some one you care about?"

"My husband," she whispered.

"You've done something to displease your husband?"

"To displease him? I ran away with another man!" There was a dismal exultation in her tone, as though she were paying Woburn off for having underrated her offense.

She had certainly surprised him; at worst he had expected a quarrel over a rival, with a possible complication of mother-in-law. He wondered how such helpless little feet could have taken so bold a step; then he remembered that there is no audacity like that of weakness.

He was wondering how to lead her to completer avowal when she added forlornly, "You see there's nothing else to do."

Woburn took a turn in the room. It was certainly a narrower strait than he had foreseen, and he hardly knew how to answer; but the first flow of confession had eased her, and she went on without farther persuasion.

"I don't know how I could ever have done it; I must have been downright crazy. I didn't care much for Joe when I married him—he wasn't exactly handsome, and girls think such a lot of that. But he just laid down and worshipped me, and I *was* getting fond of him in a way; only the life was so dull. I'd been used to a big city—I come from Detroit—and Hinksville is such a poky little place; that's where we lived; Joe is telegraph-operator on the railroad there. He'd have been in a much bigger place now, if he hadn't—well, after all, he behaved perfectly splendidly about *that*.

"I really was getting fond of him, and I believe I should have realized in time how good and noble and unselfish he was, if his mother hadn't been always sitting there and everlastingly telling me so. We learned in school about the Athenians hating some man who was always called just, and that's the way I felt about Joe. Whenever I did anything that wasn't quite right his mother would say how differently Joe would have done it. And she was forever telling me that Joe didn't approve of this and that and the other. When we were alone he approved of everything, but when his mother was round he'd sit quiet and let her say he didn't. I knew he'd let me have my way afterwards, but somehow that didn't prevent my getting mad at the time.

"And then the evenings were so long, with Joe away, and Mrs. Glenn (that's his mother) sitting there like an image knitting socks for the heathen. The only caller we ever had was the Baptist minister, and he never took any more notice of me than if I'd been a piece of furniture. I believe he was afraid to before Mrs. Glenn."

She paused breathlessly, and the tears in her eyes were now of anger.

"Well?" said Woburn gently.

"Well—then Arthur Hackett came along; he was travelling for a big publishing firm in Philadelphia. He was awfully handsome and as clever and sarcastic as anything. He used to lend me lots of novels and magazines, and tell me all about society life in New York. All the girls were after him, and Alice Sprague, whose father is the richest man in Hinksville, fell desperately in love with him and carried on like a fool; but he wouldn't take any notice of her. He never looked at anybody but me." Her face lit up with a reminiscent smile, and then clouded again. "I hate him now," she exclaimed, with a change of tone that startled Woburn. "I'd like to kill him—but he's killed me instead.

"Well, he bewitched me so I didn't know what I was doing; I was like somebody in a trance. When he wasn't there I didn't want to speak to anybody; I used to lie in bed half the day just to get away from folks; I hated Joe and Hinksville and everything else. When he came back the days went like a flash; we were together nearly all the time. I knew Joe's mother was spying on us, but I didn't care. And at last it seemed as if I couldn't let him go away again without me; so one evening he stopped at the back gate in a buggy, and we drove off together and caught the eastern express at River Bend. He promised to bring me to New York." She paused, and then added scornfully, "He didn't even do that!"

Woburn had returned to his seat and was watching her attentively. It was curious to note how her passion was spending itself in words; he saw that she would never kill herself while she had any one to talk to.

"That was five months ago," she continued, "and we travelled all through the southern states, and stayed a little while near Philadelphia, where his business is. He did things real stylishly at first. Then he was sent to Albany, and we stayed a week at the Delavan House. One afternoon I went out to do some shopping, and when I came back he was gone. He had taken his trunk with him, and hadn't left any address; but in my travelling-bag I found a fifty-dollar bill, with a slip of paper on which he had written, 'No use coming after me; I'm married.' We'd been together less than four months, and I never saw him again.

"At first I couldn't believe it. I stayed on, thinking it was a joke—or that he'd feel sorry for me and come back. But he never came and never wrote me a line. Then I began to hate him, and to see what a wicked fool I'd been to leave Joe. I was so lonesome—I thought I'd go crazy. And I kept thinking how good and patient Joe had been, and how badly I'd used him, and how lovely it would be to be back in the little parlor at Hinksville, even with Mrs. Glenn and the minister talking about free-will and predestination. So at last I wrote to Joe. I wrote him the humblest letters you ever read, one after another; but I never got any answer.

"Finally I found I'd spent all my money, so I sold my watch and my rings—Joe gave me a lovely turquoise ring when we were married—and came to New York. I felt ashamed to stay alone any longer in Albany; I was afraid that some of Arthur's friends, who had met me with him on the road, might come there and recognize me. After I got here I wrote to Susy Price, a great friend of mine who lives in Hinksville, and she answered at once, and told me just what I had expected—that Joe was ready to forgive me and crazy to have me back, but that his mother wouldn't let him stir a step or write me a line, and that she and the minister were at him all day long, telling him how bad I was and what a sin it would be to forgive me. I got Susy's letter two or three days ago, and after that I saw it was no use writing to Joe. He'll never dare go against his mother and she watches him like a cat. I suppose I deserve it—but he might have given me another chance! I know he would if he could only see me."

Her voice had dropped from anger to lamentation, and her tears again overflowed.

Woburn looked at her with the pity one feels for a child who is suddenly confronted with the result of some unpremeditated naughtiness.

"But why not go back to Hinksville," he suggested, "if your husband is ready to forgive you? You could go to your friend's house, and once your husband knows you are there you can easily persuade him to see you."

"Perhaps I could—Susy thinks I could. But I can't go back; I haven't got a cent left."

"But surely you can borrow money? Can't you ask your friend to forward you the amount of your fare?"

She shook her head.

"Susy ain't well off; she couldn't raise five dollars, and it costs twenty-five to get back to Hinksville. And besides, what would become of me while I waited for the money? They'll turn me out of here to-morrow; I haven't paid my last week's board, and I haven't got anything to give them; my bag's empty; I've pawned everything."

"And don't you know any one here who would lend you the money?"

"No; not a soul. At least I do know one gentleman; he's a friend of Arthur's, a Mr. Devine; he was staying at Rochester when we were there. I met him in the street the other day, and I didn't mean to speak to him, but he came up to me, and said he knew all about Arthur and how meanly he had behaved, and he wanted to know if he couldn't help me—I suppose he saw I was in trouble. He tried to persuade me to go and stay with his aunt, who has a lovely house right round here in Twenty-fourth Street; he must be very rich, for he offered to lend me as much money as I wanted."

"You didn't take it?"

"No," she returned; "I daresay he meant to be kind, but I didn't care to be beholden to any friend of Arthur's. He came here again yesterday, but I wouldn't see him, so he left a note giving me his aunt's address and saying she'd have a room ready for me at any time."

There was a long silence; she had dried her tears and sat looking at Woburn with eyes full of helpless reliance.

"Well," he said at length, "you did right not to take that man's money; but this isn't the only alternative," he added, pointing to the revolver.

"I don't know any other," she answered wearily. "I'm not smart enough to get employment; I can't make dresses or do type-writing, or any of the useful things they teach girls now; and besides, even if I could get work I couldn't stand the loneliness. I can never hold my head up again—I can't bear the disgrace. If I can't go back to Joe I'd rather be dead."

"And if you go back to Joe it will be all right?" Woburn suggested with a smile.

"Oh," she cried, her whole face alight, "if I could only go back to Joe!"

They were both silent again; Woburn sat with his hands in his pockets gazing at the floor. At length his silence seemed to rouse her to the unwontedness of the situation, and she rose from her seat, saying in a more constrained tone, "I don't know why I've told you all this."

"Because you believed that I would help you," Woburn answered, rising also; "and you were right; I'm going to send you home."

She colored vividly.

"You told me I was right not to take Mr. Devine's money," she faltered.

"Yes," he answered, "but did Mr. Devine want to send you home?"

"He wanted me to wait at his aunt's a little while first and then write to Joe again."

"I don't—I want you to start to-morrow morning; this morning, I mean. I'll take you to the station and buy your ticket, and your husband can send me back the money."

"Oh, I can't—I can't—you mustn't—" she stammered, reddening and paling. "Besides, they'll never let me leave here without paying."

"How much do you owe?"

"Fourteen dollars."

"Very well; I'll pay that for you; you can leave me your revolver as a pledge. But you must start by the first train; have you any idea at what time it leaves the Grand Central?"

"I think there's one at eight."

He glanced at his watch.

"In less than two hours, then; it's after six now."

She stood before him with fascinated eyes.

"You must have a very strong will," she said. "When you talk like that you make me feel as if I had to do everything you say."

"Well, you must," said Woburn lightly. "Man was made to be obeyed."

"Oh, you're not like other men," she returned; "I never heard a voice like yours; it's so strong and kind. You must be a very good man; you remind me of Joe; I'm sure you've got just such a nature; and Joe is the best man I've ever seen."

Woburn made no reply, and she rambled on, with little pauses and fresh bursts of confidence.

"Joe's a real hero, you know; he did the most splendid thing you ever heard of. I think I began to tell you about it, but I didn't finish. I'll tell you now. It happened just after we were married; I was mad with him at the time, I'm afraid, but now I see how splendid he was. He'd been telegraph operator at Hinksville for four years and was hoping that he'd get promoted to a bigger place; but he was afraid to ask for a raise. Well, I was very sick with a bad attack of pneumonia and one night the doctor said he wasn't sure whether he could pull me through. When they sent word to Joe at the telegraph office he couldn't stand being away from me another minute. There was a poor consumptive boy always hanging round the station; Joe had taught him how to operate, just to help him along; so he left him in the office and tore home for half an hour, knowing he could get back before the eastern express came along.

"He hadn't been gone five minutes when a freight-train ran off the rails about a mile up the track. It was a very still night, and the boy heard the smash and shouting, and knew something had happened. He couldn't tell what it was, but the minute he heard it he sent a message over the wires like a flash, and caught the eastern express just as it was pulling out of the station above Hinksville. If he'd hesitated a second, or made any mistake, the express would have come on, and the loss of life would have been fearful. The next day the Hinksville papers were full of Operator Glenn's presence of mind; they all said he'd be promoted. That was early in November and Joe didn't hear anything from the company till the first of January. Meanwhile the boy had gone home to his father's farm out in the country, and before Christmas he was dead. Well, on New Year's day Joe got a notice from the company saying that his pay was to be raised, and that he was to be promoted to a big junction near Detroit, in recognition of his presence of mind in stopping the eastern express. It was just what we'd both been pining for and I was nearly wild with joy; but I noticed Joe didn't say much. He just telegraphed for leave, and the next day he went right up to Detroit and told the directors there what had really happened. When he came back he told us they'd suspended him; I cried every night for a week, and even his mother said he was a fool. After that we just lived on at Hinksville, and six months later the company took him back; but I don't suppose they'll ever promote him now."

Her voice again trembled with facile emotion.

"Wasn't it beautiful of him? Ain't he a real hero?" she said. "And I'm sure you'd behave just like him; you'd be just as gentle about little things, and you'd never move an inch about big ones. You'd never do a mean action, but you'd be sorry for people who did; I can see it in your face; that's why I trusted you right off."

Woburn's eyes were fixed on the window; he hardly seemed to hear her. At length he walked across the room and pulled up the shade. The electric lights were dissolving in the gray alembic of the dawn. A milk-cart rattled down the street and, like a witch returning late from the Sabbath, a stray cat whisked into an area. So rose the appointed day.

Woburn turned back, drawing from his pocket the roll of bills which he had thrust there with so different a purpose. He counted them out, and handed her fifteen dollars.

"That will pay for your board, including your breakfast this morning," he said. "We'll breakfast together presently if you like; and meanwhile suppose we sit down and watch the sunrise. I haven't seen it for years."

He pushed two chairs toward the window, and they sat down side by side. The light came gradually, with the icy reluctance of winter; at last a red disk pushed itself above the opposite house-tops and a long cold gleam slanted across their window. They did not talk much; there was a silencing awe in the spectacle.

Presently Woburn rose and looked again at his watch.

"I must go and cover up my dress-coat," he said, "and you had better put on your hat and jacket. We shall have to be starting in half an hour."

As he turned away she laid her hand on his arm.

"You haven't even told me your name," she said.

"No," he answered; "but if you get safely back to Joe you can call me Providence."

"But how am I to send you the money?"

"Oh—well, I'll write you a line in a day or two and give you my address; I don't know myself what it will be; I'm a wanderer on the face of the earth."

"But you must have my name if you mean to write to me."

"Well, what is your name?"

"Ruby Glenn. And I think—I almost think you might send the letter right to Joe's—send it to the Hinksville station."

"Very well."

"You promise?"

"Of course I promise."

He went back into his room, thinking how appropriate it was that she should have an absurd name like Ruby. As he re-entered the room, where the gas sickened in the daylight, it seemed to him that he was returning to some forgotten land; he had passed, with the last few hours, into a wholly new phase of consciousness. He put on his fur coat, turning up the collar and crossing the lapels to hide his white tie. Then he put his cigar-case in his pocket, turned out the gas, and, picking up his hat and stick, walked back through the open doorway.

Ruby Glenn had obediently prepared herself for departure and was standing before the mirror, patting her curls into place. Her eyes were still red, but she had the happy look of a child that has outslept its grief. On the floor he noticed the tattered fragments of the letter which, a few hours earlier, he had seen her place before the mirror.

"Shall we go down now?" he asked.

"Very well," she assented; then, with a quick movement, she stepped close to him, and putting her hands on his shoulders lifted her face to his.

"I believe you're the best man I ever knew," she said, "the very best—except Joe."

She drew back blushing deeply, and unlocked the door which led into the passage-way. Woburn picked up her bag, which she had forgotten, and followed her out of the room. They passed a frowzy chambermaid, who stared at them with a yawn. Before the doors the row of boots still waited; there was a faint new aroma of coffee mingling with the smell of vanished dinners, and a fresh blast of heat had begun to tingle through the radiators.

In the unventilated coffee-room they found a waiter who had the melancholy air of being the last survivor of an exterminated race, and who reluctantly brought them some tea made with water which had not boiled, and a supply of stale rolls and staler butter. On this meagre diet they fared in silence, Woburn occasionally glancing at his watch; at length he rose, telling his companion to go and pay her bill while he called a hansom. After all, there was no use in economizing his remaining dollars.

In a few moments she joined him under the portico of the hotel. The hansom stood waiting and he sprang in after her, calling to the driver to take them to the Forty-second Street station.

When they reached the station he found a seat for her and went to buy her ticket. There were several people ahead of him at the window, and when he had bought the ticket he found that it was time to put her in the train. She rose in answer to his glance, and together they walked down the long platform in the murky chill of the roofed-in air. He followed her into the railway carriage, making sure that she had her bag, and that the ticket was safe inside it; then he held out his hand, in its pearl-coloured evening glove: he felt that the people in the other seats were staring at them.

"Good-bye," he said.

"Good-bye," she answered, flushing gratefully. "I'll never forget—never. And you *will* write, won't you? Promise."

"Of course, of course," he said, hastening from the carriage.

He retraced his way along the platform, passed through the dismal waiting-room and stepped out into the early sunshine. On the sidewalk outside the station he hesitated awhile; then he strolled slowly down Forty-second Street and, skirting the melancholy flank of the Reservoir, walked across Bryant Park. Finally he sat down on one of the benches near the Sixth Avenue and lit a cigar.

The signs of life were multiplying around him; he watched the cars roll by with their increasing freight of dingy toilers, the shop-girls hurrying to their work, the children trudging schoolward, their small vague noses red with cold, their satchels clasped in woollen-gloved hands. There is nothing very imposing in the first stirring of a great city's activities; it is a slow reluctant process, like the waking of a heavy sleeper; but to Woburn's mood the sight of that obscure renewal of humble duties was more moving than the spectacle of an army with banners.

He sat for a long time, smoking the last cigar in his case, and murmuring to himself a line from Hamlet—the saddest, he thought, in the play—

For every man hath business and desire.

Suddenly an unpremeditated movement made him feel the pressure of Ruby Glenn's revolver in his pocket; it was like a devil's touch on his arm, and he sprang up hastily. In his other pocket there were just four dollars and fifty cents; but that didn't matter now. He had no thought of flight.

For a few minutes he loitered vaguely about the park; then the cold drove him on again, and with the rapidity born of a sudden resolve he began to walk down the Fifth Avenue towards his lodgings. He brushed past a maid-servant who was washing the vestibule and ran up stairs to his room. A fire was burning in the grate and his books and photographs greeted him cheerfully from the walls; the tranquil air of the whole room seemed to take it for granted that he meant to have his bath and breakfast and go down town as usual.

He threw off his coat and pulled the revolver out of his pocket; for some moments he held it curiously in his hand, bending over to examine it as Ruby Glenn had done; then he laid it in the top drawer of a small cabinet, and locking the drawer threw the key into the fire.

After that he went quietly about the usual business of his toilet. In taking off his dress-coat he noticed the Legion of Honor which Miss Talcott had given him at the ball. He pulled it out of his buttonhole and tossed it into the fire-place. When he had finished dressing he saw with surprise that it was nearly ten o'clock. Ruby Glenn was already two hours nearer home.

Woburn stood looking about the room of which he had thought to take final leave the night before; among the ashes beneath the grate he caught sight of a little white heap which symbolized to his fancy the remains of his brief correspondence with Miss Talcott. He roused himself from this unseasonable musing and with a final glance at the familiar setting of his past, turned to face the future which the last hours had prepared for him.

He went down stairs and stepped out of doors, hastening down the street towards Broadway as though he were late for an appointment. Every now and then he encountered an acquaintance, whom he greeted with a nod and smile; he carried his head high, and shunned no man's recognition.

At length he reached the doors of a tall granite building honey-combed with windows. He mounted the steps of the portico, and passing through the double doors of plate-glass, crossed a vestibule floored with mosaic to another glass door on which was emblazoned the name of the firm.

This door he also opened, entering a large room with wainscotted subdivisions, behind which appeared the stooping shoulders of a row of clerks.

As Woburn crossed the threshold a gray-haired man emerged from an inner office at the opposite end of the room.

At sight of Woburn he stopped short.

"Mr. Woburn!" he exclaimed; then he stepped nearer and added in a low tone: "I was requested to tell you when you came that the members of the firm are waiting; will you step into the private office?"

"Professor Joslin, who, as our readers are doubtless aware, is engaged in writing the life of Mrs. Aubyn, asks us to state that he will be greatly indebted to any of the famous novelist's friends who will furnish him with information concerning the period previous to her coming to England. Mrs. Aubyn had so few intimate friends, and consequently so few regular correspondents, that letters will be of special value. Professor Joslin's address is 10 Augusta Gardens, Kensington, and he begs us to say that he will promptly return any documents entrusted to him."

G LENNARD dropped the *Spectator* and sat looking into the fire. The club was filling up, but he still had to himself the small inner room with its darkening outlook down the rain-streaked prospect of Fifth Avenue. It was all dull and dismal enough, yet a moment earlier his boredom had been perversely tinged by a sense of resentment at the thought that, as things were going, he might in time have to surrender even the despised privilege of boring himself within those particular four walls. It was not that he cared much for the club, but that the remote contingency of having to give it up stood to him, just then, perhaps by very reason of its insignificance and remoteness, for the symbol of his increasing abnegations; of that perpetual paring-off that was gradually reducing existence to the naked business of keeping himself alive. It was the futility of his multiplied shifts and privations that made them seem unworthy of a high attitude—the sense that, however rapidly he eliminated the superfluous, his cleared horizon was likely to offer no nearer view of the one prospect toward which he strained. To give up things in order to marry the woman one loves is easier than to give them up without being brought appreciably nearer to such a conclusion.

Through the open door he saw young Hollingsworth rise with a yawn from the ineffectual solace of a brandy-and-soda and transport his purposeless person to the window. Glennard measured his course with a contemptuous eye. It was so like Hollingsworth to get up and look out of the window just as it was growing too dark to see anything! There was a man rich enough to do what he pleased—had he been capable of being pleased—yet barred from all conceivable achievement by his own impervious dullness; while, a few feet off, Glennard, who wanted only enough to keep a decent coat on his back and a roof over the head of the woman he loved— Glennard, who had sweated, toiled, denied himself for the scant measure of opportunity that his zeal would have converted into a kingdom—sat wretchedly calculating that, even when he had resigned from the club, and knocked off his cigars, and given up his Sundays out of town, he would still be no nearer to attainment.

The *Spectator* had slipped to his feet, and as he picked it up his eye fell again on the paragraph addressed to the friends of Mrs. Aubyn. He had read it for the first time with a scarcely perceptible quickening of attention: her name had so long been public property that his eye passed it unseeingly, as the crowd in the street hurries without a glance by some familiar monument.

"Information concerning the period previous to her coming to England. . . ." The words were an evocation. He saw her again as she had looked at their first meeting, the poor woman of genius with her long pale face and short-sighted eyes, softened a little by the grace of youth and inexperience, but so incapable even then of any hold upon the pulses. When she spoke, indeed, she was wonderful, more wonderful, perhaps, than when later, to Glennard's fancy at least, the consciousness of memorable things uttered seemed to take from even her most intimate speech the perfect bloom of privacy. It was in those earliest days, if ever, that he had come near loving her; though even then his sentiment had lived only in the intervals of its expression. Later, when to be loved by her had been a state to touch any man's imagination, the physical reluctance had, inexplicably, so overborne the intellectual attraction, that the last years had been, to both of them, an agony of conflicting impulses. Even now, if, in turning over old papers his hand lit on her letters, the touch filled him with inarticulate misery. . . .

"She had so few intimate friends . . . that letters will be of special value." So few intimate friends! For years she had had but one; one who in the last years had requited her wonderful pages, her tragic outpourings of love, humility and pardon, with the scant phrases by which a man evades the vulgarest of sentimental importunities. He had been a brute in spite of himself, and sometimes, now that the re-membrance of her face had faded, and only her voice and words remained with him, he chafed at his own inadequacy, his stupid inability to rise to the height of her passion. His egoism was not of a kind to mirror its complacency in the adventure. To have been loved by the most brilliant woman of her day, and to have been incapable of loving her, seemed to him, in looking back, derisive evidence of his limitations; and his remorseful tenderness for her memory was compli-cated with a sense of irritation against her for having given him once for all the measure of his emotional capacity. It was not often, however, that he thus probed the past. The pub-lic, in taking possession of Mrs. Aubyn, had eased his shoul-ders of their burden. There was something fatuous in an attitude of sentimental apology toward a memory already classic: to reproach one's self for not having loved Margaret Aubyn was a good deal like being disturbed by an inability to admire the Venus of Milo. From her cold niche of fame she looked down ironically enough on his self-flagellations. . . . It was only when he came on something that belonged to her that he felt a sudden renewal of the old feeling, the strange dual impulse that drew him to her voice but drove him from her hand, so that even now, at sight of anything she had touched, his heart contracted painfully. It happened seldom nowadays. Her little presents, one by one, had dis-appeared from his rooms, and her letters, kept from some unacknowledged puerile vanity in the possession of such treasures, seldom came beneath his hand. . . .

"Her letters will be of special value—" Her letters! Why, he must have hundreds of them—enough to fill a volume. Sometimes it used to seem to him that they came with every post—he used to avoid looking in his letter-box when he came home to his rooms—but her writing seemed to spring out at him as he put his key in the door.

He stood up and strolled into the other room. Hollings-worth, lounging away from the window, had joined himself to a languidly convivial group of men, to whom, in phrases as halting as though they struggled to define an ultimate idea, he was expounding the cursed nuisance of living in a hole with such a damned climate that one had to get out of it by February, with the contingent difficulty of there being no place to take one's yacht to in winter but that other played-out hole, the Riviera. From the outskirts of this group Glennard wandered to another, where a voice as different as possible from Hollingsworth's colorless organ dominated another circle of languid listeners.

"Come and hear Dinslow talk about his patent: admission free," one of the men sang out in a tone of mock resignation.

Dinslow turned to Glennard the confident pugnacity of his smile. "Give it another six months and it'll be talking about itself," he declared. "It's pretty nearly articulate now."

"Can it say papa?" someone else inquired.

Dinslow's smile broadened. "You'll be deuced glad to say papa to *it* a year from now," he retorted. "It'll be able to support even you in affluence. Look here, now, just let me explain to you—"

Glennard moved away impatiently. The men at the club—all but those who were "in it"—were proverbially "tired" of Dinslow's patent, and none more so than Glennard, whose knowledge of its merits made it loom large in the depressing catalogue of lost opportunities. The relations between the two men had always been friendly, and Dinslow's urgent offers to "take him in on the ground floor" had of late intensified Glennard's sense of his own inability to meet good luck half-way. Some of the men who had paused to listen were already in evening clothes, others on their way home to dress; and Glennard, with an accustomed twinge of humiliation, said to himself that if he lingered among them it was in the miserable hope that one of the number might ask him to dine. Miss Trent had told him that she was to go to the opera that evening with her rich aunt; and if he should have the luck to pick up a dinner invitation he might join her there without extra outlay.

He moved about the room, lingering here and there in a tentative affectation of interest; but though the men greeted him pleasantly, no one asked him to dine. Doubtless they were all engaged, these men who could afford to pay for their dinners, who did not have to hunt for invitations as a beggar rummages for a crust in an ash-barrel! But no—as Hollingsworth left the lessening circle about the table, an admiring youth called out, "Holly, stop and dine!"

Hollingsworth turned on him the crude countenance that looked like the wrong side of a more finished face. "Sorry I can't. I'm in for a beastly banquet."

Glennard threw himself into an arm-chair. Why go home in the rain to dress? It was folly to take a cab to the opera, it was worse folly to go there at all. His perpetual meetings with Alexa Trent were as unfair to the girl as they were unnerving to himself. Since he couldn't marry her, it was time to stand aside and give a better man the chance—and his thought admitted the ironical implication that in the terms of expediency the phrase might stand for Hollingsworth.

II

He dined alone and walked home to his rooms in the rain. As he turned into Fifth Avenue he caught the wet gleam of carriages on their way to the opera, and he took the first side street, in a moment of irritation against the petty restrictions that thwarted every impulse. It was ridiculous to give up the opera, not because one might possibly be bored there, but because one must pay for the experiment.

In his sitting-room, the tacit connivance of the inanimate had centred the lamplight on a photograph of Alexa Trent, placed, in the obligatory silver frame, just where, as memory officiously reminded him, Margaret Aubyn's picture had long throned in its stead. Miss Trent's features cruelly justified the usurpation. She had the kind of beauty that comes of a happy accord of face and spirit. It is not given to many to have the lips and eyes of their rarest mood, and some women go through life behind a mask expressing only their anxiety about the butcher's bill or their inability to see a joke. With Miss Trent, face and mind had the same high serious contour. She looked like a throned Justice by some grave Florentine painter; and it seemed to Glennard that her most salient attribute, or that at least to which her conduct gave most consistent expression, was a kind of passionate justness—the

intuitive feminine justness that is so much rarer than a reasoned impartiality. Circumstances had tragically combined to
develop this instinct into a conscious habit. She had seen
more than most girls of the shabby side of life, of the perpetual tendency of want to cramp the noblest attitude. Poverty
and misfortune had overhung her childhood, and she had
none of the pretty delusions about life that are supposed to be
the crowning grace of girlhood. This very competence, which
gave her a touching reasonableness, made Glennard's situation more difficult than if he had aspired to a princess.
Between them they asked so little—they knew so well how to
make that little do; but they understood also, and she especially did not for a moment let him forget, that without that
little the future they dreamed of was impossible.

The sight of her photograph quickened Glennard's exasperation. He was sick and ashamed of the part he was playing.
He had loved her now for two years, with the tranquil tenderness that gathers depth and volume as it nears fulfilment;
he knew that she would wait for him—but the certitude
was an added pang. There are times when the constancy of
the woman one cannot marry is almost as trying as that of the
woman one does not want to.

Glennard turned up his reading-lamp and stirred the fire.
He had a long evening before him, and he wanted to crowd
out thought with action. He had brought some papers from
his office and he spread them out on his table and squared
himself to the task. . . .

It must have been an hour later that he found himself au-
tomatically fitting a key into a locked drawer. He had no
more notion than a somnambulist of the mental process that
had led up to this action. He was just dimly aware of having
pushed aside the papers and the heavy calf volumes that a moment before had bounded his horizon, and of laying in their
place, without a trace of conscious volition, the parcel he had
taken from the drawer.

The letters were tied in packets of thirty or forty. There
were a great many packets. On some of the envelopes the ink
was fading; on others, which bore the English postmark, it
was still fresh. She had been dead hardly three years, and she
had written, at lengthening intervals, to the last. . . .

He undid one of the early packets—little notes written during their first acquaintance at Hillbridge. Glennard, on leaving college, had begun life in his uncle's law office in the old university town. It was there that, at the house of her father, Professor Forth, he had first met the young lady then chiefly distinguished for having, after two years of a conspicuously unhappy marriage, returned to the protection of the paternal roof.

Mrs. Aubyn was at that time an eager and somewhat tragic young woman, of complex mind and undeveloped manners, whom her crude experience of matrimony had fitted out with a stock of generalizations that exploded like bombs in the academic air of Hillbridge. In her choice of a husband she had been fortunate enough, if the paradox be permitted, to light on one so signally gifted with the faculty of putting himself in the wrong that her leaving him had the dignity of a manifesto —made her, as it were, the spokeswoman of outraged wifehood. In this light she was cherished by that dominant portion of Hillbridge society which was least indulgent to conjugal differences, and which found a proportionate pleasure in being for once able to feast openly on a dish liberally seasoned with the outrageous. So much did this endear Mrs. Aubyn to the university ladies, that they were disposed from the first to allow her more latitude of speech and action than the ill-used wife was generally accorded in Hillbridge, where misfortune was still regarded as a visitation designed to put people in their proper place and make them feel the superiority of their neighbors. The young woman so privileged combined with a kind of personal shyness an intellectual audacity that was like a deflected impulse of coquetry: one felt that if she had been prettier she would have had emotions instead of ideas. She was in fact even then what she had always remained: a genius capable of the acutest generalizations, but curiously undiscerning where her personal susceptibilities were concerned. Her psychology failed her just where it serves most women, and one felt that her brains would never be a guide to her heart. Of all this, however, Glennard thought little in the first year of their acquaintance. He was at an age when all the gifts and graces are but so much undiscriminated food to the ravening egoism of youth. In seeking

Mrs. Aubyn's company he was prompted by an intuitive taste for the best as a pledge of his own superiority. The sympathy of the cleverest woman in Hillbridge was balm to his craving for distinction; it was public confirmation of his secret sense that he was cut out for a bigger place. It must not be understood that Glennard was vain. Vanity contents itself with the coarsest diet; there is no palate so fastidious as that of self-distrust. To a youth of Glennard's aspirations the encouragement of a clever woman stood for the symbol of all success. Later, when he had begun to feel his way, to gain a foothold, he would not need such support; but it served to carry him lightly and easily over what is often a period of insecurity and discouragement.

It would be unjust, however, to represent his interest in Mrs. Aubyn as a matter of calculation. It was as instinctive as love, and it missed being love by just such a hair-breadth deflection from the line of beauty as had determined the curve of Mrs. Aubyn's lips. When they met she had just published her first novel, and Glennard, who afterward had an ambitious man's impatience of distinguished women, was young enough to be dazzled by the semi-publicity it gave her. It was the kind of book that makes elderly ladies lower their voices and call each other "my dear" when they furtively discuss it; and Glennard exulted in the superior knowledge of the world that enabled him to take as a matter of course sentiments over which the university shook its head. Still more delightful was it to hear Mrs. Aubyn waken the echoes of academic drawing-rooms with audacities surpassing those of her printed page. Her intellectual independence gave a touch of comradeship to their intimacy, prolonging the illusion of college friendships based on a joyous interchange of heresies. Mrs. Aubyn and Glennard represented to each other the augur's wink behind the Hillbridge idol: they walked together in that light of young omniscience from which fate so curiously excludes one's elders.

Husbands, who are notoriously inopportune, may even die inopportunely, and this was the revenge that Mr. Aubyn, some two years after her return to Hillbridge, took upon his injured wife. He died precisely at the moment when Glennard was beginning to criticise her. It was not that she bored him;

she did what was infinitely worse—she made him feel his inferiority. The sense of mental equality had been gratifying to his raw ambition; but as his self-knowledge defined itself, his understanding of her also increased; and if man is at times indirectly flattered by the moral superiority of woman, her mental ascendancy is extenuated by no such oblique tribute to his powers. The attitude of looking up is a strain on the muscles; and it was becoming more and more Glennard's opinion that brains, in a woman, should be merely the obverse of beauty. To beauty Mrs. Aubyn could lay no claim; and while she had enough prettiness to exasperate him by her incapacity to make use of it, she seemed invincibly ignorant of any of the little artifices whereby women contrive to hide their defects and even to turn them into graces. Her dress never seemed a part of her; all her clothes had an impersonal air, as though they had belonged to someone else and been borrowed in an emergency that had somehow become chronic. She was conscious enough of her deficiencies to try to amend them by rash imitations of the most approved models; but no woman who does not dress well intuitively will ever do so by the light of reason, and Mrs. Aubyn's plagiarisms, to borrow a metaphor of her trade, somehow never seemed to be incorporated with the text.

Genius is of small use to a woman who does not know how to do her hair. The fame that came to Mrs. Aubyn with her second book left Glennard's imagination untouched, or had at most the negative effect of removing her still farther from the circle of his contracting sympathies. We are all the sport of time; and fate had so perversely ordered the chronology of Margaret Aubyn's romance that when her husband died Glennard felt as though he had lost a friend.

It was not in his nature to be needlessly unkind; and though he was in the impregnable position of the man who has given a woman no more definable claim on him than that of letting her fancy that he loves her, he would not for the world have accentuated his advantage by any betrayal of indifference. During the first year of her widowhood their friendship dragged on with halting renewals of sentiment, becoming more and more a banquet of empty dishes from which the covers were never removed; then Glennard went to

New York to live and exchanged the faded pleasures of inter-course for the comparative novelty of correspondence. Her letters, oddly enough, seemed at first to bring her nearer than her presence. She had adopted, and she successfully main-tained, a note as affectionately impersonal as his own; she wrote ardently of her work, she questioned him about his, she even bantered him on the inevitable pretty girl who was cer-tain before long to divert the current of his confidences. To Glennard, who was almost a stranger in New York, the sight of Mrs. Aubyn's writing was like a voice of reassurance in sur-roundings as yet insufficiently aware of him. His vanity found a retrospective enjoyment in the sentiment his heart had re-jected, and this factitious emotion drove him once or twice to Hillbridge, whence, after scenes of evasive tenderness, he re-turned dissatisfied with himself and her. As he made room for himself in New York and peopled the space he had cleared with the sympathies at the disposal of agreeable and self-confident young men, it seemed to him natural to infer that Mrs. Aubyn had refurnished in the same manner the void he was not unwilling his departure should have left. But in the dissolution of sentimental partnerships it is seldom that both associates are able to withdraw their funds at the same time; and Glennard gradually learned that he stood for the venture on which Mrs. Aubyn had irretrievably staked her all. It was not the kind of figure he cared to cut. He had no fancy for leaving havoc in his wake and would have preferred to sow a quick growth of oblivion in the spaces wasted by his uncon-sidered inroads; but if he supplied the seed, it was clearly Mrs. Aubyn's business to see to the raising of the crop. Her atti-tude seemed indeed to throw his own reasonableness into dis-tincter relief; so that they might have stood for thrift and improvidence in an allegory of the affections.

It was not that Mrs. Aubyn permitted herself to be a pen-sioner on his bounty. He knew she had no wish to keep her-self alive on the small change of sentiment; she simply fed on her own funded passion, and the luxuries it allowed her made him, even then, dimly aware that she had the secret of an in-exhaustible alchemy.

Their relations remained thus negatively tender till she sud-denly wrote him of her decision to go abroad to live. Her father had died, she had no near ties in Hillbridge, and London offered more scope than New York to her expanding personality. She was already famous, and her laurels were yet unharvested.

For a moment the news roused Glennard to a jealous sense of lost opportunities. He wanted, at any rate, to reassert his power before she made the final effort of escape. They had not met for over a year, but of course he could not let her sail without seeing her. She came to New York the day before her departure, and they spent its last hours together. Glennard had planned no course of action—he simply meant to let himself drift. They both drifted, for a long time, down the languid current of reminiscence; she seemed to sit passive, letting him push his way back through the overgrown channels of the past. At length she reminded him that they must bring their explorations to an end. He rose to leave, and stood looking at her with the same uncertainty in his heart. He was tired of her already—he was always tired of her—yet he was not sure that he wanted her to go.

"I may never see you again," he said, as though confidently appealing to her compassion.

Her look enveloped him. "And I shall see you always—always!"

"Why go then—?" escaped him.

"To be nearer you," she answered; and the words dismissed him like a closing door.

The door was never to reopen; but through its narrow crack Glennard, as the years went on, became more and more conscious of an inextinguishable light directing its small ray toward the past which consumed so little of his own commemorative oil. The reproach was taken from this thought by Mrs. Aubyn's gradual translation into terms of universality. In becoming a personage she so naturally ceased to be a person that Glennard could almost look back to his explorations of her spirit as on a visit to some famous shrine, immortalized, but in a sense desecrated, by popular veneration.

Her letters from London continued to come with the same tender punctuality; but the altered conditions of her life, the vistas of new relationships disclosed by every phrase, made her communications as impersonal as a piece of journalism. It was as though the state, the world, indeed, had taken her off his hands, assuming the maintenance of a temperament that had long exhausted his slender store of reciprocity.

In the retrospective light shed by the letters he was blinded to their specific meaning. He was not a man who concerned himself with literature, and they had been to him, at first, simply the extension of her brilliant talk, later the dreaded vehicle of a tragic importunity. He knew, of course, that they were wonderful; that, unlike the authors who give their essence to the public and keep only a dry rind for their friends, Mrs. Aubyn had stored of her rarest vintage for this hidden sacrament of tenderness. Sometimes, indeed, he had been oppressed, humiliated almost, by the multiplicity of her allusions, the wide scope of her interests, her persistence in forcing her superabundance of thought and emotion into the shallow receptacle of his sympathy; but he had never thought of the letters objectively, as the production of a distinguished woman; had never measured the literary significance of her oppressive prodigality. He was almost frightened now at the wealth in his hands; the obligation of her love had never weighed on him like this gift of her imagination: it was as though he had accepted from her something to which even a reciprocal tenderness could not have justified his claim.

He sat a long time staring at the scattered pages on his desk; and in the sudden realization of what they meant he could almost fancy some alchemistic process changing them to gold as he stared.

He had the sense of not being alone in the room, of the presence of another self observing from without the stirring of sub-conscious impulses that sent flushes of humiliation to his forehead. At length he stood up, and with the gesture of a man who wishes to give outward expression to his purpose —to establish, as it were, a moral alibi—swept the letters into a heap and carried them toward the grate. But it would have taken too long to burn all the packets. He turned back to the table and one by one fitted the pages into their envelopes; then he tied up the letters and put them back into the locked drawer.

III

It was one of the laws of Glennard's intercourse with Miss Trent that he always went to see her the day after he had resolved to give her up. There was a special charm about the moments thus snatched from the jaws of renunciation; and his sense of their significance was on this occasion so keen that he hardly noticed the added gravity of her welcome.

His feeling for her had become so vital a part of him that her nearness had the quality of imperceptibly readjusting his point of view, of making the jumbled phenomena of experience fall at once into a rational perspective. In this redistribution of values the sombre retrospect of the previous evening shrank to a mere cloud on the edge of consciousness. Perhaps the only service an unloved woman can render the man she loves is to enhance and prolong his illusions about her rival. It was the fate of Margaret Aubyn's memory to serve as a foil to Miss Trent's presence, and never had the poor lady thrown her successor into more vivid relief.

Miss Trent had the charm of still waters that are felt to be renewed by rapid currents. Her attention spread a tranquil surface to the demonstrations of others, and it was only in days of storm that one felt the pressure of the tides. This inscrutable composure was perhaps her chief grace in Glennard's eyes. Reserve, in some natures, implies merely the locking of empty rooms or the dissimulation of awkward encumbrances; but Miss Trent's reticence was to Glennard like the closed door to the sanctuary, and his certainty of divining the hidden treasure made him content to remain outside in the happy expectancy of the neophyte.

"You didn't come to the opera last night," she began, in the tone that seemed always rather to record a fact than to offer a reflection on it.

He answered with a discouraged gesture. "What was the use? We couldn't have talked."

"Not as well as here," she assented; adding, after a meditative pause, "As you didn't come I talked to Aunt Virginia instead."

"Ah!" he returned, the fact being hardly striking enough to detach him from the contemplation of her hands, which had fallen, as was their wont, into an attitude full of plastic possibilities. One felt them to be hands that, moving only to some purpose, were capable of intervals of serene inaction.

"We had a long talk," Miss Trent went on; and she waited again before adding, with the increased absence of stress that marked her graver communications, "Aunt Virginia wants me to go abroad with her."

Glennard looked up with a start. "Abroad? When?"

"Now—next month. To be gone two years."

He permitted himself a movement of tender derision. "Does she really? Well, I want you to go abroad with *me*—for any number of years. Which offer do you accept?"

"Only one of them seems to require immediate consideration," she returned with a smile.

Glennard looked at her again. "You're not thinking of it?"

Her gaze dropped and she unclasped her hands. Her movements were so rare that they might have been said to italicize her words. "Aunt Virginia talked to me very seriously. It will be a great relief to mother and the others to have me provided for in that way for two years. I must think of that, you know." She glanced down at her gown, which, under a renovated surface, dated back to the first days of Glennard's wooing. "I try not to cost much—but I do."

"Good Lord!" Glennard groaned.

They sat silent till at length she gently took up the argument. "As the eldest, you know, I'm bound to consider these things. Women are such a burden. Jim does what he can for mother, but with his own children to provide for it isn't very much. You see we're all poor together."

"Your aunt isn't. She might help your mother."

"She does—in her own way."

"Exactly—that's the rich relation all over! You may be miserable in any way you like, but if you're to be happy you must be so in her way—and in her old gowns."

"I could be very happy in Aunt Virginia's old gowns," Miss Trent interposed.

"Abroad, you mean?"

"I mean wherever I felt that I was helping. And my going abroad will help."

"Of course—I see that. And I see your considerateness in putting its advantages negatively."

"Negatively?"

"In dwelling simply on what the going will take you from, not on what it will bring you to. It means a lot to a woman, of course, to get away from a life like this." He summed up in a disparaging glance the background of indigent furniture. "The question is how you'll like coming back to it."

She seemed to accept the full consequences of his thought. "I only know I don't like leaving it."

He flung back sombrely, "You don't even put it conditionally then?"

Her gaze deepened. "On what?"

He stood up and walked across the room. Then he came back and paused before her. "On the alternative of marrying me."

The slow color—even her blushes seemed deliberate—rose to her lower lids; her lips stirred, but the words resolved themselves into a smile and she waited.

He took another turn, with the thwarted step of the man whose nervous exasperation escapes through his muscles.

"And to think that in fifteen years I shall have a big practice!"

Her eyes triumphed for him. "In less!"

"The cursed irony of it! What do I care for the man I shall be then? It's slaving one's life away for a stranger!" He took her hands abruptly. "You'll go to Cannes, I suppose, or Monte Carlo? I heard Hollingsworth say to-day that he meant to take his yacht over to the Mediterranean—"

She released herself. "If you think that—"

"I don't. I almost wish I did. It would be easier, I mean." He broke off incoherently. "I believe your Aunt Virginia does, though. She somehow connotes Hollingsworth and the Mediterranean." He caught her hands again. "Alexa—if we could manage a little hole somewhere out of town?"

"Could we?" she sighed, half yielding.

"In one of those places where they make jokes about the mosquitoes," he pressed her. "Could you get on with one servant?"

"Could you get on without varnished boots?"

"Promise me you won't go, then!"

"What are you thinking of, Stephen?"

"I don't know," he stammered, the question giving unexpected form to his intention. "It's all in the air yet, of course; but I picked up a tip the other day—"

"You're not speculating?" she cried, with a kind of super-stitious terror.

"Lord, no. This is a sure thing—I almost wish it wasn't; I mean if I can work it—" He had a sudden vision of the comprehensiveness of the temptation. If only he had been less sure of Dinslow! His assurance gave the situation the base element of safety.

"I don't understand you," she faltered.

"Trust me, instead!" he adjured her with sudden energy; and turning on her abruptly, "If you go, you know, you go free," he concluded.

She drew back, paling a little. "Why do you make it harder for me?"

"To make it easier for myself," he retorted.

IV

The next afternoon Glennard, leaving his office earlier than usual, turned, on his way home, into one of the public libraries.

He had the place to himself at that closing hour, and the librarian was able to give an undivided attention to his tentative request for letters—collections of letters. The librarian suggested Walpole.

"I meant women—women's letters."

The librarian proffered Hannah More and Miss Martineau. Glennard cursed his own inarticulateness. "I mean letters to—to some one person—a man; their husband—or—"

"Ah," said the inspired librarian, "Eloise and Abailard."

"Well—something a little nearer, perhaps," said Glennard, with lightness. "Didn't Mérimée—"

"The lady's letters, in that case, were not published."

"Of course not," said Glennard, vexed at his blunder.

"There are George Sand's letters to Flaubert."

"Ah!" Glennard hesitated. "Was she—were they—?" He chafed at his own ignorance of the sentimental by-paths of literature.

"If you want love-letters, perhaps some of the French eighteenth-century correspondences might suit you better—Mlle. Aïssé or Madame de Sabran—"

But Glennard insisted. "I want something modern—English or American. I want to look something up," he lamely concluded.

The librarian could only suggest George Eliot.

"Well, give me some of the French things, then—and I'll have Mérimée's letters. It was the woman who published them, wasn't it?"

He caught up his armful, transferring it, on the doorstep, to a cab which carried him to his rooms. He dined alone, hurriedly, at a small restaurant near by, and returned at once to his books.

Late that night, as he undressed, he wondered what contemptible impulse had forced from him his last words to Alexa Trent. It was bad enough to interfere with the girl's chances by hanging about her to the obvious exclusion of other men, but it was worse to seem to justify his weakness by dressing up the future in delusive ambiguities. He saw himself sinking from depth to depth of sentimental cowardice in his reluctance to renounce his hold on her; and it filled him with self-disgust to think that the highest feeling of which he supposed himself capable was blent with such base elements.

His awakening was hardly cheered by the sight of her writing. He tore her note open and took in the few lines—she seldom exceeded the first page—with the lucidity of apprehension that is the forerunner of evil.

"My aunt sails on Saturday and I must give her my answer the day after to-morrow. Please don't come till then—I want to think the question over by myself. I know I ought to go. Won't you help me to be reasonable?"

It was settled, then. Well, he would help her to be reasonable; he wouldn't stand in her way; he would let her go. For two years he had been living some other, luckier man's life; the time had come when he must drop back into his own. He no longer tried to look ahead, to grope his way through the endless labyrinth of his material difficulties; a sense of dull resignation closed in on him like a fog.

"Hullo, Glennard!" a voice said, as an electric car, late that afternoon, dropped him at an uptown corner.

He looked up and met the interrogative smile of Barton Flamel, who stood on the curbstone watching the retreating car with the eye of a man philosophic enough to remember that it will be followed by another.

Glennard felt his usual impulse of pleasure at meeting Flamel; but it was not in this case curtailed by the reaction of contempt that habitually succeeded it. Probably even the few men who had known Flamel since his youth could have given no good reason for the vague mistrust that he inspired. Some people are judged by their actions, others by their ideas; and perhaps the shortest way of defining Flamel is to say that his well-known leniency of view was vaguely divined to include himself. Simple minds may have resented the discovery that his opinions were based on his perceptions; but there was certainly no more definite charge against him than that implied in the doubt as to how he would behave in an emergency, and his company was looked upon as one of those mildly unwholesome dissipations to which the prudent may occasionally yield. It now offered itself to Glennard as an easy escape from the obsession of moral problems, which somehow could no more be worn in Flamel's presence than a surplice in the street.

"Where are you going? To the club?" Flamel asked; adding, as the younger man assented, "Why not come to my studio instead? You'll see one bore instead of twenty."

The apartment which Flamel described as his studio showed, as its one claim to the designation, a perennially empty easel, the rest of its space being filled with the evidences of a comprehensive dilettanteism. Against this background, which seemed the visible expression of its owner's intellectual tolerance, rows of fine books detached themselves with a prominence showing them to be Flamel's chief care.

Glennard glanced with the eye of untrained curiosity at the lines of warm-toned morocco, while his host busied himself with the uncorking of Apollinaris.

"You've got a splendid lot of books," he said.

"They're fairly decent," the other assented, in the curt tone of the collector who will not talk of his passion for fear of talking of nothing else; then, as Glennard, his hands in his pockets, began to stroll perfunctorily down the long line of bookcases— "Some men," Flamel irresistibly added, "think of books merely as tools, others as tooling. I'm between the two; there are days when I use them as scenery, other days when I want them as society; so that, as you see, my library represents a makeshift compromise between looks and brains, and the collectors look down on me almost as much as the students."

Glennard, without answering, was mechanically taking one book after another from the shelves. His hands slipped curiously over the smooth covers and the noiseless subsidence of opening pages. Suddenly he came on a thin volume of faded manuscript.

"What's this?" he asked with a listless sense of wonder.

"Ah, you're at my manuscript shelf. I've been going in for that sort of thing lately." Flamel came up and looked over his shoulders. "That's a bit of Stendhal—one of the Italian stories —and here are some letters of Balzac to Madame Surville."

Glennard took the book with sudden eagerness. "Who was Madame Surville?"

"His sister." He was conscious that Flamel was looking at him with the smile that was like an interrogation point. "I didn't know you cared for this kind of thing."

"I don't—at least I've never had the chance. Have you many collections of letters?"

"Lord, no—very few. I'm just beginning, and most of the interesting ones are out of my reach. Here's a queer little collection, though—the rarest thing I've got—half a dozen of Shelley's letters to Harriet Westbrook. I had a devil of a time getting them—a lot of collectors were after them."

Glennard, taking the volume from his hand, glanced with a kind of repugnance at the interleaving of yellow crisscrossed sheets. "She was the one who drowned herself, wasn't she?"

Flamel nodded. "I suppose that little episode adds about fifty per cent. to their value," he said meditatively.

Glennard laid the book down. He wondered why he had joined Flamel. He was in no humor to be amused by the older man's talk, and a recrudescence of personal misery rose about him like an icy tide.

"I believe I must take myself off," he said. "I'd forgotten an engagement."

He turned to go; but almost at the same moment he was conscious of a duality of intention wherein his apparent wish to leave revealed itself as a last effort of the will against the overmastering desire to stay and unbosom himself to Flamel.

The older man, as though divining the conflict, laid a detaining pressure on his arm.

"Won't the engagement keep? Sit down and try one of these cigars. I don't often have the luck of seeing you here."

"I'm rather driven just now," said Glennard vaguely. He found himself seated again, and Flamel had pushed to his side a low stand holding a bottle of Apollinaris and a decanter of cognac.

Flamel, thrown back in his capacious arm-chair, surveyed him through a cloud of smoke with the comfortable tolerance of the man to whom no inconsistencies need be explained. Connivance was implicit in the air. It was the kind of atmosphere in which the outrageous loses its edge. Glennard felt a gradual relaxing of his nerves.

"I suppose one has to pay a lot for letters like that?" he heard himself asking, with a glance in the direction of the volume he had laid aside.

"Oh, so-so—depends on circumstances." Flamel viewed him thoughtfully. "Are you thinking of collecting?"

Glennard laughed. "Lord, no. The other way round."

"Selling?"

"Oh, I hardly know. I was thinking of a poor chap—"

Flamel filled the pause with a nod of interest.

"A poor chap I used to know—who died—he died last year—and who left me a lot of letters, letters he thought a great deal of—he was fond of me and left 'em to me outright, with the idea, I suppose, that they might benefit me somehow—I don't know—I'm not much up on such things—" He reached his hand to the tall glass his host had filled.

"A collection of autograph letters, eh? Any big names?"

"Oh, only one name. They're all letters written to him—by one person, you understand; a woman, in fact—"

"Oh, a woman," said Flamel negligently.

Glennard was nettled by his obvious loss of interest. "I rather think they'd attract a good deal of notice if they were published."

Flamel still looked uninterested. "Love-letters, I suppose?"

"Oh, just—the letters a woman would write to a man she knew well. They were tremendous friends, he and she."

"And she wrote a clever letter?"

"Clever? It was Margaret Aubyn."

A great silence filled the room. It seemed to Glennard that the words had burst from him as blood gushes from a wound.

"Great Scott!" said Flamel sitting up. "A collection of Margaret Aubyn's letters? Did you say *you* had them?"

"They were left me—by my friend."

"I see. Was he—well, no matter. You're to be congratulated, at any rate. What are you going to do with them?"

Glennard stood up with a sense of weariness in all his bones. "Oh, I don't know. I haven't thought much about it. I just happened to see that some fellow was writing her life—"

"Joslin; yes. You didn't think of giving them to him?"

Glennard had lounged across the room and stood staring up at a bronze Bacchus who drooped his garlanded head above the pediment of an Italian cabinet. "What ought I to do? You're just the fellow to advise me." He felt the blood in his cheek as he spoke.

Flamel sat with meditative eye. "What do you *want* to do with them?" he asked.

"I want to publish them," said Glennard, swinging round with sudden energy—"If I can—"

"If you can? They're yours, you say?"

"They're mine fast enough. There's no one to prevent—I mean there are no restrictions—" he was arrested by the sense that these accumulated proofs of impunity might precisely stand as the strongest check on his action.

"And Mrs. Aubyn had no family, I believe?"

"No."

"Then I don't see who's to interfere," said Flamel, studying his cigar-tip.

Glennard had turned his unseeing stare on an ecstatic Saint Catherine framed in tarnished gilding.

"It's just this way," he began again, with an effort. "When letters are as personal as—as these of my friend's. . . . Well, I don't mind telling you that the cash would make a heap of difference to me; such a lot that it rather obscures my judgment—the fact is, if I could lay my hand on a few thousands now I could get into a big thing, and without appreciable risk; and I'd like to know whether you think I'd be justified—under the circumstances. . . ." He paused with a dry throat. It seemed to him at the moment that it would be impossible for him ever to sink lower in his own estimation. He was in truth less ashamed of weighing the temptation than of submitting his scruples to a man like Flamel, and affecting to appeal to sentiments of delicacy on the absence of which he had consciously reckoned. But he had reached a point where each word seemed to compel another, as each wave in a stream is forced forward by the pressure behind it; and before Flamel could speak he had faltered out—"You don't think people could say . . . could criticise the man. . . ."

"But the man's dead, isn't he?"

"He's dead—yes; but can I assume the responsibility without—"

Flamel hesitated; and almost immediately Glennard's scruples gave way to irritation. If at this hour Flamel were to affect an inopportune reluctance—!

The older man's answer reassured him. "Why need you assume any responsibility? Your name won't appear, of course; and as to your friend's, I don't see why his should either. He wasn't a celebrity himself, I suppose?"

"No, no."

"Then the letters can be addressed to Mr. Blank. Doesn't that make it all right?"

Glennard's hesitation revived. "For the public, yes. But I don't see that it alters the case for me. The question is, ought I to publish them at all?"

"Of course you ought to." Flamel spoke with invigorating emphasis. "I doubt if you'd be justified in keeping them back. Anything of Margaret Aubyn's is more or less public property by this time. She's too great for any one of us. I was only wondering how you could use them to the best advantage—to yourself, I mean. How many are there?"

"Oh, a lot; perhaps a hundred—I haven't counted. There may be more. . . ."

"Gad! What a haul! When were they written?"

"I don't know—that is—they corresponded for years. What's the odds?" He moved toward his hat with a vague impulse of flight.

"It all counts," said Flamel imperturbably. "A long correspondence—one, I mean, that covers a great deal of time—is obviously worth more than if the same number of letters had been written within a year. At any rate, you won't give them to Joslin? They'd fill a book, wouldn't they?"

"I suppose so. I don't know how much it takes to fill a book."

"Not love-letters, you say?"

"Why?" flashed from Glennard.

"Oh, nothing—only the big public is sentimental, and if they *were*—why, you could get any money for Margaret Aubyn's love-letters."

Glennard was silent.

"Are the letters interesting in themselves? I mean apart from the association with her name?"

"I'm no judge." Glennard took up his hat and thrust himself into his overcoat. "I dare say I sha'n't do anything about it. And, Flamel—you won't mention this to any one?"

"Lord, no. Well, I congratulate you. You've got a big thing." Flamel was smiling at him from the hearth.

Glennard, on the threshold, forced a response to the smile, while he questioned with loitering indifference—"Financially, eh?"

"Rather; I should say so."

Glennard's hand lingered on the knob. "How much—should you say? You know about such things."

"Oh, I should have to see the letters; but I should say—well, if you've got enough to fill a book and they're fairly readable, and the book is brought out at the right time—say ten thousand down from the publisher, and possibly one or two more in royalties. If you got the publishers bidding against each other you might do even better; but of course I'm talking in the dark."

"Of course," said Glennard, with sudden dizziness. His hand had slipped from the knob and he stood staring down at the exotic spirals of the Persian rug beneath his feet.

"I'd have to see the letters," Flamel repeated.

"Of course—you'd have to see them. . . ." Glennard stammered; and, without turning, he flung over his shoulder an inarticulate "Good-bye. . . ."

v

The little house, as Glennard strolled up to it between the trees, seemed no more than a gay tent pitched against the sunshine. It had the crispness of a freshly starched summer gown, and the geraniums on the veranda bloomed as simultaneously as the flowers in a bonnet. The garden was prospering absurdly. Seed they had sown at random—amid laughing counter-charges of incompetence—had shot up in fragrant defiance of their blunders. He smiled to see the clematis unfolding its punctual wings about the porch. The tiny lawn was smooth as a shaven cheek, and a crimson rambler mounted to the nursery window of a baby who never cried. A breeze shook the awning above the tea-table, and his wife, as he drew near, could be seen bending above a kettle that was just about to boil. So vividly did the whole scene suggest the painted bliss of a stage setting, that it would have been hardly surprising to see her step forward among the flowers and trill out her virtuous happiness from the veranda rail.

The stale heat of the long day in town, the dusty promiscuity of the suburban train, were now but the requisite foil to an evening of scented breezes and tranquil talk. They had been married more than a year, and each home-coming still reflected the freshness of their first day together. If, indeed, their happiness had a flaw, it was in resembling too closely the bright impermanence of their surroundings. Their love as yet was but the gay tent of holiday-makers.

His wife looked up with a smile. The country life suited her, and her beauty had gained depth from a stillness in which certain faces might have grown opaque.

"Are you very tired?" she asked, pouring his tea.

"Just enough to enjoy this." He rose from the chair in which he had thrown himself and bent over the tray for his cream. "You've had a visitor?" he commented, noticing a half-empty cup beside her own.

"Only Mr. Flamel," she said indifferently.

"Flamel? Again?"

She answered without show of surprise. "He left just now. His yacht is down at Laurel Bay and he borrowed a trap of the Dreshams to drive over here."

Glennard made no comment, and she went on, leaning her head back against the cushions of her bamboo seat, "He wants us to go for a sail with him next Sunday."

Glennard meditatively stirred his tea. He was trying to think of the most natural and unartificial thing to say, and his voice seemed to come from the outside, as though he were speaking behind a marionette. "Do you want to?"

"Just as you please," she said compliantly. No affectation of indifference could have been as baffling as her compliance. Glennard, of late, was beginning to feel that the surface which, a year ago, he had taken for a sheet of clear glass, might, after all, be a mirror reflecting merely his own conception of what lay behind it.

"Do you like Flamel?" he suddenly asked; to which, still engaged with her tea, she returned the feminine answer—"I thought you did."

"I do, of course," he agreed, vexed at his own incorrigible tendency to magnify Flamel's importance by hovering about the topic. "A sail would be rather jolly; let's go."

She made no reply and he drew forth the rolled-up evening papers which he had thrust into his pocket on leaving the train. As he smoothed them out his own countenance seemed to undergo the same process. He ran his eye down the list of stocks, and Flamel's importunate personality receded behind the rows of figures pushing forward into notice like so many bearers of good news. Glennard's investments were flowering like his garden: the dryest shares blossomed into dividends and a golden harvest awaited his sickle.

He glanced at his wife with the tranquil air of a man who digests good luck as naturally as the dry ground absorbs a shower. "Things are looking uncommonly well. I believe we shall be able to go to town for two or three months next winter if we can find something cheap."

She smiled luxuriously: it was pleasant to be able to say, with an air of balancing relative advantages, "Really, on the baby's account I shall be almost sorry; but if we do go, there's Kate Erskine's house . . . she'll let us have it for almost nothing. . . ."

"Well, write her about it," he recommended, his eye travelling on in search of the weather report. He had turned to the wrong page; and suddenly a line of black characters leapt out at him as from an ambush.

"Margaret Aubyn's Letters.
"Two volumes. Out To-day. First Edition of five thousand sold out before leaving the press. Second Edition ready next week. The Book of the Year. . . ."

He looked up stupidly. His wife still sat with her head thrown back, her pure profile detached against the cushions. She was smiling a little over the prospect his last words had opened. Behind her head shivers of sun and shade ran across the striped awning. A row of maples and a privet hedge hid their neighbor's gables, giving them undivided possession of their leafy half-acre; and life, a moment before, had been like their plot of ground, shut off, hedged in from importunities, impenetrably his and hers. Now it seemed to him that every maple-leaf, every privet-bud, was a relentless human gaze, pressing close upon their privacy. It was as though they sat in a brightly lit room, uncurtained from a darkness full of hostile watchers. . . . His wife still smiled; and her unconsciousness of danger seemed in some horrible way to put her beyond the reach of rescue. . . .

He had not known that it would be like this. After the first odious weeks, spent in preparing the letters for publication, in submitting them to Flamel, and in negotiating with the publishers, the transaction had dropped out of his consciousness into that unvisited limbo to which we relegate the deeds we would rather not have done but have no notion of undoing. From the moment he had obtained Miss Trent's promise not to sail with her aunt he had tried to imagine himself irrevocably committed. After that, he argued, his first duty was to her—she had become his conscience. The sum obtained from the publishers by Flamel's adroit manipulations, and opportunely transferred to Dinslow's successful venture, already yielded a return which, combined with Glennard's professional earnings, took the edge of compulsion from their way

of living, making it appear the expression of a graceful preference for simplicity. It was the mitigated poverty which can
subscribe to a review or two and have a few flowers on the
dinner-table. And already in a small way Glennard was beginning to feel the magnetic quality of prosperity. Clients who
had passed his door in the hungry days sought it out now that
it bore the name of a successful man. It was understood that
a small inheritance, cleverly invested, was the source of his
fortune; and there was a feeling that a man who could do so
well for himself was likely to know how to turn over other
people's money.

But it was in the more intimate reward of his wife's happiness that Glennard tasted the full flavor of success. Coming
out of conditions so narrow that those he offered her seemed
spacious, she fitted into her new life without any of those
manifest efforts at adjustment that are as sore to a husband's
pride as the critical rearrangement of the bridal furniture. She
had given him, instead, the delicate pleasure of watching her
expand like a sea-creature restored to its element, stretching
out the atrophied tentacles of girlish vanity and enjoyment to
the rising tide of opportunity. And somehow—in the windowless inner cell of his consciousness where self-criticism
cowered—Glennard's course seemed justified by its merely
material success. How could such a crop of innocent blessed-
ness have sprung from tainted soil? . . .

Now he had the injured sense of a man entrapped into a
disadvantageous bargain. He had not known it would be like
this; and a dull anger gathered at his heart. Anger against
whom? Against his wife, for not knowing what he suffered?
Against Flamel, for being the unconscious instrument of his
wrongdoing? Or against that mute memory to which his own
act had suddenly given a voice of accusation? Yes, that was it;
and his punishment henceforth would be the presence, the
unescapable presence, of the woman he had so persistently
evaded. She would always be there now. It was as though he
had married her instead of the other. It was what she had always wanted—to be with him—and she had gained her point
at last. . . .

He sprang up, as though in an impulse of flight. . . . The
sudden movement lifted his wife's lids, and she asked, in the

incurious voice of the woman whose life is enclosed in a magic circle of prosperity—"Any news?"

"No—none—" he said, roused to a sense of immediate peril. The papers lay scattered at his feet—what if she were to see them? He stretched his arm to gather them up, but his next thought showed him the futility of such concealment. The same advertisement would appear every day, for weeks to come, in every newspaper; how could he prevent her seeing it? He could not always be hiding the papers from her. . . . Well, and what if she did see it? It would signify nothing to her; the chances were that she would never even read the book. . . . As she ceased to be an element of fear in his calculations the distance between them seemed to lessen and he took her again, as it were, into the circle of his conjugal protection. . . . Yet a moment before he had almost hated her! . . . He laughed aloud at his senseless terrors. . . . He was off his balance, decidedly. . . .

"What are you laughing at?" she asked.

He explained, elaborately, that he was laughing at the recollection of an old woman in the train, an old woman with a lot of bundles, who couldn't find her ticket. . . . But somehow, in the telling, the humor of the story seemed to evaporate, and he felt the conventionality of her smile. He glanced at his watch. "Isn't it time to dress?"

She rose with serene reluctance. "It's a pity to go in. The garden looks so lovely."

They lingered side by side, surveying their domain. There was not space in it, at this hour, for the shadow of the elm tree in the angle of the hedge: it crossed the lawn, cut the flower-border in two, and ran up the side of the house to the nursery window. She bent to flick a caterpillar from the honeysuckle; then, as they turned indoors, "If we mean to go on the yacht next Sunday," she suggested, "oughtn't you to let Mr. Flamel know?"

Glennard's exasperation deflected suddenly. "Of course I shall let him know. You always seem to imply that I'm going to do something rude to Flamel."

The words reverberated through her silence; she had a way of thus leaving one space in which to contemplate one's folly at arm's length. Glennard turned on his heel and went upstairs. As he dropped into a chair before his dressing-table, he said to himself that in the last hour he had sounded the depths of his humiliation, and that the lowest dregs of it, the very bottom-slime, was the hateful necessity of having always, as long as the two men lived, to be civil to Barton Flamel.

VI

The week in town had been sultry, and the men, in the Sunday emancipation of white flannel and duck, filled the deck chairs of the yacht with their outstretched apathy, following, through a mist of cigarette smoke, the flitting inconsequences of the women. The party was a small one—Flamel had few intimate friends—but composed of more heterogeneous atoms than the little pools into which society usually runs. The reaction from the chief episode of his earlier life had bred in Glennard an uneasy distaste for any kind of personal saliency. Cleverness was useful in business; but in society it seemed to him as futile as the sham cascades formed by a stream that might have been used to drive a mill. He liked the collective point of view that goes with the civilized uniformity of dress clothes, and his wife's attitude implied the same preference; yet they found themselves slipping more and more into Flamel's intimacy. Alexa had once or twice said that she enjoyed meeting clever people; but her enjoyment took the negative form of a smiling receptivity; and Glennard felt a growing preference for the kind of people who have their thinking done for them by the community.

Still, the deck of the yacht was a pleasant refuge from the heat on shore, and his wife's profile, serenely projected against the changing blue, lay on his retina like a cool hand on the nerves. He had never been more impressed by the kind of absoluteness that lifted her beauty above the transient effects of other women, making the most harmonious face seem an accidental collocation of features.

The ladies who directly suggested this comparison were of a kind accustomed to take similar risks with more gratifying results. Mrs. Armiger had in fact long been the triumphant alternative of those who couldn't "see" Alexa Glennard's looks; and Mrs. Touchett's claims to consideration were founded on that distribution of effects which is the wonder of those who admire a highly cultivated country. The third lady of the trio which Glennard's fancy had put to such unflattering uses was bound by circumstances to support the claims of the other two. This was Mrs. Dresham, the wife of the editor of the *Radiator*. Mrs. Dresham was a lady who had rescued herself from social obscurity by assuming the rôle of her husband's exponent and interpreter; and Dresham's leisure being devoted to the cultivation of remarkable women, his wife's attitude committed her to the public celebration of their remarkableness. For the conceivable tedium of this duty, Mrs. Dresham was repaid by the fact that there were people who took *her* for a remarkable woman; and who in turn probably purchased similar distinction with the small change of her reflected importance. As to the other ladies of the party, they were simply the wives of some of the men—the kind of women who expect to be talked to collectively and to have their questions left unanswered.

Mrs. Armiger, the latest embodiment of Dresham's instinct for the remarkable, was an innocent beauty who for years had distilled dulness among a set of people now self-condemned by their inability to appreciate her. Under Dresham's tutelage she had developed into a "thoughtful woman," who read his leaders in the *Radiator* and bought the works he recommended. When a new book appeared, people wanted to know what Mrs. Armiger thought of it; and a young gentleman who had made a trip in Touraine had recently inscribed to her the wide-margined result of his explorations.

Glennard, leaning back with his head against the rail and a slit of fugitive blue between his half-closed lids, vaguely wished she wouldn't spoil the afternoon by making people talk; though he reduced his annoyance to the minimum by not listening to what was said, there remained a latent irritation against the general futility of words.

His wife's gift of silence seemed to him the most vivid commentary on the clumsiness of speech as a means of intercourse, and his eyes had turned to her in renewed appreciation of this finer faculty when Mrs. Armiger's voice abruptly brought home to him the underrated potentialities of language.

"You've read them, of course, Mrs. Glennard?" he heard her ask; and, in reply to Alexa's vague interrogation—"Why, the *Aubyn Letters*—it's the only book people are talking of this week."

Mrs. Dresham immediately saw her advantage. "You *haven't* read them? How very extraordinary! As Mrs. Armiger says, the book's in the air: one breathes it in like the influenza."

Glennard sat motionless, watching his wife.

"Perhaps it hasn't reached the suburbs yet," she said with her unruffled smile.

"Oh, *do* let me come to you, then!" Mrs. Touchett cried; "anything for a change of air! I'm positively sick of the book and I can't put it down. Can't you sail us beyond its reach, Mr. Flamel?"

Flamel shook his head. "Not even with this breeze. Literature travels faster than steam nowadays. And the worst of it is that we can't any of us give up reading: it's as insidious as a vice and as tiresome as a virtue."

"I believe it *is* a vice, almost, to read such a book as the *Letters*," said Mrs. Touchett. "It's the woman's soul, absolutely torn up by the roots—her whole self laid bare; and to a man who evidently didn't care; who couldn't have cared. I don't mean to read another line: it's too much like listening at a keyhole."

"But if she wanted it published?"

"Wanted it? How do we know she did?"

"Why, I heard she'd left the letters to the man—whoever he is—with directions that they should be published after his death—"

"I don't believe it," Mrs. Touchett declared.

"He's dead then, is he?" one of the men asked.

"Why, you don't suppose if he were alive he could ever hold up his head again, with these letters being read by everybody?" Mrs. Touchett protested. "It must have been horrible enough to know they'd been written to him; but to publish them! No man could have done it and no woman could have told him to—"

"Oh, come, come," Dresham judicially interposed; "after all, they're not love-letters."

"No—that's the worst of it; they're unloved letters," Mrs. Touchett retorted.

"Then, obviously, she needn't have written them; whereas the man, poor devil, could hardly help receiving them."

"Perhaps he counted on the public to save him the trouble of reading them," said young Hartly, who was in the cynical stage.

Mrs. Armiger turned her reproachful loveliness to Dresham. "From the way you defend him I believe you know who he is."

Every one looked at Dresham, and his wife smiled with the superior air of the woman who is in her husband's professional secrets. Dresham shrugged his shoulders.

"What have I said to defend him?"

"You called him a poor devil—you pitied him."

"A man who could let Margaret Aubyn write to him in that way? Of course I pity him."

"Then you *must* know who he is," cried Mrs. Armiger with a triumphant air of penetration.

Hartly and Flamel laughed and Dresham shook his head. "No one knows; not even the publishers; so they tell me at least."

"So they tell you to tell us," Hartly astutely amended; and Mrs. Armiger added, with the appearance of carrying the argument a point farther, "But even if *he's* dead and *she's* dead, somebody must have given the letters to the publishers."

"A little bird, probably," said Dresham, smiling indulgently on her deduction.

"A little bird of prey then—a vulture, I should say—" another man interpolated.

"Oh, I'm not with you there," said Dresham easily. "Those letters belonged to the public."

"How can any letters belong to the public that weren't written to the public?" Mrs. Touchett interposed.

"Well, these were, in a sense. A personality as big as Margaret Aubyn's belongs to the world. Such a mind is part of the general fund of thought. It's the penalty of greatness—one becomes a *monument historique*. Posterity pays the cost of keeping one up, but on condition that one is always open to the public."

"I don't see that that exonerates the man who gives up the keys of the sanctuary, as it were."

"Who *was* he?" another voice inquired.

"Who was he? Oh, nobody, I fancy—the letter-box, the slit in the wall through which the letters passed to posterity. . . ."

"But she never meant them for posterity!"

"A woman shouldn't write such letters if she doesn't mean them to be published. . . ."

"She shouldn't write them to such a man!" Mrs. Touchett scornfully corrected.

"I never keep letters," said Mrs. Armiger, under the obvious impression that she was contributing a valuable point to the discussion.

There was a general laugh, and Flamel, who had not spoken, said lazily, "You women are too incurably subjective. I venture to say that most men would see in those letters merely their immense literary value, their significance as documents. The personal side doesn't count where there's so much else."

"Oh, we all know you haven't any principles," Mrs. Armiger declared; and Alexa Glennard, lifting an indolent smile, said: "I shall never write you a love-letter, Mr. Flamel."

Glennard moved away impatiently. Such talk was as tedious as the buzzing of gnats. He wondered why his wife had wanted to drag him on such a senseless expedition. . . . He hated Flamel's crowd—and what business had Flamel himself to interfere in that way, standing up for the publication of the letters as though Glennard needed his defence? . . .

Glennard turned his head and saw that Flamel had drawn a seat to Alexa's elbow and was speaking to her in a low tone. The other groups had scattered, straying in twos along the deck. It came over Glennard that he should never again be able to see Flamel speaking to his wife without the sense of sick mistrust that now loosened his joints. . . .

Alexa, the next morning, over their early breakfast, surprised her husband by an unexpected request.

"Will you bring me those letters from town?" she asked.

"What letters?" he said, putting down his cup. He felt himself as vulnerable as a man who is lunged at in the dark.

"Mrs. Aubyn's. The book they were all talking about yesterday."

Glennard, carefully measuring his second cup of tea, said with deliberation, "I didn't know you cared about that sort of thing."

She was, in fact, not a great reader, and a new book seldom reached her till it was, so to speak, on the home stretch; but she replied with a gentle tenacity, "I think it would interest me because I read her life last year."

"Her life? Where did you get that?"

"Some one lent it to me when it came out—Mr. Flamel, I think."

His first impulse was to exclaim, "Why the devil do you borrow books of Flamel? I can buy you all you want—" but he felt himself irresistibly forced into an attitude of smiling compliance. "Flamel always has the newest books going, hasn't he? You must be careful, by the way, about returning what he lends you. He's rather crotchety about his library."

"Oh, I'm always very careful," she said, with a touch of competence that struck him; and she added, as he caught up his hat: "Don't forget the letters."

Why had she asked for the book? Was her sudden wish to see it the result of some hint of Flamel's? The thought turned Glennard sick, but he preserved sufficient lucidity to tell himself, a moment later, that his last hope of self-control would be lost if he yielded to the temptation of seeing a hidden purpose in everything she said and did. How much Flamel guessed, he had no means of divining; nor could he predicate, from what he knew of the man, to what use his inferences might be put. The very qualities that had made Flamel a useful adviser made him the most dangerous of accomplices. Glennard felt himself agrope among alien forces that his own act had set in motion. . . .

Alexa was a woman of few requirements; but her wishes, even in trifles, had a definiteness that distinguished them from the fluid impulses of her kind. He knew that, having once asked for the book, she would not forget it; and he put aside, as an ineffectual expedient, his momentary idea of applying for it at the circulating library and telling her that all the copies were out. If the book was to be bought, it had better be bought at once. He left his office earlier than usual and turned in at the first bookshop on his way to the train. The show-window was stacked with conspicuously lettered volumes. *Margaret Aubyn* flashed back at him in endless iteration. He plunged into the shop and came on a counter where the name repeated itself on row after row of bindings. It seemed to have driven the rest of literature to the back shelves. He caught up a copy, tossing the money to an astonished clerk, who pursued him to the door with the unheeded offer to wrap up the volumes.

In the street he was seized with a sudden apprehension. What if he were to meet Flamel? The thought was intolerable. He called a cab and drove straight to the station, where, amid the palm-leaf fans of a perspiring crowd, he waited a long half-hour for his train to start.

He had thrust a volume in either pocket, and in the train he dared not draw them out; but the detested words leaped at him from the folds of the evening paper. The air seemed full of Margaret Aubyn's name; the motion of the train set it dancing up and down on the page of a magazine that a man in front of him was reading. . . .

At the door he was told that Mrs. Glennard was still out, and he went upstairs to his room and dragged the books from his pocket. They lay on the table before him like live things that he feared to touch. . . . At length he opened the first volume. A familiar letter sprang out at him, each word quickened by its glaring garb of type. The little broken phrases fled across the page like wounded animals in the open. . . . It was a horrible sight . . . a *battue* of helpless things driven savagely out of shelter. He had not known it would be like this. . . .

He understood now that, at the moment of selling the letters, he had viewed the transaction solely as it affected himself: as an unfortunate blemish on an otherwise presentable record. He had scarcely considered the act in relation to Margaret Aubyn; for death, if it hallows, also makes innocuous. Glennard's God was a god of the living, of the immediate, the actual, the tangible; all his days he had lived in the presence of that god, heedless of the divinities who, below the surface of our deeds and passions, silently forge the fatal weapons of the dead.

VII

A knock roused him, and looking up he saw his wife. He met her glance in silence, and she faltered out, "Are you ill?"

The words restored his self-possession. "Ill? Of course not. They told me you were out and I came upstairs."

The books lay between them on the table; he wondered when she would see them. She lingered tentatively on the threshold, with the air of leaving his explanation on his hands. She was not the kind of woman who could be counted on to fortify an excuse by appearing to dispute it.

"Where have you been?" Glennard asked, moving forward so that he obstructed her vision of the books.

"I walked over to the Dreshams' for tea."

"I can't think what you see in those people," he said with a shrug; adding, uncontrollably—"I suppose Flamel was there?"

"No; he left on the yacht this morning."

An answer so obstructing to the natural escape of his irritation left Glennard with no momentary resource but that of strolling impatiently to the window. As her eyes followed him they lit on the books.

"Ah, you've brought them! I'm so glad," she said.

He answered over his shoulder, "For a woman who never reads you make the most astounding exceptions!"

Her smile was an exasperating concession to the probability that it had been hot in town or that something had bothered him.

"Do you mean it's not nice to want to read the book?" she asked. "It was not nice to publish it, certainly; but after all, I'm not responsible for that, am I?" She paused, and, as he made no answer, went on, still smiling, "I do read sometimes, you know; and I'm very fond of Margaret Aubyn's books. I was reading *Pomegranate Seed* when we first met. Don't you remember? It was then you told me all about her."

Glennard had turned back into the room and stood staring at his wife. "All about her?" he repeated, and with the words remembrance came to him. He had found Miss Trent one afternoon with the novel in her hand, and moved by the lover's fatuous impulse to associate himself in some way with whatever fills the mind of the beloved, had broken through his habitual silence about the past. Rewarded by the consciousness of figuring impressively in Miss Trent's imagination, he had gone on from one anecdote to another, reviving dormant details of his old Hillbridge life, and pasturing his vanity on the eagerness with which she listened to his reminiscences of a being already clothed in the impersonality of greatness.

The incident had left no trace in his mind; but it sprang up now like an old enemy, the more dangerous for having been forgotten. The instinct of self-preservation—sometimes the most perilous that man can exercise—made him awkwardly declare: "Oh, I used to see her at people's houses, that was all;" and her silence as usual leaving room for a multiplication of blunders, he added, with increased indifference, "I simply can't see what you can find to interest you in such a book."

She seemed to consider this intently. "You've read it, then?"

"I glanced at it—I never read such things."

"Is it true that she didn't wish the letters to be published?"

Glennard felt the sudden dizziness of the mountaineer on a narrow ledge, and with it the sense that he was lost if he looked more than a step ahead.

"I'm sure I don't know," he said; then, summoning a smile, he passed his hand through her arm. "*I* didn't have tea at the Dreshams', you know; won't you give me some now?" he suggested.

That evening Glennard, under pretext of work to be done, shut himself into the small study opening off the drawing-room. As he gathered up his papers he said to his wife: "You're not going to sit indoors on such a night as this? I'll join you presently outside."

But she had drawn her arm-chair to the lamp. "I want to look at my book," she said, taking up the first volume of the *Letters*.

Glennard, with a shrug, withdrew into the study. "I'm going to shut the door; I want to be quiet," he explained from the threshold; and she nodded without lifting her eyes from the book.

He sank into a chair, staring aimlessly at the outspread papers. How was he to work, while on the other side of the door she sat with that volume in her hand? The door did not shut her out—he saw her distinctly, felt her close to him in a contact as painful as the pressure on a bruise.

The sensation was part of the general strangeness that made him feel like a man waking from a long sleep to find himself in an unknown country among people of alien tongue. We live in our own souls as in an unmapped region, a few acres of which we have cleared for our habitation; while of the nature of those nearest us we know but the boundaries that march with ours. Of the points in his wife's character not in direct contact with his own, Glennard now discerned his ignorance; and the baffling sense of her remoteness was intensified by the discovery that, in one way, she was closer to him than ever before. As one may live for years in happy unconsciousness of the possession of a sensitive nerve, he had lived beside his wife unaware that her individuality had become a part of the texture of his life, ineradicable as some growth on a vital organ; and he now felt himself at once incapable of forecasting her judgment and powerless to evade its effects.

To escape, the next morning, the confidences of the breakfast-table, he went to town earlier than usual. His wife, who read slowly, was given to talking over what she read, and at present his first object in life was to postpone the inevitable discussion of the letters. This instinct of protection, in the afternoon, on his way up town, guided him to the club in search of a man who might be persuaded to come out to the country to dine. The only man in the club was Flamel.

Glennard, as he heard himself almost involuntarily pressing Flamel to come and dine, felt the full irony of the situation. To use Flamel as a shield against his wife's scrutiny was only a shade less humiliating than to reckon on his wife as a defence against Flamel.

He felt a contradictory movement of annoyance at the latter's ready acceptance, and the two men drove in silence to the station. As they passed the book-stall in the waiting-room Flamel lingered a moment, and the eyes of both fell on Margaret Aubyn's name, conspicuously displayed above a counter stacked with the familiar volumes.

"We shall be late, you know," Glennard remonstrated, pulling out his watch.

"Go ahead," said Flamel imperturbably. "I want to get something—"

Glennard turned on his heel and walked down the platform. Flamel rejoined him with an innocent-looking magazine in his hand; but Glennard dared not even glance at the cover, lest it should show the syllables he feared.

The train was full of people they knew, and they were kept apart till it dropped them at the little suburban station. As they strolled up the shaded hill, Glennard talked volubly, pointing out the improvements in the neighborhood, deploring the threatened approach of an electric railway, and screening himself by a series of reflex adjustments from the risk of any allusion to the *Letters*. Flamel suffered his discourse with the bland inattention that we accord to the affairs of some one else's suburb, and they reached the shelter of Alexa's tea-table without a perceptible turn toward the dreaded topic.

The dinner passed off safely. Flamel, always at his best in Alexa's presence, gave her the kind of attention which is like a becoming light thrown on the speaker's words: his answers seemed to bring out a latent significance in her phrases, as the sculptor draws his statue from the block. Glennard, under his wife's composure, detected a sensibility to this manœuvre, and the discovery was like the lightning-flash across a nocturnal landscape. Thus far these momentary illuminations had served only to reveal the strangeness of the intervening country: each fresh observation seemed to increase the sum-total of his ignorance. Her simplicity of outline was more puzzling than a complex surface. One may conceivably work one's way through a labyrinth; but Alexa's candor was like a snow-covered plain, where, the road once lost, there are no landmarks to travel by.

Dinner over, they returned to the veranda, where a moon, rising behind the old elm, was combining with that complaisant tree a romantic enlargement of their borders. Glennard had forgotten the cigars. He went to his study to fetch them, and in passing through the drawing-room he saw the second volume of the *Letters* lying open on his wife's table. He picked up the book and looked at the date of the letter she had been reading. It was one of the last . . . he knew the few lines by heart. He dropped the book and leaned against the wall. Why had he included that one among the others? Or was it possible that now they would all seem like that . . . ?

Alexa's voice came suddenly out of the dusk. "May Touchett was right—it *is* like listening at a keyhole. I wish I hadn't read it!"

Flamel returned, in the leisurely tone of the man whose phrases are punctuated by a cigarette, "It seems so to us, perhaps; but to another generation the book will be a classic."

"Then it ought not to have been published till it had time to become a classic. It's horrible, it's degrading almost, to read the secrets of a woman one might have known." She added, in a lower tone, "Stephen *did* know her—"

"Did he?" came from Flamel.

"He knew her very well, at Hillbridge, years ago. The book has made him feel dreadfully . . . he wouldn't read it . . . he didn't want me to read it. I didn't understand at first, but now I can see how horribly disloyal it must seem to him. It's so much worse to surprise a friend's secrets than a stranger's."

"Oh, Glennard's such a sensitive chap," Flamel said easily; and Alexa almost rebukingly rejoined, "If you'd known her I'm sure you'd feel as he does. . . ."

Glennard stood motionless, overcome by the singular infelicity with which he had contrived to put Flamel in possession of the two points most damaging to his case: the fact that he had been a friend of Margaret Aubyn's and that he had concealed from Alexa his share in the publication of the letters. To a man of less than Flamel's astuteness it must now be clear to whom the letters were addressed; and the possibility once suggested, nothing could be easier than to confirm it by discreet research. An impulse of self-accusal drove Glennard to the window. Why not anticipate betrayal by telling his wife the truth in Flamel's presence? If the man had a drop of decent feeling in him, such a course would be the surest means of securing his silence; and above all, it would rid Glennard of the necessity of defending himself against the perpetual criticism of his wife's belief in him. . . .

The impulse was strong enough to carry him to the window; but there a reaction of defiance set in. What had he done, after all, to need defence and explanation? Both Dresham and Flamel had, in his hearing, declared the publication of the letters to be not only justifiable but obligatory; and if the disinterestedness of Flamel's verdict might be questioned, Dresham's at least represented the impartial view of the man of letters. As to Alexa's words, they were simply the conventional utterance of the "nice" woman on a question already decided for her by other "nice" women. She had said the proper thing as mechanically as she would have put on the appropriate gown or written the correct form of dinner invitation. Glennard had small faith in the abstract judgments of the other sex: he knew that half the women who were horrified by the publication of Mrs. Aubyn's letters would have betrayed her secrets without a scruple.

The sudden lowering of his emotional pitch brought a proportionate relief. He told himself that now the worst was over and things would fall into perspective again. His wife and Flamel had turned to other topics, and coming out on the veranda, he handed the cigars to Flamel, saying cheerfully— and yet he could have sworn they were the last words he meant to utter!—"Look here, old man, before you go down to Newport you must come out and spend a few days with us—mustn't he, Alexa?"

VIII

Glennard, perhaps unconsciously, had counted on the continuance of this easier mood. He had always taken pride in a certain robustness of fibre that enabled him to harden himself against the inevitable, to convert his failures into the building materials of success. Though it did not even now occur to him that what he called the inevitable had hitherto been the alternative he happened to prefer, he was yet obscurely aware that his present difficulty was one not to be conjured by any affectation of indifference. Some griefs build the soul a spacious house, but in this misery of Glennard's he could not stand upright. It pressed against him at every turn. He told himself that this was because there was no escape from the visible evidences of his act. The *Letters* confronted him everywhere. People who had never opened a book discussed them with critical reservations; to have read them had become a social obligation in circles to which literature never penetrates except in a personal guise.

Glennard did himself injustice. It was from the unexpected discovery of his own pettiness that he chiefly suffered. Our self-esteem is apt to be based on the hypothetical great act we have never had occasion to perform; and even the most self-scrutinizing modesty credits itself negatively with a high standard of conduct. Glennard had never thought himself a hero; but he had been certain that he was incapable of baseness. We all like our wrongdoings to have a becoming cut, to be made to order, as it were; and Glennard found himself suddenly thrust into a garb of dishonor surely meant for a meaner figure.

The immediate result of his first weeks of wretchedness was the resolve to go to town for the winter. He knew that such a course was just beyond the limit of prudence; but it was easy to allay the fears of Alexa, who, scrupulously vigilant in the management of the household, preserved the American wife's usual aloofness from her husband's business cares. Glennard felt that he could not trust himself to a winter's solitude with her. He had an unspeakable dread of her learning the truth about the letters, yet could not be sure of steeling himself against the suicidal impulse of avowal. His very soul was parched for sympathy; he thirsted for a voice of pity and comprehension. But would his wife pity? Would she understand? Again he found himself brought up abruptly against his incredible ignorance of her nature. The fact that he knew well enough how she would behave in the ordinary emergencies of life, that he could count, in such contingencies, on the kind of high courage and directness he had always divined in her, made him the more hopeless of her entering into the tortuous psychology of an act that he himself could no longer explain or understand. It would have been easier had she been more complex, more feminine—if he could have counted on her imaginative sympathy or her moral obtuseness—but he was sure of neither. He was sure of nothing but that, for a time, he must avoid her. Glennard could not rid himself of the delusion that by and by his action would cease to make its consequences felt. He would not have cared to own to himself that he counted on the dulling of his sensibilities: he preferred to indulge the vague hypothesis that extraneous circumstances would somehow efface the blot upon his conscience. In his worst moments of self-abasement he tried to find solace in the thought that Flamel had sanctioned his course. Flamel, at the outset, must have guessed to whom the letters were addressed; yet neither then nor afterward had he hesitated to advise their publication. This thought drew Glennard to him in fitful impulses of friendliness, from each of which there was a sharper reaction of distrust and aversion. When Flamel was not at the house, he missed the support of his tacit connivance; when he was there, his presence seemed the assertion of an intolerable claim.

Early in the winter the Glennards took possession of the little house that was to cost them almost nothing. The change brought Glennard the relief of seeing less of his wife, and of being protected, in her presence, by the multiplied preoccupations of town life. Alexa, who could never appear hurried, showed the smiling abstraction of a pretty woman to whom the social side of married life has not lost its novelty. Glennard, with the recklessness of a man fresh from his first financial imprudence, encouraged her in such little extravagances as her good sense at first resisted. Since they had come to town, he argued, they might as well enjoy themselves. He took a sympathetic view of the necessity of new gowns, he gave her a set of furs at Christmas, and before the New Year they had agreed on the necessity of adding a parlor-maid to their small establishment.

Providence the very next day hastened to justify this measure by placing on Glennard's breakfast-plate an envelope bearing the name of the publishers to whom he had sold Mrs. Aubyn's letters. It happened to be the only letter the early post had brought, and he glanced across the table at his wife, who had come down before him and had probably laid the envelope on his plate. She was not the woman to ask awkward questions, but he felt the conjecture of her glance, and he was debating whether to affect surprise at the receipt of the letter, or to pass it off as a business communication that had strayed to his house, when a check fell from the envelope. It was the royalty on the first edition of the letters. His first feeling was one of simple satisfaction. The money had come with such infernal opportuneness that he could not help welcoming it. Before long, too, there would be more; he knew the book was still selling far beyond the publishers' previsions. He put the check in his pocket and left the room without looking at his wife.

On the way to his office the habitual reaction set in. The money he had received was the first tangible reminder that he was living on the sale of his self-esteem. The thought of material benefit had been overshadowed by his sense of the intrinsic baseness of making the letters known: now he saw what an element of sordidness it added to the situation and how the fact that he needed the money, and must use it, pledged him more irrevocably than ever to the consequences of his act. It seemed to him, in that first hour of misery, that he had betrayed his friend anew.

When, that afternoon, he reached home earlier than usual, Alexa's drawing-room was full of a gayety that overflowed to the stairs. Flamel, for a wonder, was not there; but Dresham and young Hartly, grouped about the tea-table, were receiving with resonant mirth a narrative delivered in the fluttered staccato that made Mrs. Armiger's conversation like the ejaculations of a startled aviary.

She paused as Glennard entered, and he had time to notice that his wife, who was busied about the tea-tray, had not joined in the laughter of the men.

"Oh, go on, go on," young Hartly rapturously groaned; and Mrs. Armiger met Glennard's inquiry with the deprecating cry that really she didn't see what there was to laugh at. "I'm sure I feel more like crying. I don't know what I should have done if Alexa hadn't been at home to give me a cup of tea. My nerves are in shreds—yes, another, dear, please—" and as Glennard looked his perplexity, she went on, after pondering on the selection of a second lump of sugar, "Why, I've just come from the reading, you know—the reading at the Waldorf."

"I haven't been in town long enough to know anything," said Glennard, taking the cup his wife handed him. "Who has been reading what?"

"That lovely girl from the South—Georgie—Georgie What's-her-name—Mrs. Dresham's protégée—unless she's *yours*, Mr. Dresham! Why, the big ball-room was *packed*, and all the women were crying like idiots—it was the most harrowing thing I ever heard—"

"What *did* you hear?" Glennard asked; and his wife interposed: "Won't you have another bit of cake, Julia? Or, Stephen, ring for some hot toast, please." Her tone betrayed a polite weariness of the topic under discussion. Glennard turned to the bell, but Mrs. Armiger pursued him with her lovely amazement.

"Why, the *Aubyn Letters*—didn't you know about it? She read them so beautifully that it was quite horrible—I should have fainted if there'd been a man near enough to carry me out."

Hartly's glee redoubled, and Dresham said jovially, "How like you women to raise a shriek over the book and then do all you can to encourage the blatant publicity of the readings!"

Mrs. Armiger met him more than half-way on a torrent of self-accusal. "It *was* horrid; it was disgraceful. I told your wife we ought all to be ashamed of ourselves for going, and I think Alexa was quite right to refuse to take any tickets—even if it was for a charity."

"Oh," her hostess murmured indifferently, "with me charity begins at home. I can't afford emotional luxuries."

"A charity? A charity?" Hartly exulted. "I hadn't seized the full beauty of it. Reading poor Margaret Aubyn's love-letters at the Waldorf before five hundred people for a charity! *What* charity, dear Mrs. Armiger?"

"Why, the Home for Friendless Women—"

"It was well chosen," Dresham commented; and Hartly buried his mirth in the sofa cushions.

When they were alone Glennard, still holding his untouched cup of tea, turned to his wife, who sat silently behind the kettle. "Who asked you to take a ticket for that reading?"

"I don't know, really—Kate Dresham, I fancy. It was she who got it up."

"It's just the sort of damnable vulgarity she's capable of! It's loathsome—it's monstrous—"

His wife, without looking up, answered gravely, "I thought so too. It was for that reason I didn't go. But you must remember that very few people feel about Mrs. Aubyn as you do—"

Glennard managed to set down his cup with a steady hand, but the room swung round with him and he dropped into the nearest chair. "As I do?" he repeated.

"I mean that very few people knew her when she lived in New York. To most of the women who went to the reading she was a mere name, too remote to have any personality. With me, of course, it was different—"

Glennard gave her a startled look. "Different? Why different?"

"Since you were her friend—"

"Her friend!" He stood up. "You speak as if she had had only one—the most famous woman of her day!" He moved vaguely about the room, bending down to look at some books on the table. "I hope," he added, "you didn't give that as a reason?"

"A reason?"

"For not going. A woman who gives reasons for getting out of social obligations is sure to make herself unpopular or ridiculous."

The words were uncalculated; but in an instant he saw that they had strangely bridged the distance between his wife and himself. He felt her close on him, like a panting foe; and her answer was a flash that showed the hand on the trigger.

"I seem," she said from the threshold, "to have done both in giving my reason to you."

The fact that they were dining out that evening made it easy for him to avoid Alexa till she came downstairs in her opera-cloak. Mrs. Touchett, who was going to the same dinner, had offered to call for her; and Glennard, refusing a precarious seat between the ladies' draperies, followed on foot. The evening was interminable. The reading at the Waldorf, at which all the women had been present, had revived the discussion of the *Aubyn Letters*, and Glennard, hearing his wife questioned as to her absence, felt himself miserably wishing that she had gone, rather than that her staying away should have been remarked. He was rapidly losing all sense of proportion where the *Letters* were concerned. He could no longer hear them mentioned without suspecting a purpose in the allusion; he even yielded himself for a moment to the extravagance of imagining that Mrs. Dresham, whom he disliked, had organized the reading in the hope of making him betray himself—for he was already sure that Dresham had divined his share in the transaction.

The attempt to keep a smooth surface on this inner tumult was as endless and unavailing as efforts made in a nightmare. He lost all sense of what he was saying to his neighbors; and once when he looked up his wife's glance struck him cold.

She sat nearly opposite him, at Flamel's side, and it appeared to Glennard that they had built about themselves one of those airy barriers of talk behind which two people can say what they please. While the reading was discussed they were silent. Their silence seemed to Glennard almost cynical—it stripped the last disguise from their complicity. A throb of anger rose in him, but suddenly it fell, and he felt, with a curious sense of relief, that at bottom he no longer cared whether Flamel had told his wife or not. The assumption that Flamel knew about the letters had become a fact to Glennard; and it now seemed to him better that Alexa should know too.

He was frightened at first by the discovery of his own indifference. The last barriers of his will seemed to be breaking down before a flood of moral lassitude. How could he continue to play his part, how keep his front to the enemy, with this poison of indifference stealing through his veins? He tried to brace himself with the remembrance of his wife's scorn. He had not forgotten the note on which their conversation had closed. If he had ever wondered how she would receive the truth he wondered no longer—she would despise him. But this lent a new insidiousness to his temptation, since her contempt would be a refuge from his own. He said to himself that, since he no longer cared for the consequences, he could at least acquit himself of speaking in self-defence. What he wanted now was not immunity but castigation: his wife's indignation might still reconcile him to himself. Therein lay his one hope of regeneration; her scorn was the moral antiseptic that he needed, her comprehension the one balm that could heal him. . . .

When they left the dinner he was so afraid of speaking that he let her drive home alone, and went to the club with Flamel.

IX

He rose next morning with the resolve to know what Alexa thought of him. It was not anchoring in a haven but lying to in a storm—he felt the need of a temporary lull in the turmoil of his sensations.

He came home late, for they were dining alone and he knew that they would have the evening together. When he followed her to the drawing-room after dinner he thought himself on the point of speaking; but as she handed him his coffee he said involuntarily: "I shall have to carry this off to the study; I've got a lot of work to-night."

Alone in the study he cursed his cowardice. What was it that had withheld him? A certain bright unapproachableness seemed to keep him at arm's length. She was not the kind of woman whose compassion could be circumvented; there was no chance of slipping past the outposts—he would never take her by surprise. Well—why not face her, then? What he shrank from could be no worse than what he was enduring. He had pushed back his chair and turned to go upstairs when a new expedient presented itself. What if, instead of telling her, he were to let her find out for herself and watch the effect of the discovery before speaking? In this way he made over to chance the burden of the revelation.

The idea had been suggested by the sight of the formula enclosing the publisher's check. He had deposited the money, but the notice accompanying it dropped from his note-case as he cleared his table for work. It was the formula usual in such cases, and revealed clearly enough that he was the recipient of a royalty on Margaret Aubyn's letters. It would be impossible for Alexa to read it without understanding at once that the letters had been written to him and that he had sold them. . . .

He sat downstairs till he heard her ring for the parlor-maid to put out the lights; then he went up to the drawing-room with a bundle of papers in his hand. Alexa was just rising from her seat, and the lamplight fell on the deep roll of hair that overhung her brow like the eaves of a temple. Her face had often the high secluded look of a shrine; and it was this touch of awe in her beauty that now made him feel himself on the brink of sacrilege.

Lest the feeling should control him, he spoke at once. "I've brought you a piece of work—a lot of old bills and things that I want you to sort for me. Some are not worth keeping—but you'll be able to judge of that. There may be a letter or two among them—nothing of much account; but I don't like to throw away the whole lot without having them looked over, and I haven't time to do it myself."

He held out the papers, and she took them with a smile that seemed to recognize in the service he asked the tacit intention of making amends for the incident of the previous day.

"Are you sure I shall know which to keep?"

"Oh, quite sure," he answered easily; "and besides, none are of much importance."

The next morning he invented an excuse for leaving the house without seeing her, and when he returned, just before dinner, he found a visitor's hat and stick in the hall. The visitor was Flamel, who was just taking leave.

He had risen, but Alexa remained seated; and their attitude gave the impression of a colloquy that had prolonged itself beyond the limits of speech. Both turned a surprised eye on Glennard, and he had the sense of walking into a room grown suddenly empty, as though their thoughts were conspirators dispersed by his approach. He felt the clutch of his old fear. What if his wife had already sorted the papers and had told Flamel of her discovery? Well, it was no news to Flamel that Glennard was in receipt of a royalty on the *Aubyn Letters*. . .

A sudden resolve to know the worst made him lift his eyes to his wife as the door closed on Flamel. But Alexa had risen also, and bending over her writing-table, with her back to Glennard, was beginning to speak precipitately.

"I'm dining out to-night—you don't mind my deserting you? Julia Armiger sent me word just now that she had an extra ticket for the last Ambrose concert. She told me to say how sorry she was that she hadn't two, but I knew *you* wouldn't be sorry!" She ended with a laugh that had the effect of being a strayed echo of Mrs. Armiger's; and before Glennard could speak she had added, with her hand on the door, "Mr. Flamel stayed so late that I've hardly time to dress. The concert begins ridiculously early, and Julia dines at half-past seven."

Glennard stood alone in the empty room that seemed somehow full of an ironical consciousness of what was happening. "She hates me," he murmured. "She hates me . . ."

The next day was Sunday, and Glennard purposely lingered late in his room. When he came downstairs his wife was already seated at the breakfast-table. She lifted her usual smile to his entrance and they took shelter in the nearest topic, like wayfarers overtaken by a storm. While he listened to her account of the concert he began to think that, after all, she had not yet sorted the papers, and that her agitation of the previous day must be ascribed to another cause, in which perhaps he had but an indirect concern. He wondered it had never before occurred to him that Flamel was the kind of man who might very well please a woman at his own expense, without need of fortuitous assistance. If this possibility cleared the outlook it did not brighten it. Glennard merely felt himself left alone with his baseness.

Alexa left the breakfast-table before him, and when he went up to the drawing-room he found her dressed to go out.

"Aren't you a little early for church?" he asked.

She replied that, on the way there, she meant to stop a moment at her mother's; and while she drew on her gloves he fumbled among the knick-knacks on the mantelpiece for a match to light his cigarette.

"Well, good-bye," she said, turning to go; and from the threshold she added: "By the way, I've sorted the papers you gave me. Those that I thought you would like to keep are on your study table." She went downstairs and he heard the door close behind her.

She had sorted the papers—she knew, then—she *must* know—and she had made no sign!

Glennard, he hardly knew how, found himself once more in the study. On the table lay the packet he had given her. It was much smaller—she had evidently gone over the papers with care, destroying the greater number. He loosened the elastic band and spread the remaining envelopes on his desk. The publisher's notice was among them.

X

His wife knew and she made no sign. Glennard found himself in the case of the seafarer who, closing his eyes at nightfall on a scene he thinks to put leagues behind him before day, wakes to a port-hole framing the same patch of shore. From the kind of exaltation to which his resolve had lifted him he dropped to an unreasoning apathy. His impulse of confession had acted as a drug to self-reproach. He had tried to shift a portion of his burden to his wife's shoulders; and now that she had tacitly refused to carry it, he felt the load too heavy to be taken up.

A fortunate interval of hard work brought respite from this phase of sterile misery. He went West to argue an important case, won it, and came back to fresh preoccupations. His own affairs were thriving enough to engross him in the pauses of his professional work, and for over two months he had little time to look himself in the face. Not unnaturally—for he was as yet unskilled in the subtleties of introspection—he mistook his temporary insensibility for a gradual revival of moral health.

He told himself that he was recovering his sense of proportion, getting to see things in their true light; and if he now thought of his rash appeal to his wife's sympathy it was as an act of folly from the consequences of which he had been saved by the providence that watches over madmen. He had little leisure to observe Alexa; but he concluded that the common sense momentarily denied him had counselled her silent acceptance of the inevitable. If such a quality was a poor substitute for the passionate justness that had once seemed to distinguish her, he accepted the alternative as a part of that general lowering of the key that seems needful to the maintenance of the matrimonial duet. What woman ever retained her abstract sense of justice where another woman was concerned? Possibly the thought that he had profited by Mrs. Aubyn's tenderness was not wholly disagreeable to his wife.

When the pressure of work began to lessen, and he found himself, in the lengthening afternoons, able to reach home somewhat earlier, he noticed that the little drawing-room was always full and that he and his wife seldom had an evening alone together. When he was tired, as often happened, she went out alone; the idea of giving up an engagement to remain with him seemed not to occur to her. She had shown, as a girl, little fondness for society, nor had she seemed to regret it during the year they had spent in the country. He reflected, however, that he was sharing the common lot of husbands, who proverbially mistake the early ardors of housekeeping for a sign of settled domesticity. Alexa, at any rate, was refuting his theory as inconsiderately as a seedling defeats the gardener's expectations. An indefinable change had come over her. In one sense it was a happy one, since she had grown, if not handsomer, at least more vivid and expressive; her beauty had become more communicable: it was as though she had learned the conscious exercise of intuitive attributes and now used her effects with the discrimination of an artist skilled in values. To a dispassionate critic (as Glennard now rated himself) the art may at times have been a little too obvious. Her attempts at lightness lacked spontaneity, and she sometimes rasped him by laughing like Julia Armiger; but he had enough imagination to perceive that, in respect of his wife's social arts, a husband necessarily sees the wrong side of the tapestry.

In this ironical estimate of their relation Glennard found himself strangely relieved of all concern as to his wife's feelings for Flamel. From an Olympian pinnacle of indifference he calmly surveyed their inoffensive antics. It was surprising how his cheapening of his wife put him at ease with himself. Far as he and she were from each other they yet had, in a sense, the tacit nearness of complicity. Yes, they were accomplices; he could no more be jealous of her than she could despise him. The jealousy that would once have seemed a blur on her whiteness now appeared like a tribute to ideals in which he no longer believed.

Glennard was little given to exploring the outskirts of literature. He always skipped the "literary notices" in the papers, and he had small leisure for the intermittent pleasures of the periodical. He had therefore no notion of the prolonged re-verberations which the *Aubyn Letters* had awakened. When the book ceased to be talked about he supposed it had ceased to be read; and this apparent subsidence of the agitation about it brought the reassuring sense that he had exaggerated its vitality. The conviction, if it did not ease his conscience, at least offered him the relative relief of obscurity; he felt like an offender taken down from the pillory and thrust into the soothing darkness of a cell.

But one evening, when Alexa had left him to go to a dance, he chanced to turn over the magazines on her table, and the copy of the *Horoscope* to which he settled down with his cigar confronted him, on its first page, with a portrait of Margaret Aubyn. It was a reproduction of the photograph that had stood so long on his desk. The desiccating air of memory had turned her into the mere abstraction of a woman, and this un-expected evocation seemed to bring her nearer than she had ever been in life. Was it because he understood her better? He looked long into her eyes; little personal traits reached out to him like caresses—the tired droop of her lids, her quick way of leaning forward as she spoke, the movements of her long expressive hands. All that was feminine in her, the quality he had always missed, stole toward him from her unreproachful gaze; and now that it was too late, life had developed in him the subtler perceptions which could detect it in even this poor semblance of herself. For a moment he found consolation in the thought that, at any cost, they had thus been brought to-gether; then a sense of shame rushed over him. Face to face with her, he felt himself laid bare to the inmost fold of con-sciousness. The shame was deep, but it was a renovating an-guish: he was like a man whom intolerable pain has roused from the creeping lethargy of death. . .

He rose next morning to as fresh a sense of life as though his hour of communion with Margaret Aubyn had been a more exquisite renewal of their earlier meetings. His waking thought was that he must see her again; and as consciousness affirmed itself he felt an intense fear of losing the sense of her nearness. But she was still close to him: her presence re-mained the one reality in a world of shadows. All through his working hours he was re-living with incredible minuteness every incident of their obliterated past: as a man who has mastered the spirit of a foreign tongue turns with renewed wonder to the pages his youth has plodded over. In this lucidity of retrospection the most trivial detail had its meaning, and the joy of recovery was embittered to Glennard by the perception of all that he had missed. He had been pitiably, grotesquely stupid; and there was irony in the thought that, but for the crisis through which he was passing, he might have lived on in complacent ignorance of his loss. It was as though she had bought him with her blood. . .

That evening he and Alexa dined alone. After dinner he followed her to the drawing-room. He no longer felt the need of avoiding her; he was hardly conscious of her presence. After a few words they lapsed into silence, and he sat smoking with his eyes on the fire. It was not that he was unwilling to talk to her; he felt a curious desire to be as kind as possible; but he was always forgetting that she was there. Her full bright presence, through which the currents of life flowed so warmly, had grown as tenuous as a shadow, and he saw so far beyond her.

Presently she rose and began to move about the room. She seemed to be looking for something, and he roused himself to ask what she wanted.

"Only the last number of the *Horoscope*. I thought I'd left it on this table." He said nothing, and she went on: "You haven't seen it?"

"No," he returned coldly. The magazine was locked in his desk.

His wife had moved to the mantelpiece. She stood facing him, and as he looked up he met her tentative gaze. "I was reading an article in it—a review of Mrs. Aubyn's *Letters*," she added slowly, with her deep deliberate blush.

Glennard stooped to toss his cigar into the fire. He felt a savage wish that she would not speak the other woman's name; nothing else seemed to matter.

"You seem to do a lot of reading," he said.

She still confronted him. "I was keeping this for you—I thought it might interest you," she said with an air of gentle insistence.

He stood up and turned away. He was sure she knew that he had taken the review, and he felt that he was beginning to hate her again.

"I haven't time for such things," he said indifferently. As he moved to the door he heard her take a hurried step forward; then she paused, and sank without speaking into the chair from which he had risen.

XI

As Glennard, in the raw February sunlight, mounted the road to the cemetery, he felt the beatitude that comes with an abrupt cessation of physical pain. He had reached the point where self-analysis ceases; the impulse that moved him was purely intuitive. He did not even seek a reason for it, beyond the obvious one that his desire to stand by Margaret Aubyn's grave was prompted by no attempt at a sentimental reparation, but rather by the need to affirm in some way the reality of the tie between them.

The ironical promiscuity of death had brought Mrs. Aubyn back to share the hospitality of her husband's last lodging; but though Glennard knew she had been buried near New York he had never visited her grave. He was oppressed, as he now threaded the long avenues, by a chilling vision of her return. There was no family to follow her hearse; she had died alone, as she had lived; and the "distinguished mourners" who had formed the escort of the famous writer knew nothing of the woman they were committing to the grave. Glennard could not even remember at what season she had been buried; but his mood indulged the fancy that it must have been on some such day of harsh sunlight, the incisive February brightness that gives perspicuity without warmth. The white avenues stretched before him interminably, lined with stereotyped emblems of affliction, as though all the platitudes ever uttered had been turned to marble and set up over the unresisting dead. Here and there, no doubt, a frigid urn or an insipid angel imprisoned some fine-fibred grief, as the most hackneyed words may become the vehicle of rare meanings; but for the most part the endless alignment of monuments seemed to embody those easy generalizations about death that do not disturb the repose of the living. Glennard's eye, as he followed the way pointed out to him, had instinctively sought some low mound with a quiet headstone. He had forgotten that the dead seldom plan their own houses, and with a pang he discovered the name he sought on the cyclopean base of a shaft rearing its aggressive height at the angle of two avenues.

"How she would have hated it!" he murmured.

A bench stood near and he seated himself. The monument rose before him like some pretentious uninhabited dwelling: he could not believe that Margaret Aubyn lay there. It was a Sunday morning, and black figures moved among the paths, placing flowers on the frost-bound hillocks. Glennard noticed that the neighboring graves had been thus newly dressed, and he fancied a blind stir of expectancy through the sod, as though the bare mounds spread a parched surface to that commemorative rain. He rose presently and walked back to the entrance of the cemetery. Several greenhouses stood near the gates, and turning in at the first he asked for some flowers.

"Anything in the emblematic line?" asked the anæmic man behind the dripping counter.

Glennard shook his head.

"Just cut flowers? This way then." The florist unlocked a glass door and led him down a moist green aisle. The hot air was choked with the scent of white azaleas, white lilies, white lilacs; all the flowers were white: they were like a prolongation, a mystic efflorescence, of the long rows of marble tombstones, and their perfume seemed to cover an odor of decay. The rich atmosphere made Glennard dizzy. As he leaned in the doorway, waiting for the flowers, he had a penetrating sense of Margaret Aubyn's nearness—not the imponderable presence of his inner vision, but a life that beat warm in his arms. . .

The sharp air caught him as he stepped out into it again. He walked back and scattered the flowers over the grave. The edges of the white petals shrivelled like burnt paper in the cold; and as he watched them the illusion of her nearness faded, shrank back frozen.

XII

The motive of his visit to the cemetery remained undefined save as a final effort of escape from his wife's inexpressive acceptance of his shame. It seemed to him that as long as he could keep himself alive to that shame he would not wholly have succumbed to its consequences. His chief fear was that he should become the creature of his act. His wife's indifference degraded him: it seemed to put him on a level with his dishonor. Margaret Aubyn would have abhorred the deed in proportion to her pity for the man. The sense of her potential pity drew him back to her. The one woman knew but did not understand; the other, it sometimes seemed, understood without knowing.

In its last disguise of retrospective remorse, his self-pity affected a desire for solitude and meditation. He lost himself in morbid musings, in futile visions of what life with Margaret Aubyn might have been. There were moments when, in the strange dislocation of his view, the wrong he had done her seemed a tie between them.

To indulge these emotions he fell into the habit, on Sunday afternoons, of solitary walks prolonged till after dusk. The days were lengthening, there was a touch of spring in the air, and his wanderings now usually led him to the Park and its outlying regions.

One Sunday, tired of aimless locomotion, he took a cab at the Park gates and let it carry him out to the Riverside Drive. It was a gray afternoon streaked with east wind. Glennard's cab advanced slowly, and as he leaned back, gazing with absent intentness at the deserted paths that wound under bare boughs between grass banks of premature vividness, his attention was arrested by two figures walking ahead of him. This couple, who had the path to themselves, moved at an uneven pace, as though adapting their gait to a conversation marked by meditative intervals. Now and then they paused, and in one of these pauses the lady, turning toward her companion, showed Glennard the outline of his wife's profile. The man was Flamel.

The blood rushed to Glennard's forehead. He sat up with a jerk and pushed back the lid in the roof of the hansom; but when the cabman bent down he dropped into his seat without speaking. Then, becoming conscious of the prolonged interrogation of the lifted lid, he called out—"Turn—drive back —anywhere—I'm in a hurry—"

As the cab swung round he caught a last glimpse of the two figures. They had not moved; Alexa, with bent head, stood listening.

"My God, my God—" he groaned.

It was hideous—it was abominable—he could not understand it. The woman was nothing to him—less than nothing —yet the blood hummed in his ears and hung a cloud before him. He knew it was only the stirring of the primal instinct, that it had no more to do with his reasoning self than any reflex impulse of the body; but that merely lowered anguish to disgust. Yes, it was disgust he felt—almost a physical nausea. The poisonous fumes of life were in his lungs. He was sick, unutterably sick. . .

He drove home and went to his room. They were giving a little dinner that night, and when he came down the guests were arriving. He looked at his wife: her beauty was extraordinary, but it seemed to him the beauty of a smooth sea along an unlit coast. She frightened him.

He sat late in his study. He heard the parlor-maid lock the front door; then his wife went upstairs and the lights were put out. His brain was like some great empty hall with an echo in it: one thought reverberated endlessly. . . At length he drew his chair to the table and began to write. He addressed an envelope and then slowly re-read what he had written.

"My dear Flamel,

"Many apologies for not sending you sooner the enclosed check, which represents the customary percentage on the sale of the 'Letters.'

"Trusting you will excuse the oversight,

"Yours truly

"Stephen Glennard."

He let himself out of the darkened house and dropped the letter in the post-box at the corner.

The next afternoon he was detained late at his office, and as he was preparing to leave he heard some one asking for him in the outer room. He seated himself again and Flamel was shown in.

The two men, as Glennard pushed aside an obstructive chair, had a moment to measure each other; then Flamel advanced, and drawing out his note-case, laid a slip of paper on the desk.

"My dear fellow, what on earth does this mean?"

Glennard recognized his check.

"That I was remiss, simply. It ought to have gone to you before."

Flamel's tone had been that of unaffected surprise, but at this his accent changed and he asked quickly: "On what ground?"

Glennard had moved away from the desk and stood leaning against the calf-backed volumes of the bookcase. "On the ground that you sold Mrs. Aubyn's letters for me, and that I find the intermediary in such cases is entitled to a percentage on the sale."

Flamel paused before answering. "You find, you say. It's a recent discovery?"

"Obviously, from my not sending the check sooner. You see I'm new to the business."

"And since when have you discovered that there was any question of business, as far as I was concerned?"

Glennard flushed and his voice rose slightly. "Are you reproaching me for not having remembered it sooner?"

Flamel, who had spoken in the rapid repressed tone of a man on the verge of anger, stared a moment at this and then, in his natural voice, rejoined good-humoredly, "Upon my soul, I don't understand you!"

The change of key seemed to disconcert Glennard. "It's simple enough," he muttered.

"Simple enough—your offering me money in return for a friendly service? I don't know what your other friends expect!"

"Some of my friends wouldn't have undertaken the job. Those who would have done so would probably have expected to be paid."

He lifted his eyes to Flamel and the two men looked at each other. Flamel had turned white and his lips stirred, but he held his temperate note. "If you mean to imply that the job was not a nice one you lay yourself open to the retort that you proposed it. But for my part I've never seen, I never shall see, any reason for not publishing the letters."

"That's just it!"

"What—?"

"The certainty of your not seeing was what made me go to you. When a man's got stolen goods to pawn he doesn't take them to the police-station."

"Stolen?" Flamel echoed. "The letters were stolen?"

Glennard burst into a laugh. "How much longer do you expect me to keep up that pretence about the letters? You knew well enough they were written to me."

Flamel looked at him in silence. "Were they?" he said at length. "I didn't know it."

"And didn't suspect it, I suppose," Glennard sneered.

The other was again silent; then he said, "I may remind you that, supposing I had felt any curiosity about the matter, I had no way of finding out that the letters were written to you. You never showed me the originals."

"What does that prove? There were fifty ways of finding out. It's the kind of thing one can easily do."

Flamel glanced at him with contempt. "Our ideas probably differ as to what a man can easily do. It would not have been easy for me."

Glennard's anger vented itself in the words uppermost in his thought. "It may, then, interest you to hear that my wife *does* know about the letters—has known for some months. . ."

"Ah," said the other, slowly.

Glennard saw that, in his blind clutch at a weapon, he had seized the one most apt to wound. Flamel's muscles were under control, but his face showed the undefinable change produced by the slow infiltration of poison. Every implication that the words contained had reached its mark; but Glennard felt that their obvious intent was lost in the anguish of what they suggested. He was sure now that Flamel would never have betrayed him; but the inference only made a wider outlet for his anger. He paused breathlessly for Flamel to speak.

"If she knows, it's not through me." It was what Glennard had waited for.

"Through you, by God? Who said it was through you? Do you suppose I leave it to you, or to anybody else, for that matter, to keep my wife informed of my actions? I didn't suppose even such egregious conceit as yours could delude a man to that degree!" Struggling for a foothold in the landslide of his dignity, he added in a steadier tone, "My wife learned the facts from me."

Flamel received this in silence. The other's outbreak seemed to have restored his self-control, and when he spoke it was with a deliberation implying that his course was chosen. "In that case I understand still less—"

"Still less—?"

"The meaning of this." He pointed to the check. "When you began to speak I supposed you had meant it as a bribe; now I can only infer it was intended as a random insult. In either case, here's my answer."

He tore the slip of paper in two and tossed the fragments across the desk to Glennard. Then he turned and walked out of the office.

Glennard dropped his head on his hands. If he had hoped to restore his self-respect by the simple expedient of assailing Flamel's, the result had not justified his expectation. The blow he had struck had blunted the edge of his anger, and the unforeseen extent of the hurt inflicted did not alter the fact that his weapon had broken in his hands. He now saw that his rage against Flamel was only the last projection of a passionate self-disgust. This consciousness did not dull his dislike of the man; it simply made reprisals ineffectual. Flamel's unwillingness to quarrel with him was the last stage of his abasement.

In the light of this final humiliation his assumption of his wife's indifference struck him as hardly so fatuous as the sentimental resuscitation of his past. He had been living in a factitious world wherein his emotions were the sycophants of his vanity, and it was with instinctive relief that he felt its ruins crash about his head.

It was nearly dark when he left his office, and he walked slowly homeward in the complete mental abeyance that follows on such a crisis. He was not aware that he was thinking of his wife; yet when he reached his own door he found that, in the involuntary readjustment of his vision, she had once more become the central point of consciousness.

XIII

It had never before occurred to him that she might, after all, have missed the purport of the document he had put in her way. What if, in her hurried inspection of the papers, she had passed it over as related to the private business of some client? What, for instance, was to prevent her concluding that Glennard was the counsel of the unknown person who had sold the *Aubyn Letters*? The subject was one not likely to fix her attention—she was not a curious woman.

Glennard at this point laid down his fork and glanced at her between the candle-shades. The alternative explanation of her indifference was not slow in presenting itself. Her head had the same listening droop as when he had caught sight of her the day before in Flamel's company; the attitude revived the vividness of his impression. It was simple enough, after all. She had ceased to care for him because she cared for some one else.

As he followed her upstairs he felt a sudden stirring of his dormant anger. His sentiments had lost their artificial complexity. He had already acquitted her of any connivance in his baseness, and he felt only that he loved her and that she had escaped him. This was now, strangely enough, his dominant thought: the sense that he and she had passed through the fusion of love and had emerged from it as incommunicably apart as though the transmutation had never taken place. Every other passion, he mused, left some mark upon the nature; but love passed like the flight of a ship across the waters.

She dropped into her usual seat near the lamp, and he leaned against the chimney, moving about with an inattentive hand the knick-knacks on the mantel.

Suddenly he caught sight of her reflection in the mirror. She was looking at him. He turned and their eyes met.

He moved across the room.

"There's something that I want to say to you," he began.

She held his gaze, but her color deepened. He noticed again, with a jealous pang, how her beauty had gained in warmth and meaning. It was as though a transparent cup had been filled with wine. He looked at her ironically.

"I've never prevented your seeing your friends here," he broke out. "Why do you meet Flamel in out-of-the-way places? Nothing makes a woman so cheap—"

She rose abruptly and they faced each other a few feet apart.

"What do you mean?" she asked.

"I saw you with him last Sunday on the Riverside Drive," he went on, the utterance of the charge reviving his anger.

"Ah," she murmured. She sank into her chair again and began to play with a paper-knife that lay on the table at her elbow.

Her silence exasperated him.

"Well?" he burst out. "Is that all you have to say?"

"Do you wish me to explain?" she asked proudly.

"Do you imply I haven't the right to?"

"I imply nothing. I will tell you whatever you wish to know. I went for a walk with Mr. Flamel because he asked me to."

"I didn't suppose you went uninvited. But there are certain things a sensible woman doesn't do. She doesn't slink about in out-of-the-way streets with men. Why couldn't you have seen him here?"

She hesitated. "Because he wanted to see me alone."

"Did he indeed? And may I ask if you gratify all his wishes with equal alacrity?"

"I don't know that he has any others where I am concerned." She paused again and then continued, in a voice that somehow had an under-note of warning, "He wished to bid me good-bye. He's going away."

Glennard turned on her a startled glance. "Going away?"

"He's going to Europe to-morrow. He goes for a long time. I supposed you knew."

The last phrase revived his irritation. "You forget that I depend on you for my information about Flamel. He's your friend and not mine. In fact, I've sometimes wondered at your going out of your way to be so civil to him when you must see plainly enough that I don't like him."

Her answer to this was not immediate. She seemed to be choosing her words with care, not so much for her own sake as for his, and his exasperation was increased by the suspicion that she was trying to spare him.

"He was your friend before he was mine. I never knew him till I was married. It was you who brought him to the house and who seemed to wish me to like him."

Glennard gave a short laugh. The defence was feebler than he had expected: she was certainly not a clever woman.

"Your deference to my wishes is really beautiful; but it's not the first time in history that a man has made a mistake in introducing his friends to his wife. You must, at any rate, have seen since then that my enthusiasm had cooled; but so, perhaps, has your eagerness to oblige me."

She met this with a silence that seemed to rob the taunt of half its efficacy.

"Is that what you imply?" he pressed her.

"No," she answered with sudden directness. "I noticed some time ago that you seemed to dislike him, but since then—"

"Well—since then?"

"I've imagined that you had reasons for still wishing me to be civil to him, as you call it."

"Ah," said Glennard with an effort at lightness; but his irony dropped, for something in her voice made him feel that he and she stood at last in that naked desert of apprehension where meaning skulks vainly behind speech.

"And why did you imagine this?" The blood mounted to his forehead. "Because he told you that I was under obligations to him?"

She turned pale. "Under obligations?"

"Oh, don't let's beat about the bush. Didn't he tell you it was I who published Mrs. Aubyn's letters? Answer me that."

"No," she said; and after a moment which seemed given to the weighing of alternatives, she added: "No one told me."

"You didn't know, then?"

She seemed to speak with an effort. "Not until—not until—"

"Till I gave you those papers to sort?"

Her head sank.

"You understood then?"

"Yes."

He looked at her immovable face. "Had you suspected—
before?" was slowly wrung from him.

"At times—yes—." Her voice dropped to a whisper.

"Why? From anything that was said—?"

There was a shade of pity in her glance. "No one said anything—no one told me anything." She looked away from
him. "It was your manner—"

"My manner?"

"Whenever the book was mentioned. Things you said—
once or twice—your irritation—I can't explain."

Glennard, unconsciously, had moved nearer. He breathed
like a man who has been running. "You knew, then, you
knew—" he stammered. The avowal of her love for Flamel
would have hurt him less, would have rendered her less remote. "You knew—you knew—" he repeated; and suddenly
his anguish gathered voice. "My God!" he cried, "you suspected it first, you say—and then you knew it—this damnable,
this accursed thing; you knew it months ago—it's months
since I put that paper in your way—and yet you've done nothing, you've said nothing, you've made no sign, you've lived
alongside of me as if it had made no difference—no difference
in either of our lives. What are you made of, I wonder? Don't
you see the hideous ignominy of it? Don't you see how you've
shared in my disgrace? Or haven't you any sense of shame?"

He preserved sufficient lucidity, as the words poured from
him, to see how fatally they invited her derision; but something told him they had both passed beyond the phase of obvious retaliations, and that if any chord in her responded it
would not be that of scorn.

He was right. She rose slowly and moved toward him.

"Haven't you had enough—without that?" she said in a
strange voice of pity.

He stared at her. "Enough—?"

"Of misery. . ."

An iron band seemed loosened from his temples. "You saw
then . . ?" he whispered.

"Oh, God—oh, God—" she sobbed. She dropped beside
him and hid her anguish against his knees. They clung thus in
silence a long time, driven together down the same fierce
blast of shame.

When at length she lifted her face he averted his. Her scorn would have hurt him less than the tears on his hands.

She spoke languidly, like a child emerging from a passion of weeping. "It was for the money—?"

His lips shaped an assent.

"That was the inheritance—that we married on?"

"Yes."

She drew back and rose to her feet. He sat watching her as she wandered away from him.

"You hate me," broke from him.

She made no answer.

"Say you hate me!" he persisted.

"That would have been so simple," she answered with a strange smile. She dropped into a chair near the writing-table and rested a bowed forehead on her hand.

"Was it much—?" she began at length.

"Much—?" he returned vaguely.

"The money."

"The money?" That part of it seemed to count so little that for a moment he did not follow her thought.

"It must be paid back," she insisted. "Can you do it?"

"Oh, yes," he returned listlessly. "I can do it."

"I would make any sacrifice for that!" she urged.

He nodded. "Of course." He sat staring at her in dry-eyed self-contempt. "Do you count on its making much difference?"

"Much difference?"

"In the way I feel—or you feel about me?"

She shook her head.

"It's the least part of it," he groaned.

"It's the only part we can repair."

"Good heavens! If there were any reparation—" He rose quickly and crossed the space that divided them. "Why did you never speak?"

"Haven't you answered that yourself?"

"Answered it?"

"Just now—when you told me you did it for me."

She paused a moment and then went on with a deepening note—"I would have spoken if I could have helped you."

"But you must have despised me."

impregnable refuge of self-esteem, and we hate the eye that reaches to our nakedness. If Glennard did not hate his wife it was slowly, sufferingly, that there was born in him that profounder passion which made his earlier feeling seem a mere commotion of the blood. He was like a child coming back to the sense of an enveloping presence: her nearness was a breast on which he leaned.

They did not, at first, talk much together, and each beat a devious track about the outskirts of the subject that lay between them like a haunted wood. But every word, every action, seemed to glance at it, to draw toward it, as though a fount of healing sprang in its poisoned shade. If only they might cut a way through the thicket to that restoring spring!

Glennard, watching his wife with the intentness of a wanderer to whom no natural sign is negligeable, saw that she had taken temporary refuge in the purpose of renouncing the money. If both, theoretically, owned the inefficacy of such amends, the woman's instinctive subjectiveness made her find relief in this crude form of penance. Glennard saw that she meant to live as frugally as possible till what she deemed their debt was discharged; and he prayed she might not discover how far-reaching, in its merely material sense, was the obligation she thus hoped to acquit. Her mind was fixed on the sum originally paid for the letters, and this he knew he could lay aside in a year or two. He was touched, meanwhile, by the spirit that made her discard the petty luxuries which she regarded as the sign of their bondage. Their shared renunciations drew her nearer to him, helped, in their evidence of her helplessness, to restore the full protecting stature of his love. And still they did not speak.

It was several weeks later that, one afternoon by the drawing-room fire, she handed him a letter that she had been reading when he entered.

"I've heard from Mr. Flamel," she said.

It was as though a latent presence had become visible to both. Glennard took the letter mechanically.

"It's from Smyrna," she said. "Won't you read it?"

He handed it back. "You can tell me about it—his hand's so illegible." He wandered to the other end of the room and then turned and stood before her. "I've been thinking of writing to Flamel," he said.

She looked up.

"There's one point," he continued slowly, "that I ought to clear up. I told him you'd known about the letters all along; for a long time, at least; and I saw how it hurt him. It was just what I meant to do, of course; but I can't leave him to that false impression; I must write him."

She received this without outward movement, but he saw that the depths were stirred. At length she returned in a hesitating tone, "Why do you call it a false impression? I did know."

"Yes, but I implied you didn't care."

"Ah!"

He still stood looking down on her. "Don't you want me to set that right?" he pursued.

She lifted her head and fixed him bravely. "It isn't necessary," she said.

Glennard flushed with the shock of the retort; then, with a gesture of comprehension, "No," he said, "with you it couldn't be; but I might still set myself right."

She looked at him gently. "Don't I," she murmured, "do that?"

"In being yourself merely? Alas, the rehabilitation's too complete! You make me seem—to myself even—what I'm not; what I can never be. I can't, at times, defend myself from the delusion; but I can at least enlighten others."

The flood was loosened, and kneeling by her he caught her hands. "Don't you see that it's become an obsession with me? That if I could strip myself down to the last lie—only there'd always be another one left under it!—and do penance naked in the market-place, I should at least have the relief of easing one anguish by another? Don't you see that the worst of my torture is the impossibility of such amends?"

Her hands lay in his without returning pressure. "Ah, poor woman, poor woman," he heard her sigh.

"Don't pity her, pity me! What have I done to her or to you, after all? You're both inaccessible! It was myself I sold."

He took an abrupt turn away from her; then halted before her again. "How much longer," he burst out, "do you suppose

you can stand it? You've been magnificent, you've been inspired, but what's the use? You can't wipe out the ignominy
of it. It's miserable for you and it does *her* no good!"

She lifted a vivid face. "That's the thought I can't bear!"
she cried.

"What thought?"

"That it does her no good—all you're feeling, all you're
suffering. Can it be that it makes no difference?"

He avoided her challenging glance. "What's done is done,"
he muttered.

"Is it ever, quite, I wonder?" she mused. He made no answer and they lapsed into one of the pauses that are a subter-
ranean channel of communication.

It was she who, after a while, began to speak, with a new
suffusing diffidence that made him turn a roused eye on her.

"Don't they say," she asked, feeling her way as in a kind of
tender apprehensiveness, "that the early Christians, instead of
pulling down the heathen temples—the temples of the unclean gods—purified them by turning them to their own uses?
I've always thought one might do that with one's actions—
the actions one loathes but can't undo. One can make, I
mean, a wrong the door to other wrongs or an impassable wall
against them. . ." Her voice wavered on the word. "We can't
always tear down the temples we've built to the unclean gods,
but we can put good spirits in the house of evil—the spirits of
mercy and shame and understanding, that might never have
come to us if we hadn't been in such great need. . ."

She moved over to him and laid a hand on his. His head
was bent and he did not change his attitude. She sat down beside him without speaking; but their silences now were fertile
as rain-clouds—they quickened the seeds of understanding.

At length he looked up. "I don't know," he said, "what
spirits have come to live in the house of evil that I built—but
you're there and that's enough. It's strange," he went on after another pause, "she wished the best for me so often, and
now, at last, it's through her that it's come to me. But for her
I shouldn't have known you—it's through her that I've found
you. Sometimes—do you know?—that makes it hardest—
makes me most intolerable to myself. Can't you see that it's
the worst thing I've got to face? I sometimes think I could

have borne it better if you hadn't understood! I took everything from her—everything—even to the poor shelter of loyalty she'd trusted in—the only thing I *could* have left her!—I took everything from her, I deceived her, I despoiled her, I destroyed her—and she's given me *you* in return!"

His wife's cry caught him up. "It isn't that she's given *me* to you—it is that she's given you to yourself." She leaned to him as though swept forward on a wave of pity. "Don't you see," she went on, as his eyes hung on her, "that that's the gift you can't escape from, the debt you're pledged to acquit? Don't you see that you've never before been what she thought you, and that now, so wonderfully, she's made you into the man she loved? *That's* worth suffering for, worth dying for, to a woman—that's the gift she would have wished to give!"

"Ah," he cried, "but woe to him by whom it cometh. What did I ever give her?"

"The happiness of giving," she said.

The Duchess at Prayer

Hᴀᴠᴇ you ever questioned the long shuttered front of an old Italian house, that motionless mask, smooth, mute, equivocal as the face of a priest behind which buzz the secrets of the confessional? Other houses declare the activities they shelter; they are the clear expressive cuticle of a life flowing close to the surface; but the old palace in its narrow street, the villa on its cypress-hooded hill, are as impenetrable as death. The tall windows are like blind eyes, the great door is a shut mouth. Inside there may be sunshine, the scent of myrtles, and a pulse of life through all the arteries of the huge frame; or a mortal solitude, where bats lodge in the disjointed stones and the keys rust in unused doors. . .

II

From the loggia, with its vanishing frescoes, I looked down an avenue barred by a ladder of cypress-shadows to the ducal escutcheon and multilated vases of the gate. Flat noon lay on the gardens, on fountains, porticoes and grottoes. Below the terrace, where a chrome-colored lichen had sheeted the balustrade as with fine *laminæ* of gold, vineyards stooped to the rich valley clasped in hills. The lower slopes were strewn with white villages like stars spangling a summer dusk; and beyond these, fold on fold of blue mountain, clear as gauze against the sky. The August air was lifeless, but it seemed light and vivifying after the atmosphere of the shrouded rooms through which I had been led. Their chill was on me and I hugged the sunshine.

"The Duchess's apartments are beyond," said the old man.

He was the oldest man I had ever seen; so sucked back into the past that he seemed more like a memory than a living being. The one trait linking him with the actual was the fixity with which his small saurian eye held the pocket that, as I entered, had yielded a *lira* to the gate-keeper's child. He went on, without removing his eye:

"For two hundred years nothing has been changed in the apartments of the Duchess."

"And no one lives here now?"

"No one, sir. The Duke goes to Como for the summer season."

I had moved to the other end of the loggia. Below me, through hanging groves, white roofs and domes flashed like a smile.

"And that's Vicenza?"

"Proprio!" The old man extended fingers as lean as the hands fading from the walls behind us. "You see the palace roof over there, just to the left of the Basilica? The one with the row of statues like birds taking flight? That's the Duke's town palace, built by Palladio."

"And does the Duke come there?"

"Never. In winter he goes to Rome."

"And the palace and the villa are always closed?"

"As you see—always."

"How long has this been?"

"Since I can remember."

I looked into his eyes: they were like tarnished metal mirrors reflecting nothing. "That must be a long time," I said involuntarily.

"A long time," he assented.

I looked down on the gardens. An opulence of dahlias overran the box-borders, between cypresses that cut the sunshine like basalt shafts. Bees hung above the lavender; lizards sunned themselves on the benches and slipped through the cracks of the dry basins. Everywhere were vanishing traces of that fantastic horticulture of which our dull age has lost the art. Down the alleys maimed statues stretched their arms like rows of whining beggars; faun-eared terms grinned in the thickets, and above the laurustinus walls rose the mock ruin of a temple, falling into real ruin in the bright disintegrating air. The glare was blinding.

"Let us go in," I said.

The old man pushed open a heavy door, behind which the cold lurked like a knife.

"The Duchess's apartments," he said.

Overhead and around us the same evanescent frescoes, under foot the same scagliola volutes, unrolled themselves interminably. Ebony cabinets, with inlay of precious marbles in cunning perspective, alternated down the room with the tarnished efflorescence of gilt consoles supporting Chinese monsters; and from the chimney-panel a gentleman in the Spanish habit haughtily ignored us.

"Duke Ercole II.," the old man explained, "by the Genoese Priest."

It was a narrow-browed face, sallow as a wax effigy, high-nosed and cautious-lidded, as though modelled by priestly hands; the lips weak and vain rather than cruel; a quibbling mouth that would have snapped at verbal errors like a lizard catching flies, but had never learned the shape of a round yes or no. One of the Duke's hands rested on the head of a dwarf, a simian creature with pearl ear-rings and fantastic dress; the other turned the pages of a folio propped on a skull.

"Beyond is the Duchess's bedroom," the old man reminded me.

Here the shutters admitted but two narrow shafts of light, gold bars deepening the subaqueous gloom. On a dais the bedstead, grim, nuptial, official, lifted its baldachin; a yellow Christ agonized between the curtains, and across the room a lady smiled at us from the chimney-breast.

The old man unbarred a shutter and the light touched her face. Such a face it was, with a flicker of laughter over it like the wind on a June meadow, and a singular tender pliancy of mien, as though one of Tiepolo's lenient goddesses had been busked into the stiff sheath of a seventeenth century dress!

"No one has slept here," said the old man, "since the Duchess Violante."

"And she was—?"

"The lady there—first Duchess of Duke Ercole II."

He drew a key from his pocket and unlocked a door at the farther end of the room. "The chapel," he said. "This is the Duchess's balcony." As I turned to follow him the Duchess tossed me a sidelong smile.

I stepped into a grated tribune above a chapel festooned with stucco. Pictures of bituminous saints mouldered between the pilasters; the artificial roses in the altar-vases were gray with dust and age, and under the cobwebby rosettes of the vaulting a bird's nest clung. Before the altar stood a row of tattered arm-chairs, and I drew back at sight of a figure kneeling near them.

"The Duchess," the old man whispered. "By the Cavaliere Bernini."

It was the image of a woman in furred robes and spreading fraise, her hand lifted, her face addressed to the tabernacle. There was a strangeness in the sight of that immovable presence locked in prayer before an abandoned shrine. Her face was hidden, and I wondered whether it were grief or gratitude that raised her hands and drew her eyes to the altar, where no living prayer joined her marble invocation. I followed my guide down the tribune steps, impatient to see what mystic version of such terrestrial graces the ingenious artist had found—the Cavaliere was master of such arts. The Duchess's attitude was one of transport, as though heavenly airs fluttered her laces and the love-locks escaping from her coif. I saw how admirably the sculptor had caught the poise of her head, the tender slope of the shoulder; then I crossed over and looked into her face—it was a frozen horror. Never have hate, revolt and agony so possessed a human countenance. . .

The old man crossed himself and shuffled his feet on the marble.

"The Duchess Violante," he repeated.

"The same as in the picture?"

"Eh—the same."

"But the face—what does it mean?"

He shrugged his shoulders and turned deaf eyes on me. Then he shot a glance round the sepulchral place, clutched my sleeve and said, close to my ear: "It was not always so."

"What was not?"

"The face—so terrible."

"The Duchess's face?"

"The statue's. It changed after—"

"After?"

"It was put here."

"The statue's face *changed*—?"

He mistook my bewilderment for incredulity and his confidential finger dropped from my sleeve. "Eh, that's the story.

I tell what I've heard. What do I know?" He resumed his se-
nile shuffle across the marble. "This is a bad place to stay in—
no one comes here. It's too cold. But the gentleman said, *I
must see everything!*"

I let the *lire* sound. "So I must—and hear everything. This
story, now—from whom did you have it?"

His hand stole back. "One that saw it, by God!"

"That saw it?"

"My grandmother, then. I'm a very old man."

"Your grandmother? Your grandmother was—?"

"The Duchess's serving girl, with respect to you."

"Your grandmother? Two hundred years ago?"

"Is it too long ago? That's as God pleases. I am a very old
man and she was a very old woman when I was born. When
she died she was as black as a miraculous Virgin and her
breath whistled like the wind in a keyhole. She told me the
story when I was a little boy. She told it to me out there in
the garden, on a bench by the fish-pond, one summer night
of the year she died. It must be true, for I can show you the
very bench we sat on. . ."

III

Noon lay heavier on the gardens; not our live humming
warmth but the stale exhalation of dead summers. The very
statues seemed to drowse like watchers by a death-bed.
Lizards shot out of the cracked soil like flames and the bench
in the laurustinus-niche was strewn with the blue varnished
bodies of dead flies. Before us lay the fish-pond, a yellow
marble slab above rotting secrets. The villa looked across it,
composed as a dead face, with the cypresses flanking it for
candles. . .

IV

.   .   .   .

"Impossible, you say, that my mother's mother should have
been the Duchess's maid? What do I know? It is so long since
anything has happened here that the old things seem nearer,

perhaps, than to those who live in cities. . . But how else did she know about the statue then? Answer me that, sir! That she saw with her eyes, I can swear to, and never smiled again, so she told me, till they put her first child in her arms . . . for she was taken to wife by the steward's son, Antonio, the same who had carried the letters. . . But where am I? Ah, well . . . she was a mere slip, you understand, my grandmother, when the Duchess died, a niece of the upper maid, Nencia, and suffered about the Duchess because of her pranks and the funny songs she knew. It's possible, you think, she may have heard from others what she afterward fancied she had seen herself? How that is, it's not for an unlettered man to say; though indeed I myself seem to have seen many of the things she told me. This is a strange place. No one comes here, nothing changes, and the old memories stand up as distinct as the statues in the garden. . .

"It began the summer after they came back from the Brenta. Duke Ercole had married the lady from Venice, you must know; it was a gay city, then, I'm told, with laughter and music on the water, and the days slipped by like boats running with the tide. Well, to humor her he took her back the first autumn to the Brenta. Her father, it appears, had a grand palace there, with such gardens, bowling-alleys, grottoes and casinos as never were; gondolas bobbing at the water-gates, a stable full of gilt coaches, a theatre full of players, and kitchens and offices full of cooks and lackeys to serve up chocolate all day long to the fine ladies in masks and furbelows, with their pet dogs and their blackamoors and their *abates*. Eh! I know it all as if I'd been there, for Nencia, you see, my grandmother's aunt, travelled with the Duchess, and came back with her eyes round as platters, and not a word to say for the rest of the year to any of the lads who'd courted her here in Vicenza.

"What happened there I don't know—my grandmother could never get at the rights of it, for Nencia was mute as a fish where her lady was concerned—but when they came back to Vicenza the Duke ordered the villa set in order; and in the spring he brought the Duchess here and left her. She looked happy enough, my grandmother said, and seemed no object for pity. Perhaps, after all, it was better than being shut up in

Vicenza, in the tall painted rooms where priests came and
went as softly as cats prowling for birds, and the Duke was
forever closeted in his library, talking with learned men. The
Duke was a scholar; you noticed he was painted with a book?
Well, those that can read 'em make out that they're full of
wonderful things; as a man that's been to a fair across the
mountains will always tell his people at home it was beyond
anything *they'll* ever see. As for the Duchess, she was all for
music, play-acting and young company. The Duke was a silent
man, stepping quietly, with his eyes down, as though he'd just
come from confession; when the Duchess's lap-dog yapped at
his heels he danced like a man in a swarm of hornets; when
the Duchess laughed he winced as if you'd drawn a diamond
across a window-pane. And the Duchess was always laughing.

"When she first came to the villa she was very busy laying
out the gardens, designing grottoes, planting groves and
planning all manner of agreeable surprises in the way of water-
jets that drenched you unexpectedly, and hermits in caves,
and wild men that jumped at you out of thickets. She had a
very pretty taste in such matters, but after a while she tired of
it, and there being no one for her to talk to but her maids and
the chaplain—a clumsy man deep in his books—why, she
would have strolling players out from Vicenza, mountebanks
and fortune-tellers from the market-place, travelling doctors
and astrologers, and all manner of trained animals. Still it
could be seen that the poor lady pined for company, and her
waiting women, who loved her, were glad when the Cavaliere
Ascanio, the Duke's cousin, came to live at the vineyard
across the valley—you see the pinkish house over there in the
mulberries, with a red roof and a pigeon-cote?

"The Cavaliere Ascanio was a cadet of one of the great
Venetian houses, *pezzi grossi* of the Golden Book. He had
been meant for the Church, I believe, but what! he set fight-
ing above praying and cast in his lot with the captain of the
Duke of Mantua's *bravi*, himself a Venetian of good standing,
but a little at odds with the law. Well, the next I know, the
Cavaliere was in Venice again, perhaps not in good odor on
account of his connection with the gentleman I speak of.
Some say he tried to carry off a nun from the convent of
Santa Croce; how that may be I can't say; but my grand-

mother declared he had enemies there, and the end of it was that on some pretext or other the Ten banished him to Vicenza. There, of course, the Duke, being his kinsman, had to show him a civil face; and that was how he first came to the villa.

"He was a fine young man, beautiful as a Saint Sebastian, a rare musician, who sang his own songs to the lute in a way that used to make my grandmother's heart melt and run through her body like mulled wine. He had a good word for everybody, too, and was always dressed in the French fashion, and smelt as sweet as a bean-field; and every soul about the place welcomed the sight of him.

"Well, the Duchess, it seemed, welcomed it too; youth will have youth, and laughter turns to laughter; and the two matched each other like the candlesticks on an altar. The Duchess—you've seen her portrait—but to hear my grandmother, sir, it no more approached her than a weed comes up to a rose. The Cavaliere, indeed, as became a poet, paragoned her in his song to all the pagan goddesses of antiquity; and doubtless these were finer to look at than mere women; but so, it seemed, was she; for, to believe my grandmother, she made other women look no more than the big French fashion-doll that used to be shown on Ascension days in the Piazza. She was one, at any rate, that needed no outlandish finery to beautify her; whatever dress she wore became her as feathers fit the bird; and her hair didn't get its color by bleaching on the house-top. It glittered of itself like the threads in an Easter chasuble, and her skin was whiter than fine wheaten bread and her mouth as sweet as a ripe fig. . .

"Well, sir, you could no more keep them apart than the bees and the lavender. They were always together, singing, bowling, playing cup and ball, walking in the gardens, visiting the aviaries and petting her grace's trick-dogs and monkeys. The Duchess was as gay as a foal, always playing pranks and laughing, tricking out her animals like comedians, disguising herself as a peasant or a nun (you should have seen her one day pass herself off to the chaplain as a mendicant sister), or teaching the lads and girls of the vineyards to dance and sing madrigals together. The Cavaliere had a singular ingenuity in planning such entertainments and the days were hardly long

enough for their diversions. But toward the end of the summer the Duchess fell quiet and would hear only sad music,
and the two sat much together in the gazebo at the end of
the garden. It was there the Duke found them one day when
he drove out from Vicenza in his gilt coach. He came but
once or twice a year to the villa, and it was, as my grandmother said, just a part of her poor lady's ill-luck to be wearing that day the Venetian habit, which uncovered the
shoulders in a way the Duke always scowled at, and her curls
loose and powdered with gold. Well, the three drank chocolate in the gazebo, and what happened no one knew, except
that the Duke, on taking leave, gave his cousin a seat in his
carriage; but the Cavaliere never returned.

"Winter approaching, and the poor lady thus finding herself once more alone, it was surmised among her women
that she must fall into a deeper depression of spirits. But far
from this being the case, she displayed such cheerfulness and
equanimity of humor that my grandmother, for one, was
half-vexed with her for giving no more thought to the poor
young man who, all this time, was eating his heart out in the
house across the valley. It is true she quitted her gold-laced
gowns and wore a veil over her head; but Nencia would have
it she looked the lovelier for the change and so gave the
Duke greater displeasure. Certain it is that the Duke drove
out oftener to the villa, and though he found his lady always
engaged in some innocent pursuit, such as embroidery or
music, or playing games with her young women, yet he always went away with a sour look and a whispered word to
the chaplain. Now as to the chaplain, my grandmother
owned there had been a time when her grace had not handled him overwisely. For, according to Nencia, it seems that
his reverence, who seldom approached the Duchess, being
buried in his library like a mouse in a cheese—well, one day
he made bold to appeal to her for a sum of money, a large
sum, Nencia said, to buy certain tall books, a chest full of
them, that a foreign pedlar had brought him; whereupon the
Duchess, who could never abide a book, breaks out at him
with a laugh and a flash of her old spirit—'Holy Mother of
God, must I have more books about me? I was nearly
smothered with them in the first year of my marriage;' and

the chaplain turning red at the affront, she added: 'You may buy them and welcome, my good chaplain, if you can find the money; but as for me, I am yet seeking a way to pay for my turquoise necklace, and the statue of Daphne at the end of the bowling-green, and the Indian parrot that my black boy brought me last Michaelmas from the Bohemians—so you see I've no money to waste on trifles;' and as he backs out awkwardly she tosses at him over her shoulder: 'You should pray to Saint Blandina to open the Duke's pocket!' to which he returned, very quietly, 'Your excellency's suggestion is an admirable one, and I have already entreated that blessed martyr to open the Duke's understanding.'

"Thereat, Nencia said (who was standing by), the Duchess flushed wonderfully red and waved him out of the room; and then 'Quick!' she cried to my grandmother (who was too glad to run on such errands), 'Call me Antonio, the gardener's boy, to the box-garden; I've a word to say to him about the new clove-carnations. . .'

"Now I may not have told you, sir, that in the crypt under the chapel there has stood, for more generations than a man can count, a stone coffin containing a thigh-bone of the blessed Saint Blandina of Lyons, a relic offered, I've been told, by some great Duke of France to one of our own dukes when they fought the Turk together; and the object, ever since, of particular veneration in this illustrious family. Now, since the Duchess had been left to herself, it was observed she affected a fervent devotion to this relic, praying often in the chapel and even causing the stone slab that covered the entrance to the crypt to be replaced by a wooden one, that she might at will descend and kneel by the coffin. This was matter of edification to all the household and should have been peculiarly pleasing to the chaplain; but, with respect to you, he was the kind of man who brings a sour mouth to the eating of the sweetest apple.

"However that may be, the Duchess, when she dismissed him, was seen running to the garden, where she talked earnestly with the boy Antonio about the new clove-carnations; and the rest of the day she sat indoors and played sweetly on the virginal. Now Nencia always had it in mind that her grace had made a mistake in refusing that request of the chaplain's; but she said nothing, for to talk reason to the Duchess was of no more use than praying for rain in a drought.

"Winter came early that year, there was snow on the hills by All Souls, the wind stripped the gardens, and the lemon-trees were nipped in the lemon-house. The Duchess kept her room in this black season, sitting over the fire, embroidering, reading books of devotion (which was a thing she had never done) and praying frequently in the chapel. As for the chaplain, it was a place he never set foot in but to say mass in the morning, with the Duchess overhead in the tribune, and the servants aching with rheumatism on the marble floor. The chaplain himself hated the cold, and galloped through the mass like a man with witches after him. The rest of the day he spent in his library, over a brazier, with his eternal books. . .

"You'll wonder, sir, if I'm ever to get to the gist of the story; and I've gone slowly, I own, for fear of what's coming. Well, the winter was long and hard. When it fell cold the Duke ceased to come out from Vicenza, and not a soul had the Duchess to speak to but her maid-servants and the gardeners about the place. Yet it was wonderful, my grandmother said, how she kept her brave colors and her spirits; only it was remarked that she prayed longer in the chapel, where a brazier was kept burning for her all day. When the young are denied their natural pleasures they turn often enough to religion; and it was a mercy, as my grandmother said, that she, who had scarce a live sinner to speak to, should take such comfort in a dead saint.

"My grandmother seldom saw her that winter, for though she showed a brave front to all she kept more and more to herself, choosing to have only Nencia about her and dismissing even her when she went to pray. For her devotion had that mark of true piety, that she wished it not to be observed; so that Nencia had strict orders, on the chaplain's approach, to warn her mistress if she happened to be in prayer.

"Well, the winter passed, and spring was well forward, when my grandmother one evening had a bad fright. That it was her own fault I won't deny, for she'd been down the lime-walk with Antonio when her aunt fancied her to be stitching in her chamber; and seeing a sudden light in Nencia's window, she took fright lest her disobedience be found out, and ran up quickly through the laurel-grove to the house. Her way lay by the chapel, and as she crept past it, meaning to slip in through the scullery, and groping her way, for the dark had fallen and the moon was scarce up, she heard a crash close behind her, as though someone had dropped from a window of the chapel. The young fool's heart turned over, but she looked round as she ran, and there, sure enough, was a man scuttling across the terrace; and as he doubled the corner of the house my grandmother swore she caught the whisk of the chaplain's skirts. Now that was a strange thing, certainly; for why should the chaplain be getting out of the chapel window when he might have passed through the door? For you may have noticed, sir, there's a door leads from the chapel into the saloon on the ground floor; the only other way out being through the Duchess's tribune.

"Well, my grandmother turned the matter over, and next time she met Antonio in the lime-walk (which, by reason of her fright, was not for some days) she laid before him what had happened; but to her surprise he only laughed and said, 'You little simpleton, he wasn't getting out of the window, he was trying to look in'; and not another word could she get from him.

"So the season moved on to Easter, and news came the Duke had gone to Rome for that holy festivity. His comings and goings made no change at the villa, and yet there was no one there but felt easier to think his yellow face was on the far side of the Apennines, unless perhaps it was the chaplain.

"Well, it was one day in May that the Duchess, who had walked long with Nencia on the terrace, rejoicing at the sweetness of the prospect and the pleasant scent of the gilly-flowers in the stone vases, the Duchess toward midday withdrew to her rooms, giving orders that her dinner should be served in her bed-chamber. My grandmother helped to carry in the dishes, and observed, she said, the singular beauty of the Duchess, who in honor of the fine weather had put on a gown of shot-silver and hung her bare shoulders with pearls, so that she looked fit to dance at court with an emperor. She had ordered, too, a rare repast for a lady that heeded so little what she ate—jellies, game-pasties, fruits in syrup, spiced cakes and a flagon of Greek wine; and she nodded and clapped her hands as the women set it before her, saying again and again, 'I shall eat well to-day.'

"But presently another mood seized her; she turned from the table, called for her rosary, and said to Nencia: 'The fine weather has made me neglect my devotions. I must say a litany before I dine.'

"She ordered the women out and barred the door, as her custom was; and Nencia and my grandmother went downstairs to work in the linen-room.

"Now the linen-room gives on the court-yard, and suddenly my grandmother saw a strange sight approaching. First up the avenue came the Duke's carriage (whom all thought to be in Rome), and after it, drawn by a long string of mules and oxen, a cart carrying what looked like a kneeling figure wrapped in death-clothes. The strangeness of it struck the girl dumb and the Duke's coach was at the door before she had the wit to cry out that it was coming. Nencia, when she saw it, went white and ran out of the room. My grandmother followed, scared by her face, and the two fled along the corridor to the chapel. On the way they met the chaplain, deep in a book, who asked in surprise where they were running, and when they said, to announce the Duke's arrival, he fell into such astonishment and asked them so many questions and uttered such ohs and ahs, that by the time he let them by the Duke was at their heels. Nencia reached the chapel-door first and cried out that the Duke was coming; and before she had a reply he was at her side, with the chaplain following.

"A moment later the door opened and there stood the Duchess. She held her rosary in one hand and had drawn a scarf over her shoulders; but they shone through it like the moon in a mist, and her countenance sparkled with beauty.

"The Duke took her hand with a bow. 'Madam,' he said, 'I could have had no greater happiness than thus to surprise you at your devotions.'

" 'My own happiness,' she replied, 'would have been greater had your excellency prolonged it by giving me notice of your arrival.'

" 'Had you expected me, Madam,' said he, 'your appearance could scarcely have been more fitted to the occasion.

Few ladies of your youth and beauty array themselves to venerate a saint as they would to welcome a lover.'

" 'Sir,' she answered, 'having never enjoyed the latter opportunity, I am constrained to make the most of the former. —What's that?' she cried, falling back, and the rosary dropped from her hand.

"There was a loud noise at the other end of the saloon, as of a heavy object being dragged down the passage; and presently a dozen men were seen haling across the threshold the shrouded thing from the ox-cart. The Duke waved his hand toward it. 'That,' said he, 'Madam, is a tribute to your extraordinary piety. I have heard with peculiar satisfaction of your devotion to the blessed relics in this chapel, and to commemorate a zeal which neither the rigors of winter nor the sultriness of summer could abate I have ordered a sculptured image of you, marvellously executed by the Cavaliere Bernini, to be placed before the altar over the entrance to the crypt.'

"The Duchess, who had grown pale, nevertheless smiled playfully at this. 'As to commemorating my piety,' she said, 'I recognize there one of your excellency's pleasantries—'

" 'A pleasantry?' the Duke interrupted; and he made a sign to the men, who had now reached the threshold of the chapel. In an instant the wrappings fell from the figure, and there knelt the Duchess to the life. A cry of wonder rose from all, but the Duchess herself stood whiter than the marble.

" 'You will see,' says the Duke, 'this is no pleasantry, but a triumph of the incomparable Bernini's chisel. The likeness was done from your miniature portrait by the divine Elisabetta Sirani, which I sent to the master some six months ago, with what results all must admire.'

" 'Six months!' cried the Duchess, and seemed about to fall; but his excellency caught her by the hand.

" 'Nothing,' he said, 'could better please me than the excessive emotion you display, for true piety is ever modest, and your thanks could not take a form that better became you. And now,' says he to the men, 'let the image be put in place.'

"By this, life seemed to have returned to the Duchess, and she answered him with a deep reverence. 'That I should be overcome by so unexpected a grace, your excellency admits to be natural; but what honors you accord it is my privilege to

in her excellency's words, but I would suggest, sir, that her pious wish might be met, and the saint more conspicuously honored, by transferring the relics from the crypt to a place beneath the altar.'

" 'True!' cried the Duke, 'and it shall be done at once.'

"But thereat the Duchess rose to her feet with a terrible look.

" 'No,' she cried, 'by the body of God! For it shall not be said that, after your excellency has chosen to deny every request I addressed to him, I owe his consent to the solicitation of another!'

"The chaplain turned red and the Duke yellow, and for a moment neither spoke.

"Then the Duke said, 'Here are words enough, Madam. Do you wish the relics brought up from the crypt?'

" 'I wish nothing that I owe to another's intervention!'

" 'Put the image in place then,' says the Duke furiously; and handed her grace to a chair.

"She sat there, my grandmother said, straight as an arrow, her hands locked, her head high, her eyes on the Duke, while the statue was dragged to its place; then she stood up and turned away. As she passed by Nencia, 'Call me Antonio,' she whispered; but before the words were out of her mouth the Duke stepped between them.

" 'Madam,' says he, all smiles now, 'I have travelled straight from Rome to bring you the sooner this proof of my esteem. I lay last night at Monselice and have been on the road since daybreak. Will you not invite me to supper?'

" 'Surely, my lord,' said the Duchess. 'It shall be laid in the dining-parlor within the hour.'

" 'Why not in your chamber and at once, Madam? Since I believe it is your custom to sup there.'

" 'In my chamber?' says the Duchess, in disorder.

" 'Have you anything against it?' he asked.

" 'Assuredly not, sir, if you will give me time to prepare myself.'

" 'I will wait in your cabinet,' said the Duke.

"At that, said my grandmother, the Duchess gave one look, as the souls in hell may have looked when the gates closed on our Lord; then she called Nencia and passed to her chamber.

"What happened there my grandmother could never learn, but that the Duchess, in great haste, dressed herself with extraordinary splendor, powdering her hair with gold, painting her face and bosom, and covering herself with jewels till she shone like our Lady of Loreto; and hardly were these preparations complete when the Duke entered from the cabinet, followed by the servants carrying supper. Thereupon the Duchess dismissed Nencia, and what follows my grandmother learned from a pantry-lad who brought up the dishes and waited in the cabinet; for only the Duke's body-servant entered the bed-chamber.

"Well, according to this boy, sir, who was looking and listening with his whole body, as it were, because he had never before been suffered so near the Duchess, it appears that the noble couple sat down in great good humor, the Duchess playfully reproving her husband for his long absence, while the Duke swore that to look so beautiful was the best way of punishing him. In this tone the talk continued, with such gay sallies on the part of the Duchess, such tender advances on the Duke's, that the lad declared they were for all the world like a pair of lovers courting on a summer's night in the vineyard; and so it went till the servant brought in the mulled wine.

" 'Ah,' the Duke was saying at that moment, 'this agreeable evening repays me for the many dull ones I have spent away from you; nor do I remember to have enjoyed such laughter since the afternoon last year when we drank chocolate in the gazebo with my cousin Ascanio. And that reminds me,' he said, 'is my cousin in good health?'

" 'I have no reports of it,' says the Duchess. 'But your excellency should taste these figs stewed in malmsey—'

" 'I am in the mood to taste whatever you offer,' said he; and as she helped him to the figs he added, 'If my enjoyment were not complete as it is, I could almost wish my cousin Ascanio were with us. The fellow is rare good company at supper. What do you say, Madam? I hear he's still in the country; shall we send for him to join us?'

" 'Ah,' said the Duchess, with a sigh and a languishing look, 'I see your excellency wearies of me already.'

" 'I, Madam? Ascanio is a capital good fellow, but to my mind his chief merit at this moment is his absence. It inclines me so tenderly to him that, by God, I could empty a glass to his good health.'

"With that the Duke caught up his goblet and signed to the servant to fill the Duchess's.

" 'Here's to the cousin,' he cried, standing, 'who has the good taste to stay away when he's not wanted. I drink to his very long life—and you, Madam?'

"At this the Duchess, who had sat staring at him with a changed face, rose also and lifted her glass to her lips.

" 'And I to his happy death,' says she in a wild voice; and as she spoke the empty goblet dropped from her hand and she fell face down on the floor.

"The Duke shouted to her women that she had swooned, and they came and lifted her to the bed. . . She suffered horribly all night, Nencia said, twisting herself like a heretic at the stake, but without a word escaping her. The Duke watched her, and toward daylight sent for the chaplain; but by this she was unconscious and, her teeth being locked, our Lord's body could not be passed through them.

.   .   .   .

"The Duke announced to his relations that his lady had died after partaking too freely of spiced wine and an omelet of carp's roe, at a supper she had prepared in honor of his return; and the next year he brought home a new Duchess, who gave him a son and five daughters. . ."

v

The sky had turned to a steel gray, against which the villa stood out sallow and inscrutable. A wind strayed through the gardens, loosening here and there a yellow leaf from the sycamores; and the hills across the valley were purple as thunder-clouds.

.   .   .   .

"And the statue—?" I asked.

"Ah, the statue. Well, sir, this is what my grandmother told me, here on this very bench where we're sitting. The poor child, who worshipped the Duchess as a girl of her years will worship a beautiful kind mistress, spent a night of horror, you may fancy, shut out from her lady's room, hearing the cries that came from it, and seeing, as she crouched in her corner, the women rush to and fro with wild looks, the Duke's lean face in the door, and the chaplain skulking in the antechamber with his eyes on his breviary. No one minded her that night or the next morning; and toward dusk, when it became known the Duchess was no more, the poor girl felt the pious wish to say a prayer for her dead mistress. She crept to the chapel and stole in unobserved. The place was empty and dim, but as she advanced she heard a low moaning, and coming in front of the statue she saw that its face, the day before so sweet and smiling, had the look on it that you know—and the moaning seemed to come from its lips. My grandmother turned cold, but something, she said afterward, kept her from calling or shrieking out, and she turned and ran from the place. In the passage she fell in a swoon; and when she came to her senses, in her own chamber, she heard that the Duke had locked the chapel door and forbidden any to set foot there. . . The place was never opened again till the Duke died, some ten years later; and then it was that the other servants, going in with the new heir, saw for the first time the horror that my grandmother had kept in her bosom. . ."

"And the crypt?" I asked. "Has it never been opened?"

"Heaven forbid, sir!" cried the old man, crossing himself. "Was it not the Duchess's express wish that the relics should not be disturbed?"

The Angel at the Grave

THE HOUSE stood a few yards back from the elm-shaded village street, in that semi-publicity sometimes cited as a democratic protest against old-world standards of domestic exclusiveness. This candid exposure to the public eye is more probably a result of the gregariousness which, in the New England bosom, oddly coexists with a shrinking from direct social contact; most of the inmates of such houses preferring that furtive intercourse which is the result of observations through shuttered windows and a categorical acquaintance with the neighboring clothes-lines. The House, however, faced its public with a difference. For sixty years it had written itself with a capital letter, had self-consciously squared itself in the eye of an admiring nation. The most searching inroads of village intimacy hardly counted in a household that opened on the universe; and a lady whose door-bell was at any moment liable to be rung by visitors from London or Vienna was not likely to flutter up-stairs when she observed a neighbor "stepping over."

The solitary inmate of the Anson House owed this induration of the social texture to the most conspicuous accident in her annals: the fact that she was the only granddaughter of the great Orestes Anson. She had been born, as it were, into a museum, and cradled in a glass case with a label; the first foundations of her consciousness being built on the rock of her grandfather's celebrity. To a little girl who acquires her earliest knowledge of literature through a *Reader* embellished with fragments of her ancestor's prose, that personage necessarily fills an heroic space in the foreground of life. To communicate with one's past through the impressive medium of print, to have, as it were, a footing in every library in the country, and an acknowledged kinship with that world-diffused clan, the descendants of the great, was to be pledged to a standard of manners that amazingly simplified the lesser relations of life. The village street on which Paulina Anson's youth looked out led to all the capitals of Europe; and over the roads of intercommunication unseen caravans bore back to the elm-shaded House the tribute of an admiring world.

Fate seemed to have taken a direct share in fitting Paulina for her part as the custodian of this historic dwelling. It had long been secretly regarded as a "visitation" by the great man's family that he had left no son and that his daughters were not "intellectual." The ladies themselves were the first to lament their deficiency, to own that nature had denied them the gift of making the most of their opportunities. A profound veneration for their parent and an unswerving faith in his doctrines had not amended their congenital incapacity to understand what he had written. Laura, who had her moments of mute rebellion against destiny, had sometimes thought how much easier it would have been if their progenitor had been a poet; for she could recite, with feeling, portions of *The Culprit Fay* and of the poems of Mrs. Hemans; and Phœbe, who was more conspicuous for memory than imagination, kept an album filled with "selections." But the great man was a philosopher; and to both daughters respiration was difficult on the cloudy heights of metaphysic. The situation would have been intolerable but for the fact that, while Phœbe and Laura were still at school, their father's fame had passed from the open ground of conjecture to the chill privacy of certitude. Dr. Anson had in fact achieved one of those anticipated immortalities not uncommon at a time when people were apt to base their literary judgments on their emotions, and when to affect plain food and despise England went a long way toward establishing a man's intellectual pre-eminence. Thus, when the daughters were called on to strike a filial attitude about their parent's pedestal, there was little to do but to pose gracefully and point upward; and there are spines to which the immobility of worship is not a strain. A legend had by this time crystallized about the great Orestes, and it was of more immediate interest to the public to hear what brand of tea he drank, and whether he took off his boots in the hall, than to rouse the drowsy echo of his dialectic. A great man never draws so near his public as when it has become unnecessary to read his books and is still interesting to know what he eats for breakfast.

As recorders of their parent's domestic habits, as pious scavengers of his waste-paper basket, the Misses Anson were unexcelled. They always had an interesting anecdote to impart to the literary pilgrim, and the tact with which, in later years, they intervened between the public and the growing inaccessibility of its idol, sent away many an enthusiast satisfied to have touched the veil before the sanctuary. Still it was felt, especially by old Mrs. Anson, who survived her husband for some years, that Phœbe and Laura were not worthy of their privileges. There had been a third daughter so unworthy of hers that she had married a distant cousin, who had taken her to live in a new Western community where the *Works of Orestes Anson* had not yet become a part of the civic consciousness; but of this daughter little was said, and she was tacitly understood to be excluded from the family heritage of fame. In time, however, it appeared that the traditional penny with which she had been cut off had been invested to unexpected advantage; and the interest on it, when she died, returned to the Anson House in the shape of a granddaughter who was at once felt to be what Mrs. Anson called a "compensation." It was Mrs. Anson's firm belief that the remotest operations of nature were governed by the centripetal force of her husband's greatness and that Paulina's exceptional intelligence could be explained only on the ground that she was designed to act as the guardian of the family temple.

The House, by the time Paulina came to live in it, had already acquired the publicity of a place of worship; not the perfumed chapel of a romantic idolatry but the cold clean empty meeting-house of ethical enthusiasms. The ladies lived on its outskirts, as it were, in cells that left the central fane undisturbed. The very position of the furniture had come to have a ritual significance: the sparse ornaments were the offerings of kindred intellects, the steel engravings by Raphael Morghen marked the Via Sacra of a European tour, and the black-walnut desk with its bronze ink-stand modelled on the Pantheon was the altar of this bleak temple of thought.

To a child compact of enthusiasms, and accustomed to pasture them on the scanty herbage of a new social soil, the atmosphere of the old house was full of floating nourishment.

In the compressed perspective of Paulina's outlook it stood for a monument of ruined civilizations, and its white portico opened on legendary distances. Its very aspect was impressive to eyes that had first surveyed life from the jig-saw "residence" of a raw-edged Western town. The high-ceilinged rooms, with their panelled walls, the polished mahogany, their portraits of triple-stocked ancestors and of ringleted "females" in crayon, furnished the child with the historic scenery against which a young imagination constructs its vision of the past. To other eyes the cold spotless thinly-furnished interior might have suggested the shuttered mind of a maiden-lady who associates fresh air and sunlight with dust and discoloration; but it is the eye which supplies the coloring-matter, and Paulina's brimmed with the richest hues.

Nevertheless, the House did not immediately dominate her. She had her confused out-reachings toward other centres of sensation, her vague intuition of a heliocentric system; but the attraction of habit, the steady pressure of example, gradually fixed her roving allegiance and she bent her neck to the yoke. Vanity had a share in her subjugation; for it had early been discovered that she was the only person in the family who could read her grandfather's works. The fact that she had perused them with delight at an age when (even presupposing a metaphysical bias) it was impossible for her to understand them, seemed to her aunts and grandmother sure evidence of predestination. Paulina was to be the interpreter of the oracle, and the philosophic fumes so vertiginous to meaner minds would throw her into the needed condition of clairvoyance. Nothing could have been more genuine than the emotion on which this theory was based. Paulina, in fact, delighted in her grandfather's writings. His sonorous periods, his mystic vocabulary, his bold flights into the rarefied air of the abstract, were thrilling to a fancy unhampered by the need of definitions. This purely verbal pleasure was supplemented later by the excitement of gathering up crumbs of meaning from the rhetorical board. What could have been more stimulating than to construct the theory of a girlish world out of the fragments of this Titanic cosmogony? Before Paulina's opinions had reached the stage when ossification sets in their form was fatally predetermined.

The fact that Dr. Anson had died and that his apotheosis had taken place before his young priestess's induction to the temple, made her ministrations easier and more inspiring. There were no little personal traits—such as the great man's manner of helping himself to salt, or the guttural cluck that started the wheels of speech—to distract the eye of young veneration from the central fact of his divinity. A man whom one knows only through a crayon portrait and a dozen yellowing tomes on free-will and intuition is at least secure from the belittling effects of intimacy.

Paulina thus grew up in a world readjusted to the fact of her grandfather's greatness; and as each organism draws from its surroundings the kind of nourishment most needful to its growth, so from this somewhat colorless conception she absorbed warmth, brightness and variety. Paulina was the type of woman who transmutes thought into sensation and nurses a theory in her bosom like a child.

In due course Mrs. Anson "passed away"—no one died in the Anson vocabulary—and Paulina became more than ever the foremost figure of the commemorative group. Laura and Phœbe, content to leave their father's glory in more competent hands, placidly lapsed into needlework and fiction, and their niece stepped into immediate prominence as the chief "authority" on the great man. Historians who were "getting up" the period wrote to consult her and to borrow documents; ladies with inexplicable yearnings begged for an interpretation of phrases which had "influenced" them, but which they had not quite understood; critics applied to her to verify some doubtful citation or to decide some disputed point in chronology; and the great tide of thought and investigation kept up a continuous murmur on the quiet shores of her life.

An explorer of another kind disembarked there one day in the shape of a young man to whom Paulina was primarily a kissable girl, with an after-thought in the shape of a grandfather. From the outset it had been impossible to fix Hewlett Winsloe's attention on Dr. Anson. The young man behaved with the innocent profanity of infants sporting on a tomb. His excuse was that he came from New York, a Cimmerian outskirt which survived in Paulina's geography only because Dr. Anson had gone there once or twice to lecture. The curi-

ous thing was that she should have thought it worth while to
find excuses for young Winsloe. The fact that she did so had
not escaped the attention of the village; but people, after a
gasp of awe, said it was the most natural thing in the world
that a girl like Paulina Anson should think of marrying. It
would certainly seem a little odd to see a man in the House,
but young Winsloe would of course understand that the
Doctor's books were not to be disturbed, and that he must
go down to the orchard to smoke—. The village had barely
framed this *modus vivendi* when it was convulsed by the announcement that young Winsloe declined to live in the
House on any terms. Hang going down to the orchard to
smoke! He meant to take his wife to New York. The village
drew its breath and watched.

Did Persephone, snatched from the warm fields of Enna,
peer half-consentingly down the abyss that opened at her
feet? Paulina, it must be owned, hung a moment over the
black gulf of temptation. She would have found it easy to
cope with a deliberate disregard of her grandfather's rights;
but young Winsloe's unconsciousness of that shadowy claim
was as much a natural function as the falling of leaves on a
grave. His love was an embodiment of the perpetual renewal
which to some tender spirits seems a crueller process than
decay.

On women of Paulina's mould this piety toward implicit
demands, toward the ghosts of dead duties walking unap-
peased among usurping passions, has a stronger hold than any
tangible bond. People said that she gave up young Winsloe
because her aunts disapproved of her leaving them; but such
disapproval as reached her was an emanation from the walls of
the House, from the bare desk, the faded portraits, the dozen
yellowing tomes that no hand but hers ever lifted from the
shelf.

II

After that the House possessed her. As if conscious of its
victory, it imposed a conqueror's claims. It had once been
suggested that she should write a life of her grandfather, and
the task from which she had shrunk as from a too-oppressive

privilege now shaped itself into a justification of her course. In a burst of filial pantheism she tried to lose herself in the vast ancestral consciousness. Her one refuge from scepticism was a blind faith in the magnitude and the endurance of the idea to which she had sacrificed her life, and with a passionate instinct of self-preservation she labored to fortify her position.

The preparations for the *Life* led her through by-ways that the most scrupulous of the previous biographers had left unexplored. She accumulated her material with a blind animal patience unconscious of fortuitous risks. The years stretched before her like some vast blank page spread out to receive the record of her toil; and she had a mystic conviction that she would not die till her work was accomplished.

The aunts, sustained by no such high purpose, withdrew in turn to their respective divisions of the Anson "plot," and Paulina remained alone with her tasks. She was forty when the book was completed. She had travelled little in her life, and it had become more and more difficult to her to leave the House even for a day; but the dread of entrusting her document to a strange hand made her decide to carry it herself to the publisher. On the way to Boston she had a sudden vision of the loneliness to which this last parting condemned her. All her youth, all her dreams, all her renunciations lay in that neat bundle on her knee. It was not so much her grandfather's life as her own that she had written; and the knowledge that it would come back to her in all the glorification of print was of no more help than, to a mother's grief, the assurance that the lad she must part with will return with epaulets.

She had naturally addressed herself to the firm which had published her grandfather's works. Its founder, a personal friend of the philosopher's, had survived the Olympian group of which he had been a subordinate member, long enough to bestow his octogenarian approval on Paulina's pious undertaking. But he had died soon afterward; and Miss Anson found herself confronted by his grandson, a person with a brisk commercial view of his trade, who was said to have put "new blood" into the firm.

This gentleman listened attentively, fingering her manuscript as though literature were a tactile substance; then, with a confidential twist of his revolving chair, he emitted the verdict: "We ought to have had this ten years sooner."

Miss Anson took the words as an allusion to the repressed avidity of her readers. "It has been a long time for the public to wait," she solemnly assented.

The publisher smiled. "They haven't waited," he said.

She looked at him strangely. "Haven't waited?"

"No—they've gone off; taken another train. Literature's like a big railway-station now, you know: there's a train starting every minute. People are not going to hang round the waiting-room. If they can't get to a place when they want to they go somewhere else."

The application of this parable cost Miss Anson several minutes of throbbing silence. At length she said: "Then I am to understand that the public is no longer interested in—in my grandfather?" She felt as though heaven must blast the lips that risked such a conjecture.

"Well, it's this way. He's a name still, of course. People don't exactly want to be caught not knowing who he is; but they don't want to spend two dollars finding out, when they can look him up for nothing in any biographical dictionary."

Miss Anson's world reeled. She felt herself adrift among mysterious forces, and no more thought of prolonging the discussion than of opposing an earthquake with argument. She went home carrying the manuscript like a wounded thing. On the return journey she found herself travelling straight toward a fact that had lurked for months in the background of her life, and that now seemed to await her on the very threshold: the fact that fewer visitors came to the House. She owned to herself that for the last four or five years the number had steadily diminished. Engrossed in her work, she had noted the change only to feel thankful that she had fewer interruptions. There had been a time when, at the travelling season, the bell rang continuously, and the ladies of the House lived in a chronic state of "best silks" and expectancy. It would have been impossible then to carry on any consecutive work; and she now saw that the silence which had gathered round her task had been the hush of death.

Not of *his* death! The very walls cried out against the implication. It was the world's enthusiasm, the world's faith, the world's loyalty that had died. A corrupt generation that had turned aside to worship the brazen serpent. Her heart yearned with a prophetic passion over the lost sheep straying in the wilderness. But all great glories had their interlunar period; and in due time her grandfather would once more flash full-orbed upon a darkling world.

The few friends to whom she confided her adventure reminded her with tender indignation that there were other publishers less subject to the fluctuations of the market; but much as she had braved for her grandfather she could not again brave that particular probation. She found herself, in fact, incapable of any immediate effort. She had lost her way in a labyrinth of conjecture where her worst dread was that she might put her hand upon the clue.

She locked up the manuscript and sat down to wait. If a pilgrim had come just then the priestess would have fallen on his neck; but she continued to celebrate her rites alone. It was a double solitude; for she had always thought a great deal more of the people who came to see the House than of the people who came to see her. She fancied that the neighbors kept a keen eye on the path to the House; and there were days when the figure of a stranger strolling past the gate seemed to focus upon her the scorching sympathies of the village. For a time she thought of travelling; of going to Europe, or even to Boston; but to leave the House now would have seemed like deserting her post. Gradually her scattered energies centred themselves in the fierce resolve to understand what had happened. She was not the woman to live long in an unmapped country or to accept as final her private interpretation of phenomena. Like a traveller in unfamiliar regions she began to store for future guidance the minutest natural signs. Unflinchingly she noted the accumulating symptoms of indifference that marked her grandfather's descent toward posterity. She passed from the heights on which he had been grouped with the sages of his day to the lower level where he had come to be "the friend of Emerson," "the correspondent of Hawthorne," or (later still) "the Dr. Anson" mentioned in their letters. The change had taken place as slowly and imperceptibly as a natural process. She could not say that any ruthless hand had stripped the leaves from the tree: it was simply that, among the evergreen glories of his group, her grandfather's had proved deciduous.

She had still to ask herself why. If the decay had been a natural process, was it not the very pledge of renewal? It was easier to find such arguments than to be convinced by them. Again and again she tried to drug her solicitude with analogies; but at last she saw that such expedients were but the expression of a growing incredulity. The best way of proving her faith in her grandfather was not to be afraid of his critics. She had no notion where these shadowy antagonists lurked; for she had never heard of the great man's doctrine being directly combated. Oblique assaults there must have been, however, Parthian shots at the giant that none dared face; and she thirsted to close with such assailants. The difficulty was to find them. She began by re-reading the *Works*; thence she passed to the writers of the same school, those whose rhetoric bloomed perennial in *First Readers* from which her grandfather's prose had long since faded. Amid that clamor of far-off enthusiasms she detected no controversial note. The little knot of Olympians held their views in common with an early-Christian promiscuity. They were continually proclaiming their admiration for each other, the public joining as chorus in this guileless antiphon of praise; and she discovered no traitor in their midst.

What then had happened? Was it simply that the main current of thought had set another way? Then why did the others survive? Why were they still marked down as tributaries to the philosophic stream? This question carried her still farther afield, and she pressed on with the passion of a champion whose reluctance to know the worst might be construed into a doubt of his cause. At length—slowly but inevitably—an explanation shaped itself. Death had overtaken the doctrines about which her grandfather had draped his cloudy rhetoric. They had disintegrated and been re-absorbed, adding their little pile to the dust drifted about the mute lips of the Sphinx. The great man's contemporaries had survived not by reason of what they taught, but of what they were; and he, who had been the mere mask through which they mouthed their lesson, the instrument on which their tune was played, lay buried deep among the obsolete tools of thought.

The discovery came to Paulina suddenly. She looked up one evening from her reading and it stood before her like a ghost. It had entered her life with stealthy steps, creeping close before she was aware of it. She sat in the library, among the carefully-tended books and portraits; and it seemed to her that she had been walled alive into a tomb hung with the effigies of dead ideas. She felt a desperate longing to escape into the outer air, where people toiled and loved, and living sympathies went hand in hand. It was the sense of wasted labor that oppressed her; of two lives consumed in that ruthless process that uses generations of effort to build a single cell. There was a dreary parallel between her grandfather's fruitless toil and her own unprofitable sacrifice. Each in turn had kept vigil by a corpse.

III

The bell rang—she remembered it afterward—with a loud thrilling note. It was what they used to call the "visitor's ring"; not the tentative tinkle of a neighbor dropping in to borrow a sauce-pan or discuss parochial incidents, but a decisive summons from the outer world.

Miss Anson put down her knitting and listened. She sat upstairs now, making her rheumatism an excuse for avoiding the rooms below. Her interests had insensibly adjusted themselves to the perspective of her neighbors' lives, and she wondered—as the bell re-echoed—if it could mean that Mrs. Heminway's baby had come. Conjecture had time to ripen into certainty, and she was limping toward the closet where her cloak and bonnet hung, when her little maid fluttered in with the announcement: "A gentleman to see the house."

"The *House*?"

"Yes, m'm. I don't know what he means," faltered the messenger, whose memory did not embrace the period when such announcements were a daily part of the domestic routine.

Miss Anson glanced at the proffered card. The name it bore—*Mr. George Corby*—was unknown to her, but the blood rose to her languid cheek. "Hand me my Mechlin cap, Katy," she said, trembling a little, as she laid aside her walking stick. She put her cap on before the mirror, with rapid unsteady

touches. "Did you draw up the library blinds?" she breathlessly asked.

She had gradually built up a wall of commonplace between
herself and her illusions, but at the first summons of the past
filial passion swept away the frail barriers of expediency.

She walked down-stairs so hurriedly that her stick clicked
like a girlish heel; but in the hall she paused, wondering nervously if Katy had put a match to the fire. The autumn air was
cold and she had the reproachful vision of a visitor with elderly
ailments shivering by her inhospitable hearth. She thought instinctively of the stranger as a survivor of the days when such
a visit was a part of the young enthusiast's itinerary.

The fire was unlit and the room forbiddingly cold; but the
figure which, as Miss Anson entered, turned from a lingering
scrutiny of the book-shelves, was that of a fresh-eyed sanguine youth clearly independent of any artificial caloric. She
stood still a moment, feeling herself the victim of some an-
terior impression that made this robust presence an insubstantial thing; but the young man advanced with an air of
genial assurance which rendered him at once more real and
more reminiscent.

"Why this, you know," he exclaimed, "is simply immense!"

The words, which did not immediately present themselves
as slang to Miss Anson's unaccustomed ear, echoed with an
odd familiarity through the academic silence.

"The room, you know, I mean," he explained with a comprehensive gesture. "These jolly portraits, and the books—
that's the old gentleman himself over the mantelpiece, I
suppose?—and the elms outside, and—and the whole business. I do like a congruous background—don't you?"

His hostess was silent. No one but Hewlett Winsloe had
ever spoken of her grandfather as "the old gentleman."

"It's a hundred times better than I could have hoped," her
visitor continued, with a cheerful disregard of her silence.
"The seclusion, the remoteness, the philosophic atmosphere
—there's so little of that kind of flavor left! I should have simply hated to find that he lived over a grocery, you know.—I
had the deuce of a time finding out where he *did* live," he began again, after another glance of parenthetical enjoyment.
"But finally I got on the trail through some old book on

Brook Farm. I was bound I'd get the environment right before I did my article."

Miss Anson, by this time, had recovered sufficient self-possession to seat herself and assign a chair to her visitor.

"Do I understand," she asked slowly, following his rapid eye about the room, "that you intend to write an article about my grandfather?"

"That's what I'm here for," Mr. Corby genially responded; "that is, if you're willing to help me; for I can't get on without your help," he added with a confident smile.

There was another pause, during which Miss Anson noticed a fleck of dust on the faded leather of the writing-table and a fresh spot of discoloration in the right-hand upper corner of Raphael Morghen's "Parnassus."

"Then you believe in him?" she said, looking up. She could not tell what had prompted her; the words rushed out irresistibly.

"Believe in him?" Corby cried, springing to his feet. "Believe in Orestes Anson? Why, I believe he's simply the greatest—the most stupendous—the most phenomenal figure we've got!"

The color rose to Miss Anson's brow. Her heart was beating passionately. She kept her eyes fixed on the young man's face, as though it might vanish if she looked away.

"You—you mean to say this in your article?" she asked.

"Say it? Why, the facts will say it," he exulted. "The baldest kind of a statement would make it clear. When a man is as big as that he doesn't need a pedestal!"

Miss Anson sighed. "People used to say that when I was young," she murmured. "But now——"

Her visitor stared. "When you were young? But how did they know—when the thing hung fire as it did? When the whole edition was thrown back on his hands?"

"The whole edition—what edition?" It was Miss Anson's turn to stare.

"Why, of his pamphlet—*the* pamphlet—the one thing that counts, that survives, that makes him what he is! For heaven's sake," he tragically adjured her, "don't tell me there isn't a copy of it left!"

Miss Anson was trembling slightly. "I don't think I understand what you mean," she faltered, less bewildered by his

vehemence than by the strange sense of coming on an unexplored region in the very heart of her dominion.

"Why, his account of the *amphioxus*, of course! You can't
mean that his family didn't know about it—that *you* don't
know about it? I came across it by the merest accident myself,
in a letter of vindication that he wrote in 1830 to an old scientific paper; but I understood there were journals—early
journals; there must be references to it somewhere in the
'twenties. He must have been at least ten or twelve years ahead
of Yarrell; and he saw the whole significance of it, too—he
saw where it led to. As I understand it, he actually anticipated
in his pamphlet Saint Hilaire's theory of the universal type,
and supported the hypothesis by describing the notochord of
the *amphioxus* as a cartilaginous vertebral column. The specialists of the day jeered at him, of course, as the specialists in
Goethe's time jeered at the plant-metamorphosis. As far as I
can make out, the anatomists and zoologists were down on
Dr. Anson to a man; that was why his cowardly publishers
went back on their bargain. But the pamphlet must be here
somewhere—he writes as though, in his first disappointment,
he had destroyed the whole edition; but surely there must be
at least one copy left?"

His scientific jargon was as bewildering as his slang; and
there were even moments in his discourse when Miss Anson
ceased to distinguish between them; but the suspense with
which he continued to gaze on her acted as a challenge to her
scattered thoughts.

"The *amphioxus*," she murmured, half-rising. "It's an animal, isn't it—a fish? Yes, I think I remember." She sank back
with the inward look of one who retraces some lost line of
association.

Gradually the distance cleared, the details started into life.
In her researches for the biography she had patiently followed
every ramification of her subject, and one of these overgrown
paths now led her back to the episode in question. The great
Orestes's title of "Doctor" had in fact not been merely the
spontaneous tribute of a national admiration; he had actually
studied medicine in his youth, and his diaries, as his granddaughter now recalled, showed that he had passed through
a brief phase of anatomical ardor before his attention was

diverted to super-sensual problems. It had indeed seemed to
Paulina, as she scanned those early pages, that they revealed a
spontaneity, a freshness of feeling somehow absent from his
later lucubrations—as though this one emotion had reached
him directly, the others through some intervening medium.
In the excess of her commemorative zeal she had even struggled through the unintelligible pamphlet to which a few lines
in the journal had bitterly directed her. But the subject and
the phraseology were alien to her and unconnected with her
conception of the great man's genius; and after a hurried perusal she had averted her thoughts from the episode as from
a revelation of failure. At length she rose a little unsteadily,
supporting herself against the writing-table. She looked hesitatingly about the room; then she drew a key from her old-
fashioned reticule and unlocked a drawer beneath one of the
book-cases. Young Corby watched her breathlessly. With a
tremulous hand she turned over the dusty documents that
seemed to fill the drawer. "Is this it?" she said, holding out a
thin discolored volume.

He seized it with a gasp. "Oh, by George," he said, dropping into the nearest chair.

She stood observing him strangely as his eye devoured the
mouldy pages.

"Is this the only copy left?" he asked at length, looking
up for a moment as a thirsty man lifts his head from his
glass.

"I think it must be. I found it long ago, among some old
papers that my aunts were burning up after my grandmother's
death. They said it was of no use—that he'd always meant to
destroy the whole edition and that I ought to respect his
wishes. But it was something *he* had written; to burn it was
like shutting the door against his voice—against something he
had once wished to say, and that nobody had listened to. I
wanted him to feel that I was always here, ready to listen,
even when others hadn't thought it worth while; and so I
kept the pamphlet, meaning to carry out his wish and destroy
it before my death."

Her visitor gave a groan of retrospective anguish. "And but
for me—but for to-day—you would have?"

"I should have thought it my duty."

"Oh, by George—by George," he repeated, subdued afresh by the inadequacy of speech.

She continued to watch him in silence. At length he jumped up and impulsively caught her by both hands.

"He's bigger and bigger!" he almost shouted. "He simply leads the field! You'll help me go to the bottom of this, won't you? We must turn out all the papers—letters, journals, memoranda. He must have made notes. He must have left some record of what led up to this. We must leave nothing unexplored. By Jove," he cried, looking up at her with his bright convincing smile, "do you know you're the granddaughter of a Great Man?"

Her color flickered like a girl's. "Are you—sure of him?" she whispered, as though putting him on his guard against a possible betrayal of trust.

"Sure! Sure! My dear lady—" he measured her again with his quick confident glance. "Don't *you* believe in him?"

She drew back with a confused murmur. "I—used to." She had left her hands in his: their pressure seemed to send a warm current to her heart. "It ruined my life!" she cried with sudden passion. He looked at her perplexedly.

"I gave up everything," she went on wildly, "to keep *him* alive. I sacrificed myself—others—I nursed his glory in my bosom and it died—and left me—left me here alone." She paused and gathered her courage with a gasp. "Don't make the same mistake!" she warned him.

He shook his head, still smiling. "No danger of that! You're not alone, my dear lady. He's here with you—he's come back to you to-day. Don't you see what's happened? Don't you see that it's your love that has kept him alive? If you'd abandoned your post for an instant—let things pass into other hands—if your wonderful tenderness hadn't perpetually kept guard—this might have been—must have been —irretrievably lost." He laid his hand on the pamphlet. "And then—then he *would* have been dead!"

"Oh," she said, "don't tell me too suddenly!" And she turned away and sank into a chair.

The young man stood watching her in an awed silence. For a long time she sat motionless, with her face hidden, and he thought she must be weeping.

At length he said, almost shyly: "You'll let me come back, then? You'll help me work this thing out?"

She rose calmly and held out her hand. "I'll help you," she declared.

"I'll come to-morrow, then. Can we get to work early?"

"As early as you please."

"At eight o'clock, then," he said briskly. "You'll have the papers ready?"

"I'll have everything ready." She added with a half-playful hesitancy: "And the fire shall be lit for you."

He went out with his bright nod. She walked to the window and watched his buoyant figure hastening down the elm-shaded street. When she turned back into the empty room she looked as though youth had touched her on the lips.

The Recovery

To the visiting stranger Hillbridge's first question was, "Have you seen Keniston's things?"

Keniston took precedence of the colonial State House, the Gilbert Stuart Washington and the Ethnological Museum; nay, he ran neck and neck with the President of the University, a prehistoric relic who had known Emerson, and who was still sent about the country in cotton-wool to open educational institutions with a toothless oration on Brook Farm.

Keniston was sent about the country too: he opened art exhibitions, laid the foundation of academies, and acted in a general sense as the spokesman and apologist of art. Hillbridge was proud of him in his peripatetic character, but his fellow-townsmen let it be understood that to "know" Keniston one must come to Hillbridge. Never was work more dependent for its effect on "atmosphere," on *milieu*. Hillbridge was Keniston's *milieu*, and there was one lady, a devotee of his art, who went so far as to assert that once, at an exhibition in New York, she had passed a Keniston without recognizing it. "It simply didn't want to be seen in such surroundings; it was hiding itself under an incognito," she declared.

It was a source of special pride to Hillbridge that it contained all the artist's best works. Strangers were told that Hillbridge had discovered him. The discovery had come about in the simplest manner. Professor Driffert, who had a reputation for "collecting," had one day hung a sketch on his drawing-room wall, and thereafter Mrs. Driffert's visitors (always a little flurried by the sense that it was the kind of house in which one might be suddenly called upon to distinguish between a dry-point and an etching, or between Raphael Mengs and Raphael Sanzio) were not infrequently subjected to the Professor's off-hand inquiry, "By-the-way, have you seen my Keniston?" The visitors, perceptibly awed, would retreat to a critical distance and murmur the usual guarded generalities, while they tried to keep the name in mind long enough to look it up in the Encyclopædia. The

271

name was not in the Encyclopædia; but, as a compensating fact, it became known that the man himself was in Hillbridge. Hillbridge, then, owned an artist whose celebrity it was the proper thing to take for granted! Some one else, emboldened by the thought, bought a Keniston; and the next year, on the occasion of the President's golden jubilee, the Faculty, by unanimous consent, presented him with a Keniston. Two years later there was a Keniston exhibition, to which the art-critics came from New York and Boston; and not long afterward a well-known Chicago collector vainly attempted to buy Professor Driffert's sketch, which the art journals cited as a rare example of the painter's first or silvery manner. Thus there gradually grew up a small circle of connoisseurs known in artistic circles as men who collected Kenistons.

Professor Wildmarsh, of the chair of Fine Arts and Archæology, was the first critic to publish a detailed analysis of the master's methods and purpose. The article was illustrated by engravings which (though they had cost the magazine a fortune) were declared by Professor Wildmarsh to give but an imperfect suggestion of the esoteric significance of the originals. The Professor, with a tact that contrived to make each reader feel himself included among the exceptions, went on to say that Keniston's work would never appeal to any but exceptional natures; and he closed with the usual assertion that to apprehend the full meaning of the master's "message" it was necessary to see him in the surroundings of his own home at Hillbridge.

Professor Wildmarsh's article was read one spring afternoon by a young lady just speeding eastward on her first visit to Hillbridge, and already flushed with anticipation of the intellectual opportunities awaiting her. In East Onondaigua, where she lived, Hillbridge was looked on as an Oxford. Magazine writers, with the easy American use of the superlative, designated it as "the venerable Alma Mater," the "antique seat of learning," and Claudia Day had been brought up to regard it as the fountain-head of knowledge, and of that mental distinction which is so much rarer than knowledge. An innate passion for all that was thus distinguished and exceptional made her revere Hillbridge as the native soil of those intellectual amenities that were of such difficult growth in the thin air of East Onondaigua. At the first suggestion of a visit to Hillbridge—whither she went at the invitation of a girl friend who (incredible apotheosis!) had married one of the University professors—Claudia's spirit dilated with the sense of new possibilities. The vision of herself walking under the "historic elms" toward the Memorial Library, standing rapt before the Stuart Washington, or drinking in, from some obscure corner of an academic drawing-room, the President's reminiscences of the Concord group—this vividness of self-projection into the emotions awaiting her made her glad of any delay that prolonged so exquisite a moment.

It was in this mood that she opened the article on Keniston. She knew about him, of course; she was wonderfully "well up," even for East Onondaigua. She had read of him in the magazines; she had met, on a visit to New York, a man who collected Kenistons, and a photogravure of a Keniston in an "artistic" frame hung above her writing-table at home. But Professor Wildmarsh's article made her feel how little she really knew of the master; and she trembled to think of the state of relative ignorance in which, but for the timely purchase of the magazine, she might have entered Hillbridge. She had, for instance, been densely unaware that Keniston had already had three "manners," and was showing symptoms of a fourth. She was equally ignorant of the fact that he had founded a school and "created a formula"; and she learned with a thrill that no one could hope to understand him who had not seen him in his studio at Hillbridge, surrounded by his own works. "The man and the art interpret each other," their exponent declared; and Claudia Day, bending a brilliant eye on the future, wondered if she were ever to be admitted to the privilege of that double initiation.

Keniston, to his other claims to distinction, added that of being hard to know. His friends always hastened to announce the fact to strangers—adding after a pause of suspense that they "would see what they could do." Visitors in whose favor he was induced to make an exception were further warned that he never spoke unless he was interested—so that they mustn't mind if he remained silent. It was under these reassuring conditions that, some ten days after her arrival at Hillbridge, Miss Day was introduced to the master's studio.

She found him a tall listless-looking man, who appeared middle-aged to her youth, and who stood before his own pictures with a vaguely interrogative gaze, leaving the task of their interpretation to the lady who had courageously contrived the visit. The studio, to Claudia's surprise, was bare and shabby. It formed a rambling addition to the small cheerless house in which the artist lived with his mother and a widowed sister. For Claudia it added the last touch to his distinction to learn that he was poor, and that what he earned was devoted to the maintenance of the two limp women who formed a neutral-tinted background to his impressive outline. His pictures of course fetched high prices; but he worked slowly— "painfully," as his devotees preferred to phrase it—with frequent intervals of ill health and inactivity, and the circle of Keniston connoisseurs was still as small as it was distinguished. The girl's fancy instantly hailed in him that favorite figure of imaginative youth, the artist who would rather starve than paint a pot-boiler. It is known to comparatively few that the production of successful pot-boilers is an art in itself, and that such heroic abstentions as Keniston's are not always purely voluntary.

On the occasion of her first visit the artist said so little that Claudia was able to indulge to the full the harrowing sense of her inadequacy. No wonder she had not been one of the few that he cared to talk to; every word she uttered must so obviously have diminished the inducement! She had been cheap, trivial, conventional; at once gushing and inexpressive, eager and constrained. She could feel him counting the minutes till the visit was over, and as the door finally closed on the scene of her discomfiture she almost shared the hope with which she confidently credited him—that they might never meet again.

II

Mrs. Davant glanced reverentially about the studio. "I have always said," she murmured, "that they ought to be seen in Europe."

Mrs. Davant was young, credulous and emotionally extravagant: she reminded Claudia of her earlier self—the self that, ten years before, had first set an awe-struck foot on that very threshold.

"Not for *his* sake," Mrs. Davant continued, "but for Europe's."

Claudia smiled. She was glad that her husband's pictures were to be exhibited in Paris. She concurred in Mrs. Davant's view of the importance of the event; but she thought her visitor's way of putting the case a little overcharged. Ten years spent in an atmosphere of Keniston-worship had insensibly developed in Claudia a preference for moderation of speech. She believed in her husband, of course; to believe in him, with an increasing abandonment and tenacity, had become one of the necessary laws of being; but she did not believe in his admirers. Their faith in him was perhaps as genuine as her own; but it seemed to her less able to give an account of itself. Some few of his appreciators doubtless measured him by their own standards; but it was difficult not to feel that in the Hillbridge circle, where rapture ran the highest, he was accepted on what was at best but an indirect valuation; and now and then she had a frightened doubt as to the independence of her own convictions. That innate sense of relativity which even East Onondaigua had not been able to check in Claudia Day had been fostered in Mrs. Keniston by the artistic absolutism of Hillbridge, and she often wondered that her husband remained so uncritical of the quality of admiration accorded him. Her husband's uncritical attitude toward himself and his admirers had in fact been one of the surprises of her marriage. That an artist should believe in his potential powers seemed to her at once the incentive and the pledge of excellence: she knew there was no future for a hesitating talent. What perplexed her was Keniston's satisfaction in his achievement. She had always imagined that the true artist must regard himself as the imperfect vehicle of the cosmic emotion —that beneath every difficulty overcome a new one lurked, the vision widening as the scope enlarged. To be initiated into these creative struggles, to shed on the toiler's path the consolatory ray of faith and encouragement, had seemed the chief privilege of her marriage. But there is something supererogatory in believing in a man obviously disposed to perform that service for himself; and Claudia's ardor gradually spent itself against the dense surface of her husband's complacency. She could smile now at her vision of an intellectual communion which should admit her to the inmost precincts of his inspiration. She had learned that the creative processes are seldom self-explanatory, and Keniston's inarticulateness no longer discouraged her; but she could not reconcile her sense of the continuity of all high effort to his unperturbed air of finishing each picture as though he had despatched a masterpiece to posterity. In the first recoil from her disillusionment she even allowed herself to perceive that, if he worked slowly, it was not because he mistrusted his powers of expression, but because he had really so little to express.

"It's for Europe," Mrs. Davant vaguely repeated; and Claudia noticed that she was blushingly intent on tracing with the tip of her elaborate sunshade the pattern of the shabby carpet.

"It will be a revelation to them," she went on provisionally, as though Claudia had missed her cue and left an awkward interval to fill.

Claudia had in fact a sudden sense of deficient intuition. She felt that her visitor had something to communicate which required, on her own part, an intelligent co-operation; but what it was her insight failed to suggest. She was, in truth, a little tired of Mrs. Davant, who was Keniston's latest worshipper, who ordered pictures recklessly, who paid for them regally in advance, and whose gallery was, figuratively speaking, crowded with the artist's unpainted masterpieces. Claudia's impatience was perhaps complicated by the uneasy sense that Mrs. Davant was too young, too rich, too inexperienced; that somehow she ought to be warned.—Warned of what? That some of the pictures might never be painted? Scarcely that, since Keniston, who was scrupulous in business transactions, might be trusted not to take any material advantage of such evidence of faith. Claudia's impulse remained undefined. She merely felt that she would have liked to help Mrs. Davant, and that she did not know how.

"You'll be there to see them?" she asked, as her visitor lingered.

"In Paris?" Mrs. Davant's blush deepened. "We must all be there together."

Claudia smiled. "My husband and I mean to go abroad some day—but I don't see any chance of it at present."

"But he *ought* to go—you ought both to go this summer!" Mrs. Davant persisted. "I know Professor Wildmarsh and Professor Driffert and all the other critics think that Mr. Keniston's never having been to Europe has given his work much of its wonderful individuality, its peculiar flavor and meaning—but now that his talent is formed, that he has full command of his means of expression," (Claudia recognized one of Professor Driffert's favorite formulas) "they all think he ought to see the work of the *other* great masters—that he ought to visit the home of his ancestors, as Professor Wildmarsh says!" She stretched an impulsive hand to Claudia. "You ought to let him go, Mrs. Keniston!"

Claudia accepted the admonition with the philosophy of the wife who is used to being advised on the management of her husband. "I sha'n't interfere with him," she declared; and Mrs. Davant instantly caught her up with a cry of, "Oh, it's too lovely of you to say that!" With this exclamation she left Claudia to a silent renewal of wonder.

A moment later Keniston entered: to a mind curious in combinations it might have occurred that he had met Mrs. Davant on the door-step. In one sense he might, for all his wife cared, have met fifty Mrs. Davants on the door-step: it was long since Claudia had enjoyed the solace of resenting such coincidences. Her only thought now was that her husband's first words might not improbably explain Mrs. Davant's last; and she waited for him to speak.

He paused with his hands in his pockets before an unfinished picture on the easel; then, as his habit was, he began to stroll touristlike from canvas to canvas, standing before each in a musing ecstasy of contemplation that no readjustment of view ever seemed to disturb. Her eye instinctively joined his in its inspection; it was the one point where their natures merged. Thank God, there was no doubt about the pictures! She was what she had always dreamed of being— the wife of a great artist. Keniston dropped into an armchair and filled his pipe. "How should you like to go to Europe?" he asked.

His wife looked up quickly. "When?"

"Now—this spring, I mean." He paused to light the pipe. "I should like to be over there while these things are being exhibited."

Claudia was silent.

"Well?" he repeated after a moment.

"How can we afford it?" she asked.

Keniston had always scrupulously fulfilled his duty to the mother and sister whom his marriage had dislodged; and Claudia, who had the atoning temperament which seeks to pay for every happiness by making it a source of fresh obligations, had from the outset accepted his ties with an exaggerated devotion. Any disregard of such a claim would have vulgarized her most delicate pleasures; and her husband's sensitiveness to it in great measure extenuated the artistic obtuseness that often seemed to her like a failure of the moral sense. His loyalty to the dull women who depended on him was, after all, compounded of finer tissues than any mere sensibility to ideal demands.

"Oh, I don't see why we shouldn't," he rejoined. "I think we might manage it."

"At Mrs. Davant's expense?" leaped from Claudia. She could not tell why she had said it; some inner barrier seemed to have given way under a confused pressure of emotions.

He looked up at her with frank surprise. "Well, she *has* been very jolly about it—why not? She has a tremendous feeling for art—the keenest I ever knew in a woman." Claudia imperceptibly smiled. "She wants me to let her pay in advance for the four panels she has ordered for the Memorial Library. That would give us plenty of money for the trip, and my having the panels to do is another reason for my wanting to go abroad just now."

"Another reason?"

"Yes; I've never worked on such a big scale. I want to see how those old chaps did the trick; I want to measure myself with the big fellows over there. An artist ought to, once in his life."

She gave him a wondering look. For the first time his words implied a sense of possible limitation; but his easy tone seemed to retract what they conceded. What he really wanted was fresh food for his self-satisfaction: he was like an

army that moves on after exhausting the resources of the country.

Womanlike, she abandoned the general survey of the case for the consideration of a minor point.

"Are you sure you can do that kind of thing?" she asked.

"What kind of thing?"

"The panels."

He glanced at her indulgently: his self-confidence was too impenetrable to feel the pin-prick of such a doubt.

"Immensely sure," he said with a smile.

"And you don't mind taking so much money from her in advance?"

He stared. "Why should I? She'll get it back—with interest!" He laughed and drew at his pipe. "It will be an uncommonly interesting experience. I shouldn't wonder if it freshened me up a bit."

She looked at him again. This second hint of self-distrust struck her as the sign of a quickened sensibility. What if, after all, he was beginning to be dissatisfied with his work? The thought filled her with a renovating sense of his sufficiency.

III

They stopped in London to see the National Gallery.

It was thus that, in their inexperience, they had narrowly put it; but in reality every stone of the streets, every trick of the atmosphere, had its message of surprise for their virgin sensibilities. The pictures were simply the summing up, the final interpretation, of the cumulative pressure of an unimagined world; and it seemed to Claudia that long before they reached the doors of the gallery she had some intuitive revelation of what awaited them within.

They moved about from room to room without exchanging a word. The vast noiseless spaces seemed full of sound, like the roar of a distant multitude heard only by the inner ear. Had their speech been articulate their language would have been incomprehensible; and even that far-off murmur of meaning pressed intolerably on Claudia's nerves. Keniston took the onset without outward sign of disturbance. Now and then he paused before a canvas, or prolonged from one of the benches his silent communion with some miracle of line or color; but he neither looked at his wife nor spoke to her. He seemed to have forgotten her presence.

Claudia was conscious of keeping a furtive watch on him; but the sum total of her impressions was negative. She remembered thinking when she first met him that his face was rather expressionless; and he had the habit of self-engrossed silences.

All that evening, at the hotel, they talked about London, and he surprised her by an acuteness of observation that she had sometimes inwardly accused him of lacking. He seemed to have seen everything, to have examined, felt, compared, with nerves as finely adjusted as her own; but he said nothing of the pictures. The next day they returned to the National Gallery, and he began to study the paintings in detail, pointing out differences of technique, analyzing and criticising, but still without summing up his conclusions. He seemed to have a sort of provincial dread of showing himself too much impressed. Claudia's own sensations were too complex, too overwhelming, to be readily classified. Lacking the craftsman's instinct to steady her, she felt herself carried off her feet by the rush of incoherent impressions. One point she consciously avoided, and that was the comparison of her husband's work with what they were daily seeing. Art, she inwardly argued, was too various, too complex, dependent on too many inter-relations of feeling and environment, to allow of its being judged by any provisional standard. Even the subtleties of technique must be modified by the artist's changing purpose, as this in turn is acted on by influences of which he is himself unconscious. How, then, was an unprepared imagination to distinguish between such varied reflections of the elusive vision? She took refuge in a passionate exaggeration of her own ignorance and insufficiency.

After a week in London they went to Paris. The exhibition of Keniston's pictures had been opened a few days earlier; and as they drove through the streets on the way to the station an "impressionist" poster here and there invited them to the display of the American artist's work. Mrs. Davant, who had been in Paris for the opening, had already written rapturously of the impression produced, enclosing commendatory notices from one or two papers. She reported that there had been a great crowd on the first day, and that the critics had been "immensely struck."

The Kenistons arrived in the evening, and the next morning Claudia, as a matter of course, asked her husband at what time he meant to go and see the pictures.

He looked up absently from his guide-book.

"What pictures?"

"Why—yours," she said, surprised.

"Oh, they'll keep," he answered; adding with a slightly embarrassed laugh, "We'll give the other chaps a show first." Presently he laid down his book and proposed that they should go to the Louvre.

They spent the morning there, lunched at a restaurant near by, and returned to the gallery in the afternoon. Keniston had passed from inarticulateness to an eager volubility. It was clear that he was beginning to co-ordinate his impressions, to find his way about in a corner of the great imaginative universe. He seemed extraordinarily ready to impart his discoveries; and Claudia felt that her ignorance served him as a convenient buffer against the terrific impact of new sensations.

On the way home she asked when he meant to see Mrs. Davant.

His answer surprised her. "Does she know we're here?"

"Not unless you've sent her word," said Claudia, with a touch of harmless irony.

"That's all right, then," he returned simply. "I want to wait and look about a day or two longer. She'd want us to go sight-seeing with her; and I'd rather get my impressions alone."

The next two days were hampered by the necessity of eluding Mrs. Davant. Claudia, under different circumstances, would have scrupled to share in this somewhat shabby conspiracy; but she found herself in a state of suspended judgment, wherein her husband's treatment of Mrs. Davant became for the moment merely a clue to larger meanings.

They had been four days in Paris when Claudia, returning one afternoon from a parenthetical excursion to the Rue de la Paix, was confronted on her threshold by the reproachful

figure of their benefactress. It was not to her, however, that
Mrs. Davant's reproaches were addressed. Keniston, it appeared, had borne the brunt of them; for he stood leaning
against the mantelpiece of their modest *salon* in that attitude
of convicted negligence when, if ever, a man is glad to take
refuge behind his wife.

Claudia had however no immediate intention of affording
him such shelter. She wanted to observe and wait.

"He's too impossible!" cried Mrs. Davant, sweeping her at
once into the central current of her grievance.

Claudia looked from one to the other.

"For not going to see you?"

"For not going to see his pictures!" cried the other nobly.

Claudia colored and Keniston shifted his position uneasily.

"I can't make her understand," he said, turning to his wife.

"I don't care about myself!" Mrs. Davant interjected.

"*I* do, then; it's the only thing I do care about," he hurriedly protested. "I meant to go at once—to write—Claudia
wanted to go, but I wouldn't let her." He looked helplessly
about the pleasant red-curtained room, which was rapidly
burning itself into Claudia's consciousness as a visible extension of Mrs. Davant's claims.

"I can't explain," he broke off.

Mrs. Davant in turn addressed herself to Claudia.

"People think it's so odd," she complained. "So many of
the artists here are anxious to meet him; they've all been so
charming about the pictures; and several of our American
friends have come over from London expressly for the exhibition. I told every one that he would be here for the opening
—there was a private view, you know—and they were so disappointed—they wanted to give him an ovation; and I didn't
know what to say. What *am* I to say?" she abruptly ended.

"There's nothing to say," said Keniston slowly.

"But the exhibition closes the day after to-morrow."

"Well, *I* sha'n't close—I shall be here," he declared with
an effort at playfulness. "If they want to see me—all these
people you're kind enough to mention—won't there be other
chances?"

"But I wanted them to see you *among* your pictures—to
hear you talk about them, explain them in that wonderful

way. I wanted you to interpret each other, as Professor Wild-marsh says!"

"Oh, hang Professor Wildmarsh!" said Keniston, softening the commination with a smile. "If my pictures are good for anything they oughtn't to need explaining."

Mrs. Davant stared. "But I thought that was what made them so interesting!" she exclaimed.

Keniston looked down. "Perhaps it was," he murmured.

There was an awkward silence, which Claudia broke by say-ing, with a glance at her husband: "But if the exhibition is to remain open to-morrow, could we not meet you there? And perhaps you could send word to some of our friends."

Mrs. Davant brightened like a child whose broken toy is glued together. "Oh, *do* make him!" she implored. "I'll ask them to come in the afternoon—we'll make it into a little tea —a *five o'clock*. I'll send word at once to everybody!" She gathered up her beruffled boa and sunshade, settling her plumage like a reassured bird. "It will be too lovely!" she ended in a self-consoling murmur.

But in the doorway a new doubt assailed her. "You won't fail me?" she said, turning plaintively to Keniston. "You'll make him come, Mrs. Keniston?"

"I'll bring him!" Claudia promised.

IV

When, the next morning, she appeared equipped for their customary ramble, her husband surprised her by announcing that he meant to stay at home.

"The fact is I'm rather surfeited," he said, smiling. "I sup-pose my appetite isn't equal to such a plethora. I think I'll write some letters and join you somewhere later."

She detected the wish to be alone and responded to it with her usual readiness.

"I shall sink to my proper level and buy a bonnet, then," she said. "I haven't had time to take the edge off that ap-petite."

They agreed to meet at the Hôtel Cluny at mid-day, and she set out alone with a vague sense of relief. Neither she nor Keniston had made any direct reference to Mrs. Davant's visit; but its effect was implicit in their eagerness to avoid each other.

Claudia accomplished some shopping in the spirit of perfunctoriness that robs even new bonnets of their bloom; and this business despatched, she turned aimlessly into the wide inviting brightness of the streets. Never had she felt more isolated amid that ordered beauty which gives a social quality to the very stones and mortar of Paris. All about her were evidences of an artistic sensibility pervading every form of life like the nervous structure of the huge frame—a sensibility so delicate, alert and universal that it seemed to leave no room for obtuseness or error. In such a medium the faculty of plastic expression must develop as unconsciously as any organ in its normal surroundings; to be "artistic" must cease to be an attitude and become a natural function. To Claudia the significance of the whole vast revelation was centred in the light it shed on one tiny spot of consciousness—the value of her husband's work. There are moments when to the groping soul the world's accumulated experiences are but stepping-stones across a private difficulty.

She stood hesitating on a street corner. It was barely eleven, and she had an hour to spare before going to the Hôtel Cluny. She seemed to be letting her inclination float as it would on the cross-currents of suggestion emanating from the brilliant complex scene before her; but suddenly, in obedience to an impulse that she became aware of only in acting on it, she called a cab and drove to the gallery where her husband's pictures were exhibited.

A magnificent official in gold braid sold her a ticket and pointed the way up the empty crimson-carpeted stairs. His duplicate, on the upper landing, held out a catalogue with an air of recognizing the futility of the offer; and a moment later she found herself in the long noiseless impressive room full of velvet-covered ottomans and exotic plants. It was clear that the public ardor on which Mrs. Davant had expatiated had spent itself earlier in the week; for Claudia had this luxurious apartment to herself. Something about its air of rich privacy, its diffusion of that sympathetic quality in other countries so conspicuously absent from the public show-room, seemed to emphasize its present emptiness. It was as though the flowers,

the carpet, the lounges, surrounded their visitor's solitary advance with the mute assurance that they had done all they
could toward making the thing "go off," and that if they had
failed it was simply for lack of co-operation. She stood still
and looked about her. The pictures struck her instantly as odd
gaps in the general harmony; it was self-evident that they had
not co-operated. They had not been pushing, aggressive, discordant: they had merely effaced themselves. She swept a startled eye from one familiar painting to another. The canvases
were all there—and the frames—but the miracle, the mirage
of life and meaning, had vanished like some atmospheric illusion. What was it that had happened? And had it happened to
her or to the pictures? She tried to rally her frightened
thoughts; to push or coax them into a semblance of resistance; but argument was swept off its feet by the huge rush of
a single conviction—the conviction that the pictures were
bad. There was no standing up against that: she felt herself
submerged.

The stealthy fear that had been following her all these days
had her by the throat now. The great vision of beauty
through which she had been moving as one enchanted was
turned to a phantasmagoria of evil mocking shapes. She hated
the past; she hated its splendor, its power, its wicked magical
vitality. . . She dropped into a seat and continued to stare at
the wall before her. Gradually, as she stared, there stole out to
her from the dimmed humbled canvases a reminder of what
she had once seen in them, a spectral appeal to her faith to
call them back to life. What proof had she that her present estimate of them was less subjective than the other? The confused impressions of the last few days were hardly to be
pleaded as a valid theory of art. How, after all, did she know
that the pictures were bad? On what suddenly acquired technical standard had she thus decided the case against them? It
seemed as though it were a standard outside of herself, as
though some unheeded inner sense were gradually making
her aware of the presence, in that empty room, of a critical intelligence that was giving out a subtle effluence of disapproval. The fancy was so vivid that, to shake it off, she rose
and began to move about again. In the middle of the room
stood a monumental divan surmounted by a *massif* of palms

and azaleas. As Claudia's muffled wanderings carried her
around the angle of this seat, she saw that its farther side was
occupied by the figure of a man, who sat with his hands resting on his stick and his head bowed upon them. She gave a
little cry and her husband rose and faced her.

Instantly the live point of consciousness was shifted, and
she became aware that the quality of the pictures no longer
mattered. It was what *he* thought of them that counted: her
life hung on that.

They looked at each other a moment in silence; such con-
cussions are not apt to flash into immediate speech. At length
he said simply, "I didn't know you were coming here."

She colored as though he had charged her with something
underhand.

"I didn't mean to," she stammered; "but I was too early for
our appointment—"

Her words cast a revealing glare on the situation. Neither
of them looked at the pictures; but to Claudia those unob-
truding presences seemed suddenly to press upon them and
force them apart.

Keniston glanced at his watch. "It's twelve o'clock," he
said. "Shall we go on?"

v

At the door he called a cab and put her in it; then, drawing
out his watch again, he said abruptly: "I believe I'll let you go
alone. I'll join you at the hotel in time for luncheon." She
wondered for a moment if he meant to return to the gallery;
but, looking back as she drove off, she saw him walk rapidly
away in the opposite direction.

The cabman had carried her half-way to the Hôtel Cluny
before she realized where she was going, and cried out to him
to turn home. There was an acute irony in this mechanical
prolongation of the quest of beauty. She had had enough of
it, too much of it; her one longing was to escape, to hide herself away from its all-suffusing implacable light.

At the hotel, alone in her room, a few tears came to soften
her seared vision; but her mood was too tense to be eased by
weeping. Her whole being was centred in the longing to

know what her husband thought. Their short exchange of words had, after all, told her nothing. She had guessed a faint resentment at her unexpected appearance; but that might merely imply a dawning sense, on his part, of being furtively watched and criticised. She had sometimes wondered if he was never conscious of her observation; there were moments when it seemed to radiate from her in visible waves. Perhaps, after all, he was aware of it, on his guard against it, as a lurking knife behind the thick curtain of his complacency; and to-day he must have caught the gleam of the blade.

Claudia had not reached the age when pity is the first chord to vibrate in contact with any revelation of failure. Her one hope had been that Keniston should be clear-eyed enough to face the truth. Whatever it turned out to be, she wanted him to measure himself with it. But as his image rose before her she felt a sudden half-maternal longing to thrust herself between him and disaster. Her eagerness to see him tested by circumstances seemed now like a cruel scientific curiosity. She saw in a flash of sympathy that he would need her most if he fell beneath his fate.

He did not, after all, return for luncheon; and when she came up-stairs from her solitary meal their *salon* was still untenanted. She permitted herself no sensational fears; for she could not, at the height of apprehension, figure Keniston as yielding to any tragic impulse; but the lengthening hours brought an uneasiness that was fuel to her pity. Suddenly she heard the clock strike five. It was the hour at which they had promised to meet Mrs. Davant at the gallery—the hour of the "ovation." Claudia rose and went to the window, straining for a glimpse of her husband in the crowded street. Could it be that he had forgotten her, had gone to the gallery without her? Or had something happened—that veiled "something" which, for the last hour, had grimly hovered on the outskirts of her mind?

She heard a hand on the door and Keniston entered. As she turned to meet him her whole being was swept forward on a great wave of pity: she was so sure, now, that he must know.

But he confronted her with a glance of preoccupied brightness; her first impression was that she had never seen him so

vividly, so expressively pleased. If he needed her, it was not to
bind up his wounds.

He gave her a smile which was clearly the lingering reflection
of some inner light. "I didn't mean to be so late," he said, tossing aside his hat and the little red volume that served as a clue
to his explorations. "I turned in to the Louvre for a minute after I left you this morning, and the place fairly swallowed me
up—I couldn't get away from it. I've been there ever since."
He threw himself into a chair and glanced about for his pipe.

"It takes time," he continued musingly, "to get at them, to
make out what they're saying—the big fellows, I mean.
They're not a communicative lot. At first I couldn't make
much out of their lingo—it was too different from mine! But
gradually, by picking up a hint here and there, and piecing
them together, I've begun to understand; and to-day, by
Jove, I got one or two of the old chaps by the throat and
fairly turned them inside out—made them deliver up their last
drop." He lifted a brilliant eye to her. "Lord, it was tremendous!" he declared.

He had found his pipe and was musingly filling it. Claudia
waited in silence.

"At first," he began again, "I was afraid their language was
too hard for me—that I should never quite know what they
were driving at; they seemed to cold-shoulder me, to be bent
on shutting me out. But I was bound I wouldn't be beaten,
and now, to-day"—he paused a moment to strike a match—
"when I went to look at those things of mine it all came over
me in a flash. By Jove! It was as if I'd made them all into a
big bonfire to light me on my road!"

His wife was trembling with a kind of sacred terror. She
had been afraid to pray for light for him, and here he was joyfully casting his whole past upon the pyre!

"Is there nothing left?" she faltered.

"Nothing left? There's everything!" he exulted. "Why, here
I am, not much over forty, and I've found out already—already!" He stood up and began to move excitedly about the
room. "My God! Suppose I'd never known! Suppose I'd
gone on painting things like that forever! Why, I feel like
those chaps at revivalist meetings when they get up and say
they're saved! Won't somebody please start a hymn?"

Claudia, with a tremulous joy, was letting herself go on the strong current of his emotion; but it had not yet carried her beyond her depth, and suddenly she felt hard ground underfoot.

"Mrs. Davant—" she exclaimed.

He stared, as though suddenly recalled from a long distance. "Mrs. Davant?"

"We were to have met her—this afternoon—now—"

"At the gallery? Oh, that's all right. I put a stop to that; I went to see her after I left you; I explained it all to her."

"All?"

"I told her I was going to begin all over again."

Claudia's heart gave a forward bound and then sank back hopelessly.

"But the panels—?"

"That's all right too. I told her about the panels," he reassured her.

"You told her—?"

"That I can't paint them now. She doesn't understand, of course; but she's the best little woman and she trusts me."

She could have wept for joy at his exquisite obtuseness. "But that isn't all," she wailed. "It doesn't matter how much you've explained to her. It doesn't do away with the fact that we're living on those panels!"

"Living on them?"

"On the money that she paid you to paint them. Isn't that what brought us here? And—if you mean to do as you say— to begin all over again—how in the world are we ever to pay her back?"

Her husband turned on her an inspired eye. "There's only one way that I know of," he imperturbably declared, "and that's to stay out here till I learn how to paint them."

The Rembrandt

"YOU'RE *so* artistic," my cousin Eleanor Copt began.
Of all Eleanor's exordiums it is the one I most dread.
When she tells me I'm so clever I know this is merely the preamble to inviting me to meet the last literary obscurity of the
moment: a trial to be evaded or endured, as circumstances
dictate; whereas her calling me artistic fatally connotes the request to visit, in her company, some distressed gentlewoman
whose future hangs on my valuation of her old Saxe or of her
grandfather's Marc Antonios. Time was when I attempted to
resist these compulsions of Eleanor's; but I soon learned that,
short of actual flight, there was no refuge from her beneficent
despotism. It is not always easy for the curator of a museum
to abandon his post on the plea of escaping a pretty cousin's
importunities; and Eleanor, aware of my predicament, is none
too magnanimous to take advantage of it. Magnanimity is, in
fact, not in Eleanor's line. The virtues, she once explained to
me, are like bonnets: the very ones that look best on other
people may not happen to suit one's own particular style; and
she added, with a slight deflection of metaphor, that none of
the ready-made virtues ever *had* fitted her: they all pinched
somewhere, and she'd given up trying to wear them.

Therefore when she said to me, "You're *so* artistic," em-
phasizing the conjunction with a tap of her dripping umbrella
(Eleanor is out in all weathers: the elements are as powerless
against her as man), I merely stipulated, "It's not old Saxe
again?"

She shook her head reassuringly. "A picture—a Rembrandt!"

"Good Lord! Why not a Leonardo?"

"Well"—she smiled—"that, of course, depends on *you*."

"On me?"

"On your attribution. I dare say Mrs. Fontage would consent to the change—though she's very conservative."

A gleam of hope came to me and I pronounced: "One
can't judge of a picture in this weather."

"Of course not. I'm coming for you to-morrow."

"I've an engagement to-morrow."

"I'll come before or after your engagement."

The afternoon paper lay at my elbow and I contrived a furtive consultation of the weather-report. It said "Rain to-morrow," and I answered briskly: "All right, then; come at ten"—rapidly calculating that the clouds on which I counted might lift by noon.

My ingenuity failed of its due reward; for the heavens, as if in league with my cousin, emptied themselves before morning, and punctually at ten Eleanor and the sun appeared together in my office.

I hardly listened, as we descended the Museum steps and got into Eleanor's hansom, to her vivid summing-up of the case. I guessed beforehand that the lady we were about to visit had lapsed by the most distressful degrees from opulence to a "hall-bedroom"; that her grandfather, if he had not been Minister to France, had signed the Declaration of Independence; that the Rembrandt was an heirloom, sole remnant of disbanded treasures; that for years its possessor had been unwilling to part with it, and that even now the question of its disposal must be approached with the most diplomatic obliquity.

Previous experience had taught me that all Eleanor's "cases" presented a harrowing similarity of detail. No circumstance tending to excite the spectator's sympathy and involve his action was omitted from the history of her beneficiaries; the lights and shades were indeed so skilfully adjusted that any impartial expression of opinion took on the hue of cruelty. I could have produced closetfuls of "heirlooms" in attestation of this fact; for it is one more mark of Eleanor's competence that her friends usually pay the interest on her philanthropy. My one hope was that in this case the object, being a picture, might reasonably be rated beyond my means; and as our cab drew up before a blistered brown-stone door-step I formed the self-defensive resolve to place an extreme valuation on Mrs. Fontage's Rembrandt. It is Eleanor's fault if she is sometimes fought with her own weapons.

The house stood in one of those shabby provisional-looking New York streets that seem resignedly awaiting demolition. It was the kind of house that, in its high days, must have had a bow-window with a bronze in it. The bow-window had

been replaced by a plumber's *devanture*, and one might con-
ceive the bronze to have gravitated to the limbo where
Mexican onyx tables and bric-à-brac in buffalo-horn await the
first signs of our next æsthetic reaction.

Eleanor swept me through a hall that smelled of poverty,
up unlit stairs to a bare slit of a room. "And she must leave
this in a month!" she whispered across her knock.

I had prepared myself for the limp widow's weed of a
woman that one figures in such a setting; and confronted
abruptly with Mrs. Fontage's white-haired erectness I had the
disconcerting sense that I was somehow in her presence at my
own solicitation. I instinctively charged Eleanor with this re-
versal of the situation; but a moment later I saw it must be ascribed to a something about Mrs. Fontage that precluded the
possibility of her asking any one a favor. It was not that she
was of forbidding, or even majestic, demeanor; but that one
guessed, under her aquiline prettiness, a dignity nervously on
guard against the petty betrayal of her surroundings. The
room was unconcealably poor: the little faded "relics," the
high-stocked ancestral silhouettes, the steel-engravings after
Raphael and Correggio, grouped in a vain attempt to hide the
most obvious stains on the wall-paper, served only to accen-
tuate the contrast of a past evidently diversified by foreign
travel and the enjoyment of the arts. Even Mrs. Fontage's
dress had the air of being a last expedient, the ultimate outcome of a much-taxed ingenuity in darning and turning. One
felt that all the poor lady's barriers were falling save that of
her impregnable manner.

To this manner I found myself conveying my appreciation
of being admitted to a view of the Rembrandt.

Mrs. Fontage's smile took my homage for granted. "It is always," she conceded, "a privilege to be in the presence of the
great masters." Her slim wrinkled hand waved me to a dusky
canvas near the window.

"It's *so* interesting, dear Mrs. Fontage," I heard Eleanor exclaiming, "and my cousin will be able to tell you exactly—"
Eleanor, in my presence, always admits that she knows nothing about art; but she gives the impression that this is merely
because she hasn't had time to look into the matter—and has
had me to do it for her.

Mrs. Fontage seated herself without speaking, as though fearful that a breath might disturb my communion with the masterpiece. I felt that she thought Eleanor's reassuring ejaculations ill-timed; and in this I was of one mind with her; for the impossibility of telling her exactly what I thought of her Rembrandt had become clear to me at a glance.

My cousin's vivacities began to languish and the silence seemed to shape itself into a receptacle for my verdict. I stepped back, affecting a more distant scrutiny; and as I did so my eye caught Mrs. Fontage's profile. Her lids trembled slightly. I took refuge in the familiar expedient of asking the history of the picture, and she waved me brightly to a seat.

This was indeed a topic on which she could dilate. The Rembrandt, it appeared, had come into Mr. Fontage's possession many years ago, while the young couple were on their wedding-tour, and under circumstances so romantic that she made no excuse for relating them in all their parenthetic fulness. The picture belonged to an old Belgian Countess of redundant quarterings, whom the extravagances of an ungovernable nephew had compelled to part with her possessions (in the most private manner) about the time of the Fontages' arrival. By a really remarkable coincidence, it happened that their courier (an exceptionally intelligent and superior man) was an old servant of the Countess's, and had thus been able to put them in the way of securing the Rembrandt under the very nose of an English Duke, whose agent had been sent to Brussels to negotiate for its purchase. Mrs. Fontage could not recall the Duke's name, but he was a great collector and had a famous Highland castle, where somebody had been murdered, and which she herself had visited (by moonlight) when she had travelled in Scotland as a girl. The episode had in short been one of the most interesting "experiences" of a tour almost chromo-lithographic in vivacity of impression; and they had always meant to go back to Brussels for the sake of reliving so picturesque a moment. Circumstances (of which the narrator's surroundings declared the nature) had persistently interfered with the projected return to Europe, and the picture had grown doubly valuable as representing the high-water mark of their artistic emotions. Mrs. Fontage's moist eye caressed the canvas. "There is only," she added with a perceptible effort, "one slight drawback: the picture is not signed. But for that the Countess, of course, would have sold it to a museum. All the connoisseurs who have seen it pronounce it an undoubted Rembrandt, in the artist's best manner; but the museums"—she arched her brows in smiling recognition of a well-known weakness—"give the preference to signed examples—"

Mrs. Fontage's words evoked so touching a vision of the young tourists of fifty years ago, entrusting to an accomplished and versatile courier the direction of their helpless zeal for art, that I lost sight for a moment of the point at issue. The old Belgian Countess, the wealthy Duke with a feudal castle in Scotland, Mrs. Fontage's own maiden pilgrimage to Arthur's Seat and Holyrood, all the accessories of the naïf transaction, seemed a part of that vanished Europe to which our young race carried its indiscriminate ardors, its tender romantic credulity: the legendary castellated Europe of keepsakes, brigands and old masters, that compensated, by one such "experience" as Mrs. Fontage's, for an after-life of æsthetic privation.

I was restored to the present by Eleanor's looking at her watch. The action mutely conveyed that something was expected of me. I risked the temporizing statement that the picture was very interesting; but Mrs. Fontage's polite assent revealed the poverty of the expedient. Eleanor's impatience overflowed.

"You would like my cousin to give you an idea of its value?" she suggested.

Mrs. Fontage grew more erect. "No one," she corrected with great gentleness, "can know its value quite as well as I, who live with it—"

We murmured our hasty concurrence.

"But it might be interesting to hear"—she addressed herself to me—"as a mere matter of curiosity—what estimate would be put on it from the purely commercial point of view —if such a term may be used in speaking of a work of art."

I sounded a note of deprecation.

"Oh, I understand, of course," she delicately anticipated me, "that that could never be *your* view, your personal view; but since occasions *may* arise—do arise—when it becomes

necessary to—to put a price on the priceless, as it were—I
have thought—Miss Copt has suggested—"

"Some day," Eleanor encouraged her, "you might feel that
the picture ought to belong to some one who has more—
more opportunity of showing it—letting it be seen by the
public—for educational reasons—"

"I have tried," Mrs. Fontage admitted, "to see it in that
light."

The crucial moment was upon me. To escape the challenge
of Mrs. Fontage's brilliant composure I turned once more to
the picture. If my courage needed reinforcement, the picture
amply furnished it. Looking at that lamentable canvas seemed
the surest way of gathering strength to denounce it; but behind me, all the while, I felt Mrs. Fontage's shuddering pride
drawn up in a final effort of self-defense. I hated myself for
my sentimental perversion of the situation. Reason argued
that it was more cruel to deceive Mrs. Fontage than to tell her
the truth; but that merely proved the inferiority of reason to
instinct in situations involving any concession to the emotions. Along with her faith in the Rembrandt I must destroy
not only the whole fabric of Mrs. Fontage's past, but even
that life-long habit of acquiescence in untested formulas that
makes the best part of the average feminine strength. I
guessed the episode of the picture to be inextricably interwoven with the traditions and convictions which served to veil
Mrs. Fontage's destitution not only from others but from
herself. Viewed in that light the Rembrandt had perhaps been
worth its purchase-money; and I regretted that works of art
do not commonly sell on the merit of the moral support they
may have rendered.

From this unavailing flight I was recalled by the sense that
something must be done. To place a fictitious value on the picture was at best a provisional measure; while the brutal alternative of advising Mrs. Fontage to sell it for a hundred dollars
at least afforded an opening to the charitably disposed purchaser. I intended, if other resources failed, to put myself forward in that light; but delicacy of course forbade my coupling
my unflattering estimate of the Rembrandt with an immediate
offer to buy it. All I could do was to inflict the wound: the
healing unguent must be withheld for later application.

I turned to Mrs. Fontage, who sat motionless, her finely-lined cheeks touched with an expectant color, her eyes averted from the picture which was so evidently the one object they beheld.

"My dear madam—" I began. Her vivid smile was like a light held up to dazzle me. It shrouded every alternative in darkness and I had the flurried sense of having lost my way among the intricacies of my contention. Of a sudden I felt the hopelessness of finding a crack in her impenetrable conviction. My words slipped from me like broken weapons. "The picture," I faltered, "would of course be worth more if it were signed. As it is, I—I hardly think—on a conservative estimate—it can be valued at—at more—than—a thousand dollars, say—"

My deflected argument ran on somewhat aimlessly till it found itself plunging full tilt against the barrier of Mrs. Fontage's silence. She sat as impassive as though I had not spoken. Eleanor loosed a few fluttering words of congratulation and encouragement, but their flight was suddenly cut short. Mrs. Fontage had risen with a certain solemnity.

"I could never," she said gently—her gentleness was adamantine—"under any circumstances whatever, consider, for a moment even, the possibility of parting with the picture at such a price."

II

Within three weeks a tremulous note from Mrs. Fontage requested the favor of another visit. If the writing was tremulous, however, the writer's tone was firm. She named her own day and hour, without the conventional reference to her visitor's convenience.

My first impulse was to turn the note over to Eleanor. I had acquitted myself of my share in the ungrateful business of coming to Mrs. Fontage's aid, and if, as her letter denoted, she had now yielded to the closer pressure of need, the business of finding a purchaser for the Rembrandt might well be left to my cousin's ingenuity. But here conscience put in the uncomfortable reminder that it was I who, in putting a price on the picture, had raised the real obstacle in the way of Mrs.

Fontage's rescue. No one would give a thousand dollars for the Rembrandt; but to tell Mrs. Fontage so had become as unthinkable as murder. I had, in fact, on returning from my first inspection of the picture, refrained from imparting to Eleanor my opinion of its value. Eleanor is porous, and I knew that sooner or later the unnecessary truth would exude through the loose texture of her dissimulation. Not infrequently she thus creates the misery she alleviates; and I have sometimes suspected her of paining people in order that she might be sorry for them. I had, at all events, cut off retreat in Eleanor's direction; and the remaining alternative carried me straight to Mrs. Fontage.

She received me with the same commanding sweetness. The room was even barer than before—I believe the carpet was gone—but her manner built up about her a palace to which I was welcomed with high state; and it was as a mere incident of the ceremony that I was presently made aware of her decision to sell the Rembrandt. My previous unsuccess in planning how to deal with Mrs. Fontage had warned me to leave my farther course to chance; and I listened to her explanation with complete detachment. She had resolved to travel for her health; her doctor advised it, and as her absence might be indefinitely prolonged she had reluctantly decided to part with the picture in order to avoid the expense of storage and insurance. Her voice drooped at the admission, and she hurried on, detailing the vague itinerary of a journey that was to combine long-promised visits to impatient friends with various "interesting opportunities" less definitely specified. The poor lady's skill in rearing a screen of verbiage about her enforced avowal had distracted me from my own share in the situation, and it was with dismay that I suddenly caught the drift of her assumptions. She expected me to buy the Rembrandt for the Museum; she had taken my previous valuation as a tentative bid, and when I came to my senses she was in the act of accepting my offer.

Had I had a thousand dollars of my own to dispose of, the bargain would have been concluded on the spot; but I was in the impossible position of being materially unable to buy the picture and morally unable to tell her that it was not worth acquiring for the Museum.

I dashed into the first evasion in sight. I had no authority, I explained, to purchase pictures for the Museum without the consent of the committee.

Mrs. Fontage coped for a moment in silence with the incredible fact that I had rejected her offer; then she ventured, with a kind of pale precipitation: "But I understood—Miss Copt tells me that you practically decide such matters for the committee." I could guess what the effort had cost her.

"My cousin is given to generalizations. My opinion may have some weight with the committee—"

"Well, then—" she timidly prompted.

"For that very reason I can't buy the picture."

She said, with a drooping note, "I don't understand."

"Yet you told me," I reminded her, "that you knew museums didn't buy unsigned pictures."

"Not for what they are worth! Every one knows that. But I—I understood—the price you named—" Her pride shuddered back from the abasement. "It's a misunderstanding then," she faltered.

To avoid looking at her, I glanced desperately at the Rembrandt. Could I—? But reason rejected the possibility. Even if the committee had been blind—and they all *were* but Crozier—I simply shouldn't have dared to do it. I stood up, feeling that to cut the matter short was the only alleviation within reach.

Mrs. Fontage had summoned her indomitable smile; but its brilliancy dropped, as I opened the door, like a candle blown out by a draught.

"If there's any one else—if you knew any one who would care to see the picture, I should be most happy—" She kept her eyes on me, and I saw that, in her case, it hurt less than to look at the Rembrandt. "I shall have to leave here, you know," she panted, "if nobody cares to have it—"

III

That evening at my club I had just succeeded in losing sight of Mrs. Fontage in the fumes of an excellent cigar, when a voice at my elbow evoked her harassing image.

"I want to talk to you," the speaker said, "about Mrs. Fontage's Rembrandt."

"There isn't any," I was about to growl; but looking up I recognized the confiding countenance of Mr. Jefferson Rose.

Mr. Rose was known to me chiefly as a young man suffused with a vague enthusiasm for Virtue and my cousin Eleanor.

One glance at his glossy exterior conveyed the assurance that his morals were as immaculate as his complexion and his linen. Goodness exuded from his moist eye, his liquid voice, the warm damp pressure of his trustful hand. He had always struck me as one of the most uncomplicated organisms I had ever met. His ideas were as simple and inconsecutive as the propositions in a primer, and he spoke slowly, with a kind of uniformity of emphasis that made his words stand out like the raised type for the blind. An obvious incapacity for abstract conceptions made him peculiarly susceptible to the magic of generalization, and one felt he would have been at the mercy of any Cause that spelled itself with a capital letter. It was hard to explain how, with such a superabundance of merit, he managed to be a good fellow: I can only say that he performed the astonishing feat as naturally as he supported an invalid mother and two sisters on the slender salary of a banker's clerk. He sat down beside me with an air of bright expectancy.

"It's a remarkable picture, isn't it?" he said.

"You've seen it?"

"I've been so fortunate. Miss Copt was kind enough to get Mrs. Fontage's permission; we went this afternoon."

I inwardly wished that Eleanor had selected another victim; unless indeed the visit were part of a plan whereby some third person, better equipped for the cultivation of delusions, was to be made to think the Rembrandt remarkable. Knowing the limitations of Mr. Rose's resources I began to wonder if he had any rich aunts.

"And her buying it in that way, too," he went on with his limpid smile, "from that old Countess in Brussels, makes it all the more interesting, doesn't it? Miss Copt tells me it's very seldom old pictures can be traced back for more than a generation. I suppose the fact of Mrs. Fontage's knowing its history must add a good deal to its value?"

Uncertain as to his drift, I said: "In her eyes it certainly appears to."

Implications are lost on Mr. Rose, who glowingly continued: "That's the reason why I wanted to talk to you about it —to consult you. Miss Copt tells me you value it at a thousand dollars."

There was no denying this, and I grunted a reluctant assent.

"Of course," he went on earnestly, "your valuation is based on the fact that the picture isn't signed—Mrs. Fontage explained that; and it *does* make a difference, certainly. But the thing is—if the picture's really good—ought one to take advantage—? I mean—one can see that Mrs. Fontage is in a tight place, and I wouldn't for the world—"

My astonished state arrested him.

"*You* wouldn't—?"

"I mean—you see, it's just this way"; he coughed and blushed: "I can't give more than a thousand dollars myself— it's as big a sum as I can manage to scrape together—but before I make the offer I want to be sure I'm not standing in the way of her getting more money."

My astonishment lapsed to dismay. "You're going to buy the picture for a thousand dollars?"

His blush deepened. "Why, yes. It sounds rather absurd, I suppose. It isn't much in my line, of course. I can see the picture's very beautiful, but I'm no judge—it isn't the kind of thing, naturally, that I could afford to go in for; but in this case I'm very glad to do what I can; the circumstances are so distressing; and knowing what you think of the picture I feel it's a pretty safe investment—"

"I don't think!" I blurted out.

"You—?"

"I don't think the picture's worth a thousand dollars; I don't think it's worth ten cents; I simply lied about it, that's all."

Mr. Rose looked as frightened as though I had charged him with the offense.

"Hang it, man, can't you see how it happened? I saw the poor woman's pride and happiness hung on her faith in that picture. I tried to make her understand that it was worthless —but she wouldn't; I tried to tell her so—but I couldn't. I behaved like a maudlin ass, but you shan't pay for my infernal bungling—you mustn't buy the picture!"

Mr. Rose sat silent, tapping one glossy boot-tip with another. Suddenly he turned on me a glance of stored intelligence. "But you know," he said good-humoredly, "I rather think I must."

"You haven't—already?"

"Oh, no; the offer's not made."

"Well, then—"

His look gathered a brighter significance.

"But if the picture's worth nothing, nobody will buy it—" I groaned.

"Except," he continued, "some fellow like me, who doesn't know anything. *I* think it's lovely, you know; I mean to hang it in my mother's sitting-room." He rose and clasped my hand in his adhesive pressure. "I'm awfully obliged to you for telling me this; but perhaps you won't mind my asking you not to mention our talk to Miss Copt? It might bother her, you know, to think the picture isn't exactly up to the mark; and it won't make a rap of difference to me."

IV

Mr. Rose left me to a sleepless night. The next morning my resolve was formed, and it carried me straight to Mrs. Fontage's. She answered my knock by stepping out on the landing, and as she shut the door behind her I caught a glimpse of her devastated interior. She mentioned, with a careful avoidance of the note of pathos on which our last conversation had closed, that she was preparing to leave that afternoon; and the trunks obstructing the threshold showed that her preparations were nearly complete. They were, I felt certain, the same trunks that, strapped behind a rattling vettura, had accompanied the bride and groom on that memorable voyage of discovery of which the booty had till recently adorned her walls; and there was a dim consolation in the thought that those early "finds" in coral and Swiss wood-carving, in lava and alabaster, still lay behind the worn locks, in the security of worthlessness.

Mrs. Fontage, on the landing, among her strapped and corded treasures, maintained the same air of stability that made it impossible, even under such conditions, to regard her flight as anything less dignified than a departure. It was the moral support of what she tacitly assumed that enabled me to set forth with proper deliberation the object of my visit; and she received my announcement with an absence of surprise that struck me as the very flower of tact. Under cover of these mutual assumptions the transaction was rapidly concluded; and it was not till the canvas passed into my hands that, as though the physical contact had unnerved her, Mrs. Fontage suddenly faltered. "It's the giving it up—" she stammered, disguising herself to the last; and I hastened away from the collapse of her splendid effrontery.

I need hardly point out that I had acted impulsively, and that reaction from the most honorable impulses is sometimes attended by moral perturbation. My motives had indeed been mixed enough to justify some uneasiness, but this was allayed by the instinctive feeling that it is more venial to defraud an institution than a man. Since Mrs. Fontage had to be kept from starving by means not wholly defensible, it was better that the obligation should be borne by a rich institution than an impecunious youth. I doubt, in fact, if my scruples would have survived a night's sleep, had they not been complicated by some uncertainty as to my own future. It was true that, subject to the purely formal assent of the committee, I had full power to buy for the Museum, and that the one member of the committee likely to dispute my decision was opportunely travelling in Europe; but the picture once in place I must face the risk of any expert criticism to which chance might expose it. I dismissed this contingency for future study, stored the Rembrandt in the cellar of the Museum, and thanked heaven that Crozier was abroad.

Six months later he strolled into my office. I had just concluded, under conditions of exceptional difficulty, and on terms unexpectedly benign, the purchase of the great Bartley Reynolds; and this circumstance, by relegating the matter of the Rembrandt to a lower stratum of consciousness, enabled me to welcome Crozier with unmixed pleasure. My security was enhanced by his appearance. His smile was charged with amiable reminiscences, and I inferred that his trip had put him in the humor to approve of everything, or at least to

ignore what fell short of his approval. I had therefore no uneasiness in accepting his invitation to dine that evening. It is
always pleasant to dine with Crozier and never more so than
when he is just back from Europe. His conversation gives
even the food a flavor of the Café Anglais.

The repast was delightful, and it was not till we had finished a Camembert which he must have brought over with
him, that my host said, in a tone of after-dinner perfunctoriness: "I see you've picked up a picture or two since I left."

I assented. "The Bartley Reynolds seemed too good an opportunity to miss, especially as the French government was after it. I think we got it cheap—"

"*Connu, connu,*" said Crozier pleasantly. "I know all about
the Reynolds. It was the biggest kind of a haul and I congratulate you. Best stroke of business we've done yet. But tell
me about the other picture—the Rembrandt."

"I never said it was a Rembrandt." I could hardly have said
why, but I felt distinctly annoyed with Crozier.

"Of course not. There's 'Rembrandt' on the frame, but I
saw you'd modified it to 'Dutch School'; I apologize." He
paused, but I offered no explanation. "What about it?" he
went on. "Where did you pick it up?" As he leaned to the flame
of the cigar-lighter his face seemed ruddy with enjoyment.

"I got it for a song," I said.

"A thousand, I think?"

"Have you seen it?" I asked abruptly.

"Went over the place this afternoon and found it in the cellar. Why hasn't it been hung, by the way?"

I paused a moment. "I'm waiting—"

"To—?"

"To have it varnished."

"Ah!" He leaned back and poured himself a second glass of
Chartreuse. The smile he confided to its golden depths pro-
voked me to challenge him with—

"What do you think of it?"

"The Rembrandt?" He lifted his eyes from the glass. "Just
what you do."

"It isn't a Rembrandt."

"I apologize again. You call it, I believe, a picture of the
same period?"

"I'm uncertain of the period."

"H'm." He glanced appreciatively along his cigar. "What are you certain of?"

"That it's a damned bad picture," I said savagely.

He nodded. "Just so. That's all we wanted to know."

"*We?*"

"We—I—the committee, in short. You see, my dear fellow, if you hadn't been certain it was a damned bad picture our position would have been a little awkward. As it is, my remaining duty—I ought to explain that in this matter I'm acting for the committee—is as simple as it's agreeable."

"I'll be hanged," I burst out, "if I understand one word you're saying!"

He fixed me with a kind of cruel joyousness. "You will—you will," he assured me; "at least you'll begin to, when you hear that I've seen Miss Copt."

"Miss Copt?"

"And that she has told me under what conditions the picture was bought."

"She doesn't know anything about the conditions! That is," I added, hastening to restrict the assertion, "she doesn't know my opinion of the picture." I thirsted for five minutes with Eleanor.

"Are you quite sure?" Crozier took me up. "Mr. Jefferson Rose does."

"Ah—I see."

"I thought you would," he reminded me. "As soon as I'd laid eyes on the Rembrandt—I beg your pardon!—I saw that it—well, required some explanation."

"You might have come to me."

"I meant to; but I happened to meet Miss Copt, whose encyclopædic information has often before been of service to me. I always go to Miss Copt when I want to look up anything; and I found she knew all about the Rembrandt."

"*All?*"

"Precisely. The knowledge was in fact causing her sleepless nights. Mr. Rose, who was suffering from the same form of insomnia, had taken her into his confidence, and she—ultimately—took me into hers."

"Of course!"

"I must ask you to do your cousin justice. She didn't speak till it became evident to her uncommonly quick perceptions that your buying the picture on its merits would have been infinitely worse for—for everybody—than your diverting a small portion of the Museum's funds to philanthropic uses. Then she told me the moving incident of Mr. Rose. Good fellow, Rose. And the old lady's case was desperate. Somebody had to buy that picture." I moved uneasily in my seat. "Wait a moment, will you? I haven't finished my cigar. There's a little head of Il Fiammingo's that you haven't seen, by the way; I picked it up the other day in Parma. We'll go in and have a look at it presently. But meanwhile what I want to say is that I've been charged—in the most informal way—to express to you the committee's appreciation of your admirable promptness and energy in capturing the Bartley Reynolds. We shouldn't have got it at all if you hadn't been uncommonly wide-awake, and to get it at such a price is a double triumph. We'd have thought nothing of a few more thousands—"

"I don't see," I impatiently interposed, "that, as far as I'm concerned, that alters the case."

"The case—?"

"Of Mrs. Fontage's Rembrandt. I bought the picture because, as you say, the situation was desperate, and I couldn't raise a thousand myself. What I did was of course indefensible; but the money shall be refunded to-morrow—"

Crozier raised a protesting hand. "Don't interrupt me when I'm talking ex cathedrâ. The money's been refunded already. The fact is, the Museum has sold the Rembrandt."

I stared at him wildly. "Sold it? To whom?"

"Why—to the committee.—Hold on a bit, please.—Won't you take another cigar? Then perhaps I can finish what I've got to say.—Why, my dear fellow, the committee's under an obligation to you—that's the way we look at it. I've investigated Mrs. Fontage's case, and—well, the picture had to be bought. She's eating meat now, I believe, for the first time in a year. And they'd have turned her out into the street that very day, your cousin tells me. Something had to be done at once, and you've simply given a number of well-to-do and self-indulgent gentlemen the opportunity of performing, at very small individual expense, a meritorious action in the nick of time. That's the first thing I've got to thank you for. And then—you'll remember, please, that I have the floor—that I'm still speaking for the committee—and secondly, as a slight recognition of your services in securing the Bartley Reynolds at a very much lower figure than we were prepared to pay, we beg you—the committee begs you—to accept the gift of Mrs. Fontage's Rembrandt. Now we'll go in and look at that little head. . . ."

The Moving Finger

THE NEWS of Mrs. Grancy's death came to me with the shock of an immense blunder—one of fate's most irretrievable acts of vandalism. It was as though all sorts of renovating forces had been checked by the clogging of that one wheel. Not that Mrs. Grancy contributed any perceptible momentum to the social machine: her unique distinction was that of filling to perfection her special place in the world. So many people are like badly-composed statues, over-lapping their niches at one point and leaving them vacant at another. Mrs. Grancy's niche was her husband's life; and if it be argued that the space was not large enough for its vacancy to leave a very big gap, I can only say that, at the last resort, such dimensions must be determined by finer instruments than any ready-made standard of utility. Ralph Grancy's was in short a kind of disembodied usefulness: one of those constructive influences that, instead of crystallizing into definite forms, remain as it were a medium for the development of clear thinking and fine feeling. He faithfully irrigated his own dusty patch of life, and the fruitful moisture stole far beyond his boundaries. If, to carry on the metaphor, Grancy's life was a sedulously-cultivated enclosure, his wife was the flower he had planted in its midst—the embowering tree, rather, which gave him rest and shade at its foot and the wind of dreams in its upper branches.

We had all—his small but devoted band of followers—known a moment when it seemed likely that Grancy would fail us. We had watched him pitted against one stupid obstacle after another—ill-health, poverty, misunderstanding and, worst of all for a man of his texture, his first wife's soft insidious egotism. We had seen him sinking under the leaden embrace of her affection like a swimmer in a drowning clutch; but just as we despaired he had always come to the surface again, blinded, panting, but striking out fiercely for the shore. When at last her death released him it became a question as to how much of the man she had carried with her. Left alone, he revealed numb withered patches, like a tree from which a parasite has been stripped. But gradually he began to put out new leaves; and when he met the lady who was to become his second wife—his one *real* wife, as his friends reckoned—the whole man burst into flower.

The second Mrs. Grancy was past thirty when he married her, and it was clear that she had harvested that crop of middle joy which is rooted in young despair. But if she had lost the surface of eighteen she had kept its inner light; if her cheek lacked the gloss of immaturity her eyes were young with the stored youth of half a life-time. Grancy had first known her somewhere in the East—I believe she was the sister of one of our consuls out there—and when he brought her home to New York she came among us as a stranger. The idea of Grancy's remarriage had been a shock to us all. After one such calcining most men would have kept out of the fire; but we agreed that he was predestined to sentimental blunders, and we awaited with resignation the embodiment of his latest mistake. Then Mrs. Grancy came—and we understood. She was the most beautiful and the most complete of explanations. We shuffled our defeated omniscience out of sight and gave it hasty burial under a prodigality of welcome. For the first time in years we had Grancy off our minds. "He'll do something great now!" the least sanguine of us prophesied; and our sentimentalist emended: "He *has* done it—in marrying her!"

It was Claydon, the portrait-painter, who risked this hyperbole; and who soon afterward, at the happy husband's request, prepared to defend it in a portrait of Mrs. Grancy. We were all—even Claydon—ready to concede that Mrs. Grancy's unwontedness was in some degree a matter of environment. Her graces were complementary and it needed the mate's call to reveal the flash of color beneath her neutral-tinted wings. But if she needed Grancy to interpret her, how much greater was the service she rendered him! Claydon professionally described her as the right frame for him; but if she defined she also enlarged, if she threw the whole into perspective she also cleared new ground, opened fresh vistas, reclaimed whole areas of activity that had run to waste under the harsh husbandry of privation. This interaction of sympathies was not without its visible expression. Claydon was not alone in maintaining that Grancy's presence—or indeed the mere mention of his name—had a perceptible effect on his wife's appearance. It was as though a light were shifted, a curtain drawn back, as though, to borrow another of Claydon's metaphors, Love the indefatigable artist were perpetually seeking a happier "pose" for his model. In this interpretative light Mrs. Grancy acquired the charm which makes some women's faces like a book of which the last page is never turned. There was always something new to read in her eyes. What Claydon read there—or at least such scattered hints of the ritual as reached him through the sanctuary doors—his portrait in due course declared to us. When the picture was exhibited it was at once acclaimed as his masterpiece; but the people who knew Mrs. Grancy smiled and said it was flattered. Claydon, however, had not set out to paint *their* Mrs. Grancy—or ours even—but Ralph's; and Ralph knew his own at a glance. At the first confrontation he saw that Claydon had understood. As for Mrs. Grancy, when the finished picture was shown to her she turned to the painter and said simply: "Ah, you've done me facing the east!"

The picture, then, for all its value, seemed a mere incident in the unfolding of their double destiny, a foot-note to the illuminated text of their lives. It was not till afterward that it acquired the significance of last words spoken on a threshold never to be recrossed. Grancy, a year after his marriage, had given up his town house and carried his bliss an hour's journey away, to a little place among the hills. His various duties and interests brought him frequently to New York but we necessarily saw him less often than when his house had served as the rallying-point of kindred enthusiasms. It seemed a pity that such an influence should be withdrawn, but we all felt that his long arrears of happiness should be paid in whatever coin he chose. The distance from which the fortunate couple radiated warmth on us was not too great for friendship to traverse; and our conception of a glorified leisure took the form of Sundays spent in the Grancys' library, with its sedative rural outlook and the portrait of Mrs. Grancy illuminating its studious walls. The picture was at its best in that setting; and we used to accuse Claydon of visiting Mrs. Grancy in order to see her portrait. He met this by declaring that the portrait *was*

Mrs. Grancy; and there were moments when the statement seemed unanswerable. One of us, indeed—I think it must have been the novelist—said that Claydon had been saved from falling in love with Mrs. Grancy only by falling in love with his picture of her; and it was noticeable that he, to whom his finished work was no more than the shed husk of future effort, showed a perennial tenderness for this one achievement. We smiled afterward to think how often, when Mrs. Grancy was in the room, her presence reflecting itself in our talk like a gleam of sky in a hurrying current, Claydon, averted from the real woman, would sit as it were listening to the picture. His attitude, at the time, seemed only a part of the unusualness of those picturesque afternoons, when the most familiar combinations of life underwent a magical change. Some human happiness is a landlocked lake; but the Grancys' was an open sea, stretching a buoyant and illimitable surface to the voyaging interests of life. There was room and to spare on those waters for all our separate ventures; and always, beyond the sunset, a mirage of the fortunate isles toward which our prows were bent.

II

It was in Rome that, three years later, I heard of her death. The notice said "suddenly"; I was glad of that. I was glad too —basely perhaps—to be away from Grancy at a time when silence must have seemed obtuse and speech derisive.

I was still in Rome when, a few months afterward, he suddenly arrived there. He had been appointed secretary of legation at Constantinople and was on the way to his post. He had taken the place, he said frankly, "to get away." Our relations with the Porte held out a prospect of hard work, and that, he explained, was what he needed. He could never be satisfied to sit down among the ruins. I saw that, like most of us in moments of extreme moral tension, he was playing a part, behaving as he thought it became a man to behave in the eye of disaster. The instinctive posture of grief is a shuffling compromise between defiance and prostration; and pride feels the need of striking a worthier attitude in face of such a foe. Grancy, by nature musing and retrospective, had chosen the rôle of the man of action, who answers blow for blow and opposes a mailed front to the thrusts of destiny; and the completeness of the equipment testified to his inner weakness. We talked only of what we were not thinking of, and parted, after a few days, with a sense of relief that proved the inadequacy of friendship to perform, in such cases, the office assigned to it by tradition.

Soon afterward my own work called me home, but Grancy remained several years in Europe. International diplomacy kept its promise of giving him work to do, and during the year in which he acted as *chargé d'affaires* he acquitted himself, under trying conditions, with conspicuous zeal and discretion. A political redistribution of matter removed him from office just as he had proved his usefulness to the government; and the following summer I heard that he had come home and was down at his place in the country.

On my return to town I wrote him and his reply came by the next post. He answered as it were in his natural voice, urging me to spend the following Sunday with him, and suggesting that I should bring down any of the old set who could be persuaded to join me. I thought this a good sign, and yet—shall I own it?—I was vaguely disappointed. Perhaps we are apt to feel that our friends' sorrows should be kept like those historic monuments from which the encroaching ivy is periodically removed.

That very evening at the club I ran across Claydon. I told him of Grancy's invitation and proposed that we should go down together; but he pleaded an engagement. I was sorry, for I had always felt that he and I stood nearer Ralph than the others, and if the old Sundays were to be renewed I should have preferred that we two should spend the first alone with him. I said as much to Claydon and offered to fit my time to his; but he met this by a general refusal.

"I don't want to go to Grancy's," he said bluntly. I waited a moment, but he appended no qualifying clause.

"You've seen him since he came back?" I finally ventured.

Claydon nodded.

"And is he so awfully bad?"

"Bad? No: he's all right."

"All right? How can he be, unless he's changed beyond all recognition?"

"Oh, you'll recognize *him*," said Claydon, with a puzzling deflection of emphasis.

His ambiguity was beginning to exasperate me, and I felt myself shut out from some knowledge to which I had as good a right as he.

"You've been down there already, I suppose?"

"Yes; I've been down there."

"And you've done with each other—the partnership is dissolved?"

"Done with each other? I wish to God we had!" He rose nervously and tossed aside the review from which my approach had diverted him. "Look here," he said, standing before me, "Ralph's the best fellow going and there's nothing under heaven I wouldn't do for him—short of going down there again." And with that he walked out of the room.

Claydon was incalculable enough for me to read a dozen different meanings into his words; but none of my interpretations satisfied me. I determined, at any rate, to seek no farther for a companion; and the next Sunday I travelled down to Grancy's alone. He met me at the station and I saw at once that he had changed since our last meeting. Then he had been in fighting array, but now if he and grief still housed together it was no longer as enemies. Physically the transformation was as marked but less reassuring. If the spirit triumphed the body showed its scars. At five-and-forty he was gray and stooping, with the tired gait of an old man. His serenity, however, was not the resignation of age. I saw that he did not mean to drop out of the game. Almost immediately he began to speak of our old interests; not with an effort, as at our former meeting, but simply and naturally, in the tone of a man whose life has flowed back into its normal channels. I remembered, with a touch of self-reproach, how I had distrusted his reconstructive powers; but my admiration for his reserved force was now tinged by the sense that, after all, such happiness as his ought to have been paid with his last coin. The feeling grew as we neared the house and I found how inextricably his wife was interwoven with my remembrance of the place: how the whole scene was but an extension of that vivid presence.

Within doors nothing was changed, and my hand would have dropped without surprise into her welcoming clasp. It was luncheon-time, and Grancy led me at once to the dining-room, where the walls, the furniture, the very plate and porcelain, seemed a mirror in which a moment since her face had been reflected. I wondered whether Grancy, under the re-covered tranquillity of his smile, concealed the same sense of her nearness, saw perpetually between himself and the actual her bright unappeasable ghost. He spoke of her once or twice, in an easy incidental way, and her name seemed to hang in the air after he had uttered it, like a chord that continues to vibrate. If he felt her presence it was evidently as an en-veloping medium, the moral atmosphere in which he breathed. I had never before known how completely the dead may survive.

After luncheon we went for a long walk through the au-tumnal fields and woods, and dusk was falling when we re-entered the house. Grancy led the way to the library, where, at this hour, his wife had always welcomed us back to a bright fire and a cup of tea. The room faced the west, and held a clear light of its own after the rest of the house had grown dark. I remembered how young she had looked in this pale gold light, which irradiated her eyes and hair, or silhouetted her girlish outline as she passed before the windows. Of all the rooms the library was most peculiarly hers; and here I felt that her nearness might take visible shape. Then, all in a mo-ment, as Grancy opened the door, the feeling vanished and a kind of resistance met me on the threshold. I looked about me. Was the room changed? Had some desecrating hand effaced the traces of her presence? No; here too the setting was undisturbed. My feet sank into the same deep-piled Daghestan; the book-shelves took the firelight on the same rows of rich subdued bindings; her arm-chair stood in its old place near the tea-table; and from the opposite wall her face confronted me.

Her face—but *was* it hers? I moved nearer and stood look-ing up at the portrait. Grancy's glance had followed mine and I heard him move to my side.

"You see a change in it?" he said.

"What does it mean?" I asked.

"It means—that five years have passed."

"Over *her*?"

"Why not?—Look at me!" He pointed to his gray hair and furrowed temples. "What do you think kept *her* so young? It was happiness! But now—" he looked up at her with infinite tenderness. "I like her better so," he said. "It's what she would have wished."

"Have wished?"

"That we should grow old together. Do you think she would have wanted to be left behind?"

I stood speechless, my gaze travelling from his worn grief-beaten features to the painted face above. It was not furrowed like his; but a veil of years seemed to have descended on it. The bright hair had lost its elasticity, the cheek its clearness, the brow its light: the whole woman had waned.

Grancy laid his hand on my arm. "You don't like it?" he said sadly.

"Like it? I—I've lost her!" I burst out.

"And I've found her," he answered.

"In *that*?" I cried with a reproachful gesture.

"Yes; in that." He swung round on me almost defiantly. "The other had become a sham, a lie! This is the way she would have looked—does look, I mean. Claydon ought to know, oughtn't he?"

I turned suddenly. "Did Claydon do this for you?"

Grancy nodded.

"Since your return?"

"Yes. I sent for him after I'd been back a week—." He turned away and gave a thrust to the smouldering fire. I followed, glad to leave the picture behind me. Grancy threw himself into a chair near the hearth, so that the light fell on his sensitive variable face. He leaned his head back, shading his eyes with his hand, and began to speak.

III

"You fellows knew enough of my early history to guess what my second marriage meant to me. I say guess, because no one could understand—really. I've always had a feminine streak in me, I suppose: the need of a pair of eyes that should see with me, of a pulse that should keep time with mine. Life is a big thing, of course; a magnificent spectacle; but I got so tired of looking at it alone! Still, it's always good to live, and I had plenty of happiness—of the evolved kind. What I'd never had a taste of was the simple inconscient sort that one breathes in like the air. . .

"Well—I met her. It was like finding the climate in which I was meant to live. You know what she was—how indefinitely she multiplied one's points of contact with life, how she lit up the caverns and bridged the abysses! Well, I swear to you (though I suppose the sense of all that was latent in me) that what I used to think of on my way home at the end of the day, was simply that when I opened this door she'd be sitting over there, with the lamp-light falling in a particular way on one little curl in her neck. . . When Claydon painted her he caught just the look she used to lift to mine when I came in— I've wondered, sometimes, at his knowing how she looked when she and I were alone.—How I rejoiced in that picture! I used to say to her, 'You're my prisoner now—I shall never lose you. If you grew tired of me and left me you'd leave your real self there on the wall!' It was always one of our jokes that she was going to grow tired of me—

"Three years of it—and then she died. It was so sudden that there was no change, no diminution. It was as if she had suddenly become fixed, immovable, like her own portrait: as if Time had ceased at its happiest hour, just as Claydon had thrown down his brush one day and said, 'I can't do better than that.'

"I went away, as you know, and stayed over there five years. I worked as hard as I knew how, and after the first black months a little light stole in on me. From thinking that she would have been interested in what I was doing I came to feel that she *was* interested—that she was there and that she knew. I'm not talking any psychical jargon—I'm simply trying to express the sense I had that an influence so full, so abounding as hers couldn't pass like a spring shower. We had so lived into each other's hearts and minds that the consciousness of what she would have thought and felt illuminated all I did. At first she used to come back shyly, tentatively, as though not sure of finding me; then she stayed longer and longer, till at last she became again the very air I breathed. . . There were bad moments, of course, when her nearness mocked me with the loss of the real woman; but gradually the distinction between the two was effaced and the mere thought of her grew warm as flesh and blood.

"Then I came home. I landed in the morning and came straight down here. The thought of seeing her portrait possessed me and my heart beat like a lover's as I opened the library door. It was in the afternoon and the room was full of light. It fell on her picture—the picture of a young and radiant woman. She smiled at me coldly across the distance that divided us. I had the feeling that she didn't even recognize me. And then I caught sight of myself in the mirror over there —a gray-haired broken man whom she had never known!

"For a week we two lived together—the strange woman and the strange man. I used to sit night after night and question her smiling face; but no answer ever came. What did she know of me, after all? We were irrevocably separated by the five years of life that lay between us. At times, as I sat here, I almost grew to hate her; for her presence had driven away my gentle ghost, the real wife who had wept, aged, struggled with me during those awful years. . . It was the worst loneliness I've ever known. Then, gradually, I began to notice a look of sadness in the picture's eyes; a look that seemed to say: 'Don't you see that *I* am lonely too?' And all at once it came over me how she would have hated to be left behind! I remembered her comparing life to a heavy book that could not be read with ease unless two people held it together; and I thought how impatiently her hand would have turned the pages that divided us!—So the idea came to me: 'It's the picture that stands between us; the picture that is dead, and not my wife. To sit in this room is to keep watch beside a corpse.' As this feeling grew on me the portrait became like a beautiful mausoleum in which she had been buried alive: I could hear her beating against the painted walls and crying to me faintly for help. . .

"One day I found I couldn't stand it any longer and I sent for Claydon. He came down and I told him what I'd been through and what I wanted him to do. At first he refused point-blank to touch the picture. The next morning I went off for a long tramp, and when I came home I found him sitting here alone. He looked at me sharply for a moment and then he said: 'I've changed my mind; I'll do it.' I arranged one of the north rooms as a studio and he shut himself up there for a day; then he sent for me. The picture stood there as you see it now—it was as though she'd met me on the threshold and taken me in her arms! I tried to thank him, to tell him what it meant to me, but he cut me short.

" 'There's an up train at five, isn't there?' he asked. 'I'm booked for a dinner to-night. I shall just have time to make a bolt for the station and you can send my traps after me.' I haven't seen him since.

"I can guess what it cost him to lay hands on his masterpiece; but, after all, to him it was only a picture lost, to me it was my wife regained!"

IV

After that, for ten years or more, I watched the strange spectacle of a life of hopeful and productive effort based on the structure of a dream. There could be no doubt to those who saw Grancy during this period that he drew his strength and courage from the sense of his wife's mystic participation in his task. When I went back to see him a few months later I found the portrait had been removed from the library and placed in a small study up-stairs, to which he had transferred his desk and a few books. He told me he always sat there when he was alone, keeping the library for his Sunday visitors. Those who missed the portrait of course made no comment on its absence, and the few who were in his secret respected it. Gradually all his old friends had gathered about him and our Sunday afternoons regained something of their former character; but Claydon never reappeared among us.

As I look back now I see that Grancy must have been failing from the time of his return home. His invincible spirit belied and disguised the signs of weakness that afterward asserted themselves in my remembrance of him. He seemed to have an inexhaustible fund of life to draw on, and more than one of us was a pensioner on his superfluity.

Nevertheless, when I came back one summer from my European holiday and heard that he had been at the point of death, I understood at once that we had believed him well only because he wished us to.

I hastened down to the country and found him midway in a slow convalescence. I felt then that he was lost to us and he read my thought at a glance.

"Ah," he said, "I'm an old man now and no mistake. I suppose we shall have to go half-speed after this; but we shan't need towing just yet!"

The plural pronoun struck me, and involuntarily I looked up at Mrs. Grancy's portrait. Line by line I saw my fear reflected in it. It was the face of a woman *who knows that her husband is dying.* My heart stood still at the thought of what Claydon had done.

Grancy had followed my glance. "Yes, it's changed her," he said quietly. "For months, you know, it was touch and go with me—we had a long fight of it, and it was worse for her than for me." After a pause he added: "Claydon has been very kind; he's so busy nowadays that I seldom see him, but when I sent for him the other day he came down at once."

I was silent and we spoke no more of Grancy's illness; but when I took leave it seemed like shutting him in alone with his death-warrant.

The next time I went down to see him he looked much better. It was a Sunday and he received me in the library, so that I did not see the portrait again. He continued to improve and toward spring we began to feel that, as he had said, he might yet travel a long way without being towed.

One evening, on returning to town after a visit which had confirmed my sense of reassurance, I found Claydon dining alone at the club. He asked me to join him and over the coffee our talk turned to his work.

"If you're not too busy," I said at length, "you ought to make time to go down to Grancy's again."

He looked up quickly. "Why?" he asked.

"Because he's quite well again," I returned with a touch of cruelty. "His wife's prognostications were mistaken."

Claydon stared at me a moment. "Oh, *she* knows," he affirmed with a smile that chilled me.

"You mean to leave the portrait as it is then?" I persisted.

He shrugged his shoulders. "He hasn't sent for me yet!"

A waiter came up with the cigars and Claydon rose and joined another group.

It was just a fortnight later that Grancy's housekeeper telegraphed for me. She met me at the station with the news that he had been "taken bad" and that the doctors were with him. I had to wait for some time in the deserted library before the medical men appeared. They had the baffled manner of empirics who have been superseded by the great Healer; and I lingered only long enough to hear that Grancy was not suffering and that my presence could do him no harm.

I found him seated in his arm-chair in the little study. He held out his hand with a smile.

"You see she was right after all," he said.

"She?" I repeated, perplexed for the moment.

"My wife." He indicated the picture. "Of course I knew she had no hope from the first. I saw that"—he lowered his voice—"after Claydon had been here. But I wouldn't believe it at first!"

I caught his hands in mine. "For God's sake don't believe it now!" I adjured him.

He shook his head gently. "It's too late," he said. "I might have known that she knew."

"But, Grancy, listen to me," I began; and then I stopped. What could I say that would convince him? There was no common ground of argument on which we could meet; and after all it would be easier for him to die feeling that she *had* known. Strangely enough, I saw that Claydon had missed his mark. . .

V

Grancy's will named me as one of his executors; and my associate, having other duties on his hands, begged me to assume the task of carrying out our friend's wishes. This placed me under the necessity of informing Claydon that the portrait of Mrs. Grancy had been bequeathed to him; and he replied by the next post that he would send for the picture at once. I was staying in the deserted house when the portrait was taken away; and as the door closed on it I felt that Grancy's presence had vanished too. Was it his turn to follow her now, and could one ghost haunt another?

After that, for a year or two, I heard nothing more of the picture, and though I met Claydon from time to time we had little to say to each other. I had no definable grievance against the man and I tried to remember that he had done a fine thing in sacrificing his best picture to a friend; but my resentment had all the tenacity of unreason.

One day, however, a lady whose portrait he had just finished begged me to go with her to see it. To refuse was impossible, and I went with the less reluctance that I knew I was not the only friend she had invited. The others were all grouped around the easel when I entered, and after contributing my share to the chorus of approval I turned away and began to stroll about the studio. Claydon was something of a collector and his things were generally worth looking at. The studio was a long tapestried room with a curtained archway at one end. The curtains were looped back, showing a smaller apartment, with books and flowers and a few fine bits of bronze and porcelain. The tea-table standing in this inner room proclaimed that it was open to inspection, and I wandered in. A *bleu poudré* vase first attracted me; then I turned to examine a slender bronze Ganymede, and in so doing found myself face to face with Mrs. Grancy's portrait. I stared up at her blankly and she smiled back at me in all the recovered radiance of youth. The artist had effaced every trace of his later touches and the original picture had reappeared. It throned alone on the panelled wall, asserting a brilliant supremacy over its carefully-chosen surroundings. I felt in an instant that the whole room was tributary to it: that Claydon had heaped his treasures at the feet of the woman he loved. Yes—it was the woman he had loved and not the picture; and my instinctive resentment was explained.

Suddenly I felt a hand on my shoulder.

"Ah, how could you?" I cried, turning on him.

"How could I?" he retorted. "How could I *not*? Doesn't she belong to me now?"

I moved away impatiently.

"Wait a moment," he said with a detaining gesture. "The others have gone and I want to say a word to you.—Oh, I know what you've thought of me—I can guess! You think I killed Grancy, I suppose?"

I was startled by his sudden vehemence. "I think you tried to do a cruel thing," I said.

"Ah—what a little way you others see into life!" he murmured. "Sit down a moment—here, where we can look at her—and I'll tell you."

He threw himself on the ottoman beside me and sat gazing up at the picture, with his hands clasped about his knee.

"Pygmalion," he began slowly, "turned his statue into a real woman; *I* turned my real woman into a picture. Small compensation, you think—but you don't know how much of a woman belongs to you after you've painted her!—Well, I made the best of it, at any rate—I gave her the best I had in me; and she gave me in return what such a woman gives by merely being. And after all she rewarded me enough by making me paint as I shall never paint again! There was one side of her, though, that was mine alone, and that was her beauty; for no one else understood it. To Grancy even it was the mere expression of herself—what language is to thought. Even when he saw the picture he didn't guess my secret—he was so sure she was all his! As though a man should think he owned the moon because it was reflected in the pool at his door—

"Well—when he came home and sent for me to change the picture it was like asking me to commit murder. He wanted me to make an old woman of her—of her who had been so divinely, unchangeably young! As if any man who really loved a woman would ask her to sacrifice her youth and beauty for his sake! At first I told him I couldn't do it—but afterward, when he left me alone with the picture, something queer happened. I suppose it was because I was always so confoundedly fond of Grancy that it went against me to refuse what he asked. Anyhow, as I sat looking up at her, she seemed to say, 'I'm not yours but his, and I want you to make me what he wishes.' And so I did it. I could have cut my hand off when the work was done—I daresay he told you I never would go back and look at it. He thought I was too busy—he never understood. . .

"Well—and then last year he sent for me again—you remember. It was after his illness, and he told me he'd grown twenty years older and that he wanted her to grow older too—he didn't want her to be left behind. The doctors all thought he was going to get well at that time, and he thought so too; and so did I when I first looked at him. But when I turned to the picture—ah, now I don't ask you to believe me; but I swear it was *her* face that told me he was dying, and that she wanted him to know it! She had a message for him and she made me deliver it."

He rose abruptly and walked toward the portrait; then he sat down beside me again.

"Cruel? Yes, it seemed so to me at first; and this time, if I resisted, it was for *his* sake and not for mine. But all the while I felt her eyes drawing me, and gradually she made me understand. If she'd been there in the flesh (she seemed to say) wouldn't she have seen before any of us that he was dying? Wouldn't he have read the news first in her face? And wouldn't it be horrible if now he should discover it instead in strange eyes?—Well—that was what she wanted of me and I did it—I kept them together to the last!" He looked up at the picture again. "But now she belongs to me," he repeated. . .

Sanctuary

Iᴛ ɪs not often that youth allows itself to feel undividedly happy: the sensation is too much the result of selection and elimination to be within reach of the awakening clutch on life. But Kate Orme, for once, had yielded herself to happiness, letting it permeate every faculty as a spring rain soaks into a germinating meadow. There was nothing to account for this sudden sense of beatitude; but was it not this precisely which made it so irresistible, so overwhelming? There had been, within the last two months—since her engagement to Denis Peyton—no distinct addition to the sum of her happiness, and no possibility, she would have affirmed, of adding perceptibly to a total already incalculable. Inwardly and outwardly the conditions of her life were unchanged; but whereas, before, the air had been full of flitting wings, now they seemed to pause over her and she could trust herself to their shelter.

Many influences had combined to build up the centre of brooding peace in which she found herself. Her nature answered to the finest vibrations, and at first her joy in loving had been too great not to bring with it a certain confusion, a readjusting of the whole scenery of life. She found herself in a new country, wherein he who had led her there was least able to be her guide. There were moments when she felt that the first stranger in the street could have interpreted her happiness for her more easily than Denis. Then, as her eye adapted itself, as the lines flowed into each other, opening deep vistas upon new horizons, she began to enter into possession of her kingdom, to entertain the actual sense of its belonging to her. But she had never before felt that she also belonged to it; and this was the feeling which now came to complete her happiness, to give it the hallowing sense of permanence.

She rose from the writing-table where, list in hand, she had been going over the wedding-invitations, and walked toward the drawing-room window. Everything about her seemed to contribute to that rare harmony of feeling which levied a tax

on every sense. The large coolness of the room, its fine traditional air of spacious living, its outlook over field and
woodland toward the lake lying under the silver bloom of
September; the very scent of the late violets in a glass on the
writing-table; the rosy-mauve masses of hydrangea in tubs
along the terrace; the fall, now and then, of a leaf through the
still air—all, somehow, were mingled in the suffusion of well-
being that yet made them seem but so much dross upon its
current.

The girl's smile prolonged itself at the sight of a figure approaching from the lower slopes above the lake. The path was
a short cut from the Peyton place, and she had known that
Denis would appear in it at about that hour. Her smile, however, was prolonged not so much by his approach as by her
sense of the impossibility of communicating her mood to
him. The feeling did not disturb her. She could not imagine
sharing her deepest moods with any one, and the world in
which she lived with Denis was too bright and spacious to admit of any sense of constraint. Her smile was in truth a tribute to that clear-eyed directness of his which was so often a
refuge from her own complexities.

Denis Peyton was used to being met with a smile. He
might have been pardoned for thinking smiles the habitual
wear of the human countenance; and his estimate of life and
of himself was necessarily tinged by the cordial terms on
which they had always met each other. He had in fact found
life, from the start, an uncommonly agreeable business, cul-
minating fitly enough in his engagement to the only girl he
had ever wished to marry, and the inheritance, from his unhappy step-brother, of a fortune which agreeably widened his
horizon. Such a combination of circumstances might well justify a young man in thinking himself of some account in the
universe; and it seemed the final touch of fitness that the
mourning which Denis still wore for poor Arthur should lend
a new distinction to his somewhat florid good looks.

Kate Orme was not without an amused perception of her
future husband's point of view; but she could enter into it
with the tolerance which allows for the inconscient element
in all our judgments. There was, for instance, no one more
sentimentally humane than Denis's mother, the second Mrs.

Peyton, a scented silvery person whose lavender silks and neutral-tinted manner expressed a mind with its blinds drawn down toward all the unpleasantnesses of life; yet it was clear that Mrs. Peyton saw a "dispensation" in the fact that her step-son had never married, and that his death had enabled Denis, at the right moment, to step gracefully into affluence. Was it not, after all, a sign of healthy-mindedness to take the gifts of the gods in this religious spirit, discovering fresh evidence of "design" in what had once seemed the sad fact of Arthur's in-accessibility to correction? Mrs. Peyton, beautifully conscious of having done her "best" for Arthur, would have thought it unchristian to repine at the providential failure of her efforts. Denis's deductions were, of course, a little less direct than his mother's. He had, besides, been fond of Arthur, and his efforts to keep the poor fellow straight had been less didactic and more spontaneous. Their result read itself, if not in any change in Arthur's character, at least in the revised wording of his will; and Denis's moral sense was pleasantly fortified by the discov-ery that it very substantially paid to be a good fellow.

The sense of general providentialness on which Mrs. Peyton reposed had in fact been confirmed by events which reduced Denis's mourning to a mere tribute of respect—since it would have been a mockery to deplore the disappearance of any one who had left behind him such an unsavory wake as poor Arthur. Kate did not quite know what had happened: her father was as firmly convinced as Mrs. Peyton that young girls should not be admitted to any open discussion of life. She could only gather, from the silences and evasions amid which she moved, that a woman had turned up—a woman who was of course "dreadful," and whose dreadfulness ap-peared to include a sort of shadowy claim upon Arthur. But the claim, whatever it was, had been promptly discredited. The whole question had vanished and the woman with it. The blinds were drawn again on the ugly side of things, and life was resumed on the usual assumption that no such side ex-isted. Kate knew only that a darkness had crossed her sky and left it as unclouded as before.

Was it, perhaps, she now asked herself, the very lifting of the cloud—remote, unthreatening as it had been—which gave such new serenity to her heaven? It was horrible to think that one's deepest security was a mere sense of escape—that happiness was no more than a reprieve. The perversity of such ideas was emphasized by Peyton's approach. He had the gift of restoring things to their normal relations, of carrying one over the chasms of life through the closed tunnel of an incurious cheerfulness. All that was restless and questioning in the girl subsided in his presence, and she was content to take her love as a gift of grace, which began just where the office of reason ended. She was more than ever, to-day, in this mood of charmed surrender. More than ever he seemed the keynote of the accord between herself and life, the centre of a delightful complicity in every surrounding circumstance. One could not look at him without seeing that there was always a fair wind in his sails.

It was carrying him toward her, as usual, at a quick confident pace, which nevertheless lagged a little, she noticed, as he emerged from the beech-grove and struck across the lawn. He walked as though he were tired. She had meant to wait for him on the terrace, held in check by her usual inclination to linger on the threshold of her pleasures; but now something drew her toward him, and she went quickly down the steps and across the lawn.

"Denis, you look tired. I was afraid something had happened."

She had slipped her hand through his arm, and as they moved forward she glanced up at him, struck not so much by any new look in his face as by the fact that her approach had made no change in it.

"I am rather tired.—Is your father in?"

"Papa?" She looked up in surprise. "He went to town yesterday. Don't you remember?"

"Of course—I'd forgotten. You're alone, then?" She dropped his arm and stood before him. He was very pale now, with the furrowed look of extreme physical weariness.

"Denis—are you ill? *Has* anything happened?"

He forced a smile. "Yes—but you needn't look so frightened."

She drew a deep breath of reassurance. *He* was safe, after all! And all else, for a moment, seemed to swing below the rim of her world.

"Your mother—?" she then said, with a fresh start of fear.

"It's not my mother." They had reached the terrace, and he moved toward the house. "Let us go indoors. There's such a beastly glare out here."

He seemed to find relief in the cool obscurity of the drawing-room, where, after the brightness of the afternoon light, their faces were almost indistinguishable to each other. She sat down, and he moved a few paces away. Before the writing-table he paused to look at the neatly sorted heaps of wedding-cards.

"They are to be sent out to-morrow?"

"Yes."

He turned back and stood before her.

"It's about the woman," he began abruptly—"the woman who pretended to be Arthur's wife."

Kate started as at the clutch of an unacknowledged fear.

"She *was* his wife, then?"

Peyton made an impatient movement of negation. "If she was, why didn't she prove it? She hadn't a shred of evidence. The courts rejected her appeal."

"Well, then—?"

"Well, she's dead." He paused, and the next words came with difficulty. "She and the child."

"The child? There was a child?"

"Yes."

Kate started up and then sank down. These were not things about which young girls were told. The confused sense of horror had been nothing to this first sharp edge of fact.

"And both are dead?"

"Yes."

"How do you know? My father said she had gone away—gone back to the West—"

"So we thought. But this morning we found her."

"Found her?"

He motioned toward the window. "Out there—in the lake."

"Both?"

"Both."

She drooped before him shudderingly, her eyes hidden, as though to exclude the vision. "She had drowned herself?"

"Yes."

"Oh, poor thing—poor thing!"

They paused awhile, the minutes delving an abyss between them till he threw a few irrelevant words across the silence.

"One of the gardeners found them."

"Poor thing!"

"It was sufficiently horrible."

"Horrible—oh!" She had swung round again to her pole. "Poor Denis! *You* were not there—*you* didn't have to—?"

"I had to see her." She felt the instant relief in his voice. He could talk now, could distend his nerves in the warm air of her sympathy. "I had to identify her." He rose nervously and began to pace the room. "It's knocked the wind out of me. I—my God! I couldn't foresee it, could I?" He halted before her with outstretched hands of argument. "I did all I could— it's not *my* fault, is it?"

"Your fault? Denis!"

"She wouldn't take the money—" He broke off, checked by her awakened glance.

"The money? What money?" Her face changed, hardening as his relaxed. "Had you offered her *money* to give up the case?"

He stared a moment, and then dismissed the implication with a laugh.

"No—no; after the case was decided against her. She seemed hard up, and I sent Hinton to her with a cheque."

"And she refused it?"

"Yes."

"What did she say?"

"Oh, I don't know—the usual thing. That she'd only wanted to prove she was his wife—on the child's account. That she'd never wanted his money. Hinton said she was very quiet—not in the least excited—but she sent back the cheque."

Kate sat motionless, her head bent, her hands clasped about her knees. She no longer looked at Peyton.

"Could there have been a mistake?" she asked slowly.

"A mistake?"

She raised her head now, and fixed her eyes on his, with a strange insistence of observation. "Could they have been married?"

"The courts didn't think so."

"Could the courts have been mistaken?"

He started up again, and threw himself into another chair. "Good God, Kate! We gave her every chance to prove her case—why didn't she do it? You don't know what you're talking about—such things are kept from girls. Why, whenever a man of Arthur's kind dies, such—such women turn up. There are lawyers who live on such jobs—ask your father about it. Of course, this woman expected to be bought off—"

"But if she wouldn't take your money?"

"She expected a big sum, I mean, to drop the case. When she found we meant to fight it, she saw the game was up. I suppose it was her last throw, and she was desperate; we don't know how many times she may have been through the same thing before. That kind of woman is always trying to make money out of the heirs of any man who—who has—been about with them."

Kate received this in silence. She had a sense of walking along a narrow ledge of consciousness above a sheer hallucinating depth into which she dared not look. But the depth drew her, and she plunged one terrified glance into it.

"But the child—the child was Arthur's?"

Peyton shrugged his shoulders. "There again—how can we tell? Why, I don't suppose the woman herself—I wish to heaven your father were here to explain!"

She rose and crossed over to him, laying her hands on his shoulders with a gesture almost maternal.

"Don't let us talk of it," she said. "You did all you could. Think what a comfort you were to poor Arthur."

He let her hands lie where she had placed them, without response or resistance.

"I tried—I tried hard to keep him straight!"

"We all know that—every one knows it. And we know how grateful he was—what a difference it made to him in the end. It would have been dreadful to think of his dying out there alone."

She drew him down on a sofa and seated herself by his side. A deep lassitude was upon him, and the hand she had possessed herself of lay in her hold inert.

"It was splendid of you to travel day and night as you did. And then that dreadful week before he died! But for you he would have died alone among strangers."

He sat silent, his head dropping forward, his eyes fixed. "Among strangers," he repeated absently.

She looked up, as if struck by a sudden thought. "That poor woman—did you ever see her while you were out there?"

He drew his hand away and gathered his brows together as if in an effort of remembrance.

"I saw her—oh, yes, I saw her." He pushed the tumbled hair from his forehead and stood up. "Let us go out," he said. "My head is in a fog. I want to get away from it all."

A wave of compunction drew her to her feet.

"It was my fault! I ought not to have asked so many questions." She turned and rang the bell. "I'll order the ponies— we shall have time for a drive before sunset."

II

With the sunset in their faces they swept through the keen-scented autumn air at the swiftest pace of Kate's ponies. She had given the reins to Peyton, and he had turned the horses' heads away from the lake, rising by woody upland lanes to the high pastures which still held the sunlight. The horses were fresh enough to claim his undivided attention, and he drove in silence, his smooth fair profile turned to his companion, who sat silent also.

Kate Orme was engaged in one of those rapid mental excursions which were forever sweeping her from the straight path of the actual into uncharted regions of conjecture. Her survey of life had always been marked by the tendency to seek out ultimate relations, to extend her researches to the limit of her imaginative experience. But hitherto she had been like some young captive brought up in a windowless palace whose painted walls she takes for the actual world. Now the palace had been shaken to its base, and through a cleft in the walls she looked out upon life. For the first moment all was indistinguishable blackness; then she began to detect vague shapes and confused gestures in the depths. There were people be-

low there, men like Denis, girls like herself—for under the
unlikeness she felt the strange affinity—all struggling in that
awful coil of moral darkness, with agonized hands reaching
up for rescue. Her heart shrank from the horror of it, and
then, in a passion of pity, drew back to the edge of the abyss.
Suddenly her eyes turned toward Denis. His face was grave,
but less disturbed. And men knew about these things! They
carried this abyss in their bosoms, and went about smiling,
and sat at the feet of innocence. Could it be that Denis—
Denis even— Ah, no! She remembered what he had been to
poor Arthur; she understood, now, the vague allusions to
what he had tried to do for his brother. He had seen Arthur
down there, in that coiling blackness, and had leaned over
and tried to drag him out. But Arthur was too deep down,
and his arms were interlocked with other arms—they had
dragged each other deeper, poor souls, like drowning people
who fight together in the waves! Kate's visualizing habit gave
a hateful precision and persistency to the image she had
evoked—she could not rid herself of the vision of anguished
shapes striving together in the darkness. The horror of it took
her by the throat—she drew a choking breath, and felt the
tears on her face.

Peyton turned to her. The horses were climbing a hill, and
his attention had strayed from them.

"This has done me good," he began; but as he looked his
voice changed. "Kate! What is it? Why are you crying? Oh, for
God's sake, *don't*!" he ended, his hand closing on her wrist.

She steadied herself and raised her eyes to his.

"I—I couldn't help it," she stammered, struggling in the
sudden release of her pent compassion. "It seems so awful
that we should stand so close to this horror—that it might
have been you who—"

"I who—what on earth do you mean?" he broke in
stridently.

"Oh, don't you see? I found myself exulting that you and I
were so far from it—above it—safe in ourselves and each
other—and then the other feeling came—the sense of selfishness, of going by on the other side; and I tried to realize that
it might have been you and I who—who were down there in
the night and the flood—"

Peyton let the whip fall on the ponies' flanks. "Upon my soul," he said with a laugh, "you must have a nice opinion of both of us."

The words fell chillingly on the blaze of her self-immolation. Would she never learn to remember that Denis was incapable of mounting such hypothetical pyres? He might be as alive as herself to the direct demands of duty, but of its imaginative claims he was robustly unconscious. The thought brought a wholesome reaction of thankfulness.

"Ah, well," she said, the sunset dilating through her tears, "don't you see that I can bear to think such things only because they're impossibilities? It's easy to look over into the depths if one has a rampart to lean on. What I most pity poor Arthur for is that, instead of that woman lying there, so dreadfully dead, there might have been a girl like me, so exquisitely alive because of him; but it seems cruel, doesn't it, to let what he was *not* add ever so little to the value of what you are? To let him contribute ever so little to my happiness by the difference there is between you?"

She was conscious, as she spoke, of straying again beyond his reach, through intricacies of sensation new even to her exploring susceptibilities. A happy literalness usually enabled him to strike a short cut through such labyrinths, and rejoin her smiling on the other side; but now she became wonderingly aware that he had been caught in the thick of her hypothesis.

"It's the difference that makes you care for me, then?" he broke out, with a kind of violence which seemed to renew his clutch on her wrist.

"The difference?"

He lashed the ponies again, so sharply that a murmur escaped her, and he drew them up, quivering, with an inconsequent "Steady, boys," at which their back-laid ears protested.

"It's because I'm moral and respectable, and all that, that you're fond of me," he went on; "you're—you're simply in love with my virtues. You couldn't imagine caring if I were down there in the ditch, as you say, with Arthur?"

The question fell on a silence which seemed to deepen suddenly within herself. Every thought hung bated on the sense

SANCTUARY 333

that something was coming: her whole consciousness became a void to receive it.

"Denis!" she cried.

He turned on her almost savagely. "I don't want your pity, you know," he burst out. "You can keep that for Arthur. I had an idea women loved men for themselves—through everything, I mean. But I wouldn't steal your love—I don't want it on false pretenses, you understand. Go and look into other men's lives, that's all I ask of you. I slipped into it—it was just a case of holding my tongue when I ought to have spoken—but I—I—for God's sake, don't sit there staring! I suppose you've seen all along that I knew he was married to the woman."

III

The housekeeper's reminding her that Mr. Orme would be at home the next day for dinner, and did she think he would like the venison with claret sauce or jelly, roused Kate to the first consciousness of her surroundings. Her father would return on the morrow: he would give to the dressing of the venison such minute consideration as, in his opinion, every detail affecting his comfort or convenience quite obviously merited. And if it were not the venison it would be something else; if it were not the housekeeper it would be Mr. Orme, charged with the results of a conference with his agent, a committee-meeting at his club, or any of the other incidents which, by happening to himself, became events. Kate found herself caught in the inexorable continuity of life, found herself gazing over a scene of ruin lit up by the punctual recurrence of habit as nature's calm stare lights the morrow of a whirlwind.

Life was going on, then, and dragging her at its wheels. She could neither check its rush nor wrench loose from it and drop out—oh, how blessedly!—into darkness and cessation. She must go bounding on, racked, broken, but alive in every fibre. The most she could hope was a few hours' respite, not from her own terrors, but from the pressure of outward claims: the midday halt, during which the victim is unbound while his torturers rest from their efforts. Till her father's return she would have the house to herself, and, the question of the venison despatched, could give herself to long lonely pacings of the empty rooms, and shuddering subsidences upon her pillow.

Her first impulse, as the mist cleared from her brain, was the habitual one of reaching out for ultimate relations. She wanted to know the worst; and for her, as she saw in a flash, the worst of it was the core of fatality in what had happened. She shrank from her own way of putting it—nor was it even figuratively true that she had ever felt, under her faith in Denis, any such doubt as the perception implied. But that was merely because her imagination had never put him to the test. She was fond of exposing herself to hypothetical ordeals, but somehow she had never carried Denis with her on these adventures. What she saw now was that, in a world of strangeness, he remained the object least strange to her. She was not in the tragic case of the girl who suddenly sees her lover unmasked. No mask had dropped from Denis's face: the pink shades had simply been lifted from the lamps, and she saw him for the first time in an unmitigated glare.

Such exposure does not alter the features, but it lays an ugly emphasis on the most charming lines, pushing the smile to a grin, the curve of good-nature to the droop of slackness. And it was precisely into the flagging lines of extreme weakness that Denis's graceful contour flowed. In the terrible talk which had followed his avowal, and wherein every word flashed a light on his moral processes, she had been less startled by what he had done than by the way in which his conscience had already become a passive surface for the channelling of consequences. He was like a child who has put a match to the curtains, and stands agape at the blaze. It was horribly naughty to put the match—but beyond that the child's responsibility did not extend. In this business of Arthur's, where all had been wrong from the beginning—where self-defence might well find a plea for its casuistries in the absence of a definite right to be measured by—it had been easy, after the first slip, to drop a little lower with each struggle. The woman—oh, the woman was—well, of the kind who prey on such men. Arthur, out there, at his lowest ebb, had drifted into living with her as a man drifts into drink or opium. He knew what she was—he knew where she had come from. But he had fallen ill, and she had nursed him—nursed him devotedly, of course. That was her chance, and she knew it. Before he was out of the fever she had the noose around him—he came to and found himself married. Such cases were common enough—if the man recovered he bought off the woman and got a divorce. It was all a part of the business—the marriage, the bribe, the divorce. Some of those women made a big income out of it—they were married and divorced once a year. If Arthur had only got well—but, instead, he had a relapse and died. And there was the woman, made his widow by mischance as it were, with her child on her arm—whose child?—and a scoundrelly black-mailing lawyer to work up her case for her. Her claim was clear enough—the right of dower, a third of his estate. But if he had never meant to marry her? If he had been trapped as patently as a rustic fleeced in a gambling-hell? Arthur, in his last hours, had confessed to the marriage, but had also acknowledged its folly. And after his death, when Denis came to look about him and make inquiries, he found that the witnesses, if there had been any, were dispersed and undiscoverable. The whole question hinged on Arthur's statement to his brother. Suppress that statement, and the claim vanished, and with it the scandal, the humiliation, the life-long burden of the woman and child dragging the name of Peyton through heaven knew what depths. He had thought of that first, Denis swore, rather than of the money. The money, of course, had made a difference, —he was too honest not to own it—but not till afterward, he declared—would have declared on his honour, but that the word tripped him up, and sent a flush to his forehead.

Thus, in broken phrases, he flung his defence at her: a defence improvised, pieced together as he went along, to mask the crude instinctiveness of his act. For with increasing clearness Kate saw, as she listened, that there had been no real struggle in his mind; that, but for the grim logic of chance, he might never have felt the need of any justification. If the woman, after the manner of such baffled huntresses, had wandered off in search of fresh prey, he might, quite sincerely, have congratulated himself on having saved a decent name and an honest fortune from her talons. It was the price she had paid to establish her claim that for the first time brought him to a startled sense of its justice. His conscience responded only to the concrete pressure of facts.

It was with the anguish of this discovery that Kate Orme locked herself in at the end of their talk. How the talk had ended, how at length she had got him from the room and the house, she recalled but confusedly. The tragedy of the woman's death, and of his own share in it, were as nothing in the disaster of his bright irreclaimableness. Once, when she had cried out, "You would have married me and said nothing," and he groaned back, "But I *have* told you," she felt like a trainer with a lash above some bewildered animal.

But she persisted savagely. "You told me because you had to; because your nerves gave way; because you knew it couldn't hurt you to tell." The perplexed appeal of his gaze had almost checked her. "You told me because it was a relief; but nothing will really relieve you—nothing will really help you—till you have told some one who—who *will* hurt you."

"Who will hurt me—?"

"Till you have told the truth as—as openly as you lied."

He started up, ghastly with fear. "I don't understand you."

"You must confess, then—publicly—openly—you must go to the judge. I don't know how it's done."

"To the judge? When they're both dead? When everything is at an end? What good could that do?" he groaned.

"Everything is not at an end for you—everything is just beginning. You must clear yourself of this guilt; and there is only one way—to confess it. And you must give back the money."

This seemed to strike him as conclusive proof of her irrelevance. "I wish I had never heard of the money! But to whom would you have me give it back? I tell you she was a waif out of the gutter. I don't believe any one knew her real name—I don't believe she had one."

"She must have had a mother and father."

"Am I to devote my life to hunting for them through the slums of California? And how shall I know when I have found them? It's impossible to make you understand. I did wrong—I did horribly wrong—but that is not the way to repair it."

"What is, then?"

He paused, a little askance at the question. "To do better—
to do my best," he said, with a sudden flourish of firmness.
"To take warning by this dreadful—"

"Oh, be silent," she cried out, and hid her face. He looked
at her hopelessly.

At last he said: "I don't know what good it can do to go
on talking. I have only one more thing to say. Of course you
know that you are free."

He spoke simply, with a sudden return to his old voice and
accent, at which she weakened as under a caress. She lifted her
head and gazed at him. "Am I?" she said musingly.

"Kate!" burst from him; but she raised a silencing hand.

"It seems to me," she said, "that I am imprisoned—imprisoned with you in this dreadful thing. First I must help you to
get out—then it will be time enough to think of myself."

His face fell and he stammered: "I don't understand you."

"I can't say what I shall do—or how I shall feel—till I know
what you are going to do and feel."

"You must see how I feel—that I'm half dead with it."

"Yes—but that is only half."

He turned this over for a perceptible space of time before
asking slowly: "You mean that you'll give me up, if I don't do
this crazy thing you propose?"

She paused in turn. "No," she said; "I don't want to bribe
you. You must feel the need of it yourself."

"The need of proclaiming this thing publicly?"

"Yes."

He sat staring before him. "Of course you realize what it
would mean?" he began at length.

"To you?" she returned.

"I put that aside. To others—to you. I should go to prison."

"I suppose so," she said simply.

"You seem to take it very easily—I'm afraid my mother
wouldn't."

"Your mother?" This produced the effect he had expected.

"You hadn't thought of her, I suppose? It would probably
kill her."

"It would have killed her to think that you could do what
you have done!"

"It would have made her very unhappy; but there's a difference."

Yes: there was a difference; a difference which no rhetoric could disguise. The secret sin would have made Mrs. Peyton wretched, but it would not have killed her. And she would have taken precisely Denis's view of the elasticity of atonement: she would have accepted private regrets as the genteel equivalent of open expiation. Kate could even imagine her extracting a "lesson" from the providential fact that her son had not been found out.

"You see it's not so simple," he broke out, with a tinge of doleful triumph.

"No: it's not simple," she assented.

"One must think of others," he continued, gathering faith in his argument as he saw her reduced to acquiescence.

She made no answer, and after a moment he rose to go. So far, in retrospect, she could follow the course of their talk; but when, in the act of parting, argument lapsed into entreaty, and renunciation into the passionate appeal to give him at least one more hearing, her memory lost itself in a tumult of pain, and she recalled only that, when the door closed on him, he took with him her promise to see him once again.

IV

She had promised to see him again; but the promise did not imply that she had rejected his offer of freedom. In the first rush of misery she had not fully repossessed herself, had felt herself entangled in his fate by a hundred meshes of association and habit; but after a sleepless night spent with the thought of him—that dreadful bridal of their souls—she woke to a morrow in which he had no part. She had not sought her freedom, nor had he given it; but a chasm had opened at their feet, and they found themselves on different sides.

Now she was able to scan the disaster from the melancholy vantage of her independence. She could even draw a solace from the fact that she had ceased to love Denis. It was inconceivable that an emotion so interwoven with every fibre of consciousness should cease as suddenly as the flow of sap in an uprooted plant; but she had never allowed herself to be tricked by the current phraseology of sentiment, and there were no stock axioms to protect her from the truth.

It was probably because she had ceased to love him that she could look forward with a kind of ghastly composure to seeing him again. She had stipulated, of course, that the wedding should be put off, but she had named no other condition beyond asking for two days to herself—two days during which he was not even to write. She wished to shut herself in with her misery, to accustom herself to it as she had accustomed herself to happiness. But actual seclusion was impossible: the subtle reactions of life almost at once began to break down her defences. She could no more have her wretchedness to herself than any other emotion: all the lives about her were so many unconscious factors in her sensations. She tried to concentrate herself on the thought as to how she could best help poor Denis; for love, in ebbing, had laid bare an unsuspected depth of pity. But she found it more and more difficult to consider his situation in the abstract light of right and wrong. Open expiation still seemed to her the only possible way of healing; but she tried vainly to think of Mrs. Peyton as taking such a view. Yet Mrs. Peyton ought at least to know what had happened: was it not, in the last resort, she who should pronounce on her son's course? For a moment Kate was fascinated by this evasion of responsibility; she had nearly decided to tell Denis that he must begin by confessing everything to his mother. But almost at once she began to shrink from the consequences. There was nothing she so dreaded for him as that any one should take a light view of his act: should turn its irremediableness into an excuse. And this, she foresaw, was what Mrs. Peyton would do. The first burst of misery over, she would envelop the whole situation in a mist of expediency. Brought to the bar of Kate's judgment, she at once revealed herself incapable of higher action.

Kate's conception of her was still under arraignment when the actual Mrs. Peyton fluttered in. It was the afternoon of the second day, as the girl phrased it in the dismal re-creation of her universe. She had been thinking so hard of Mrs. Peyton that the lady's silvery insubstantial presence seemed hardly more than a projection of the thought; but as Kate collected

herself, and regained contact with the outer world, her preoc-
cupation yielded to surprise. It was unusual for Mrs. Peyton
to pay visits. For years she had remained enthroned in a semi-
invalidism which prohibited effort while it did not preclude
diversion; and the girl at once divined a special purpose in her
coming.

Mrs. Peyton's traditions would not have permitted any direct method of attack; and Kate had to sit through the usual
prelude of ejaculation and anecdote. Presently, however, the
elder lady's voice gathered significance, and laying her hand
on Kate's she murmured: "I have come to talk to you of this
sad affair."

Kate began to tremble. Was it possible that Denis had after
all spoken? A rising hope checked her utterance, and she saw
in a flash that it still lay with him to regain his hold on her.
But Mrs. Peyton went on delicately: "It has been a great shock
to my poor boy. To be brought in contact with Arthur's past
was in itself inexpressibly painful; but this last dreadful business—that woman's wicked act—"

"Wicked?" Kate exclaimed.

Mrs. Peyton's gentle stare reproved her. "Surely religion
teaches us that suicide is a sin? And to murder her child! I
ought not to speak to you of such things, my dear. No one has
ever mentioned anything so dreadful in my presence: my dear
husband used to screen me so carefully from the painful side of
life. Where there is so much that is beautiful to dwell upon, we
should try to ignore the existence of such horrors. But nowadays everything is in the papers; and Denis told me he thought
it better that you should hear the news first from him."

Kate nodded without speaking.

"He felt how *dreadful* it was to have to tell you. But I tell
him he takes a morbid view of the case. Of course one is
shocked at the woman's crime—but, if one looks a little
deeper, how can one help seeing that it may have been designed as the means of rescuing that poor child from a life of
vice and misery? That is the view I want Denis to take: I want
him to see how all the difficulties of life disappear when one
has learned to look for a divine purpose in human sufferings."

Mrs. Peyton rested a moment on this period, as an experienced climber pauses to be overtaken by a less agile com-

panion; but presently she became aware that Kate was still far below her, and perhaps needed a stronger incentive to the ascent.

"My dear child," she said adroitly, "I said just now that I was sorry you had been obliged to hear of this sad affair; but after all it is only you who can avert its consequences."

Kate drew an eager breath. "Its consequences?" she faltered.

Mrs. Peyton's voice dropped solemnly. "Denis has told me everything," she said.

"Everything?"

"That you insist on putting off the marriage. Oh, my dear, I do implore you to reconsider that!"

Kate sank back with the sense of having passed again into a region of leaden shadow. "Is that all he told you?"

Mrs. Peyton gazed at her with arch raillery. "All? Isn't it everything—to him?"

"Did he give you my reason, I mean?"

"He said you felt that, after this shocking tragedy, there ought, in decency, to be a delay; and I quite understand the feeling. It does seem too unfortunate that the woman should have chosen this particular time! But you will find as you grow older that life is full of such sad contrasts."

Kate felt herself slowly petrifying under the warm drip of Mrs. Peyton's platitudes.

"It seems to me," the elder lady continued, "that there is only one point from which we ought to consider the question—and that is, its effect on Denis. But for that we ought to refuse to know anything about it. But it has made my boy so unhappy. The law-suit was a cruel ordeal to him—the dreadful notoriety, the revelation of poor Arthur's infirmities. Denis is as sensitive as a woman; it is his unusual refinement of feeling that makes him so worthy of being loved by you. But such sensitiveness may be carried to excess. He ought not to let this unhappy incident prey on him: it shows a lack of trust in the divine ordering of things. That is what troubles me: his faith in life has been shaken. And—you must forgive me, dear child—you *will* forgive me, I know—but I can't help blaming you a little—"

Mrs. Peyton's accent converted the accusation into a caress, which prolonged itself in a tremulous pressure of Kate's hand.

The girl gazed at her blankly. "You blame *me*——?"

"Don't be offended, my child. I only fear that your excessive sympathy with Denis, your own delicacy of feeling, may have led you to encourage his morbid ideas. He tells me you were very much shocked—as you naturally would be—as any girl must be—I would not have you otherwise, dear Kate! It is *beautiful* that you should both feel so; most beautiful; but you know religion teaches us not to yield too much to our grief. Let the dead bury their dead; the living owe themselves to each other. And what had this wretched woman to do with either of you? It is a misfortune for Denis to have been connected in any way with a man of Arthur Peyton's character; but after all, poor Arthur did all he could to atone for the disgrace he brought on us, by making Denis his heir—and I am sure I have no wish to question the decrees of Providence." Mrs. Peyton paused again, and then softly absorbed both of Kate's hands. "For my part," she continued, "I see in it another instance of the beautiful ordering of events. Just after dear Denis's inheritance has removed the last obstacle to your marriage, this sad incident comes to show how desperately he needs you, how cruel it would be to ask him to defer his happiness."

She broke off, shaken out of her habitual placidity by the abrupt withdrawal of the girl's hands. Kate sat inertly staring, but no answer rose to her lips.

At length Mrs. Peyton resumed, gathering her draperies about her with a tentative hint of leave-taking: "I may go home and tell him that you will not put off the wedding?"

Kate was still silent, and her visitor looked at her with the mild surprise of an advocate unaccustomed to plead in vain.

"If your silence means refusal, my dear, I think you ought to realize the responsibility you assume." Mrs. Peyton's voice had acquired an edge of righteous asperity. "If Denis has a fault it is that he is too gentle, too yielding, too readily influenced by those he cares for. Your influence is paramount with him now—but if you turn from him just when he needs your help, who can say what the result will be?"

The argument, though impressively delivered, was hardly of a nature to carry conviction to its hearer; but it was perhaps for that very reason that she suddenly and unexpectedly replied to it by sinking back into her seat with a burst of tears. To Mrs. Peyton, however, tears were the signal of surrender, and, at Kate's side in an instant, she hastened to temper her triumph with magnanimity.

"Don't think I don't feel with you; but we must both forget ourselves for our boy's sake. I told him I should come back with your promise."

The arm she had slipped about Kate's shoulder fell back with the girl's start. Kate had seen in a flash what capital would be made of her emotion.

"No, no, you misunderstand me. I can make no promise," she declared.

The older lady sat a moment irresolute; then she restored her arm to the shoulder from which it had been so abruptly displaced.

"My dear child," she said, in a tone of tender confidence, "if I have misunderstood you, ought you not to enlighten me? You asked me just now if Denis had given me your reason for this strange postponement. He gave me one reason, but it seems hardly sufficient to explain your conduct. If there is any other,—and I know you well enough to feel sure there is,—will you not trust me with it? If my boy has been unhappy enough to displease you, will you not give his mother the chance to plead his cause? Remember, no one should be condemned unheard. As Denis's mother, I have the right to ask for your reason."

"My reason? My reason?" Kate stammered, panting with the exhaustion of the struggle. Oh, if only Mrs. Peyton would release her! "If you have the right to know it, why doesn't he tell you?" she cried.

Mrs. Peyton stood up, quivering. "I will go home and ask him," she said. "I will tell him he has your permission to speak."

She moved toward the door, with the nervous haste of a person unaccustomed to decisive action. But Kate sprang before her.

"No, no; don't ask him! I implore you not to ask him," she cried.

Mrs. Peyton turned on her with sudden authority of voice and gesture. "Do I understand you?" she said. "You admit that you have a reason for putting off your marriage, and yet you forbid me—me, Denis's mother—to ask him what it is? My poor child, I needn't ask, for I know already. If he has offended you, and you refuse him the chance to defend himself, I needn't look farther for your reason: it is simply that you have ceased to love him."

Kate fell back from the door which she had instinctively barricaded.

"Perhaps that is it," she murmured, letting Mrs. Peyton pass.

V

Mr. Orme's returning carriage-wheels crossed Mrs. Peyton's indignant flight; and an hour later Kate, in the bland candlelight of the dinner-hour, sat listening with practised fortitude to her father's comments on the venison.

She had wondered, as she awaited him in the drawing-room, if he would notice any change in her appearance. It seemed to her that the flagellation of her thoughts must have left visible traces. But Mr. Orme was not a man of subtle perceptions, save where his personal comfort was affected: though his egoism was clothed in the finest feelers, he did not suspect a similar surface in others. His daughter, as part of himself, came within the normal range of his solicitude; but she was an outlying region, a subject province; and Mr. Orme's was a highly centralized polity.

News of the painful incident—he often used Mrs. Peyton's vocabulary—had reached him at his club, and to some extent disturbed the assimilation of a carefully ordered breakfast; but since then two days had passed, and it did not take Mr. Orme forty-eight hours to resign himself to the misfortunes of others. It was all very nasty, of course, and he wished to heaven it hadn't happened to any one about to be connected with him; but he viewed it with the transient annoyance of a gentleman who has been splashed by the mud of a fatal runaway.

Mr. Orme affected, under such circumstances, a bluff and hearty stoicism as remote as possible from Mrs. Peyton's deprecating evasion of facts. It was a bad business; he was sorry Kate should have been mixed up with it; but she would be married soon now, and then she would see that life wasn't exactly a Sunday-school story. Everybody was exposed to such disagreeable accidents: he remembered a case in their own family—oh, a distant cousin whom Kate wouldn't have heard of—a poor fellow who had got entangled with just such a woman, and having (most properly) been sent packing by his father, had justified the latter's course by promptly forging his name—a very nasty affair altogether; but luckily the scandal had been hushed up, the woman bought off, and the prodigal, after a season of probation, safely married to a nice girl with a good income, who was told by the family that the doctors recommended his settling in California.

Luckily the scandal was hushed up: the phrase blazed out against the dark background of Kate's misery. That was doubtless what most people felt—the words represented the consensus of respectable opinion. The best way of repairing a fault was to hide it: to tear up the floor and bury the victim at night. Above all, no coroner and no autopsy!

She began to feel a strange interest in her distant cousin. "And his wife—did she know what he had done?"

Mr. Orme stared. His moral pointed, he had returned to the contemplation of his own affairs.

"His wife? Oh, of course not. The secret has been most admirably kept; but her property was put in trust, so she's quite safe with him."

Her property! Kate wondered if her faith in her husband had also been put in trust, if her sensibilities had been protected from his possible inroads.

"Do you think it quite fair to have deceived her in that way?"

Mr. Orme gave her a puzzled glance: he had no taste for the by-paths of ethical conjecture.

"His people wanted to give the poor fellow another chance: they did the best they could for him."

"And—he has done nothing dishonourable since?"

"Not that I know of: the last I heard was that they had a little boy, and that he was quite happy. At that distance he's not likely to bother *us*, at all events."

Long after Mr. Orme had left the topic, Kate remained lost in its contemplation. She had begun to perceive that the fair surface of life was honeycombed by a vast system of moral

sewage. Every respectable household had its special arrange-
ments for the private disposal of family scandals; it was only
among the reckless and improvident that such hygienic precautions were neglected. Who was she to pass judgment on
the merits of such a system? The social health must be preserved: the means devised were the result of long experience
and the collective instinct of self-preservation. She had meant
to tell her father that evening that her marriage had been put
off; but she now abstained from doing so, not from any
doubt of Mr. Orme's acquiescence—he could always be made
to feel the force of conventional scruples—but because the
whole question sank into insignificance beside the larger issue
which his words had raised.

In her own room, that night, she passed through that tra-
vail of the soul of which the deeper life is born. Her first sense
was of a great moral loneliness—an isolation more complete,
more impenetrable, than that in which the discovery of
Denis's act had plunged her. For she had vaguely leaned,
then, on a collective sense of justice that should respond to
her own ideas of right and wrong: she still believed in the logical correspondence of theory and practice. Now she saw that,
among those nearest her, there was no one who recognized
the moral need of expiation. She saw that to take her father
or Mrs. Peyton into her confidence would be but to widen
the circle of sterile misery in which she and Denis moved. At
first the aspect of life thus revealed to her seemed simply
mean and base—a world where honour was a pact of silence
between adroit accomplices. The network of circumstance
had tightened round her, and every effort to escape drew its
meshes closer. But as her struggles subsided she felt the spiritual release which comes with acceptance: not connivance in
dishonour, but recognition of evil. Out of that dark vision
light was to come, the shaft of cloud turning to the pillar of
fire. For here, at last, life lay before her as it was: not brave,
garlanded and victorious, but naked, grovelling and diseased,
dragging its maimed limbs through the mud, yet lifting
piteous hands to the stars. Love itself, once throned aloft on
an altar of dreams, how it stole to her now, storm-beaten and
scarred, pleading for the shelter of her breast! Love, indeed,
not in the old sense in which she had conceived it, but a

graver, austerer presence—the charity of the mystic three. She
thought she had ceased to love Denis—but what had she
loved in him but her happiness and his? Their affection had
been the *garden enclosed* of the Canticles, where they were to
walk forever in a delicate isolation of bliss. But now love appeared to her as something more than this—something wider,
deeper, more enduring than the selfish passion of a man and
a woman. She saw it in all its far-reaching issues, till the first
meeting of two pairs of young eyes kindled a light which
might be a high-lifted beacon across dark waters of humanity.

All this did not come to her clearly, consecutively, but in a
series of blurred and shifting images. Marriage had meant to
her, as it means to girls brought up in ignorance of life, simply the exquisite prolongation of wooing. If she had looked
beyond, to the vision of wider ties, it was as a traveller gazes
over a land veiled in golden haze, and so far distant that the
imagination delays to explore it. But now through the blur of
sensations one image strangely persisted—the image of Denis's
child. Had she ever before thought of their having a child?
She could not remember. She was like one who wakens from
a long fever: she recalled nothing of her former self or of her
former feelings. She knew only that the vision persisted—the
vision of the child whose mother she was not to be. It was impossible that she should marry Denis—her inmost soul rejected him . . . but it was just because she was not to be the
child's mother that its image followed her so pleadingly. For
she saw with perfect clearness the inevitable course of events.
Denis would marry some one else—he was one of the men
who are fated to marry, and she needed not his mother's reminder that her abandonment of him at an emotional crisis
would fling him upon the first sympathy within reach. He
would marry a girl who knew nothing of his secret—for Kate
was intensely aware that he would never again willingly confess himself—he would marry a girl who trusted him and
leaned on him, as she, Kate Orme—the earlier Kate Orme—
had done but two days since! And with this deception between them their child would be born: born to an inheritance
of secret weakness, a vice of the moral fibre, as it might be
born with some hidden physical taint which would destroy it
before the cause could be detected. . . . Well, and what of it?

Was she to hold herself responsible? Were not thousands of children born with some such unsuspected taint? . . . Ah, but if here was one that she could save? What if she, who had had so exquisite a vision of wifehood, should reconstruct from its ruins this vision of protecting maternity—if her love for her lover should be, not lost, but transformed, enlarged, into this passion of charity for his race? If she might expiate and redeem his fault by becoming a refuge from its consequences? Before this strange extension of her love all the old limitations seemed to fall. Something had cleft the surface of self, and there welled up the mysterious primal influences, the sacrificial instinct of her sex, a passion of spiritual motherhood that made her long to fling herself between the unborn child and its fate. . . .

She never knew, then or after, how she reached this mystic climax of effacement; she was only conscious, through her anguish, of that lift of the heart which made one of the saints declare that joy was the inmost core of sorrow. For it was indeed a kind of joy she felt, if old names must serve for such new meanings; a surge of liberating faith in life, the old *credo quia absurdum* which is the secret cry of all supreme endeavour.

PART II

I

Does it look nice, mother?"

Dick Peyton met her with the question on the threshold, drawing her gaily into the little square room, and adding, with a laugh with a blush in it: "You know she's an uncommonly noticing person, and little things tell with her."

He swung round on his heel to follow his mother's smiling inspection of the apartment.

"She seems to have *all* the qualities," Mrs. Denis Peyton remarked, as her circuit finally brought her to the prettily appointed tea-table.

"*All,*" he declared, taking the sting from her emphasis by his prompt adoption of it. Dick had always had a wholesome way of thus appropriating to his own use such small shafts of maternal irony as were now and then aimed at him.

Kate Peyton laughed and loosened her furs. "It looks charmingly," she pronounced, ending her survey by an approach to the window, which gave, far below, the oblique perspective of a long side-street leading to Fifth Avenue.

The high-perched room was Dick Peyton's private office, a retreat partitioned off from the larger enclosure in which, under a north light and on a range of deal tables, three or four young draughtsmen were busily engaged in elaborating his architectural projects. The outer door of the office bore the sign: *Peyton and Gill, Architects*; but Gill was an utilitarian person, as unobtrusive as his name, who contented himself with a desk in the work-room, and left Dick to lord it alone in the small apartment to which clients were introduced, and where the social part of the business was carried on.

It was to serve, on this occasion, as the scene of a tea designed, as Kate Peyton was vividly aware, to introduce a certain young lady to the scene of her son's labours. Mrs. Peyton had been hearing a great deal lately about Clemence Verney. Dick was naturally expansive, and his close intimacy with his mother—an intimacy fostered by his father's early death—if it had suffered some natural impairment in his school and college days, had of late been revived by four years of comradeship in Paris, where Mrs. Peyton, in a tiny apartment of the Rue de Varennes, had kept house for him during his course of studies at the Beaux Arts. There were indeed not lacking critics of her own sex who accused Kate Peyton of having figured too largely in her son's life; of having failed to efface herself at a period when it is agreed that young men are best left free to try conclusions with the world. Mrs. Peyton, had she cared to defend herself, might have said that Dick, if communicative, was not impressionable, and that the closeness of texture which enabled him to throw off her sarcasms preserved him also from the infiltration of her prejudices. He was certainly no knight of the apron-string, but a seemingly resolute and self-sufficient young man, whose romantic friendship with his mother had merely served to throw a veil of suavity over the hard angles of youth.

But Mrs. Peyton's real excuse was after all one which she would never have given. It was because her intimacy with her son was the one need of her life that she had, with infinite tact and discretion, but with equal persistency, clung to every step of his growth, dissembling herself, adapting herself, rejuvenating herself, in the passionate effort to be always within reach, but never in the way.

Denis Peyton had died after seven years of marriage, when his boy was barely six. During those seven years he had managed to squander the best part of the fortune he had inherited from his step-brother; so that, at his death, his widow and son were left with a scant competence. Mrs. Peyton, during her husband's life, had apparently made no effort to restrain his expenditure. She had even been accused, by those judicious persons who are always ready with an estimate of their neighbours' motives, of having encouraged poor Denis's improvidence for the gratification of her own ambition. She had in fact, in the early days of their marriage, tried to launch him in politics, and had perhaps drawn somewhat heavily on his funds in the first heat of the contest; but the experiment ending in failure, as Denis Peyton's experiments were apt to end, she had made no farther demands on his exchequer. Her personal tastes were in fact unusually simple, but her outspoken indifference to money was not, in the opinion of her critics, designed to act as a check upon her husband; and it resulted in leaving her, at his death, in straits from which it was impossible not to deduce a moral.

Her small means, and the care of the boy's education, served the widow as a pretext for secluding herself in a socially remote suburb, where it was inferred that she was expiating, on queer food and in ready-made boots, her rash defiance of fortune. Whether or not Mrs. Peyton's penance took this form, she hoarded her substance to such good purpose that she was not only able to give Dick the best of schooling, but to propose, on his leaving Harvard, that he should prolong his studies by another four years at the Beaux Arts. It had been the joy of her life that her boy had early shown a marked bent for a special line of work. She could not have borne to see him reduced to a mere money-getter, yet she was not sorry that their small means forbade the cultivation of an ornamental leisure. In his college days Dick had troubled her by a superabundance of tastes, a restless flitting from one form of artistic expression to another. Whatever art he enjoyed he wished to practise, and he passed from music to painting, from painting to architecture, with an ease which seemed to his mother to indicate lack of purpose rather than excess of talent. She had observed that these changes were usually due, not to self-criticism, but to some external discouragement. Any depreciation of his work was enough to convince him of the uselessness of pursuing that special form of art, and the reaction produced the immediate conviction that he was really destined to shine in some other line of work. He had thus swung from one calling to another till, at the end of his college career, his mother took the decisive step of transplanting him to the Beaux Arts, in the hope that a definite course of study, combined with the stimulus of competition, might fix his wavering aptitudes. The result justified her expectation, and their four years in the Rue de Varennes yielded the happiest confirmation of her belief in him. Dick's ability was recognized not only by his mother, but by his professors. He was engrossed in his work, and his first successes developed his capacity for application. His mother's only fear was that praise was still too necessary to him. She was uncertain how long his ambition would sustain him in the face of failure. He gave lavishly where he was sure of a return; but it remained to be seen if he were capable of production without recognition. She had brought him up in a wholesome scorn of material rewards, and nature seemed, in this direction, to have seconded her training. He was genuinely indifferent to money, and his enjoyment of beauty was of that happy sort which does not generate the wish for possession. As long as the inner eye had food for contemplation, he cared very little for the deficiencies in his surroundings; or, it might rather be said, he felt, in the sum-total of beauty about him, an ownership of appreciation that left him free from the fret of personal desire. Mrs. Peyton had cultivated to excess this disregard of material conditions; but she now began to ask herself whether, in so doing, she had not laid too great a strain on a temperament naturally exalted. In guarding against other tendencies she had perhaps fostered in him too exclusively those qualities which circumstances had brought to an unusual development in herself. His enthusiasms and his disdains were alike too unqualified for that happy mean of character which is the best defence against the surprises of fortune. If she had taught him to set an exaggerated value on ideal rewards, was not that but a shifting of the danger-point on which her fears had always hung? She trembled sometimes to think how little love and a lifelong vigilance had availed in the deflecting of inherited tendencies.

Her fears were in a measure confirmed by the first two years of their life in New York, and the opening of his career as a professional architect. Close on the easy triumphs of his studentship there came the chilling reaction of public indifference. Dick, on his return from Paris, had formed a partnership with an architect who had had several years of practical training in a New York office; but the quiet and industrious Gill, though he attracted to the new firm a few small jobs which overflowed from the business of his former employer, was not able to infect the public with his own faith in Peyton's talents, and it was trying to a genius who felt himself capable of creating palaces to have to restrict his efforts to the building of suburban cottages or the planning of cheap alterations in private houses.

Mrs. Peyton expended all the ingenuities of tenderness in keeping up her son's courage; and she was seconded in the task by a friend whose acquaintance Dick had made at the Beaux Arts, and who, two years before the Peytons, had returned to New York to start on his own career as an architect. Paul Darrow was a young man full of crude seriousness, who, after a youth of struggling work and study in his native northwestern state, had won a scholarship which sent him abroad for a course at the Beaux Arts. His two years there coincided with the first part of Dick's residence, and Darrow's gifts had at once attracted the younger student. Dick was unstinted in his admiration of rival talent, and Mrs. Peyton, who was romantically given to the cultivation of such generosities, had seconded his enthusiasm by the kindest offers of hospitality to the young student. Darrow thus became the grateful frequenter of their little *salon*; and after their return to New York the intimacy between the young men was renewed, though Mrs. Peyton found it more difficult to coax Dick's friend to her New York drawing-room than to the informal surroundings of the Rue de Varennes. There, no doubt, se-

cluded and absorbed in her son's work, she had seemed to
Darrow almost a fellow-student; but seen among her own associates she became once more the woman of fashion, divided
from him by the whole breadth of her ease and his awkward-
ness. Mrs. Peyton, whose tact had divined the cause of his
estrangement, would not for an instant let it affect the friendship of the two young men. She encouraged Dick to frequent
Darrow, in whom she divined a persistency of effort, an artistic self-confidence, in curious contrast to his social hesitancies.
The example of his obstinate capacity for work was just the
influence her son needed, and if Darrow would not come to
them she insisted that Dick must seek him out, must never let
him think that any social discrepancy could affect a friendship
based on deeper things. Dick, who had all the loyalties, and
who took an honest pride in his friend's growing success,
needed no urging to maintain the intimacy; and his copious
reports of midnight colloquies in Darrow's lodgings showed
Mrs. Peyton that she had a strong ally in her invisible friend.

It had been, therefore, somewhat of a shock to learn in the
course of time that Darrow's influence was being shared, if
not counteracted, by that of a young lady in whose honour
Dick was now giving his first professional tea. Mrs. Peyton
had heard a great deal about Miss Clemence Verney, first
from the usual purveyors of such information, and more recently from her son, who, probably divining that rumour had
been before him, adopted his usual method of disarming his
mother by taking her into his confidence. But, ample as her
information was, it remained perplexing and contradictory,
and even her own few meetings with the girl had not helped
her to a definite opinion. Miss Verney, in conduct and ideas,
was patently of the "new school": a young woman of feverish
activities and broad-cast judgments, whose very versatility
made her hard to define. Mrs. Peyton was shrewd enough to
allow for the accidents of environment; what she wished to
get at was the residuum of character beneath Miss Verney's
shifting surface.

"It looks charmingly," Mrs. Peyton repeated, giving a loosening touch to the chrysanthemums in a tall vase on her son's
desk.

Dick laughed, and glanced at his watch.

"They won't be here for another quarter of an hour. I think I'll tell Gill to clean out the work-room before they come."

"Are we to see the drawings for the competition?" his mother asked.

He shook his head smilingly. "Can't—I've asked one or two of the Beaux Arts fellows, you know; and besides, old Darrow's actually coming."

"Impossible!" Mrs. Peyton exclaimed.

"He swore he would last night." Dick laughed again, with a tinge of self-satisfaction. "I've an idea he wants to see Miss Verney."

"Ah," his mother murmured. There was a pause before she added: "Has Darrow really gone in for this competition?"

"Rather! I should say so! He's simply working himself to the bone."

Mrs. Peyton sat revolving her muff on a meditative hand; at length she said: "I'm not sure I think it quite nice of him."

Her son halted before her with an incredulous stare. *"Mother!"* he exclaimed.

The rebuke sent a blush to her forehead. "Well—considering your friendship—and everything."

"Everything? What do you mean by everything? The fact that he has more ability than I have and is therefore more likely to succeed? The fact that he needs the money and the success a deuced sight more than any of us? Is that the reason you think he oughtn't to have entered? Mother! I never heard you say an ungenerous thing before."

The blush deepened to crimson, and she rose with a nervous laugh. "It *was* ungenerous," she conceded. "I suppose I'm jealous for you. I hate these competitions!"

Her son smiled reassuringly. "You needn't. I'm not afraid: I think I shall pull it off this time. In fact, Paul's the only man I'm afraid of—I'm always afraid of Paul—but the mere fact that he's in the thing is a tremendous stimulus."

His mother continued to study him with an anxious tenderness. "Have you worked out the whole scheme? Do you *see* it yet?"

"Oh, broadly, yes. There's a gap here and there—a hazy bit, rather—it's the hardest problem I've ever had to tackle;

but then it's my biggest opportunity, and I've simply *got* to pull it off!"

Mrs. Peyton sat silent, considering his flushed face and illumined eye, which were rather those of the victor nearing the goal than of the runner just beginning the race. She remembered something that Darrow had once said of him: "Dick always sees the end too soon."

"You haven't too much time left," she murmured.

"Just a week. But I shan't go anywhere after this. I shall renounce the world." He glanced smilingly at the festal tea-table and the embowered desk. "When I next appear, it will either be with my heel on Paul's neck—poor old Paul—or else—or else—being dragged lifeless from the arena!"

His mother nervously took up the laugh with which he ended. "Oh, not lifeless," she said.

His face clouded. "Well, maimed for life, then," he muttered.

Mrs. Peyton made no answer. She knew how much hung on the possibility of his winning the competition which for weeks past had engrossed him. It was a design for the new museum of sculpture, for which the city had recently voted half a million. Dick's taste ran naturally to the grandiose, and the erection of public buildings had always been the object of his ambition. Here was an unmatched opportunity, and he knew that, in a competition of the kind, the newest man had as much chance of success as the firm of most established reputation, since every competitor entered on his own merits, the designs being submitted to a jury of architects who voted on them without knowing the names of the contestants. Dick, characteristically, was not afraid of the older firms; indeed, as he had told his mother, Paul Darrow was the only rival he feared. Mrs. Peyton knew that, to a certain point, self-confidence was a good sign; but somehow her son's did not strike her as being of the right substance—it seemed to have no dimension but extent. Her fears were complicated by a suspicion that, under his professional eagerness for success, lay the knowledge that Miss Verney's favour hung on the victory. It was that, perhaps, which gave a feverish touch to his ambition; and Mrs. Peyton, surveying the future from the height of her maternal apprehensions, divined that the situation depended mainly on the girl's view of it. She would have given a great deal to know Clemence Verney's conception of success.

II

Miss Verney, when she presently appeared, in the wake of the impersonal and exclamatory young married woman who served as a background to her vivid outline, seemed competent to impart at short notice any information required of her. She had never struck Mrs. Peyton as more alert and efficient. A melting grace of line and colour tempered her edges with the charming haze of youth; but it occurred to her critic that she might emerge from this morning mist as a dry and metallic old woman.

If Miss Verney suspected a personal application in Dick's hospitality, it did not call forth in her the usual tokens of self-consciousness. Her manner may have been a shade more vivid than usual, but she preserved all her bright composure of glance and speech, so that one guessed, under the rapid dispersal of words, an undisturbed steadiness of perception. She was lavishly but not indiscriminately interested in the evidences of her host's industry, and as the other guests assembled, straying with vague ejaculations through the labyrinth of scale drawings and blue prints, Mrs. Peyton noted that Miss Verney alone knew what these symbols stood for.

To his visitors' requests to be shown his plans for the competition, Peyton had opposed a laughing refusal, enforced by the presence of two fellow-architects, young men with lingering traces of the Beaux Arts in their costume and vocabulary, who stood about in Gavarni attitudes and dazzled the ladies by allusions to fenestration and entasis. The party had already drifted back to the tea-table when a hesitating knock announced Darrow's approach. He entered with his usual air of having blundered in by mistake, embarrassed by his hat and great-coat, and thrown into deeper confusion by the necessity of being introduced to the ladies grouped about the urn. To the men he threw a gruff nod of fellowship, and Dick having relieved him of his encumbrances, he retreated behind the shelter of Mrs. Peyton's welcome. The latter judiciously gave

him time to recover, and when she turned to him he was engaged in a surreptitious inspection of Miss Verney, whose
dusky slenderness, relieved against the bare walls of the office,
made her look like a young St. John of Donatello's. The girl
returned his look with one of her clear glances, and the group
having presently broken up again, Mrs. Peyton saw that she
had drifted to Darrow's side. The visitors at length wandered
back to the work-room to see a portfolio of Dick's water-
colours; but Mrs. Peyton remained seated behind the urn, listening to the interchange of talk through the open door while
she tried to coördinate her impressions.

She saw that Miss Verney was sincerely interested in Dick's
work: it was the nature of her interest that remained in doubt.
As if to solve this doubt, the girl presently reappeared alone
on the threshold, and discovering Mrs. Peyton, advanced toward her with a smile.

"Are you tired of hearing us praise Mr. Peyton's things?"
she asked, dropping into a low chair beside her hostess.
"Unintelligent admiration must be a bore to people who
know, and Mr. Darrow tells me you are almost as learned as
your son."

Mrs. Peyton returned the smile, but evaded the question.
"I should be sorry to think your admiration unintelligent,"
she said. "I like to feel that my boy's work is appreciated by
people who understand it."

"Oh, I have the usual smattering," said Miss Verney carelessly. "I *think* I know why I admire his work; but then I am
sure I see more in it when some one like Mr. Darrow tells me
how remarkable it is."

"Does Mr. Darrow say that?" the mother exclaimed, losing
sight of her object in the rush of maternal pleasure.

"He has said nothing else: it seems to be the only subject
which loosens his tongue. I believe he is more anxious to have
your son win the competition than to win it himself."

"He is a very good friend," Mrs. Peyton assented. She was
struck by the way in which the girl led the topic back to the
special application of it which interested her. She had none of
the artifices of prudery.

"He feels sure that Mr. Peyton *will* win," Miss Verney continued. "It was very interesting to hear his reasons. He is an

extraordinarily interesting man. It must be a tremendous incentive to have such a friend."

Mrs. Peyton hesitated. "The friendship is delightful; but I don't know that my son needs the incentive. He is almost too ambitious."

Miss Verney looked up brightly. "Can one be?" she said. "Ambition is so splendid! It must be so glorious to be a man and go crashing through obstacles, straight up to the thing one is after. I'm afraid I don't care for people who are superior to success. I like marriage by capture!" She rose with her wandering laugh, and stood flushed and sparkling above Mrs. Peyton, who continued to gaze at her gravely.

"What do you call success?" the latter asked. "It means so many different things."

"Oh, yes, I know—the inward approval, and all that. Well, I'm afraid I like the other kind: the drums and wreaths and acclamations. If I were Mr. Peyton, for instance, I'd much rather win the competition than—than be as disinterested as Mr. Darrow."

Mrs. Peyton smiled. "I hope you won't tell him so," she said half seriously. "He is over-stimulated already; and he is so easily influenced by any one who—whose opinion he values."

She stopped abruptly, hearing herself, with a strange inward shock, reëcho the words which another man's mother had once spoken to her. Miss Verney did not seem to take the allusion to herself, for she continued to fix on Mrs. Peyton a gaze of impartial sympathy.

"But we can't help being interested!" she declared.

"It's very kind of you; but I wish you would all help him to feel that this competition is after all of very little account compared with other things—his health and his peace of mind, for instance. He is looking horribly used up."

The girl glanced over her shoulder at Dick, who was just reëntering the room at Darrow's side.

"Oh, do you think so?" she said. "I should have thought it was his friend who was used up."

Mrs. Peyton followed the glance with surprise. She had been too preoccupied to notice Darrow, whose crudely modelled face was always of a dull pallour, to which his slow-moving grey eye lent no relief except in rare moments of expansion. Now the face had the fallen lines of a death-mask, in which only the smile he turned on Dick remained alive; and the sight smote her with compunction. Poor Darrow! He did look horribly fagged out: as if he needed care and petting and good food. No one knew exactly how he lived. His rooms, according to Dick's report, were fireless and ill kept, but he stuck to them because his landlady, whom he had fished out of some financial plight, had difficulty in obtaining other lodgers. He belonged to no club, and wandered out alone for his meals, mysteriously refusing the hospitality which his friends pressed on him. It was plain that he was very poor, and Dick conjectured that he sent what he earned to an aunt in his native village; but he was so silent about such matters that, outside of his profession, he seemed to have no personal life.

Miss Verney's companion having presently advised her of the lapse of time, there ensued a general leave-taking, at the close of which Dick accompanied the ladies to their carriage. Darrow was meanwhile blundering into his great-coat, a process which always threw him into a state of perspiring embarrassment; but Mrs. Peyton, surprising him in the act, suggested that he should defer it and give her a few moments' talk.

"Let me make you some fresh tea," she said, as Darrow blushingly shed the garment, "and when Dick comes back we'll all walk home together. I've not had a chance to say two words to you this winter."

Darrow sank into a chair at her side and nervously contemplated his boots. "I've been tremendously hard at work," he said.

"I know: *too* hard at work, I'm afraid. Dick tells me you have been wearing yourself out over your competition plans."

"Oh, well, I shall have time to rest now," he returned. "I put the last stroke to them this morning."

Mrs. Peyton gave him a quick look. "You're ahead of Dick, then."

"In point of time only," he said smiling.

"That is in itself an advantage," she answered with a tinge of asperity. In spite of an honest effort for impartiality she could not, at the moment, help regarding Darrow as an obstacle in her son's path.

"I wish the competition were over!" she exclaimed, conscious that her voice had betrayed her. "I hate to see you both looking so fagged."

Darrow smiled again, perhaps at her studied inclusion of himself.

"Oh, *Dick*'s all right," he said. "He'll pull himself together in no time."

He spoke with an emphasis which might have struck her, if her sympathies had not again been deflected by the allusion to her son.

"Not if he doesn't win," she exclaimed.

Darrow took the tea she had poured for him, knocking the spoon to the floor in his eagerness to perform the feat gracefully. In bending to recover the spoon he struck the tea-table with his shoulder, and set the cups dancing. Having regained a measure of composure, he took a swallow of the hot tea and set it down with a gasp, precariously near the edge of the tea-table. Mrs. Peyton rescued the cup, and Darrow, apparently forgetting its existence, rose and began to pace the room. It was always hard for him to sit still when he talked.

"You mean he's so tremendously set on it?" he broke out.

Mrs. Peyton hesitated. "You know him almost as well as I do," she said. "He's capable of anything where there is a possibility of success; but I'm always afraid of the reaction."

"Oh, well, Dick's a man," said Darrow bluntly. "Besides, he's going to succeed."

"I wish he didn't feel so sure of it. You mustn't think I'm afraid for him. He's a man, and I want him to take his chances with other men; but I wish he didn't care so much about what people think."

"People?"

"Miss Verney, then: I suppose you know."

Darrow paused in front of her. "Yes: he's talked a good deal about her. You think she wants him to succeed?"

"At any price!"

He drew his brows together. "What do you call any price?"

"Well—herself, in this case, I believe."

Darrow bent a puzzled stare on her. "You mean she attaches that amount of importance to this competition?"

"She seems to regard it as symbolical: that's what I gather. And I'm afraid she's given him the same impression."

Darrow's sunken face was suffused by his rare smile. "Oh, well, he'll pull it off then!" he said.

Mrs. Peyton rose with a distracted sigh. "I half hope he won't, for such a motive," she exclaimed.

"The motive won't show in his work," said Darrow. He added, after a pause probably devoted to the search for the right word: "He seems to think a great deal of her."

Mrs. Peyton fixed him thoughtfully. "I wish I knew what *you* think of her."

"Why, I never saw her before."

"No; but you talked with her to-day. You've formed an opinion: I think you came here on purpose."

He chuckled joyously at her discernment: she had always seemed to him gifted with supernatural insight. "Well, I did want to see her," he owned.

"And what do you think?"

He took a few vague steps and then halted before Mrs. Peyton. "I think," he said, smiling, "that she likes to be helped first, and to have everything on her plate at once."

III

At dinner, with a rush of contrition, Mrs. Peyton remembered that she had after all not spoken to Darrow about his health. He had distracted her by beginning to talk of Dick; and besides, much as Darrow's opinions interested her, his personality had never fixed her attention. He always seemed to her simply a vehicle for the transmission of ideas.

It was Dick who recalled her to a sense of her omission by asking if she hadn't thought that old Paul looked rather more ragged than usual.

"He did look tired," Mrs. Peyton conceded. "I meant to tell him to take care of himself."

Dick laughed at the futility of the measure. "Old Paul is never tired: he can work twenty-five hours out of the twenty-four. The trouble with him is that he's ill. Something wrong with the machinery, I'm afraid."

"Oh, I'm sorry. Has he seen a doctor?"

"He wouldn't listen to me when I suggested it the other day; but he's so deuced mysterious that I don't know what he may have done since." Dick rose, putting down his coffee-cup and half-smoked cigarette. "I've half a mind to pop in on him tonight and see how he's getting on."

"But he lives at the other end of the earth; and you're tired yourself."

"I'm not tired; only a little strung-up," he returned, smiling. "And besides, I'm going to meet Gill at the office by and by and put in a night's work. It won't hurt me to take a look at Paul first."

Mrs. Peyton was silent. She knew it was useless to contend with her son about his work, and she tried to fortify herself with the remembrance of her own words to Darrow: Dick was a man and must take his chance with other men.

But Dick, glancing at his watch, uttered an exclamation of annoyance. "Oh, by Jove, I shan't have time after all. Gill is waiting for me now; we must have dawdled over dinner." He bent to give his mother a caressing tap on the cheek. "Now don't worry," he adjured her; and as she smiled back at him he added with a sudden happy blush: "She doesn't, you know: she's so sure of me."

Mrs. Peyton's smile faded, and laying a detaining hand on his, she said with sudden directness: "Sure of you, or of your success?"

He hesitated. "Oh, she regards them as synonymous. She thinks I'm bound to get on."

"But if you don't?"

He shrugged laughingly, but with a slight contraction of his confident brows. "Why, I shall have to make way for some one else, I suppose. That's the law of life."

Mrs. Peyton sat upright, gazing at him with a kind of solemnity. "Is it the law of love?" she asked.

He looked down on her with a smile that trembled a little. "My dear romantic mother, I don't want her pity, you know!"

Dick, coming home the next morning shortly before daylight, left the house again after a hurried breakfast, and Mrs. Peyton heard nothing of him till nightfall. He had promised to be back for dinner, but a few moments before eight, as she was coming down to the drawing-room, the parlour-maid handed her a hastily pencilled note.

"Don't wait for me," it ran. "Darrow is ill and I can't leave him. I'll send a line when the doctor has seen him."

Mrs. Peyton, who was a woman of rapid reactions, read the words with a pang. She was ashamed of the jealous thoughts she had harboured of Darrow, and of the selfishness which had made her lose sight of his troubles in the consideration of Dick's welfare. Even Clemence Verney, whom she secretly accused of a want of heart, had been struck by Darrow's ill looks, while she had had eyes only for her son. Poor Darrow! How cold and self-engrossed he must have thought her! In the first rush of penitence her impulse was to drive at once to his lodgings; but the infection of his own shyness restrained her. Dick's note gave no details: the illness was evidently grave, but might not Darrow regard her coming as an intrusion? To repair her negligence of yesterday by a sudden invasion of his privacy might be only a greater failure in tact; and after a moment of deliberation she resolved on sending to ask Dick if he wished her to go to him.

The reply, which came late, was what she had expected. "No; we have all the help we need. The doctor has sent a good nurse, and is coming again later. It's pneumonia, but of course he doesn't say much yet. Let me have some beef-juice as soon as the cook can make it."

The beef-juice ordered and dispatched, she was left to a vigil in melancholy contrast to that of the previous evening. Then she had been enclosed in the narrow limits of her maternal interests; now the barriers of self were broken down, and her personal preoccupations swept away on the current of a wider sympathy. As she sat there in the radius of lamp-light which, for so many evenings, had held Dick and herself in a charmed circle of tenderness, she saw that her love for her boy had come to be merely a kind of extended egotism. Love had narrowed instead of widening her, had rebuilt between herself and life the very walls which, years and years before, she had laid low with bleeding fingers. It was horrible, how she had come to sacrifice everything to the one passion of ambition for her boy. . . .

At daylight she sent another messenger, one of her own servants, who returned without having seen Dick. Mr. Peyton had sent word that there was no change. He would write later; he wanted nothing. The day wore on drearily. Once Kate found herself computing the precious hours lost to Dick's unfinished task. She blushed at her ineradicable selfishness, and tried to turn her mind to poor Darrow. But she could not master her impulses; and now she caught herself indulging the thought that his illness would at least exclude him from the competition. But no—she remembered that he had said his work was finished. Come what might, he stood in the path of her boy's success. She hated herself for the thought, but it would not down.

Evening drew on, but there was no note from Dick. At length, in the shamed reaction from her fears, she rang for a carriage and went upstairs to dress. She could stand aloof no longer: she must go to Darrow, if only to escape from her wicked thoughts of him. As she came down again she heard Dick's key in the door. She hastened her steps, and as she reached the hall he stood before her without speaking.

She looked at him and the question died on her lips. He nodded, and walked slowly past her.

"There was no hope from the first," he said.

The next day Dick was taken up with the preparations for the funeral. The distant aunt, who appeared to be Darrow's only relation, had been duly notified of his death; but no answer having been received from her, it was left to his friend to fulfil the customary duties. He was again absent for the best part of the day; and when he returned at dusk Mrs. Peyton, looking up from the tea-table behind which she awaited him, was startled by the deep-lined misery of his face.

Her own thoughts were too painful for ready expression, and they sat for a while in a mute community of wretchedness.

"Is everything arranged?" she asked at length.

"Yes. Everything."

"And you have not heard from the aunt?"

He shook his head.

"Can you find no trace of any other relations?"

"None. I went over all his papers. There were very few, and I found no address but the aunt's." He sat thrown back in his chair, disregarding the cup of tea she had mechanically poured for him. "I found this, though," he added after a pause, drawing a letter from his pocket and holding it out to her.

She took it doubtfully. "Ought I to read it?"

"Yes."

She saw then that the envelope, in Darrow's hand, was addressed to her son. Within were a few pencilled words, dated on the first day of his illness, the morrow of the day on which she had last seen him.

"Dear Dick," she read, "I want you to use my plans for the museum if you can get any good out of them. Even if I pull out of this I want you to. I shall have other chances, and I have an idea this one means a lot to you."

Mrs. Peyton sat speechless, gazing at the date of the letter, which she had instantly connected with her last talk with Darrow. She saw that he had understood her, and the thought scorched her to the soul.

"Wasn't it glorious of him?" Dick said.

She dropped the letter, and hid her face in her hands.

IV

The funeral took place the next morning, and on the return from the cemetery Dick told his mother that he must go and look over things at Darrow's office. He had heard the day before from his friend's aunt, a helpless person to whom telegraphy was difficult and travel inconceivable, and who, in eight pages of unpunctuated eloquence, made over to Dick what she called the melancholy privilege of winding up her nephew's affairs.

Mrs. Peyton looked anxiously at her son. "Is there no one who can do this for you? He must have had a clerk or some one who knows about his work."

Dick shook his head. "Not lately. He hasn't had much to do this winter, and these last months he had chucked everything to work alone over his plans."

The word brought a faint colour to Mrs. Peyton's cheek. It was the first allusion that either of them had made to Darrow's bequest.

"Oh, of course you must do all you can," she murmured, turning alone into the house.

The emotions of the morning had stirred her deeply, and she sat at home during the day, letting her mind dwell, in a kind of retrospective piety, on the thought of poor Darrow's devotion. She had given him too little time while he lived, had acquiesced too easily in his growing habits of seclusion; and she felt it as a proof of insensibility that she had not been more closely drawn to the one person who had loved Dick as she loved him. The evidence of that love, as shown in Darrow's letter, filled her with a vain compunction. The very extravagance of his offer lent it a deeper pathos. It was wonderful that, even in the urgency of affection, a man of his almost morbid rectitude should have overlooked the restrictions of professional honour, should have implied the possibility of his friend's overlooking them. It seemed to make his sacrifice the more complete that it had, unconsciously, taken the form of a subtle temptation.

The last word arrested Mrs. Peyton's thoughts. A temptation? To whom? Not, surely, to one capable, as her son was capable, of rising to the height of his friend's devotion. The offer, to Dick, would mean simply, as it meant to her, the last touching expression of an inarticulate fidelity: the utterance of a love which at last had found its formula. Mrs. Peyton dismissed as morbid any other view of the case. She was annoyed with herself for supposing that Dick could be ever so remotely affected by the possibility at which poor Darrow's renunciation hinted. The nature of the offer removed it from practical issues to the idealizing region of sentiment.

Mrs. Peyton had been sitting alone with these thoughts for the greater part of the afternoon, and dusk was falling when Dick entered the drawing-room. In the dim light, with his pallour heightened by the sombre effect of his mourning, he came upon her almost startlingly, with a revival of some long-effaced impression which, for a moment, gave her the sense of struggling among shadows. She did not, at first, know what had produced the effect; then she saw that it was his likeness to his father.

"Well—is it over?" she asked, as he threw himself into a chair without speaking.

"Yes: I've looked through everything." He leaned back, crossing his hands behind his head, and gazing past her with a look of utter lassitude.

She paused a moment, and then said tentatively: "To-morrow you will be able to go back to your work."

"Oh—my work," he exclaimed, as if to brush aside an ill-timed pleasantry.

"Are you too tired?"

"No." He rose and began to wander up and down the room. "I'm not tired.—Give me some tea, will you?" He paused before her while she poured the cup, and then, without taking it, turned away to light a cigarette.

"Surely there is still time?" she suggested, with her eyes on him.

"Time? To finish my plans? Oh, yes—there's time. But they're not worth it."

"Not worth it?" She started up, and then dropped back into her seat, ashamed of having betrayed her anxiety. "They are worth as much as they were last week," she said with an attempt at cheerfulness.

"Not to me," he returned. "I hadn't seen Darrow's then."

There was a long silence. Mrs. Peyton sat with her eyes fixed on her clasped hands, and her son paced the room restlessly.

"Are they so wonderful?" she asked at length.

"Yes."

She paused again, and then said, lifting a tremulous glance to his face: "That makes his offer all the more beautiful."

Dick was lighting another cigarette, and his face was turned from her. "Yes—I suppose so," he said in a low tone.

"They were quite finished, he told me," she continued, un-consciously dropping her voice to the pitch of his.

"Yes."

"Then they will be entered, I suppose?"

"Of course—why not?" he answered almost sharply.

"Shall you have time to attend to all that and to finish yours too?"

"Oh, I suppose so. I've told you it isn't a question of time. I see now that mine are not worth bothering with."

She rose and approached him, laying her hands on his shoulders. "You are tired and unstrung; how can you judge? Why not let me look at both designs to-morrow?"

Under her gaze he flushed abruptly and drew back with a half-impatient gesture.

"Oh, I'm afraid that wouldn't help me; you'd be sure to think mine best," he said with a laugh.

"But if I could give you good reasons?" she pressed him.

He took her hand, as if ashamed of his impatience. "Dear mother, if you had any reasons their mere existence would prove that they were bad."

His mother did not return his smile. "You won't let me see the two designs then?" she said with a faint tinge of insistence.

"Oh, of course—if you want to—if you only won't talk about it now! Can't you see that I'm pretty nearly dead-beat?" he burst out uncontrollably; and as she stood silent, he added with a weary fall in his voice, "I think I'll go upstairs and see if I can't get a nap before dinner."

Though they had separated upon the assurance that she should see the two designs if she wished it, Mrs. Peyton knew they would not be shown to her. Dick, indeed, would not again deny her request; but had he not reckoned on the improbability of her renewing it? All night she lay confronted by that question. The situation shaped itself before her with that hallucinating distinctness which belongs to the midnight vision. She knew now why Dick had suddenly reminded her of his father: had she not once before seen the same thought moving behind the same eyes? She was sure it had occurred to Dick to use Darrow's drawings. As she lay awake in the darkness she could hear him, long after midnight, pacing the floor overhead: she held her breath, listening to the recurring beat of his foot, which seemed that of an imprisoned spirit revolving wearily in the cage of the same thought. She felt in every fibre that a crisis in her son's life had been reached, that the act now before him would have a determining effect on his whole future. The circumstances of her past had raised to clairvoyance her natural insight into human motive, had made of her a moral barometer responding to the faintest fluctuations of atmosphere, and years of anxious meditation had familiarized her with the form which her son's temptations were likely to take. The peculiar misery of her situation was that she could not, except indirectly, put this intuition, this foresight, at his service. It was a part of her discernment to be aware that life is the only real counsellor, that wisdom unfiltered through personal experience does not become a part of the moral tissues. Love such as hers had a great office, the office of preparation and direction; but it must know how to hold its hand and keep its counsel, how to attend upon its object as an invisible influence rather than as an active interference.

All this Kate Peyton had told herself again and again, during those hours of anxious calculation in which she had tried to cast Dick's horoscope; but not in her moments of most fantastic foreboding had she figured so cruel a test of her courage. If her prayers for him had taken precise shape, she might have asked that he should be spared the spectacular, the dramatic appeal to his will-power: that his temptations should slip by him in a dull disguise. She had secured him against all ordinary forms of baseness; the vulnerable point lay higher, in that region of idealizing egotism which is the seat of life in such natures.

Years of solitary foresight gave her mind a singular alertness in dealing with such possibilities. She saw at once that the peril of the situation lay in the minimum of risk it involved. Darrow had employed no assistant in working out his plans for the competition, and his secluded life made it almost certain that he had not shown them to any one, and that she and Dick alone knew them to have been completed. Moreover, it was a part of Dick's duty to examine the contents of his friend's office, and in doing this nothing would be easier than to possess himself of the drawings and make use of any part of them that might serve his purpose. He had Darrow's authority for doing so; and though the act involved a slight breach of professional probity, might not his friend's wishes be invoked as a secret justification? Mrs. Peyton found herself almost hating poor Darrow for having been the unconscious instrument of her son's temptation. But what right had she, after all, to suspect Dick of considering, even for a moment, the act of which she was so ready to accuse him? His unwillingness to let her see the drawings might have been the accidental result of lassitude and discouragement. He was tired and troubled, and she had chosen the wrong moment to make the request. His want of readiness might even be due to the wish to conceal from her how far his friend had surpassed him. She knew his sensitiveness on this point, and reproached herself for not having foreseen it. But her own arguments failed to convince her. Deep beneath her love for her boy and her faith in him there lurked a nameless doubt. She could hardly now, in looking back, define the impulse upon which she had married Denis Peyton: she knew only that the deeps of her nature had been loosened, and that she had been borne forward on their current to the very fate from which her heart recoiled. But if in one sense her marriage remained a problem, there was another in which her motherhood seemed to solve it. She had never lost the sense of having snatched her child from some dim peril which still lurked and hovered; and he became more closely hers with every effort of her vigilant love. For the act of rescue had not been accomplished once and for all in the moment of immolation: it had not been by a sudden stroke of heroism, but by ever-renewed and indefatigable effort, that she had built up for him the miraculous shelter of her love. And now that it stood there, a hallowed refuge against failure, she could not even set a light in the pane, but must let him grope his way to it unaided.

v

Mrs. Peyton's midnight musings summed themselves up in the conclusion that the next few hours would end her uncertainty. She felt the day to be decisive. If Dick offered to show her the drawings, her fears would be proved groundless; if he avoided the subject, they were justified.

She dressed early in order not to miss him at breakfast; but as she entered the dining-room the parlour-maid told her that Mr. Peyton had overslept himself, and had rung to have his breakfast sent upstairs. Was it a pretext to avoid her? She was vexed at her own readiness to see a portent in the simplest incident; but while she blushed at her doubts she let them govern her. She left the dining-room door open, determined not to miss him if he came downstairs while she was at breakfast; then she went back to the drawing-room and sat down at her writing-table, trying to busy herself with some accounts while she listened for his step. Here too she had left the door open; but presently even this slight departure from her daily usage seemed a deviation from the passive attitude she had adopted, and she rose and shut the door. She knew that she could still hear his step on the stairs—he had his father's quick swinging gait—but as she sat listening, and vainly trying to write, the closed door seemed to symbolize a refusal to share in his trial, a hardening of herself against his need of her. What if he should come down intending to speak, and should be turned from his purpose? Slighter obstacles have deflected the course of events in those indeterminate moments when the soul floats between two tides. She sprang up quickly, and as her hand touched the latch she heard his step on the stairs.

When he entered the drawing-room she had regained the writing-table and could lift a composed face to his. He came in hurriedly, yet with a kind of reluctance beneath his haste: again it was his father's step. She smiled, but looked away from him as he approached her; she seemed to be re-living her own past as one re-lives things in the distortion of fever.

"Are you off already?" she asked, glancing at the hat in his hand.

"Yes; I'm late as it is. I overslept myself." He paused and looked vaguely about the room. "Don't expect me till late—don't wait dinner for me."

She stirred impulsively. "Dick, you're overworking—you'll make yourself ill."

"Nonsense. I'm as fit as ever this morning. Don't be imagining things."

He dropped his habitual kiss on her forehead, and turned to go. On the threshold he paused, and she felt that something in him sought her and then drew back. "Good-bye," he called to her as the door closed on him.

She sat down and tried to survey the situation divested of her midnight fears. He had not referred to her wish to see the drawings: but what did the omission signify? Might he not have forgotten her request? Was she not forcing the most trivial details to fit in with her apprehensions? Unfortunately for her own reassurance, she knew that her familiarity with Dick's processes was based on such minute observation, and that, to such intimacy as theirs, no indications were trivial. She was as certain as if he had spoken, that when he had left the house that morning he was weighing the possibility of using Darrow's drawings, of supplementing his own incomplete design from the fulness of his friend's invention. And with a bitter pang she divined that he was sorry he had shown her Darrow's letter.

It was impossible to remain face to face with such conjectures, and though she had given up all her engagements during the few days since Darrow's death, she now took refuge in the thought of a concert which was to take place at a friend's house that morning. The music-room, when she entered, was thronged with acquaintances, and she found transient relief in that dispersal of attention which makes society an anæsthetic for some forms of wretchedness. Contact with the pressure of busy indifferent life often gives remoteness to questions which have clung as close as the flesh to the bone; and if Mrs. Peyton did not find such complete release, she at least interposed between herself and her anxiety the obligation to dissemble it. But the relief was only momentary, and when the first bars of the overture turned from her the smiles of recognition among which she had tried to lose herself, she felt a deeper sense of isolation. The music, which at another time would have swept her away on some rich current of emotion, now seemed to island her in her own thoughts, to create an artificial solitude in which she found herself more immitigably face to face with her fears. The silence, the *recueillement*, about her gave resonance to the inner voices, lucidity to the inner vision, till she seemed enclosed in a luminous empty horizon against which every possibility took the sharp edge of accomplished fact. With relentless precision the course of events was unrolled before her: she saw Dick yielding to his opportunity, snatching victory from dishonour, winning love, happiness and success in the act by which he lost himself. It was all so simple, so easy, so inevitable, that she felt the futility of struggling or hoping against it. He would win the competition, would marry Miss Verney, would press on to achievement through the opening which the first success had made for him.

As Mrs. Peyton reached this point in her forecast, she found her outward gaze arrested by the face of the young lady who so dominated her inner vision. Miss Verney, a few rows distant, sat intent upon the music, in that attitude of poised motion which was her nearest approach to repose. Her slender brown profile with its breezy hair, her quick eye, and the lips which seemed to listen as well as speak, all betokened to Mrs. Peyton a nature through which the obvious energies blew free, a bare open stretch of consciousness without shelter for tenderer growths. She shivered to think of Dick's frail scruples exposed to those rustling airs. And then, suddenly, a new thought struck her. What if she might turn this force to her own use, make it serve, unconsciously to Dick, as the means of his deliverance? Hitherto she had assumed that her son's worst danger lay in the chance of his confiding his difficulty to Clemence Verney; and she had, in her own past, a precedent which made her think such a confidence not unlikely. If he did carry his scruples to the girl, she argued, the latter's imperviousness, her frank inability to understand them, would have the effect of dispelling them like mist; and he was acute enough to know this and profit by it. So she had hitherto reasoned; but now the girl's presence seemed to clarify her perceptions, and she told herself that something in Dick's nature, something which she herself had put there, would resist this short cut to safety, would make him take the more tortuous way to his goal rather than gain it through the privacies of the heart he loved. For she had lifted him thus far above his father, that it would be a disenchantment to him to find that Clemence Verney did not share his scruples. On this much, his mother now exultingly felt, she could count in her passive struggle for supremacy. No, he would never, never tell Clemence Verney—and his one hope, his sure salvation, therefore lay in some one else's telling her.

The excitement of this discovery had nearly, in mid-concert, swept Mrs. Peyton from her seat to the girl's side. Fearing to miss the latter in the throng at the entrance, she slipped out during the last number and, lingering in the farther drawing-room, let the dispersing audience drift her in Miss Verney's direction. The girl shone sympathetically on her approach, and in a moment they had detached themselves from the crowd and taken refuge in the perfumed emptiness of the conservatory.

The girl, whose sensations were always easily set in motion, had at first a good deal to say of the music, for which she claimed, on her hearer's part, an active show of approval or dissent; but this dismissed, she turned a melting face on Mrs. Peyton and said with one of her rapid modulations of tone: "I was so sorry about poor Mr. Darrow."

Mrs. Peyton uttered an assenting sigh. "It was a great grief to us—a great loss to my son."

"Yes—I know. I can imagine what you must have felt. And then it was so unlucky that it should have happened just now."

Mrs. Peyton shot a reconnoitering glance at her profile. "His dying, you mean, on the eve of success?"

Miss Verney turned a frank smile upon her. "One ought to feel that, of course—but I'm afraid I am very selfish where my friends are concerned, and I was thinking of Mr. Peyton's having to give up his work at such a critical moment." She spoke without a note of deprecation: there was a pagan freshness in her opportunism.

Mrs. Peyton was silent, and the girl continued after a pause: "I suppose now it will be almost impossible for him to finish his drawings in time. It's a pity he hadn't worked out the whole scheme a little sooner. Then the details would have come of themselves."

Mrs. Peyton felt a contempt strangely mingled with exultation. If only the girl would talk in that way to Dick!

"He has hardly had time to think of himself lately," she said, trying to keep the coldness out of her voice.

"No, of course not," Miss Verney assented; "but isn't that all the more reason for his friends to think of him? It was very dear of him to give up everything to nurse Mr. Darrow—but, after all, if a man is going to get on in his career there are times when he must think first of himself."

Mrs. Peyton paused, trying to choose her words with deliberation. It was quite clear now that Dick had not spoken, and she felt the responsibility that devolved upon her.

"Getting on in a career—is that always the first thing to be considered?" she asked, letting her eyes rest musingly on the girl's.

The glance did not disconcert Miss Verney, who returned it with one of equal comprehensiveness. "Yes," she said quickly, and with a slight blush. "With a temperament like Mr. Peyton's I believe it is. Some people can pick themselves up after any number of bad falls: I am not sure that he could. I think discouragement would weaken instead of strengthening him."

Both women had forgotten external conditions in the quick reach for each other's meanings. Mrs. Peyton flushed, her maternal pride in revolt; but the answer was checked on her lips by the sense of the girl's unexpected insight. Here was some one who knew Dick as well as she did—should she say a partisan or an accomplice? A dim jealousy stirred beneath Mrs. Peyton's other emotions: she was undergoing the agony which the mother feels at the first intrusion on her privilege of judging her child; and her voice had a flutter of resentment.

"You must have a poor opinion of his character," she said.

Miss Verney did not remove her eyes, but her blush deepened beautifully. "I have, at any rate," she said, "a high one of his talent. I don't suppose many men have an equal amount of moral and intellectual energy."

"And you would cultivate the one at the expense of the other?"

"In certain cases—and up to a certain point." She shook out the long fur of her muff, one of those silvery flexible furs which clothe a woman with a delicate sumptuousness. Everything about her, at the moment, seemed rich and cold—everything, as Mrs. Peyton quickly noted, but the blush lingering under her dark skin; and so complete was the girl's self-command that the blush seemed to be there only because it had been forgotten.

"I dare say you think me strange," she continued. "Most people do, because I speak the truth. It's the easiest way of concealing one's feelings. I can, for instance, talk quite openly about Mr. Peyton under shelter of your inference that I shouldn't do so if I were what is called 'interested' in him. And as I *am* interested in him, my method has its advantages!" She ended with one of the fluttering laughs which seemed to flit from point to point of her expressive person.

Mrs. Peyton leaned toward her. "I believe you are interested," she said quietly; "and since I suppose you allow others the privilege you claim for yourself, I am going to confess that I followed you here in the hope of finding out the nature of your interest."

Miss Verney shot a glance at her, and drew away in a soft subsidence of undulating furs.

"Is this an embassy?" she asked smiling.

"No: not in any sense."

The girl leaned back with an air of relief. "I'm glad; I should have disliked—" She looked again at Mrs. Peyton. "You want to know what I mean to do?"

"Yes."

"Then I can only answer that I mean to wait and see what he does."

"You mean that everything is contingent on his success?"

"*I* am—if I'm everything," she admitted gaily.

The mother's heart was beating in her throat, and her words seemed to force themselves out through the throbs.

"I—I don't quite see why you attach such importance to this special success."

"Because he does," the girl returned instantly. "Because to him it is the final answer to his self-questioning—the questioning whether he is ever to amount to anything or not. He says if he has anything in him it ought to come out now. All the conditions are favourable—it is the chance he has always prayed for. You see," she continued, almost confidentially, but without the least loss of composure—"you see he has told me a great deal about himself and his various experiments—his phases of indecision and disgust. There are lots of tentative talents in the world, and the sooner they are crushed out by circumstances the better. But it seems as though he really had it in him to do something distinguished—as though the uncertainty lay in his character and not in his talent. That is what interests, what attracts me. One can't teach a man to have genius, but if he has it one may show him how to use it. That is what I should be good for, you see—to keep him up to his opportunities."

Mrs. Peyton had listened with an intensity of attention that left her reply unprepared. There was something startling and yet half attractive in the girl's avowal of principles which are oftener lived by than professed.

"And you think," she began at length, "that in this case he has fallen below his opportunity?"

"No one can tell, of course; but his discouragement, his *abattement*, is a bad sign. I don't think he has any hope of succeeding."

The mother again wavered a moment. "Since you are so frank," she then said, "will you let me be equally so, and ask how lately you have seen him?"

The girl smiled at the circumlocution. "Yesterday afternoon," she said simply.

"And you thought him—"

"Horribly down on his luck. He said himself that his brain was empty."

Again Mrs. Peyton felt the throb in her throat, and a slow blush rose to her cheek. "Was that all he said?"

"About himself—was there anything else?" said the girl quickly.

"He didn't tell you of—of an opportunity to make up for the time he has lost?"

"An opportunity? I don't understand."

"He didn't speak to you, then, of Mr. Darrow's letter?"

"He said nothing of any letter."

"There *was* one, which was found after poor Darrow's death. In it he gave Dick leave to use his design for the competition. Dick says the design is wonderful—it would give him just what he needs."

Miss Verney sat listening raptly, with a rush of colour that suffused her like light.

"But when was this? Where was the letter found? He never said a word of it!" she exclaimed.

"The letter was found on the day of Darrow's death."

"But I don't understand! Why has he never told me? Why should he seem so hopeless?" She turned an ignorant appealing face on Mrs. Peyton. It was prodigious, but it was true—

she felt nothing, saw nothing, but the crude fact of the opportunity.

Mrs. Peyton's voice trembled with the completeness of her triumph. "I suppose his reason for not speaking is that he has scruples."

"Scruples?"

"He feels that to use the design would be dishonest."

Miss Verney's eyes fixed themselves on her in a commiserating stare. "Dishonest? When the poor man wished it himself? When it was his last request? When the letter is there to prove it? Why, the design belongs to your son! No one else has any right to it."

"But Dick's right does not extend to passing it off as his own—at least that is his feeling, I believe. If he won the competition he would be winning it on false pretenses."

"Why should you call them false pretenses? His design might have been better than Darrow's if he had had time to carry it out. It seems to me that Mr. Darrow must have felt this—must have felt that he owed his friend some compensation for the time he took from him. I can imagine nothing more natural than his wishing to make this return for your son's sacrifice."

She positively glowed with the force of her conviction, and Mrs. Peyton, for a strange instant, felt her own resistance wavering. She herself had never considered the question in that light—the light of Darrow's viewing his gift as a justifiable compensation. But the glimpse she caught of it drove her shuddering behind her retrenchments.

"That argument," she said coldly, "would naturally be more convincing to Darrow than to my son."

Miss Verney glanced up, struck by the change in Mrs. Peyton's voice.

"Ah, then you agree with him? You think it *would* be dishonest?"

Mrs. Peyton saw that she had slipped into self-betrayal. "My son and I have not spoken of the matter," she said evasively. She caught the flash of relief in Miss Verney's face.

"You haven't spoken? Then how do you know how he feels about it?"

"I only judge from—well, perhaps from his not speaking."

The girl drew a deep breath. "I see," she murmured. "That is the very reason that prevents his speaking."

"The reason?"

"Your knowing what he thinks—and his knowing that you know."

Mrs. Peyton was startled at her subtlety. "I assure you," she said, rising, "that I have done nothing to influence him."

The girl gazed at her musingly. "No," she said with a faint smile, "nothing except to read his thoughts."

VI

Mrs. Peyton reached home in the state of exhaustion which follows on a physical struggle. It seemed to her as though her talk with Clemence Verney had been an actual combat, a measuring of wrist and eye. For a moment she was frightened at what she had done—she felt as though she had betrayed her son to the enemy. But before long she regained her moral balance, and saw that she had merely shifted the conflict to the ground on which it could best be fought out—since the prize fought for was the natural battlefield. The reaction brought with it a sense of helplessness, a realization that she had let the issue pass out of her hold; but since, in the last analysis, it had never lain there, since it was above all needful that the determining touch should be given by any hand but hers, she presently found courage to subside into inaction. She had done all she could—even more, perhaps, than prudence warranted—and now she could but await passively the working of the forces she had set in motion.

For two days after her talk with Miss Verney she saw little of Dick. He went early to his office and came back late. He seemed less tired, more self-possessed, than during the first days after Darrow's death; but there was a new inscrutableness in his manner, a note of reserve, of resistance almost, as though he had barricaded himself against her conjectures. She had been struck by Miss Verney's reply to the anxious asseveration that she had done nothing to influence Dick—"Nothing," the girl had answered, "except to read his thoughts." Mrs. Peyton shrank from this detection of a tacit

interference with her son's liberty of action. She longed—
how passionately he would never know—to stand apart from
him in this struggle between his two destinies, and it was almost a relief that he on his side should hold aloof, should, for
the first time in their relation, seem to feel her tenderness as
an intrusion.

Only four days remained before the date fixed for the sending in of the designs, and still Dick had not referred to his
work. Of Darrow, also, he had made no mention. His mother
longed to know if he had spoken to Clemence Verney—or
rather if the girl had forced his confidence. Mrs. Peyton was
almost certain that Miss Verney would not remain silent—
there were times when Dick's renewed application to his work
seemed an earnest of her having spoken, and spoken convincingly. At the thought Kate's heart grew chill. What if her experiment should succeed in a sense she had not intended? If
the girl should reconcile Dick to his weakness, should pluck
the sting from his temptation? In this round of uncertainties
the mother revolved for two interminable days; but the second evening brought an answer to her question.

Dick, returning earlier than usual from the office, had
found, on the hall-table, a note which, since morning, had
been under his mother's observation. The envelope, fashionable in tint and texture, was addressed in a rapid staccato
hand which seemed the very imprint of Miss Verney's utterance. Mrs. Peyton did not know the girl's writing; but such
notes had of late lain often enough on the hall-table to make
their attribution easy. This communication Dick, as his
mother poured his tea, looked over with a face of shifting
lights; then he folded it into his note-case, and said, with a
glance at his watch: "If you haven't asked any one for this
evening I think I'll dine out."

"Do, dear; the change will be good for you," his mother
assented.

He made no answer, but sat leaning back, his hands clasped
behind his head, his eyes fixed on the fire. Every line of his
body expressed a profound physical lassitude, but the face remained alert and guarded. Mrs. Peyton, in silence, was busy-
ing herself with the details of the tea-making, when suddenly,
inexplicably, a question forced itself to her lips.

"And your work—?" she said, strangely hearing herself speak.

"My work—?" He sat up, on the defensive almost, but without a tremor of the guarded face.

"You're getting on well? You've made up for lost time?"

"Oh, yes: things are going better." He rose, with another glance at his watch. "Time to dress," he said, nodding to her as he turned to the door.

It was an hour later, during her own solitary dinner, that a ring at the door was followed by the parlour-maid's announcement that Mr. Gill was there from the office. In the hall, in fact, Kate found her son's partner, who explained apologetically that he had understood Peyton was dining at home, and had come to consult him about a difficulty which had arisen since he had left the office. On hearing that Dick was out, and that his mother did not know where he had gone, Mr. Gill's perplexity became so manifest that Mrs. Peyton, after a moment, said hesitatingly: "He may be at a friend's house; I could give you the address."

The architect caught up his hat. "Thank you; I'll have a try for him."

Mrs. Peyton hesitated again. "Perhaps," she suggested, "it would be better to telephone."

She led the way into the little study behind the drawing-room, where a telephone stood on the writing-table. The folding doors between the two rooms were open: should she close them as she passed back into the drawing-room? On the threshold she wavered an instant; then she walked on and took her usual seat by the fire.

Gill, meanwhile, at the telephone, had "rung up" the Verney house, and inquired if his partner were dining there. The reply was evidently affirmative; and a moment later Kate knew that he was in communication with her son. She sat motionless, her hands clasped on the arms of her chair, her head erect, in an attitude of avowed attention. If she listened she would listen openly: there should be no suspicion of eavesdropping. Gill, engrossed in his message, was probably hardly conscious of her presence; but if he turned his head he should at least have no difficulty in seeing her, and in being aware that she could hear what he said. Gill, however, as she was quick to remember, was doubtless ignorant of any need for secrecy in his communication to Dick. He had often heard the affairs of the office discussed openly before Mrs. Peyton, had been led to regard her as familiar with all the details of her son's work. He talked on unconcernedly, and she listened.

Ten minutes later, when he rose to go, she knew all that she had wanted to find out. Long familiarity with the technicalities of her son's profession made it easy for her to translate the stenographic jargon of the office. She could lengthen out all Gill's abbreviations, interpret all his allusions, and reconstruct Dick's answers from the questions addressed to him. And when the door closed on the architect she was left face to face with the fact that her son, unknown to any one but herself, was using Darrow's drawings to complete his work.

Mrs. Peyton, left alone, found it easier to continue her vigil by the drawing-room fire than to carry up to the darkness and silence of her own room the truth she had been at such pains to acquire. She had no thought of sitting up for Dick. Doubtless, his dinner over, he would rejoin Gill at the office, and prolong through the night the task in which she now knew him to be engaged. But it was less lonely by the fire than in the wide-eyed darkness which awaited her upstairs. A mortal loneliness enveloped her. She felt as though she had fallen by the way, spent and broken in a struggle of which even its object had been unconscious. She had tried to deflect the natural course of events, she had sacrificed her personal happiness to a fantastic ideal of duty, and it was her punishment to be left alone with her failure, outside the normal current of human strivings and regrets.

She had no wish to see her son just then: she would have preferred to let the inner tumult subside, to repossess herself in this new adjustment to life, before meeting his eyes again. But as she sat there, far adrift on her misery, she was aroused by the turning of his key in the latch. She started up, her heart sounding a retreat, but her faculties too dispersed to obey it; and while she stood wavering, the door opened and he was in the room.

In the room, and with face illumined: a Dick she had not seen since the strain of the contest had cast its shade on him.

Now he shone as if in a sunrise of victory, holding out exultant hands from which she hung back instinctively.

"Mother! I knew you'd be waiting for me!" He had her on his breast now, and his kisses were in her hair. "I've always said you knew everything that was happening to me, and now you've guessed that I wanted you to-night."

She was struggling faintly against the dear endearments. "What *has* happened?" she murmured, drawing back for a dazzled look at him.

He had drawn her to the sofa, had dropped beside her, regaining his hold of her in the boyish need that his happiness should be touched and handled.

"My engagement has happened!" he cried out to her. "You stupid dear, do you need to be told?"

VII

She had indeed needed to be told: the surprise was complete and overwhelming. She sat silent under it, her hands trembling in his, till the blood mounted to his face and she felt his confident grasp relax.

"You didn't guess it, then?" he exclaimed, starting up and moving away from her.

"No; I didn't guess it," she confessed in a dead-level voice.

He stood above her, half challenging, half defensive. "And you haven't a word to say to me? Mother!" he adjured her.

She rose too, putting her arms about him with a kiss. "Dick! Dear Dick!" she murmured.

"She imagines you don't like her; she says she's always felt it. And yet she owns you've been delightful, that you've tried to make friends with her. And I thought you knew how much it would mean to me, just now, to have this uncertainty over, and that you'd actually been trying to help me, to put in a good word for me. I thought it was you who had made her decide."

"I?"

"By your talk with her the other day. She told me of your talk with her."

His mother's hands slipped from his shoulders and she sank back into her seat. She felt the cruelty of her silence, but only an inarticulate murmur found a way to her lips. Before speaking she must clear a space in the suffocating rush of her sensations. For the moment she could only repeat inwardly that Clemence Verney had yielded before the final test, and that she herself was somehow responsible for this fresh entanglement of fate. For she saw in a flash how the coils of circumstance had tightened; and as her mind cleared it was filled with the perception that this, precisely, was what the girl intended, that this was why she had conferred the crown before the victory. By pledging herself to Dick she had secured his pledge in return: had put him on his honour in a cynical inversion of the term. Kate saw the succession of events spread out before her like a map, and the astuteness of the girl's policy frightened her. Miss Verney had conducted the campaign like a strategist. She had frankly owned that her interest in Dick's future depended on his capacity for success, and in order to key him up to his first achievement she had given him a foretaste of its results.

So much was almost immediately clear to Mrs. Peyton; but in a moment her inferences had carried her a point farther. For it was now plain to her that Miss Verney had not risked so much without first trying to gain her point at less cost: that if she had had to give herself as a prize, it was because no other bribe had been sufficient. This then, as the mother saw with a throb of hope, meant that Dick, who since Darrow's death had held to his purpose unwaveringly, had been deflected from it by the first hint of Clemence Verney's connivance. Kate had not miscalculated: things had happened as she had foreseen. In the light of the girl's approval his act had taken an odious look. He had recoiled from it, and it was to revive his flagging courage that she had had to promise herself, to take him in the meshes of her surrender.

Kate, looking up, saw above her the young perplexity of her boy's face, the suspended happiness waiting to brim over. With a fresh touch of misery she said to herself that this was his hour, his one irrecoverable moment, and that she was darkening it by her silence. Her memory went back to the same hour in her own life: she could feel its heat in her pulses still. What right had she to stand in Dick's light? Who was she to decide between his code and hers? She put out her hand and drew him down to her.

"She'll be the making of me, you know, mother," he said, as they leaned together. "She'll put new life in me—she'll help me get my second wind. Her talk is like a fresh breeze blowing away the fog in my head. I never knew any one who saw so straight to the heart of things, who had such a grip on values. She goes straight up to life and catches hold of it, and you simply can't make her let go."

He got up and walked the length of the room; then he came back and stood smiling above his mother.

"You know you and I are rather complicated people," he said. "We're always walking around things to get new views of them—we're always rearranging the furniture. And somehow she simplifies life so tremendously." He dropped down beside her with a deprecating laugh. "Not that I mean, dear, that it hasn't been good for me to argue things out with myself, as you've taught me to—only the man who stops to talk is apt to get shoved aside nowadays, and I don't believe Milton's archangels would have had much success in active business."

He had begun in a strain of easy confidence, but as he went on she detected an effort to hold the note, she felt that his words were being poured out in a vain attempt to fill the silence which was deepening between them. She longed, in her turn, to pour something into that menacing void, to bridge it with a reconciling word or look; but her soul hung back, and she had to take refuge in a vague murmur of tenderness.

"My boy! My boy!" she repeated; and he sat beside her without speaking, their hand-clasp alone spanning the distance which had widened between their thoughts.

The engagement, as Kate subsequently learned, was not to be made known till later. Miss Verney had even stipulated that for the present there should be no recognition of it in her own family or in Dick's. She did not wish to interfere with his final work for the competition, and had made him promise, as he laughingly owned, that he would not see her again till the drawings were sent in. His mother noticed that he made no other allusion to his work; but when he bade her good-night he added that he might not see her the next morning, as he had to go to the office early. She took this as a hint that he wished to be left alone, and kept her room the next day till the closing door told her that he was out of the house.

She herself had waked early, and it seemed to her that the day was already old when she came downstairs. Never had the house appeared so empty. Even in Dick's longest absences something of his presence had always hung about the rooms: a fine dust of memories and associations, which wanted only the evocation of her thought to float into a palpable semblance of him. But now he seemed to have taken himself quite away, to have broken every fibre by which their lives had hung together. Where the sense of him had been there was only a deeper emptiness: she felt as if a strange man had gone out of the house.

She wandered from room to room, aimlessly, trying to adjust herself to their solitude. She had known such loneliness before, in the years when most women's hearts are fullest; but that was long ago, and the solitude had after all been less complete, because of the sense that it might still be filled. Her son had come: her life had brimmed over; but now the tide ebbed again, and she was left gazing over a bare stretch of wasted years. Wasted! There was the mortal pang, the stroke from which there was no healing. Her faith and hope had been marsh-lights luring her to the wilderness, her love a vain edifice reared on shifting ground.

In her round of the rooms she came at last to Dick's study upstairs. It was full of his boyhood: she could trace the history of his past in its quaint relics and survivals, in the school-books lingering on his crowded shelves, the school-photographs and college-trophies hung among his later treasures. All his successes and failures, his exaltations and inconsistencies, were recorded in the warm huddled heterogeneous room. Everywhere she saw the touch of her own hand, the vestiges of her own steps. It was she alone who held the clue to the labyrinth, who could thread a way through the confusions and contradictions of his past; and her soul rejected the thought that his future could ever escape from her. She dropped down into his shabby college armchair and hid her face in the papers on his desk.

VIII

The day dwelt in her memory as a long stretch of aimless hours: blind alleys of time that led up to a dead wall of inaction.

Toward afternoon she remembered that she had promised to dine out and go to the opera. At first she felt that the contact of life would be unendurable; then she shrank from shutting herself up with her misery. In the end she let herself drift passively on the current of events, going through the mechanical routine of the day without much consciousness of what was happening.

At twilight, as she sat in the drawing-room, the evening paper was brought in, and in glancing over it her eye fell on a paragraph which seemed printed in more vivid type than the rest. It was headed, *The New Museum of Sculpture*, and underneath she read: "The artists and architects selected to pass on the competitive designs for the new Museum will begin their sittings on Monday, and to-morrow is the last day on which designs may be sent in to the committee. Great interest is felt in the competition, as the conspicuous site chosen for the new building, and the exceptionally large sum voted by the city for its erection, offer an unusual field for the display of architectural ability."

She leaned back, closing her eyes. It was as though a clock had struck, loud and inexorably, marking off some irrecoverable hour. She was seized by a sudden longing to seek Dick out, to fall on her knees and plead with him: it was one of those physical obsessions against which the body has to stiffen its muscles as well as the mind its thoughts. Once she even sprang up to ring for a cab; but she sank back again, breathing as if after a struggle, and gripping the arms of her chair to keep herself down.

"I can only wait for him—only wait for him—" she heard herself say; and the words loosened the sobs in her throat.

At length she went upstairs to dress for dinner. A ghost-like self looked back at her from her toilet-glass: she watched it performing the mechanical gestures of the toilet, dressing her, as it appeared, without help from her actual self. Each little act stood out sharply against the blurred background of her

brain: when she spoke to her maid her voice sounded extraordinarily loud. Never had the house been so silent; or, stay—
yes, once she had felt the same silence, once when Dick, in his
school-days, had been ill of a fever, and she had sat up with
him on the decisive night. The silence had been as deep and
as terrible then; and as she dressed she had before her the vision of his room, of the cot in which he lay, of his restless
head working a hole in the pillow, his face so pinched and
alien under the familiar freckles. It might be his death-watch
she was keeping: the doctors had warned her to be ready. And
in the silence her soul had fought for her boy, her love had
hung over him like wings, her abundant useless hateful life
had struggled to force itself into his empty veins. And she had
succeeded, she had saved him, she had poured her life into
him; and in place of the strange child she had watched all
night, at daylight she held her own boy to her breast.

That night had once seemed to her the most dreadful of
her life; but she knew now that it was one of the agonies
which enrich, that the passion thus spent grows fourfold from
its ashes. She could not have borne to keep this new vigil
alone. She must escape from its sterile misery, must take
refuge in other lives till she regained courage to face her own.
At the opera, in the illumination of the first *entr'acte*, as she
gazed about the house, wondering through the numb ache of
her wretchedness how others could talk and smile and be indifferent, it seemed to her that all the jarring animation about
her was suddenly focussed in the face of Clemence Verney.
Miss Verney sat opposite, in the front of a crowded box, a box
in which, continually, the black-coated background shifted
and renewed itself. Mrs. Peyton felt a throb of anger at the
girl's bright air of unconcern. She forgot that she too was
talking, smiling, holding out her hand to newcomers, in a
studied mimicry of life, while her real self played out its
tragedy behind the scenes. Then it occurred to her that, to
Clemence Verney, there was no tragedy in the situation.
According to the girl's calculations, Dick was virtually certain
of success; and unsuccess was to her the only conceivable
disaster.

All through the opera the sense of that opposing force, that
negation of her own beliefs, burned itself into Mrs. Peyton's

consciousness. The space between herself and the girl seemed to vanish, the throng about them to disperse, till they were face to face and alone, enclosed in their mortal enmity. At length the feeling of humiliation and defeat grew unbearable to Mrs. Peyton. The girl seemed to flout her in the insolence of victory, to sit there as the visible symbol of her failure. It was better after all to be at home alone with her thoughts.

As she drove away from the opera she thought of that other vigil which, only a few streets away, Dick was perhaps still keeping. She wondered if his work were over, if the final stroke had been drawn. And as she pictured him there, signing his pact with evil in the loneliness of the conniving night, an uncontrollable impulse possessed her. She must drive by his windows and see if they were still alight. She would not go up to him,—she dared not,—but at least she would pass near to him, would invisibly share his watch and hover on the edge of his thoughts. She lowered the window and called out the address to the coachman.

The tall office-building loomed silent and dark as she approached it; but presently, high up, she caught a light in the familiar windows. Her heart gave a leap, and the light swam on her through tears. The carriage drew up, and for a moment she sat motionless. Then the coachman bent down toward her, and she saw that he was asking if he should drive on. She tried to shape a yes, but her lips refused it, and she shook her head. He continued to lean down perplexedly, and at length, under the interrogation of his attitude, it became impossible to sit still, and she opened the door and stepped out. It was equally impossible to stand on the sidewalk, and her next steps carried her to the door of the building. She groped for the bell and rang it, feeling still dimly accountable to the coachman for some consecutiveness of action, and after a moment the night watchman opened the door, drawing back amazed at the shining apparition which confronted him. Recognizing Mrs. Peyton, whom he had seen about the building by day, he tried to adapt himself to the situation by a vague stammer of apology.

"I came to see if my son is still here," she faltered.

"Yes, ma'am, he's here. He's been here most nights lately till after twelve."

"And is Mr. Gill with him?"

"No: Mr. Gill he went away just after I come on this evening."

She glanced up into the cavernous darkness of the stairs.

"Is he alone up there, do you think?"

"Yes, ma'am, I know he's alone, because I seen his men leaving soon after Mr. Gill."

Kate lifted her head quickly. "Then I will go up to him," she said.

The watchman apparently did not think it proper to offer any comment on this unusual proceeding, and a moment later she was fluttering and rustling up through the darkness, like a night-bird hovering among rafters. There were ten flights to climb: at every one her breath failed her, and she had to stand still and press her hands against her heart. Then the weight on her breast lifted, and she went on again, upward and upward, the great dark building dropping away from her, in tier after tier of mute doors and mysterious corridors. At last she reached Dick's floor, and saw the light shining down the passage from his door. She leaned against the wall, her breath coming short, the silence throbbing in her ears. Even now it was not too late to turn back. She bent over the stairs, letting her eyes plunge into the nether blackness, with the single glimmer of the watchman's light in its depths; then she turned and stole toward her son's door.

There again she paused and listened, trying to catch, through the hum of her pulses, any noise that might come to her from within. But the silence was unbroken—it seemed as though the office must be empty. She pressed her ear to the door, straining for a sound. She knew he never sat long at his work, and it seemed unaccountable that she should not hear him moving about the drawing-board. For a moment she fancied he might be sleeping; but sleep did not come to him readily after prolonged mental effort—she recalled the restless straying of his feet above her head for hours after he returned from his night work in the office.

She began to fear that he might be ill. A nervous trembling seized her, and she laid her hand on the latch, whispering "Dick!"

Her whisper sounded loudly through the silence, but there was no answer, and after a pause she called again. With each call the hush seemed to deepen: it closed in on her, mysterious and impenetrable. Her heart was beating in short frightened leaps: a moment more and she would have cried out. She drew a quick breath and turned the door-handle.

The outer room, Dick's private office, with its red carpet and easy-chairs, stood in pleasant lamp-lit emptiness. The last time she had entered it, Darrow and Clemence Verney had been there, and she had sat behind the urn observing them. She paused a moment, struck now by a faint sound from beyond; then she slipped noiselessly across the carpet, pushed open the swinging door, and stood on the threshold of the work-room. Here the gas-lights hung a green-shaded circle of brightness over the great draughting-table in the middle of the floor. Table and floor were strewn with a confusion of papers —torn blue-prints and tracings, crumpled sheets of tracing-paper wrenched from the draughting-boards in a sudden fury of destruction; and in the centre of the havoc, his arms stretched across the table and his face hidden in them, sat Dick Peyton.

He did not seem to hear his mother's approach, and she stood looking at him, her breast tightening with a new fear.

"Dick!" she said, "Dick—!" and he sprang up, staring with dazed eyes. But gradually, as his gaze cleared, a light spread in it, a mounting brightness of recognition.

"You've come—you've come—" he said, stretching his hands to her; and all at once she had him in her breast as in a shelter.

"You wanted me?" she whispered as she held him.

He looked up at her, tired, breathless, with the white radiance of the runner near the goal.

"I *had* you, dear!" he said, smiling strangely on her; and her heart gave a great leap of understanding.

Her arms had slipped from his neck, and she stood leaning on him, deep-suffused in the shyness of her discovery. For it might still be that he did not wish her to know what she had done for him.

But he put his arm about her, boyishly, and drew her toward one of the hard seats between the tables; and there, on the bare floor, he knelt before her, and hid his face in her lap. She sat motionless, feeling the dear warmth of his head against her knees, letting her hands stray in faint caresses through his hair.

Neither spoke for awhile; then he raised his head and looked at her. "I suppose you know what has been happening to me," he said.

She shrank from seeming to press into his life a hair's-breadth farther than he was prepared to have her go. Her eyes turned from him toward the scattered drawings on the table.

"You have given up the competition?" she said.

"Yes—and a lot more." He stood up, the wave of emotion ebbing, yet leaving him nearer, in his recovered calmness, than in the shock of their first moment.

"I didn't know, at first, how much you guessed," he went on quietly. "I was sorry I'd shown you Darrow's letter; but it didn't worry me much because I didn't suppose you'd think it possible that I should—take advantage of it. It's only lately that I've understood that you knew everything." He looked at her with a smile. "I don't know yet how I found it out, for you're wonderful about keeping things to yourself, and you never made a sign. I simply felt it in a kind of nearness—as if I couldn't get away from you.—Oh, there were times when I should have preferred not having you about—when I tried to turn my back on you, to see things from other people's standpoint. But you were always there—you wouldn't be discouraged. And I got tired of trying to explain things to you, of trying to bring you round to my way of thinking. You wouldn't go away and you wouldn't come any nearer—you just stood there and watched everything that I was doing."

He broke off, taking one of his restless turns down the long room. Then he drew up a chair beside her, and dropped into it with a great sigh.

"At first, you know, I hated it most awfully. I wanted to be let alone and to work out my own theory of things. If you'd said a word—if you'd tried to influence me—the spell would have been broken. But just because the actual *you* kept apart and didn't meddle or pry, the other, the you in my heart, seemed to get a tighter hold on me. I don't know how to tell you,—it's all mixed up in my head—but old things you'd said and done kept coming back to me, crowding between me and what I was trying for, looking at me without speaking, like old friends I'd gone back on, till I simply couldn't stand it any longer. I fought it off till to-night, but when I came back to finish the work there you were again—and suddenly, I don't know how, you weren't an obstacle any longer, but a refuge— and I crawled into your arms as I used to when things went against me at school."

His hands stole back into hers, and he leaned his head against her shoulder like a boy.

"I'm an abysmally weak fool, you know," he ended; "I'm not worth the fight you've put up for me. But I want you to know that it's your doing—that if you had let go an instant I should have gone under—and that if I'd gone under I should never have come up again alive."

The Descent of Man

WHEN Professor Linyard came back from his holiday in the Maine woods the air of rejuvenation he brought with him was due less to the influences of the climate than to the companionship he had enjoyed on his travels. To Mrs. Linyard's observant eye he had appeared to set out alone; but an invisible traveller had in fact accompanied him, and if his heart beat high it was simply at the pitch of his adventure: for the Professor had eloped with an idea.

No one who has not tried the experiment can divine its exhilaration. Professor Linyard would not have changed places with any hero of romance pledged to a flesh-and-blood abduction. The most fascinating female is apt to be encumbered with luggage and scruples: to take up a good deal of room in the present and overlap inconveniently into the future; whereas an idea can accommodate itself to a single molecule of the brain or expand to the circumference of the horizon. The Professor's companion had to the utmost this quality of adaptability. As the express train whirled him away from the somewhat inelastic circle of Mrs. Linyard's affections, his idea seemed to be sitting opposite him, and their eyes met every moment or two in a glance of joyous complicity; yet when a friend of the family presently joined him and began to talk about college matters, the idea slipped out of sight in a flash, and the Professor would have had no difficulty in proving that he was alone.

But if, from the outset, he found his idea the most agreeable of fellow-travellers, it was only in the aromatic solitude of the woods that he tasted the full savour of his adventure. There, during the long cool August days, lying full length on the pine-needles and gazing up into the sky, he would meet the eyes of his companion bending over him like a nearer heaven. And what eyes they were!—clear yet unfathomable, bubbling with inexhaustible laughter, yet drawing their freshness and sparkle from the central depths of thought! To a man who for twenty years had faced an eye reflecting the commonplace with perfect accuracy, these escapes into the inscrutable had always been peculiarly inviting; but hitherto the Professor's mental infidelities had been restricted by an unbroken and relentless domesticity. Now, for the first time since his marriage, chance had given him six weeks to himself, and he was coming home with his lungs full of liberty.

It must not be inferred that the Professor's domestic relations were defective: they were in fact so complete that it was almost impossible to get away from them. It is the happy husbands who are really in bondage; the little rift within the lute is often a passage to freedom. Marriage had given the Professor exactly what he had sought in it: a comfortable lining to life. The impossibility of rising to sentimental crises had made him scrupulously careful not to shirk the practical obligations of the bond. He took as it were a sociological view of his case, and modestly regarded himself as a brick in that foundation on which the state is supposed to rest. Perhaps if Mrs. Linyard had cared about entomology, or had taken sides in the war over the transmission of acquired characteristics, he might have had a less impersonal notion of marriage; but he was unconscious of any deficiency in their relation, and if consulted would probably have declared that he didn't want any woman bothering with his beetles. His real life had always lain in the universe of thought, in that enchanted region which, to those who have lingered there, comes to have so much more colour and substance than the painted curtain hanging before it. The Professor's particular veil of Maia was a narrow strip of homespun woven in a monotonous pattern; but he had only to lift it to step into an empire.

This unseen universe was thronged with the most seductive shapes: the Professor moved Sultan-like through a seraglio of ideas. But of all the lovely apparitions that wove their spells about him, none had ever worn quite so persuasive an aspect as this latest favourite. For the others were mostly rather grave companions, serious-minded and elevating enough to have passed muster in a Ladies' Debating Club; but this new fancy of the Professor's was simply one embodied laugh. It was, in other words, the smile of relaxation at the end of a long day's toil: the flash of irony which the laborious mind projects, irresistibly, over labour conscientiously performed. The Professor had always been a hard worker. If he was an indulgent friend to his ideas he was also a stern taskmaster to them. For, in addition to their other duties, they had to support his family: to pay the butcher and baker, and provide for Jack's schooling and Millicent's dresses. The Professor's household was a modest one, yet it tasked his ideas to keep it up to his wife's standard. Mrs. Linyard was not an exacting wife, and she took enough pride in her husband's attainments to pay for her honours by turning Millicent's dresses and darning Jack's socks and going to the College receptions year after year in the same black silk with shiny seams. It consoled her to see an occasional mention of Professor Linyard's remarkable monograph on the Ethical Reactions of the Infusoria, or an allusion to his investigations into the Unconscious Cerebration of the Amœba.

Still there were moments when the healthy indifference of Jack and Millicent reacted on the maternal sympathies; when Mrs. Linyard would have made her husband a railway director, if by this transformation she might have increased her boy's allowance and given her daughter a new hat, or a set of furs such as the other girls were wearing. Of such moments of rebellion the Professor himself was not wholly unconscious. He could not indeed understand why any one should want a new hat; and as to an allowance, he had had much less money at college than Jack, and had yet managed to buy a microscope and collect a few "specimens"; while Jack was free from such expensive tastes! But the Professor did not let his want of sympathy interfere with the discharge of his paternal obligations. He worked hard to keep the wants of his family gratified, and it was precisely in the endeavour to attain this end that he at length broke down and had to cease from work altogether.

To cease from work was not to cease from thought of it; and in the unwonted pause from effort the Professor found himself taking a general survey of the field he had travelled. At last it was possible to lift his nose from the loom, to step a moment in front of the tapestry he had been weaving. From this first inspection of the pattern so long wrought over from behind, it was natural to glance a little farther and seek its reflection in the public eye. It was not indeed of his special task that he thought in this connection. He was but one of the great army of weavers at work among the threads of that cosmic woof; and what he sought was the general impression their labour had produced.

When Professor Linyard first plied his microscope, the audience of the man of science had been composed of a few fellow-students, sympathetic or hostile as their habits of mind predetermined, but versed in the jargon of the profession and familiar with the point of departure. In the intervening quarter of a century, however, this little group had been swallowed up in a larger public. Every one now read scientific books and expressed an opinion on them. The ladies and the clergy had taken them up first; now they had passed to the school-room and the kindergarten. Daily life was regulated on scientific principles; the daily papers had their "Scientific Jottings"; nurses passed examinations in hygienic science, and babies were fed and dandled according to the new psychology.

The very fact that scientific investigation still had, to some minds, the flavor of heterodoxy, gave it a perennial interest. The mob had broken down the walls of tradition to batten in the orchard of forbidden knowledge. The inaccessible goddess whom the Professor had served in his youth now offered her charms in the market-place. And yet it was not the same goddess, after all, but a pseudo-science masquerading in the garb of the real divinity. This false goddess had her ritual and her literature. She had her sacred books, written by false priests and sold by millions to the faithful. In the most successful of these works, ancient dogma and modern discovery were depicted in a close embrace under the lime-lights of a hazy transcendentalism; and the tableau never failed of its effect. Some of the books designed on this popular model had lately fallen into the Professor's hands, and they filled him with mingled rage and hilarity. The rage soon died: he came to regard this mass of pseudo-literature as protecting the truth from desecration. But the hilarity remained, and flowed into the form of his idea. And the idea—the divine incomparable idea—was simply that he should avenge his goddess by satirising her false interpreters. He would write a skit on the "popular" scientific book; he would so heap platitude on platitude, fallacy on fallacy, false analogy on false analogy, so use

his superior knowledge to abound in the sense of the ignorant, that even the gross crowd would join in the laugh
against its augurs. And the laugh should be something more
than the distention of mental muscles; it should be the trum-
pet-blast bringing down the walls of ignorance, or at least the
little stone striking the giant between the eyes.

II

The Professor, on presenting his card, had imagined that it
would command prompt access to the publisher's sanctuary;
but the young man who read his name was not moved to
immediate action. It was clear that Professor Linyard of
Hillbridge University was not a specific figure to the purveyors of popular literature. But the publisher was an old friend;
and when the card had finally drifted to his office on the languid tide of routine he came forth at once to greet his visitor.

The warmth of his welcome convinced the Professor that
he had been right in bringing his manuscript to Ned Harviss.
He and Harviss had been at Hillbridge together, and the future publisher had been one of the wildest spirits in that band
of college outlaws which yearly turns out so many inoffensive
citizens and kind husbands and fathers. The Professor knew
the taming qualities of life. He was aware that many of his
most reckless comrades had been transformed into prudent
capitalists or cowed wage-earners; but he was almost sure that
he could count on Harviss. So rare a sense of irony, so keen a
perception of relative values, could hardly have been blunted
even by twenty years' intercourse with the obvious.

The publisher's appearance was a little disconcerting. He
looked as if he had been fattened on popular fiction; and his fat
was full of optimistic creases. The Professor seemed to see him
bowing into the office a long train of spotless heroines laden
with the maiden tribute of the hundredth thousand volume.

Nevertheless, his welcome was reassuring. He did not dis-
own his early enormities, and capped his visitor's tentative allusions by such flagrant references to the past that the
Professor produced his manuscript without a scruple.

"What—you don't mean to say you've been doing something in our line?"

The Professor smiled. "You publish scientific books some-times, don't you?"

The publisher's optimistic creases relaxed a little. "H'm—it all depends—I'm afraid you're a little *too* scientific for us. We have a big sale for scientific breakfast foods, but not for the concentrated essences. In your case, of course, I should be delighted to stretch a point; but in your own interest I ought to tell you that perhaps one of the educational houses would do you better."

The Professor leaned back, still smiling luxuriously.

"Well, look it over—I rather think you'll take it."

"Oh, we'll *take* it, as I say; but the terms might not—"

"No matter about the terms—"

The publisher threw his head back with a laugh. "I had no idea that science was so profitable; we find our popular nov-elists are the hardest hands at a bargain."

"Science is disinterested," the Professor corrected him. "And I have a fancy to have you publish this thing."

"That's immensely good of you, my dear fellow. Of course your name goes with a certain public—and I rather like the originality of our bringing out a work so out of our line. I daresay it may boom us both." His creases deepened at the thought, and he shone encouragingly on the Professor's leave-taking.

Within a fortnight, a line from Harviss recalled the Pro-fessor to town. He had been looking forward with immense zest to this second meeting; Harviss's college roar was in his tympanum, and he could already hear the protracted chuckle which would follow his friend's progress through the manu-script. He was proud of the adroitness with which he had kept his secret from Harviss, had maintained to the last the pre-tence of a serious work, in order to give the keener edge to his reader's enjoyment. Not since under-graduate days had the Professor tasted such a draught of pure fun as his antici-pations now poured for him.

This time his card brought instant admission. He was bowed into the office like a successful novelist, and Harviss grasped him with both hands.

"Well—do you mean to take it?" he asked with a lingering coquetry.

"Take it? Take it, my dear fellow? It's in press already—you'll excuse my not waiting to consult you? There will be no difficulty about terms, I assure you, and we had barely time to catch the autumn market. My dear Linyard, why didn't you *tell* me?" His voice sank to a reproachful solemnity, and he pushed forward his own arm-chair.

The Professor dropped into it with a chuckle. "And miss the joy of letting you find out?"

"Well—it *was* a joy." Harviss held out a box of his best cigars. "I don't know when I've had a bigger sensation. It was so deucedly unexpected—and, my dear fellow, you've brought it so exactly to the right shop."

"I'm glad to hear you say so," said the Professor modestly.

Harviss laughed in rich appreciation. "I don't suppose you had a doubt of it; but of course I was quite unprepared. And it's so extraordinarily out of your line—"

The Professor took off his glasses and rubbed them with a slow smile.

"Would you have thought it so—at college?"

Harviss stared. "At college?—Why, you were the most iconoclastic devil—"

There was a perceptible pause. The Professor restored his glasses and looked at his friend. "Well—?" he said simply.

"Well—?" echoed the other, still staring. "Ah—I see; you mean that that's what explains it. The swing of the pendulum, and so forth. Well, I admit it's not an uncommon phenomenon. I've conformed myself, for example; most of our crowd have, I believe; but somehow I hadn't expected it of you."

The close observer might have detected a faint sadness under the official congratulation of his tone; but the Professor was too amazed to have an ear for such fine shades.

"Expected it of me? Expected what of me?" he gasped. "What in heaven do you think this thing is?" And he struck his fist on the manuscript which lay between them.

Harviss had recovered his optimistic creases. He rested a benevolent eye on the document.

"Why, your apologia—your confession of faith, I should call it. You surely must have seen which way you were going? You can't have written it in your sleep?"

"Oh, no, I was wide awake enough," said the Professor faintly.

"Well, then, why are you staring at me as if I were *not*?" Harviss leaned forward to lay a reassuring hand on his visitor's worn coat-sleeve. "Don't mistake me, my dear Linyard. Don't fancy there was the least unkindness in my allusion to your change of front. What is growth but the shifting of the stand-point? Why should a man be expected to look at life with the same eyes at twenty and—at our age? It never occurred to me that you could feel the least delicacy in admitting that you have come round a little—have fallen into line, so to speak."

But the Professor had sprung up as if to give his lungs more room to expand; and from them there issued a laugh which shook the editorial rafters.

"Oh, Lord, oh, Lord—is it really as good as that?"

Harviss had glanced instinctively toward the electric bell on his desk; he was evidently prepared for an emergency.

"My dear fellow—" he began in a soothing tone.

"Oh, let me have my laugh out, do," implored the Professor. "I'll—I'll quiet down in a minute; you needn't ring for the young man." He dropped into his chair again and grasped its arms to steady his shaking. "This is the best laugh I've had since college," he brought out between his paroxysms. And then, suddenly, he sat up with a groan. "But if it's as good as that it's a failure!" he exclaimed.

Harviss, stiffening a little, examined the tip of his cigar. "My dear Linyard," he said at length, "I don't understand a word you're saying."

The Professor succumbed to a fresh access, from the vortex of which he managed to fling out—"But that's the very core of the joke!"

Harviss looked at him resignedly. "What is?"

"Why, your not seeing—your not understanding—"

"Not understanding *what*?"

"Why, what the book is meant to be." His laughter subsided again and he sat gazing thoughtfully at the publisher. "Unless it means," he wound up, "that I've over-shot the mark."

"If I am the mark, you certainly have," said Harviss, with a glance at the clock.

The Professor caught the glance and interpreted it. "The book is a skit," he said, rising.

The other stared. "A skit? It's not serious, you mean?"

"Not to me—but it seems you've taken it so."

"You never told me—" began the publisher in a ruffled tone.

"No, I never told you," said the Professor.

Harviss sat staring at the manuscript between them. "I don't pretend to be up in such recondite forms of humour," he said stiffly. "Of course you address yourself to a very small class of readers."

"Oh, infinitely small," admitted the Professor, extending his hand toward the manuscript.

Harviss appeared to be pursuing his own train of thought. "That is," he continued, "if you insist on an ironical interpretation."

"If I insist on it—what do you mean?"

The publisher smiled faintly. "Well—isn't the book susceptible of another? If *I* read it without seeing—"

"Well?" murmured the other, fascinated.

—"why shouldn't the rest of the world?" declared Harviss boldly. "I represent the Average Reader—that's my business, that's what I've been training myself to do for the last twenty years. It's a mission like another—the thing is to do it thoroughly; not to cheat and compromise. I know fellows who are publishers in business hours and dilettantes the rest of the time. Well, they never succeed: convictions are just as necessary in business as in religion. But that's not the point—I was going to say that if you'll let me handle this book as a genuine thing I'll guarantee to make it go."

The Professor stood motionless, his hand still on the manuscript.

"A genuine thing?" he echoed.

"A serious piece of work—the expression of your convictions. I tell you there's nothing the public likes as much as convictions—they'll always follow a man who believes in his own ideas. And this book is just on the line of popular interest. You've got hold of a big thing. It's full of hope and enthusiasm: it's written in the religious key. There are passages in it that would do splendidly in a Birthday Book—things that popular preachers would quote in their sermons. If you'd wanted to catch a big public you couldn't have gone about it in a better way. The thing's perfect for my purpose—I wouldn't let you alter a word of it. It will sell like a popular novel if you'll let me handle it in the right way."

III

When the Professor left Harviss's office the manuscript remained behind. He thought he had been taken by the huge irony of the situation—by the enlarged circumference of the joke. In its original form, as Harviss had said, the book would have addressed itself to a very limited circle: now it would include the world. The elect would understand; the crowd would not; and his work would thus serve a double purpose. And, after all, nothing was changed in the situation; not a word of the book was to be altered. The change was merely in the publisher's point of view, and in the "tip" he was to give the reviewers. The Professor had only to hold his tongue and look serious.

These arguments found a strong reinforcement in the large premium which expressed Harviss's sense of his opportunity. As a satire the book would have brought its author nothing; in fact, its cost would have come out of his own pocket, since, as Harviss assured him, no publisher would have risked taking it. But as a profession of faith, as the recantation of an eminent biologist, whose leanings had hitherto been supposed to be toward a cold determinism, it would bring in a steady income to author and publisher. The offer found the Professor in a moment of financial perplexity. His illness, his unwonted holiday, the necessity of postponing a course of well-paid lectures, had combined to diminish his resources; and when Harviss offered him an advance of a thousand dollars the esoteric savour of the joke became irresistible. It was still as a joke that he persisted in regarding the transaction; and though he had pledged himself not to betray the real intent of the book, he held *in petto* the notion of some day being able to take the public into his confidence. As for the initiated, they would know at once: and however long a face he pulled his colleagues would see the tongue in his cheek.

Meanwhile it fortunately happened that, even if the book should achieve the kind of triumph prophesied by Harviss, it would not appreciably injure its author's professional standing. Professor Linyard was known chiefly as a microscopist. On the structure and habits of a certain class of coleoptera he was the most distinguished living authority; but none save his intimate friends knew what generalizations on the destiny of man he had drawn from these special studies. He might have published a treatise on the Filioque without shaking the confidence of those on whose approval his reputation rested; and moreover he was sustained by the thought that one glance at his book would let them into its secret. In fact, so sure was he of this that he wondered the astute Harviss had cared to risk such speedy exposure. But Harviss had probably reflected that even in this reverberating age the opinions of the laboratory do not easily reach the street; and the Professor, at any rate, was not bound to offer advice on this point.

The determining cause of his consent was the fact that the book was already in press. The Professor knew little about the workings of the press, but the phrase gave him a sense of finality, of having been caught himself in the toils of that mysterious engine. If he had had time to think the matter over his scruples might have dragged him back; but his conscience was eased by the futility of resistance.

IV

Mrs. Linyard did not often read the papers; and there was therefore a special significance in her approaching her husband one evening after dinner with a copy of the *New York Investigator* in her hand. Her expression lent solemnity to the act: Mrs. Linyard had a limited but distinctive set of expressions, and she now looked as she did when the President of the University came to dine.

"You didn't tell me of this, Samuel," she said in a slightly tremulous voice.

"Tell you of what?" returned the Professor, reddening to the margin of his baldness.

"That you had published a book—I might never have heard of it if Mrs. Pease hadn't brought me the paper."

Her husband rubbed his eye-glasses and groaned. "Oh, you would have heard of it," he said gloomily.

Mrs. Linyard stared. "Did you wish to keep it from me, Samuel?" And as he made no answer, she added with irresistible pride: "Perhaps you don't know what beautiful things have been said about it."

He took the paper with a reluctant hand. "Has Pease been saying beautiful things about it?"

"The Professor? Mrs. Pease didn't say he had mentioned it."

The author heaved a sigh of relief. His book, as Harviss had prophesied, had caught the autumn market: had caught and captured it. The publisher had conducted the campaign like an experienced strategist. He had completely surrounded the enemy. Every newspaper, every periodical, held in ambush an advertisement of "The Vital Thing." Weeks in advance the great commander had begun to form his lines of attack. Allusions to the remarkable significance of the coming work had appeared first in the scientific and literary reviews, spreading thence to the supplements of the daily journals. Not a moment passed without a quickening touch to the public consciousness: seventy millions of people were forced to remember at least once a day that Professor Linyard's book was on the verge of appearing. Slips emblazoned with the question: *Have you read "The Vital Thing"?* fell from the pages of popular novels and whitened the floors of crowded street-cars. The query, in large lettering, assaulted the traveller at the railway bookstall, confronted him on the walls of "elevated" stations, and seemed, in its ascending scale, about to supplant the interrogations as to sapolio and stove-polish which animate our rural scenery.

On the day of publication the Professor had withdrawn to his laboratory. The shriek of the advertisements was in his ears and his one desire was to avoid all knowledge of the event they heralded. A reaction of self-consciousness had set in, and if Harviss's cheque had sufficed to buy up the first edition of "The Vital Thing" the Professor would gladly have devoted it to that purpose. But the sense of inevitableness gradually subdued him, and he received his wife's copy of the *Investigator* with a kind of impersonal curiosity. The review was a long one, full of extracts: he saw, as he glanced over the latter, how

well they would look in a volume of "Selections." The reviewer began by thanking his author "for sounding with no
uncertain voice that note of ringing optimism, of faith in
man's destiny and the supremacy of good, which has too long
been silenced by the whining chorus of a decadent nihilism.
. . . It is well," the writer continued, "when such reminders
come to us not from the moralist but from the man of science
—when from the desiccating atmosphere of the laboratory
there rises this glorious cry of faith and reconstruction."

The review was minute and exhaustive. Thanks no doubt to
Harviss's diplomacy, it had been given to the *Investigator's*
"best man," and the Professor was startled by the bold eye
with which his emancipated fallacies confronted him. Under
the reviewer's handling they made up admirably as truths, and
their author began to understand Harviss's regret that they
should be be used for any less profitable purpose.

The *Investigator*, as Harviss phrased it, "set the pace," and
the other journals followed, finding it easier to let their critical man-of-all-work play a variation on the first reviewer's
theme than to secure an expert to "do" the book afresh. But
it was evident that the Professor had captured his public, for
all the resources of the profession could not, as Harviss glee-
fully pointed out, have carried the book so straight to the
heart of the nation. There was something noble in the way in
which Harviss belittled his own share in the achievement, and
insisted on the inutility of shoving a book which had started
with such headway on.

"All I ask you is to admit that I saw what would happen,"
he said with a touch of professional pride. "I knew you'd
struck the right note—I knew they'd be quoting you from
Maine to San Francisco. Good as fiction? It's better—it'll
keep going longer."

"Will it?" said the Professor with a slight shudder. He was
resigned to an ephemeral triumph, but the thought of the
book's persistency frightened him.

"I should say so! Why, you fit in everywhere—science, the-
ology, natural history—and then the all-for-the-best element
which is so popular just now. Why, you come right in with the
How-to-Relax series, and they sell way up in the millions.
And then the book's so full of tenderness—there are such

lovely things in it about flowers and children. I didn't know an old Dryasdust like you could have such a lot of sentiment in him. Why, I actually caught myself snivelling over that passage about the snowdrops piercing the frozen earth; and my wife was saying the other day that, since she's read 'The Vital Thing,' she begins to think you must write the 'What-Cheer Column,' in the *Inglenook*." He threw back his head with a laugh which ended in the inspired cry: "And, by George, sir, when the thing begins to slow off we'll start somebody writing against it, and that will run us straight up into another hundred thousand."

And as earnest of this belief he drew the Professor a supplementary cheque.

V

Mrs. Linyard's knock cut short the importunities of the lady who had been trying to persuade the Professor to be taken by flashlight at his study-table for the Christmas number of the *Inglenook*. On this point the Professor had fancied himself impregnable; but the unwonted smile with which he welcomed his wife's intrusion showed that his defences were weakening.

The lady from the *Inglenook* took the hint with professional promptness, but said brightly, as she snapped the elastic around her note-book: "I sha'n't let you forget me, Professor."

The groan with which he followed her retreat was interrupted by his wife's question: "Do they pay you for these interviews, Samuel?"

The Professor looked at her with sudden attention. "Not directly," he said, wondering at her expression.

She sank down with a sigh. "Indirectly, then?"

"What is the matter, my dear? I gave you Harviss's second cheque the other day—"

Her tears arrested him. "Don't be hard on the boy, Samuel! I really believe your success has turned his head."

"The boy—what boy? My success—? Explain yourself, Susan!"

"It's only that Jack has—has borrowed some money— which he can't repay. But you mustn't think him altogether to blame, Samuel. Since the success of your book he has been asked about so much—it's given the children quite a different position. Millicent says that wherever they go the first question asked is, 'Are you any relation of the author of "The Vital Thing"?' Of course we're all very proud of the book; but it entails obligations which you may not have thought of in writing it."

The Professor sat gazing at the letters and newspaper clippings on the study-table which he had just successfully defended from the camera of the *Inglenook*. He took up an envelope bearing the name of a popular weekly paper.

"I don't know that the *Inglenook* would help much," he said, "but I suppose this might."

Mrs. Linyard's eyes glowed with maternal avidity.

"What is it, Samuel?"

"A series of 'Scientific Sermons' for the Round-the-Gas-Log column of *The Woman's World*. I believe that journal has a larger circulation than any other weekly, and they pay in proportion."

He had not even asked the extent of Jack's indebtedness. It had been so easy to relieve recent domestic difficulties by the timely production of Harviss's two cheques that it now seemed natural to get Mrs. Linyard out of the room by promising further reinforcements. The Professor had indignantly rejected Harviss's suggestion that he should follow up his success by a second volume on the same lines. He had sworn not to lend more than a passive support to the fraud of "The Vital Thing"; but the temptation to free himself from Mrs. Linyard prevailed over his last scruples, and within an hour he was at work on the Scientific Sermons.

The Professor was not an unkind man. He really enjoyed making his family happy; and it was his own business if his reward for so doing was that it kept them out of his way. But the success of "The Vital Thing" gave him more than this negative satisfaction. It enlarged his own existence and opened new doors into other lives. The Professor, during fifty virtuous years, had been cognizant of only two types of women: the fond and foolish, whom one married, and the earnest and intellectual, whom one did not. Of the two, he infinitely preferred the former, even for conversational purposes. But as a social instrument woman was unknown to him; and it was not till he was drawn into the world on the tide of his literary success that he discovered the deficiencies in his classification of the sex. Then he learned with astonishment of the existence of a third type: the woman who is fond without foolishness and intellectual without earnestness. Not that the Professor inspired, or sought to inspire, sentimental emotions; but he expanded in the warm atmosphere of personal interest which some of his new acquaintances contrived to create about him. It was delightful to talk of serious things in a setting of frivolity, and to be personal without being domestic.

Even in this new world, where all subjects were touched on lightly, and emphasis was the only indelicacy, the Professor found himself constrained to endure an occasional reference to his book. It was unpleasant at first; but gradually he slipped into the habit of hearing it talked of, and grew accustomed to telling pretty women just how "it had first come to him."

Meanwhile the success of the Scientific Sermons was facilitating his family relations. His photograph in the *Inglenook*, to which the lady of the note-book had succeeded in appending a vivid interview, carried his fame to circles inaccessible even to "The Vital Thing"; and the Professor found himself the man of the hour. He soon grew used to the functions of the office, and gave out hundred-dollar interviews on every subject, from labour-strikes to Babism, with a frequency which reacted agreeably on the domestic exchequer. Presently his head began to figure in the advertising pages of the magazines. Admiring readers learned the name of the only breakfast-food in use at his table, of the ink with which "The Vital Thing" had been written, the soap with which the author's hands were washed, and the tissue-builder which fortified him for further effort. These confidences endeared the Professor to millions of readers, and his head passed in due course from the magazine and the newspaper to the biscuit-tin and the chocolate-box.

VI

The Professor, all the while, was leading a double life. While the author of "The Vital Thing" reaped the fruits of popular approval, the distinguished microscopist continued

his laboratory work unheeded save by the few who were engaged in the same line of investigations. His divided allegiance had not hitherto affected the quality of his work: it
seemed to him that he returned to the laboratory with greater
zest after an afternoon in a drawing-room where readings
from "The Vital Thing" had alternated with plantation
melodies and tea. He had long ceased to concern himself with
what his colleagues thought of his literary career. Of the few
whom he frequented, none had referred to "The Vital
Thing"; and he knew enough of their lives to guess that their
silence might as fairly be attributed to indifference as to disapproval. They were intensely interested in the Professor's
views on beetles but they really cared very little what he
thought of the Almighty.

The Professor entirely shared their feelings, and one of his
chief reasons for cultivating the success which accident had
bestowed on him, was that it enabled him to command a
greater range of appliances for his real work. He had known
what it was to lack books and instruments; and "The Vital
Thing" was the magic wand which summoned them to his
aid. For some time he had been feeling his way along the
edge of a discovery: balancing himself with professional skill
on a plank of hypothesis flung across an abyss of uncertainty.
The conjecture was the result of years of patient gathering of
facts: its corroboration would take months more of comparison and classification. But at the end of the vista victory
loomed. The Professor felt within himself that assurance of
ultimate justification which, to the man of science, makes a
life-time seem the mere comma between premiss and deduction. But he had reached the point where his conjectures required formulation. It was only by giving them expression, by
exposing them to the comment and criticism of his associates,
that he could test their final value; and this inner assurance
was confirmed by the only friend whose confidence he invited.

Professor Pease, the husband of the lady who had opened
Mrs. Linyard's eyes to the triumph of "The Vital Thing," was
the repository of her husband's scientific experiences. What
he thought of "The Vital Thing" had never been divulged;
and he was capable of such vast exclusions that it was quite
possible that pervasive work had not yet reached him. In any

case, it was not likely to affect his judgment of the author's professional capacity.

"You want to put that all in a book, Linyard," was Professor Pease's conclusion, after listening to the summary of his friend's projected work. "I'm sure you've got hold of something big; but to see it clearly yourself you ought to outline it for others. Take my advice—chuck everything else and get to work to-morrow. It's time you wrote a book, anyhow."

It's time you wrote a book, anyhow! The words smote the Professor with mingled pain and ecstasy: he could have wept over their significance. But his friend's other phrase reminded him with a start of Harviss. "You have got hold of a big thing—" it had been the publisher's first comment on "The Vital Thing." But what a world of meaning lay between the two phrases! It was the world in which the powers who fought for the Professor were destined to wage their final battle; and for the moment he had no doubt of the outcome.

"By George, I'll do it, Pease!" he said, stretching his hand to his friend.

The next day he went to town to see Harviss. He wanted to ask for an advance on the new popular edition of "The Vital Thing." He had determined to drop a course of supplementary lectures at the University and to give himself up for a year to his book. To do this additional funds were necessary; but thanks to "The Vital Thing" they would be forthcoming.

The publisher received him as cordially as usual; but the response to his demand was not as prompt as his previous experience had entitled him to expect.

"Of course we'll be glad to do what we can for you, Linyard; but the fact is we've decided to give up the idea of the new edition for the present."

"You've given up the new edition?"

"Why, yes—we've done pretty well by 'The Vital Thing,' and we're inclined to think it's *your* turn to do something for it now."

The Professor looked at him blankly. "What can I do for it?" he asked—"what *more*" his accent added.

"Why, put a little new life in it by writing something else. The secret of perpetual motion hasn't yet been discovered, you know, and it's one of the laws of literature that books which start with a rush are apt to slow down sooner than the crawlers. We've kept 'The Vital Thing' going for eighteen months—but, hang it, it ain't so vital any more. We simply couldn't see our way to a new edition. Oh, I don't say it's dead yet—but it's moribund, and you're the only man who can resuscitate it."

The Professor continued to stare. "I—what can I do about it?" he stammered.

"Do? Why, write another like it—go it one better: you know the trick. The public isn't tired of you by any means; but you want to make yourself heard again before anybody else cuts in. Write another book—write two, and we'll sell them in sets in a box: The Vital Thing Series. That will take tremendously in the holidays. Try and let us have a new volume by October—I'll be glad to give you a big advance if you'll sign a contract on that."

The Professor sat silent: there was too cruel an irony in the coincidence.

Harviss looked up at him in surprise.

"Well, what's the matter with taking my advice—you're not going out of literature, are you?"

The Professor rose from his chair. "No—I'm going into it," he said simply.

"Going into it?"

"I'm going to write a real book—a serious one."

"Good Lord! Most people think 'The Vital Thing' 's serious."

"Yes—but I mean something different."

"In your old line—beetles and so forth?"

"Yes," said the Professor solemnly.

Harviss looked at him with equal gravity. "Well, I'm sorry for that," he said, "because it takes you out of our bailiwick. But I suppose you've made enough money out of 'The Vital Thing' to permit yourself a little harmless amusement. When you want more cash come back to us—only don't put it off too long, or some other fellow will have stepped into your shoes. Popularity don't keep, you know; and the hotter the success the quicker the commodity perishes."

He leaned back, cheerful and sententious, delivering his axioms with conscious kindliness.

The Professor, who had risen and moved to the door, turned back with a wavering step.

"When did you say another volume would have to be ready?" he faltered.

"I said October—but call it a month later. You don't need any pushing nowadays."

"And—you'd have no objection to letting me have a little advance now? I need some new instruments for my real work."

Harviss extended a cordial hand. "My dear fellow, that's talking—I'll write the cheque while you wait; and I daresay we can start up the cheap edition of 'The Vital Thing' at the same time, if you'll pledge yourself to give us the book by November.—How much?" he asked, poised above his cheque-book.

In the street, the Professor stood staring about him, uncertain and a little dazed.

"After all, it's only putting it off for six months," he said to himself; "and I can do better work when I get my new instruments."

He smiled and raised his hat to the passing victoria of a lady in whose copy of "The Vital Thing" he had recently written:

Labor est etiam ipsa voluptas.

The Mission of Jane

LETHBURY, surveying his wife across the dinner table, found his transient glance arrested by an indefinable change in her appearance.

"How smart you look! Is that a new gown?" he asked.

Her answering look seemed to deprecate his charging her with the extravagance of wasting a new gown on him, and he now perceived that the change lay deeper than any accident of dress. At the same time, he noticed that she betrayed her consciousness of it by a delicate, almost frightened blush. It was one of the compensations of Mrs. Lethbury's protracted childishness that she still blushed as prettily as at eighteen. Her body had been privileged not to outstrip her mind, and the two, as it seemed to Lethbury, were destined to travel together through an eternity of girlishness.

"I don't know what you mean," she said.

Since she never did, he always wondered at her bringing this out as a fresh grievance against him; but his wonder was unresentful, and he said good-humouredly: "You sparkle so that I thought you had on your diamonds."

She sighed and blushed again.

"It must be," he continued, "that you've been to a dressmaker's opening. You're absolutely brimming with illicit enjoyment."

She stared again, this time at the adjective. His adjectives always embarrassed her: their unintelligibleness savoured of impropriety.

"In short," he summed up, "you've been doing something that you're thoroughly ashamed of."

To his surprise she retorted: "I don't see why I should be ashamed of it!"

Lethbury leaned back with a smile of enjoyment. When there was nothing better going he always liked to listen to her explanations.

"Well—?" he said.

She was becoming breathless and ejaculatory. "Of course you'll laugh—you laugh at everything!"

"That rather blunts the point of my derision, doesn't it?" he interjected; but she pushed on without noticing:

"It's so easy to laugh at things."

"Ah," murmured Lethbury with relish, "that's Aunt Sophronia's, isn't it?"

Most of his wife's opinions were heirlooms, and he took a quaint pleasure in tracing their descent. She was proud of their age, and saw no reason for discarding them while they were still serviceable. Some, of course, were so fine that she kept them for state occasions, like her great-grandmother's Crown Derby; but from the lady known as Aunt Sophronia she had inherited a stout set of every-day prejudices that were practically as good as new; whereas her husband's, as she noticed, were always having to be replaced. In the early days she had fancied there might be a certain satisfaction in taxing him with the fact; but she had long since been silenced by the reply: "My dear, I'm not a rich man, but I never use an opinion twice if I can help it."

She was reduced, therefore, to dwelling on his moral deficiencies; and one of the most obvious of these was his refusal to take things seriously. On this occasion, however, some ulterior purpose kept her from taking up his taunt.

"I'm not in the least ashamed!" she repeated, with the air of shaking a banner to the wind; but the domestic atmosphere being calm, the banner drooped unheroically.

"That," said Lethbury judicially, "encourages me to infer that you ought to be, and that, consequently, you've been giving yourself the unusual pleasure of doing something I shouldn't approve of."

She met this with an almost solemn directness. "No," she said. "You won't approve of it. I've allowed for that."

"Ah," he exclaimed, setting down his liqueur-glass. "You've worked out the whole problem, eh?"

"I believe so."

"That's uncommonly interesting. And what is it?"

She looked at him quietly. "A baby."

If it was seldom given her to surprise him, she had attained the distinction for once.

"A baby?"

"Yes."

"A—human baby?"

"Of course!" she cried, with the virtuous resentment of the woman who has never allowed dogs in the house.

Lethbury's puzzled stare broke into a fresh smile. "A baby I sha'n't approve of? Well, in the abstract I don't think much of them, I admit. Is this an abstract baby?"

Again she frowned at the adjective; but she had reached a pitch of exaltation at which such obstacles could not deter her.

"It's the loveliest baby—" she murmured.

"Ah, then it's concrete. It exists. In this harsh world it draws its breath in pain—"

"It's the healthiest child I ever saw!" she indignantly corrected.

"You've seen it, then?"

Again the accusing blush suffused her. "Yes—I've seen it."

"And to whom does the paragon belong?"

And here indeed she confounded him. "To me—I hope," she declared.

He pushed his chair back with an articulate murmur. "To *you*—?"

"To *us*," she corrected.

"Good Lord!" he said. If there had been the least hint of hallucination in her transparent gaze—but no: it was as clear, as shallow, as easily fathomable as when he had first suffered the sharp surprise of striking bottom in it.

It occurred to him that perhaps she was trying to be funny: he knew that there is nothing more cryptic than the humour of the unhumourous.

"Is it a joke?" he faltered.

"Oh, I hope not. I want it so much to be a reality—"

He paused to smile at the limitations of a world in which jokes were not realities, and continued gently: "But since it is one already—"

"To us, I mean: to you and me. I want—" her voice wavered, and her eyes with it. "I have always wanted so dreadfully . . . it has been such a disappointment . . . not to . . ."

"I see," said Lethbury slowly.

But he had not seen before. It seemed curious now that he had never thought of her taking it in that way, had never surmised any hidden depths beneath her outspread obviousness. He felt as though he had touched a secret spring in her mind.

There was a moment's silence, moist and tremulous on her part, awkward and slightly irritated on his.

"You've been lonely, I suppose?" he began. It was odd, having suddenly to reckon with the stranger who gazed at him out of her trivial eyes.

"At times," she said.

"I'm sorry."

"It was not your fault. A man has so many occupations; and women who are clever—or very handsome—I suppose that's an occupation too. Sometimes I've felt that when dinner was ordered I had nothing to do till the next day."

"Oh," he groaned.

"It wasn't your fault," she insisted. "I never told you—but when I chose that rose-bud paper for the front room upstairs, I always thought—"

"Well—?"

"It would be such a pretty paper—for a baby—to wake up in. That was years ago, of course; but it was rather an expensive paper . . . and it hasn't faded in the least . . ." she broke off incoherently.

"It hasn't faded?"

"No—and so I thought . . . as we don't use the room for anything . . . now that Aunt Sophronia is dead . . . I thought I might . . . you might . . . oh, Julian, if you could only have seen it just waking up in its crib!"

"Seen what—where? You haven't got a baby upstairs?"

"Oh, no—not *yet*," she said, with her rare laugh—the girlish bubbling of merriment that had seemed one of her chief graces in the early days. It occurred to him that he had not given her enough things to laugh about lately. But then she needed such very elementary things: she was as difficult to amuse as a savage. He concluded that he was not sufficiently simple.

"Alice," he said almost solemnly, "what *do* you mean?"

She hesitated a moment: he saw her gather her courage for a supreme effort. Then she said slowly, gravely, as though she were pronouncing a sacramental phrase:

"I'm so lonely without a little child—and I thought perhaps you'd let me adopt one. . . . It's at the hospital . . . its mother is dead . . . and I could . . . pet it, and dress it, and do things for it . . . and it's such a good baby . . . you can ask any of the nurses . . . it would never, *never* bother you by crying . . ."

II

Lethbury accompanied his wife to the hospital in a mood of chastened wonder. It did not occur to him to oppose her wish. He knew, of course, that he would have to bear the brunt of the situation: the jokes at the club, the enquiries, the explanations. He saw himself in the comic rôle of the adopted father and welcomed it as an expiation. For in his rapid reconstruction of the past he found himself cutting a shabbier figure than he cared to admit. He had always been intolerant of stupid people, and it was his punishment to be convicted of stupidity. As his mind traversed the years between his marriage and this unexpected assumption of paternity, he saw, in the light of an overheated imagination, many signs of unwonted crassness. It was not that he had ceased to think his wife stupid: she *was* stupid, limited, inflexible; but there was a pathos in the struggles of her swaddled mind, in its blind reachings toward the primal emotions. He had always thought she would have been happier with a child; but he had thought it mechanically, because it had so often been thought before, because it was in the nature of things to think it of every woman, because his wife was so eminently one of a species that she fitted into all the generalisations of the sex. But he had regarded this generalisation as merely typical of the triumph of tradition over experience. Maternity was no doubt the supreme function of primitive woman, the one end to which her whole organism tended; but the law of increasing complexity had operated in both sexes, and he had not seriously supposed that, outside the world of Christmas fiction and anecdotic art, such truisms had any special hold on the feminine imagination. Now he saw that the arts in question were kept alive by the vitality of the sentiments they appealed to.

Lethbury was in fact going through a rapid process of readjustment. His marriage had been a failure, but he had preserved toward his wife the exact fidelity of act that is sometimes supposed to excuse any divagation of feeling; so that, for years, the tie between them had consisted mainly in his abstaining from making love to other women. The abstention had not always been easy, for the world is surprisingly well-stocked with the kind of woman one ought to have married but did not; and Lethbury had not escaped the solicitation of such alternatives. His immunity had been purchased at the cost of taking refuge in the somewhat rarefied atmosphere of his perceptions; and his world being thus limited, he had given unusual care to its details, compensating himself for the narrowness of his horizon by the minute finish of his foreground. It was a world of fine shadings and the nicest proportions, where impulse seldom set a blundering foot, and the feast of reason was undisturbed by an intemperate flow of soul. To such a banquet his wife naturally remained uninvited. The diet would have disagreed with her, and she would probably have objected to the other guests. But Lethbury, miscalculating her needs, had hitherto supposed that he had made ample provision for them, and was consequently at liberty to enjoy his own fare without any reproach of mendicancy at his gates. Now he beheld her pressing a starved face against the windows of his life, and in his imaginative reaction he invested her with a pathos borrowed from the sense of his own shortcomings.

In the hospital the imaginative process continued with increasing force. He looked at his wife with new eyes. Formerly she had been to him a mere bundle of negations, a labyrinth of dead walls and bolted doors. There was nothing behind the walls, and the doors led no whither: he had sounded and listened often enough to be sure of that. Now he felt like a traveller who, exploring some ancient ruin, comes on an inner cell, intact amid the general dilapidation, and painted with images which reveal the forgotten uses of the building.

His wife stood by a white crib in one of the wards. In the crib lay a child, a year old, the nurse affirmed, but to Lethbury's eye a mere dateless fragment of humanity projected against a background of conjecture. Over this anonymous particle of life Mrs. Lethbury leaned, such ecstasy reflected in her face as strikes up, in Correggio's Night-piece, from the child's body to the mother's countenance. It was a

light that irradiated and dazzled her. She looked up at an en-
quiry of Lethbury's, but as their glances met he perceived
that she no longer saw him, that he had become as invisible
to her as she had long been to him. He had to transfer his
question to the nurse.

"What is the child's name?" he asked.

"We call her Jane," said the nurse.

III

Lethbury, at first, had resisted the idea of a legal adoption;
but when he found that his wife could not be brought to regard the child as hers till it had been made so by process of
law, he promptly withdrew his objection. On one point only
he remained inflexible; and that was the changing of the
waif's name. Mrs. Lethbury, almost at once, had expressed a
wish to rechristen it: she fluctuated between Muriel and
Gladys, deferring the moment of decision like a lady wavering
between two bonnets. But Lethbury was unyielding. In the
general surrender of his prejudices this one alone held out.

"But Jane is so dreadful," Mrs. Lethbury protested.

"Well, we don't know that *she* won't be dreadful. She may
grow up a Jane."

His wife exclaimed reproachfully. "The nurse says she's the
loveliest—"

"Don't they always say that?" asked Lethbury patiently. He
was prepared to be inexhaustibly patient now that he had
reached a firm foothold of opposition.

"It's cruel to call her Jane," Mrs. Lethbury pleaded.

"It's ridiculous to call her Muriel."

"The nurse is *sure* she must be a lady's child."

Lethbury winced: he had tried, all along, to keep his mind
off the question of antecedents.

"Well, let her prove it," he said, with a rising sense of exasperation. He wondered how he could ever have allowed himself to be drawn into such a ridiculous business; for the first
time he felt the full irony of it. He had visions of coming
home in the afternoon to a house smelling of linseed and
paregoric, and of being greeted by a chronic howl as he went

up stairs to dress for dinner. He had never been a club-man, but he saw himself becoming one now.

The worst of his anticipations were unfulfilled. The baby was surprisingly well and surprisingly quiet. Such infantile remedies as she absorbed were not potent enough to be perceived beyond the nursery; and when Lethbury could be induced to enter that sanctuary, there was nothing to jar his nerves in the mild pink presence of his adopted daughter. Jars there were, indeed: they were probably inevitable in the disturbed routine of the household; but they occurred between Mrs. Lethbury and the nurses, and Jane contributed to them only a placid stare which might have served as a rebuke to the combatants.

In the reaction from his first impulse of atonement, Lethbury noted with sharpened perceptions the effect of the change on his wife's character. He saw already the error of supposing that it could work any transformation in her. It simply magnified her existing qualities. She was like a dried sponge put in water: she expanded, but she did not change her shape. From the stand-point of scientific observation it was curious to see how her stored instincts responded to the pseudo-maternal call. She overflowed with the petty maxims of the occasion. One felt in her the epitome, the consummation, of centuries of animal maternity, so that this little woman, who screamed at a mouse and was nervous about burglars, came to typify the cave-mother rending her prey for her young.

It was less easy to regard philosophically the practical effects of her borrowed motherhood. Lethbury found with surprise that she was becoming assertive and definite. She no longer represented the negative side of his life; she showed, indeed, a tendency to inconvenient affirmations. She had gradually expanded her assumption of motherhood till it included his own share in the relation, and he suddenly found himself regarded as the father of Jane. This was a contingency he had not foreseen, and it took all his philosophy to accept it; but there were moments of compensation. For Mrs. Lethbury was undoubtedly happy for the first time in years; and the thought that he had tardily contributed to this end reconciled him to the irony of the means.

At first he was inclined to reproach himself for still viewing the situation from the outside, for remaining a spectator instead of a participant. He had been allured, for a moment, by the vision of severed hands meeting over a cradle, as the whole body of domestic fiction bears witness to their doing; and the fact that no such conjunction took place he could explain only on the ground that it was a borrowed cradle. He did not dislike the little girl. She still remained to him a hypothetical presence, a query rather than a fact; but her nearness was not unpleasant, and there were moments when her tentative utterances, her groping steps, seemed to loosen the dry accretions enveloping his inner self. But even at such moments—moments which he invited and caressed—she did not bring him nearer to his wife. He now perceived that he had made a certain place in his life for Mrs. Lethbury, and that she no longer fitted into it. It was too late to enlarge the space, and so she overflowed and encroached. Lethbury struggled against the sense of submergence. He let down barrier after barrier, yielding privacy after privacy; but his wife's personality continued to dilate. She was no longer herself alone: she was herself and Jane. Gradually, in a monstrous fusion of identity, she became herself, himself and Jane; and instead of trying to adapt her to a spare crevice of his character, he found himself carelessly squeezed into the smallest compartment of the domestic economy.

IV

He continued to tell himself that he was satisfied if his wife was happy; and it was not till the child's tenth year that he felt a doubt of her happiness.

Jane had been a preternaturally good child. During the eight years of her adoption she had caused her foster-parents no anxiety beyond those connected with the usual succession of youthful diseases. But her unknown progenitors had given her a robust constitution, and she passed unperturbed through measles, chicken-pox and whooping-cough. If there was any suffering it was endured vicariously by Mrs. Lethbury, whose temperature rose and fell with the patient's, and who could not hear Jane sneeze without visions of a marble

angel weeping over a broken column. But though Jane's
prompt recoveries continued to belie such premonitions,
though her existence continued to move forward on an even
keel of good health and good conduct, Mrs. Lethbury's satisfaction showed no corresponding advance. Lethbury, at first,
was disposed to add her disappointment to the long list of
feminine inconsistencies with which the sententious observer
of life builds up his favourable induction; but circumstances
presently led him to take a kindlier view of the case.

Hitherto his wife had regarded him as a negligible factor in
Jane's evolution. Beyond providing for his adopted daughter,
and effacing himself before her, he was not expected to contribute to her well-being. But as time passed he appeared to
his wife in a new light. It was he who was to educate Jane. In
matters of the intellect, Mrs. Lethbury was the first to declare
her deficiencies—to proclaim them, even, with a certain virtuous superiority. She said she did not pretend to be clever, and
there was no denying the truth of the assertion. Now, however, she seemed less ready, not to own her limitations, but to
glory in them. Confronted with the problem of Jane's in-
struction she stood in awe of the child.

"I have always been stupid, you know," she said to
Lethbury with a new humility, "and I'm afraid I sha'n't know
what is best for Jane. I'm sure she has a wonderfully good
mind, and I should reproach myself if I didn't give her every
opportunity." She looked at him helplessly. "You must tell me
what ought to be done."

Lethbury was not unwilling to oblige her. Somewhere in
his mental lumber-room there rusted a theory of education
such as usually lingers among the impedimenta of the childless. He brought this out, refurbished it, and applied it to
Jane. At first he thought his wife had not overrated the
quality of the child's mind. Jane seemed extraordinarily intelligent. Her precocious definiteness of mind was encour-
aging to her inexperienced preceptor. She had no difficulty
in fixing her attention, and he felt that every fact he imparted was being etched in metal. He helped his wife to en-
gage the best teachers, and for a while continued to take an
ex-official interest in his adopted daughter's studies. But
gradually his interest waned. Jane's ideas did not increase

with her acquisitions. Her young mind remained a mere receptacle for facts: a kind of cold-storage from which anything which had been put there could be taken out at a moment's notice, intact but congealed. She developed, moreover, an inordinate pride in the capacity of her mental storehouse, and a tendency to pelt her public with its contents. She was overheard to jeer at her nurse for not knowing when the Saxon Heptarchy had fallen, and she alternately dazzled and depressed Mrs. Lethbury by the wealth of her chronological allusions. She showed no interest in the significance of the facts she amassed: she simply collected dates as another child might have collected stamps or marbles. To her foster-mother she seemed a prodigy of wisdom; but Lethbury saw, with a secret movement of sympathy, how the aptitudes in which Mrs. Lethbury gloried were slowly estranging her from her child.

"She is getting too clever for me," his wife said to him, after one of Jane's historical flights, "but I am so glad that she will be a companion to you."

Lethbury groaned in spirit. He did not look forward to Jane's companionship. She was still a good little girl: but there was something automatic and formal in her goodness, as though it were a kind of moral calisthenics which she went through for the sake of showing her agility. An early consciousness of virtue had moreover constituted her the natural guardian and adviser of her elders. Before she was fifteen she had set about reforming the household. She took Mrs. Lethbury in hand first; then she extended her efforts to the servants, with consequences more disastrous to the domestic harmony; and lastly she applied herself to Lethbury. She proved to him by statistics that he smoked too much, and that it was injurious to the optic nerve to read in bed. She took him to task for not going to church more regularly, and pointed out to him the evils of desultory reading. She suggested that a regular course of study encourages mental concentration, and hinted that inconsecutiveness of thought is a sign of approaching age.

To her adopted mother her suggestions were equally pertinent. She instructed Mrs. Lethbury in an improved way of making beef stock, and called her attention to the unhygienic qualities of carpets. She poured out distracting facts about bacilli and vegetable mould, and demonstrated that curtains and picture-frames are a hot-bed of animal organisms. She learned by heart the nutritive ingredients of the principal articles of diet, and revolutionised the cuisine by an attempt to establish a scientific average between starch and phosphates. Four cooks left during this experiment, and Lethbury fell into the habit of dining at his club.

Once or twice, at the outset, he had tried to check Jane's ardour; but his efforts resulted only in hurting his wife's feelings. Jane remained impervious, and Mrs. Lethbury resented any attempt to protect her from her daughter. Lethbury saw that she was consoled for the sense of her own inferiority by the thought of what Jane's intellectual companionship must be to him; and he tried to keep up the illusion by enduring with what grace he might the blighting edification of Jane's discourse.

V

As Jane grew up he sometimes avenged himself by wondering if his wife was still sorry that they had not called her Muriel. Jane was not ugly; she developed, indeed, a kind of categorical prettiness which might have been a projection of her mind. She had a creditable collection of features, but one had to take an inventory of them to find out that she was good-looking. The fusing grace had been omitted.

Mrs. Lethbury took a touching pride in her daughter's first steps in the world. She expected Jane to take by her complexion those whom she did not capture by her learning. But Jane's rosy freshness did not work any perceptible ravages. Whether the young men guessed the axioms on her lips and detected the encyclopædia in her eye, or whether they simply found no intrinsic interest in these features, certain it is, that, in spite of her mother's heroic efforts, and of incessant calls on Lethbury's purse, Jane, at the end of her first season, had dropped hopelessly out of the running. A few duller girls found her interesting, and one or two young men came to the house with the object of meeting other young women; but she was rapidly becoming one of the social supernumeraries who are asked out only because they are on people's lists.

The blow was bitter to Mrs. Lethbury; but she consoled herself with the idea that Jane had failed because she was too clever. Jane probably shared this conviction; at all events she betrayed no consciousness of failure. She had developed a pronounced taste for society, and went out, unweariedly and obstinately, winter after winter, while Mrs. Lethbury toiled in her wake, showering attentions on oblivious hostesses. To Lethbury there was something at once tragic and exasperating in the sight of their two figures, the one conciliatory, the other dogged, both pursuing with unabated zeal the elusive prize of popularity. He even began to feel a personal stake in the pursuit, not as it concerned Jane but as it affected his wife. He saw that the latter was the victim of Jane's disappointment: that Jane was not above the crude satisfaction of "taking it out" of her mother. Experience checked the impulse to come to his wife's defence; and when his resentment was at its height, Jane disarmed him by giving up the struggle.

Nothing was said to mark her capitulation; but Lethbury noticed that the visiting ceased and that the dressmaker's bills diminished. At the same time Mrs. Lethbury made it known that Jane had taken up charities; and before long Jane's conversation confirmed this announcement. At first Lethbury congratulated himself on the change; but Jane's domesticity soon began to weigh on him. During the day she was sometimes absent on errands of mercy; but in the evening she was always there. At first she and Mrs. Lethbury sat in the drawing-room together, and Lethbury smoked in the library; but presently Jane formed the habit of joining him there, and he began to suspect that he was included among the objects of her philanthropy.

Mrs. Lethbury confirmed the suspicion. "Jane has grown very serious-minded lately," she said. "She imagines that she used to neglect you and she is trying to make up for it. Don't discourage her," she added innocently.

Such a plea delivered Lethbury helpless to his daughter's ministrations; and he found himself measuring the hours he spent with her by the amount of relief they must be affording